# Do No Harm

Carol Topolski is a psychoanalytic psychotherapist. Her many previous roles include working on the Woodstock festival, in advertising, and as a prison teacher, nursery-school director, director of a rape crisis centre and refuge for battered women, probation officer and film censor. She lives in London and is married with two daughters and two grandchildren. Her first novel, *Monster Love*, is available in Penguin.

# Do No Harm

CAROL TOPOLSKI

FIG TREE
*an imprint of*
PENGUIN BOOKS

FIG TREE

Published by the Penguin Group

Penguin Group (Australia), 250 Camberwell Road, Camberwell, Victoria 3124, Australia
(a division of Pearson Australia Group Pty Ltd)

Penguin Group (USA) Inc., 375 Hudson Street, New York, New York 10014, USA

Penguin Group (Canada), 90 Eglinton Avenue East, Suite 700, Toronto ON M4P 2Y3, Canada
(a division of Pearson Penguin Canada Inc.)

Penguin Books Ltd, 80 Strand, London WC2R 0RL, England

Penguin Ireland, 25 St Stephen's Green, Dublin 2, Ireland
(a division of Penguin Books Ltd)

Penguin Books India Pvt Ltd, 11 Community Centre, Panchsheel Park, New Delhi – 110 017, India

Penguin Books (NZ) Ltd, 67 Apollo Drive, Rosedale, North Shore 0632, New Zealand
(a division of Pearson New Zealand Ltd)

Penguin Books (South Africa) (Pty) Ltd, 24 Sturdee Avenue, Rosebank,
Johannesburg 2196, South Africa

Penguin Books Ltd, Registered Offices: 80 Strand, London, WC2R 0RL, England

First published in Great Britain by Penguin Books 2010
This edition published by Penguin Group (Australia) 2011

1  3  5  7  9  10  8  6  4  2

Set in Dante MT Std
Typeset by Palimpsest Book Production Limited, Grangemouth, Stirlingshire
Printed and bound in Australia by McPherson's Printing Group, Maryborough, Victoria

A CIP catalogue record for this book is available from the British Library

ISBN: 978-1-905-49028-8

penguin.com.au

FSC
www.fsc.org
MIX
Paper from
responsible sources
FSC® C001695

For Michael, Cassie, Clea, Alessia and Luca. Of course.
And Peter Hildebrand (1928–2001). My friend.

If only there were evil people somewhere insidiously committing evil deeds and it were necessary only to separate them from the rest of us and destroy them. But the line dividing good and evil cuts through the heart of every human being. And who is willing to destroy a piece of his own heart?

Aleksandr Solzhenitsyn

# 1979

Look at the woman. See her potter. See her shoulders drop as she drifts into the garden. Her eyes take in the dank piles of leaves and the shrubs giving up the ghost after this year's blink-and-you'll-miss-it summer. There are four chrysanthemums huddling by the wall and she breaks them off, takes them into the kitchen and puts them in the arty vase shaped like a milk bottle. Her husband sometimes fills it with milk. Says something about emperors. And new clothes. Says it every time, and every time she grins back.

Today feels like one long grin stretching out ahead, empty of appointments and commitments and clients. She lifts out her gypsy skirt and twirls by the fridge like the ballerina in the musical box she got for her ninth birthday. She twirls into the living room and round the sofa, over the carpet still smelling of chemicals. Beige. Bonkers with a small child, but it's washable – and rather piss-elegant, she thought when they chose it. She shakes off her shoes to feel the bouclé against her feet. Doesn't matter if she looks idiotic twirling round the room. Round and round, then round again. There's no one here. Just her. And the grinning day.

She considers lolling on the sofa. Or doing handstands against the wall. Or playing the moany music she likes, loudly, but it's been a while since breakfast and she's ready for elevenses. Half past elevenses, more like. She boils the kettle, plumps for Earl Grey and is just cosying the teapot when she hears the front gate squeak. *Must remember to oil it*, she thinks. *But not now. No chores today.* The knock on the door is imperious and she's mildly irritated when the bell rings too. *I'm coming, I'm coming*, she thinks, *keep your flipping hair on!*

Her visitor is unexpected. Especially with the beard. But she's heard tales, so she steps aside and says, 'Do come in.' The day shifts into a different gear. She can find out more than she already knows. Swap stories with her mother when they meet up later. She spends her working days winkling people's stories out of them, so she'll find out the truth. Get her visitor to spill the beans. She fetches the teapot and brings it in with a bottle of milk and two mugs.

The visitor says, 'I take sugar – is that OK?' and she goes to find it.

'Sorry,' she calls from the kitchen, 'I always forget.'

It's at the back of the cupboard, behind the mustard, so she has to move things around to get at it. She brings the bag into the living room, and a spoon. The tea's been poured.

They talk, and she hears surprising things. She doesn't have to probe, her visitor wants to tell her. And there's another surprise. She's feeling sleepy. Not just passing-yawn sleepy, but heavy sleepy, as though she's been awake for days. She apologises, twice, but she's losing the thread and just has time to put the mug on the table before she feels herself falling. Off the chair, on to the carpet. When her eyes are at half mast, before she closes them forever, she sees the hand reach into the holdall. Sees the flash of metal.

# 1974

Sunday, 6.49 p.m.

The blade winks in the fierce blue light as it turns in my fingers. Its edge is as fine as a split hair. Its handle presses urgently into my palm. Its heft is perfect. I hold it in my right hand over the flesh, settling my left hand on the skin slipping idly over the musculature beneath. I can tease out this whiff of anticipation almost infinitely and I've hovered, knife in hand, for minutes before now like a falcon frozen on a thermal, waiting . . . waiting . . . for the twitch of its prey in the scrub below. My left thumb splays along the curvature to hold the flesh still as I inhale so slowly someone watching would be hard pressed to say whether I breathed at all. But there is only me here. Me and the knife. I lower my hand in slow motion and push the blade against the flesh. The tiny pop of entry makes me smile.

*Here we go.*

My left hand tightens its grip as I draw the knife down, the metal's glissade buttery smooth through the skin's minute follicular pocks. The subcutaneous fat creams into view as the wound pulls back its lips. I deepen the cut, slicing through the fragile caul into the muscle's heart. Transferring the knife to my left hand, I slide my right forefinger into the skeins of tissue to poke a pocket about the size of my fingernail between the sticky layers. When I pull my finger out, the flesh exhales sleepily over the hole, but I know where it is. It can't escape. To my right on the steel top there's a small pile of green and white fragments in a bowl. I take a pinch and push it into the pocket.

3

I ease the incision shut and poise the knife to make the next one exactly one and a half centimetres away.

*Damn, I'm good.*

When I've made ten deposits in ten parallel cuts, I lift the loin of pork on to the onions lolling in olive oil and sprinkle the last of the rosemary and garlic round the roasting tin. I grind sea salt and black pepper over the meat – just enough – before sliding the dish into the upper oven.

In the lower oven layers of potatoes are sweltering in cream. By the time they're ready the pork will be calling herbily from its lair, crisped, moist and tender. My culinary timing is immaculate. Always. I go to the sink where two heads of broccoli nudge each other on the draining board. I used to call them trees when I was small, but Mother was affronted by baby speak and insisted I learned to spell the word, tapping out each letter on the dining table. 'B . . . r . . . o . . . double c . . . o . . . l . . . i. Broccoli. That's double c, Virginia, if you please.' If I got it wrong, she'd tap it out on my fingers, sometimes with the back of a spoon.

I can call it trees now if I choose, and sometimes I do.

I fill the left-hand sink with water and drop the broccoli heads into it. I reach for my glass of wine, a sly Bourgogne Aligoté, and suck in a mouthful, cruising my palate and swooshing it from cheek to cheek before gulping it down. I reach to my right to settle the glass by the sink but it trips against the plate rack and smashes on the floor. *Shit, shit, shit, oh buggery shit!* I go to get cloths and kitchen paper and broom and bucket and this time manage to clear up the mess without cutting myself. After I've chucked the debris, wrapping it in newspaper to protect the dustmen, I go to the unit above the sink where I keep my wine glasses. I buy them by the dozen. Often. I refill my glass and set it down at the other end of the kitchen, well away from my elbows or shoulders or hips or knees. When I've washed and trimmed the trees, I find the pine nuts I brought back from Tuscany after the symposium. I dry fry them in a pan, watching as they turn from cream to caramel, snatching them away before they carbonise.

When the pork is nearly ready, I'll stir-fry the broccoli and sprinkle it with the pinolas and a hint of argan oil.

The cheese has been sitting in the kitchen's exhalations since this morning and I go over to it now to check on its vital signs. I push my thumb against its coarse battered-orange skin, testing the ooze beneath. In a world where almost any food can be bought at almost any time of the year, Vacherin is resolutely seasonal, and I love it like a missing friend who shows up only every now and again with a cheesy grin on her face.

I've bought endive for the salad I have with every meal, despite the postprandial long haul of defoliating my teeth, and decide that a sweet dressing might temper the leaves' bitter twist. I pull Dijon mustard from one cupboard and honey from another. I read the label out loud, *Miele di Millefiori*, rolling the words round my mouth like cherries, and tip a languid arc over the mustard splat in a bowl. I add sea salt and pepper, oil and lemon juice and beat it till the dressing gloops off the spoon. I wash and dry the salad and put it back in the fridge next to the cheesecake in front of the double cream. I wish there were such a thing as treble cream. Quadruple cream even.

I've tried tolerating a messy kitchen, but it makes me nervous. Apart from the glasses – and the plates and the cups and the dishes and the vases – I am never untidy in here, though I don't give a shit in the rest of the house. I suffered punishing heartburn the one time I ate in the dining room with a cabal of pans and utensils loitering next door, so I clear the worktops now and put everything back in its place. When it's all done, I take my wine and go to the door, turning round for one last check. Gleams of steel on both sides of the room brace themselves for my next onslaught, and cupboards and drawers and carousels crouch behind a façade so expertly engineered that anyone else would need a map to get in. Every kind of tool and gadget lurks in the kitchen's belly, and I use them all.

It is a tasty kitchen. A kitchen whose mother tongue is food.

I switch on the light as I turn into the hall. The lampshade's nylon is busy with brown and orange wriggles that remind me of sperm. I called it 'Shades of Spermatozoa' when I bought it fifteen years ago, thinking it would make a good title for a book. Or a song, though I don't listen to music much. My bare feet chill on the hall's tessellated tiles but their happy slaps are smothered by the shagpile as I go into the dining room.

This was the reason I bought the house, a room in which to eat languidly, with pleasure, until I'm satisfied. FTB, as Mother would say. Full to bursting, though I've yet to burst. Its height, ornate cornices and ceiling rose smack of the hubris of empire builders, and a chandelier emerges from a sudden burst of plaster leaves and up-themselves lilies. It looks a little tipsy because I once smacked a broom into it while clearing a spider's web and smashed a great swathe of its prisms. I thought its asymmetry was a thing of strange beauty so never replaced it. I go over to the French windows at the back of the room and draw the curtains against the expiring light outside. The rings clack along the pole as the curtain edges strive to meet. And fail. They've never exactly been on speaking terms. A pair of Habitat metal uplighters pose on one wall opposite the two candelabra lights on the other. One of their shades burned when it lounged against the bulb, but I let it be because its scorch is a measure of the life it has lived. Like a scar on a knee or an anxious groove on a forehead.

It took four sweating, cursing men to manoeuvre the table into the room, which I think it will probably never leave. Magda, my cleaning lady, polishes it twice a week with the beeswax whose heady fragrance lingers in the air like incense. It reminds her of back home, she says. The old way of doing things. You English have no idea, she says. Around the table are its ten minions, headed by an oak carver of patrician mien, followed by a pair of 1930s kitchen chairs, three Regency chairs with weary seats, a mock Rennie Mackintosh ladder-back chair and three Formica chairs, circa 1954. I was sixteen then, but never sweet.

I go over to the mahogany sideboard to lay the table.

I lift out a tablecloth edged and interrupted by handmade lace. Magda does her best, but there are red and brown and black stains here and there, like telling chapters in my alimentary history. I spread it on the table and set silver candelabra at each end, their arms semaphoring each other across the lacy wastes between. I lay two places in case Ruby shows up, setting the posh cutlery round the plates in the prescribed order. Mother's pernickety about that, even when it's just a snack in the garden. A plastic-handled kitchen knife seems to have sneaked into the cutlery drawer, so I put it at Ruby's place, where it sits like a common-as-muck pleb at a king's banquet. She'll snicker when she sees it.

If she comes.

Needing a refill, I pop back to the kitchen. I empty the bottle of Bourgogne and sniff at the Gigondas, which I uncorked two hours ago. I think it will do, unlike the flimsy Châteauneuf-du-Pape I had to ditch yesterday.

I am neither a believer in frugality on days like today, nor a believer in popes at any time.

I go upstairs to shower, adjusting one of the tepid watercolours on the wall in passing. I bought the six of them as a job lot at auction: I suppose they're British landscapes, but they could be anywhere. Well, maybe not Africa. Taking off my clothes in the bedroom I inadvertently catch sight of myself in the mirror. I usually manage to avoid my reflection, but if I fail I have a good long stare because sometimes I slip my mind.

I wouldn't turn anyone's head or stop anyone's heart or create an admiring stir. When puberty hit and I shot up like a cabbage past its prime, Mother used to tell me I was ungainly, which I suppose offended her gainliness. In my Birkenstocks I scrape the six-foot mark if I stand up straight, which is rare, but they're the nearest thing to walking barefoot and I am forced by convention to wear shoes. I've had the same pudding-basin haircut since childhood and I'd shave it off if I could, but a shiny head might frighten the horses, so I grudgingly wash it once a week. My mid-mud locks gave up the fag of curling before I went to school and now just kink listlessly over my head. I found my first grey hair when I was twenty-five, a year before my first grey pube, three years before my early menopause, and was relieved. No more shrugging on the pretence of femininity in the morning; no more wearing it like a scratchy wool coat in the summer heat; no more beastly girly stuff. My hedgerow brows clamber across a face which has never quite mastered the art of pretty. Never learned how to charm. I'm not bothered. As long as I can smell, as long as I can see and taste and hear and touch – as long as I can work – I'm content.

My neck leads to wide shoulders and arms ending with the dispro-
portionate hands of an adolescent. Or a gambolling puppy, though
I've never knowingly gambolled. All year round, my spatulate fingers
look as though they've been scrubbed with wire wool, their nails cut
riskily close to the quick. Mother paid a great deal of attention to her
nails, which were perfectly oval and shone with colours whose names
could have come out of the *Rubaiyat*. My small breasts perch above
my body's perpendiculars and my long legs, which might be called
coltish on another woman, drop with no nonsense to my feet.

Having committed myself to memory, I go across the landing to
the bathroom. After boiling my skin as close to lobster as possible
without actually cooking, I lavish Yves St Laurent creams on my body
and my face and return to the bedroom. My scents congregate on a
bookshelf and I toy with Joy before settling on Cabochard. I spray
my neck and my wrists and the backs of my knees and look in the
wardrobe for the silk blouse with the myriad buttons that usually
elude my fingers. They comply this time, except for one that jackknifes behind a radiator. I'll hunt the bastard down later. Skulking
among the M&S work clothes are my favourite trousers. They are
the colour of dried blood, and chains and buckles and straps loop
and whoop along their length.

'But they're men's trousers,' the furry woman in the charity shop
said when I bought them.

'Ah yes. They're for my niece,' I replied. 'She's a tall girl and is
rather keen on that punk nonsense.'

I strap them on and clank over to my jewellery hanging on the
coat stand.

During the two years I worked in Sierra Leone, my patients' rela-
tives would press necklaces into my hands when I pulled off the
impossible. The whole family – sometimes twenty, thirty people
strong – would gather outside the hospital and sing and dance their
thanks in febrile rhythms that almost unglued me. These beads, they
said, these shells and bones and stones, would ward off the spirits
that so nearly claimed their sister. Their mother, their daughter, their
aunt. I settle some seed pods round my neck and slip on my shoes.

I drink the last of my wine and go downstairs.

I know how to feed myself well. And with gusto. The meat begs to be carved, the potatoes hide the lubricious heart of a lover under their crust, the pine nuts perk against the broccoli and the salad is dressed lightly, because an overdressed salad is like a ball gown at a barbecue. I sit in my chair and toast myself and Ruby with the queen of red wines. Then several times more for the sheer hell of it.

Ruby's habit is just to pitch up. 'Like a bad penny,' she'll say, waiting for the next line. I know my cue. 'No, no, Ruby,' I'll say, 'more like a gold sovereign,' and she'll smirk.

I won't wait for her tonight, nor will I save her any food. If she comes when the meal is finished, I can always make something simple, like fresh linguine with truffle oil, and open another bottle of red.

There's one slice of pork left when I've finished my first course. I'll save it for next door's dog because today is the last of the trips. The quads are due in tomorrow. I reach over to the sideboard for the Vacherin, palpate it one more time and gently ease off its crust. I dip chunks of bread into its custardy guts and the cheese drips on to my chin and my blouse and my lap. I finish it all, running my finger round the inside to scoop out its last vestiges. I drink three glasses of five-year-old Vin Santo with the cheesecake, taking a fourth through to the living room when I've cleared up.

I stretch out on the battered chesterfield and rest my hands on my midriff. I close my eyes and imagine my meal churning inside me. Shreds of broccoli and bopping raisins and clumps of pork reeling around in a mongrel dance. Bubbles popping into my tiny domed fundus, boiling up my oesophagus and bursting into my mouth, where they trail along my palate and up my nose and into the next four days. I must have dozed off because when I next look at my watch, twenty minutes have passed. I stand up, slightly fuzzy, and go to the door. As I pass the console table, I let my fingers trail along its top, skittering over the altar cloth, circling the brass candlesticks and skating like a slow-motion leaf on water over the rosewood case quietly shining at its centre.

I've got a long surgical list tomorrow, so I have to be up at sparrow's fart. I've often wondered what a sparrow's fart might look like. A small feathered blip on the wind smelling of worms, I suppose.

# 1943

I've been sitting on this knobbly chair for a long time. I can't tell the time yet, but I know it's a long time because my this-hand-side leg has gone to sleep. I pretend to read clock faces sometimes, but only in my head because Mother tuts when I do it wrong. I look over at the goldy clock on the mantelpiece and I count for a bit because I know that each tick means something. It's seventeen o'clock and probably a few minutes, excepting I don't know how to do minutes yet. I pick up my sewing from the table. I hope the horrid needle didn't lose its horrid thread when I chucked it down crossly. If it has, I'll have to go and ask Nana to put it back through the little hole and she'll tut like Mother, only faster. The sewing is damp at the edges from my hands. It's a very hot day today – 'Too hot to be playing outside with the chickens,' Nana said, 'so you just sit quietly and do your sewing, Virginia, and if you're a good girl maybe you can go outside when it's cooler.'

Being a good girl means sticking the needle – which has kept the red thread, hurrah, hooray – into the material and pulling it back through without pricking my finger like Sleeping Beauty. I'm not like Sleeping Beauty even a bit because when I prick my finger I don't have a nice long sleep for a hundred years, I just bleed and I'm scared I'll get blood on my sewing. When I prick myself I look hardly at my finger and wait for the pretty bobble of blood to come out. It looks like a fairy football. Only then it squooshes and makes a mess.

Mother was a good sewer, Nana says, and she keeps showing me some sewing Mother did when she was a little girl even though she was a lot bigger than I am now. She was ten, Nana says, and points to the sewing that's on the wall, where it says *Eleanor Redford, Aged 10* and *Home*

*Is Where The Heart Is* next to a house with a tree and some flowers and some stars in the sky. And a moon. The sky's the bit I like best because it looks like somewhere you could fly off to and have magic adventures on your own. Not somewhere where you have to do silly sewing and wash your hands before meals. I don't say 'silly sewing' to grown-ups because of the tutting, but I say it over and over in my head like this: *silly sewing silly sewing silly sewing*, and it sounds a bit like a snake. Well, I think it sounds like a snake, only I've never seen a real one. I don't think there are many snakes in Yorkshire. Excepting sometimes when I go for a walk in the fields by myself I think they might be hiding in hedges. Or up in trees, ready to drop down on my head and squeeze me to death. Or bite my eyes off. There's a snake in my flappy book and sometimes I give him elephant legs.

I can hear Nana banging pots and pans in the kitchen. She's probably making tea for Grandpa and my uncles for when they come home all hot and smelly. I've got three uncles: the two ones who live here at the farm, and Uncle Edgar who's at Granny and Papa Denham's house, only I've never met him. I think he might be God because there's this big picture of him in Granny's drawing room with a baby light at the top and loads of other pictures on a table underneath with shiny candlesticks like at the front bit at church, which is God's house. If Uncle Edgar's God then he'll be out doing God things all the time, like making people better who've died, so he'd be very busy. Perhaps he's off trying to stop the War, that'd be something God would do, and then Father would come home, though I don't know what he looks like now. I've seen Granny's picture of him in the kitchen, but he might have changed at War because of killing and things. You never know. Sometimes I see Granny standing in front of the big gold picture and she looks jolly sad. Once I thought I saw her crying when she looked at the picture of Uncle Edgar-god, excepting grown-ups don't cry.

I've been at Nana's for days and days and days. I always come here when Mother's doing her important war work. Only the way the grown-ups say it, it's *Important War Work*, and it's also *Top Secret*, so I'm not allowed to ask what kind of work it is. If I did, I'd be a nosy parker which is not a good person to be. I think maybe it's making guns or planes because probably Mother knows how to do making things because of Father's factory. Excepting she doesn't work there and anyway the factory makes tractors, but he might have taught her something before he went away to War, you never know. I'm not sure what he's doing at War, but I'm sure it must be something to do with being brave because grown-ups talk about *Our Brave Troops*.

Mother's usually grumpy when she comes back from Important War Work, like she wishes she was still doing it and not having to make my tea and teach me my letters, so I walk around on my tippy-toes and try not to break things. And I hope Ruby won't just pop in because that makes Mother even more grumpy. Ruby can always go away when Mother gets even more grumpy, but she hasn't taught me how to fly yet.

Ruby's here now, sitting on the chair over there, twisting a bit of her yellow hair and kicking her red shoes against the thing for your feet at the bottom. The bar thing.

'I'm bored,' she says, only she says it like this: I'm *boooo-ored*. 'Can't we go outside? We could go and find those kittens we saw yesterday, or we could throw stones at the cows and make them moo all over the place.'

'No, we can't,' I say, 'because Nana would be really cross and then she'll tell Mother and she might even smack me, you never know.'

Ruby's face gets scrunched, which makes me know I've got to do something quickly. 'I know,' I say, 'let's play doctors. We could play it in here so Nana thinks I'm doing sewing and we can play very, very softly so she won't hear.'

Ruby bucks up and says, 'Oo, yes, yes, yes – that would be super!'

'You stay there while I go and get our special things,' I say, 'and whistle our special whistle if Nana comes to see if I'm doing my sewing.'

Mustn't let Ruby do the sewing while I'm away because she'll spill ink on it or something, even though I don't think there's any ink in the dining room. But Ruby's like Spike the sheepdog, she'd sniffle and snuffle around and find some in a Top Secret hidey-hole that only grown-ups know about and then she'd splosh it on the sewing and on the tablecloth and maybe even down Nana's bosom if she came in to see what the noise was about. Ruby's very noisy when she's having fun, not like me – I'm as quiet as a caterpillar.

'Now, don't you move from your chair,' I say as I take off my sandals and creep to the door, and Ruby grins and shakes her head.

Hurrah, hooray, the kitchen door's nearly closed and I can't hear Nana banging any more, so perhaps she's out in the yard or in the scullery doing the washing. I slide my foot on to each stair really slowly, not standing on the bits of the five stairs that make horrid noises. Sometimes I get frightened in the night when I hear cracks and creaks because I think it's the bogeyman coming to eat me with his tiger teeth, but Nana says, 'Oh, don't be such a mouse, Virginia,' so I just sing a happy song to myself very quietly until he's gone away.

I slip into the bedroom I sleep in when I'm here, which was Mother's when she was a little girl. It has lots of flowers on the curtains and the eiderdown, and a real dressing table with a mirror that you can see the back of your head in. What the grown-ups don't know is that I'm Top Secret too, and I go to my hidey-hole at the bottom of the cupboard.

When I was staying with Nana before today, I saw that one of the floorboards at the bottom of the cupboard was loose, so I sat on my BTM and wriggled it for a long, long time till I could lift it up and look into the dusty spider's webs underneath. There must have been mice there too because I saw some mouse poo, but I mustn't say poo because it's very common, Mother says. I have to say Number Twos. Excepting I can say poo to myself and when I'm talking to Ruby. When I cleared out the cobwebs and the poo, I saw a little gap between the stones the house is made of, so I found another stone and put it in the front of the hole so no one can look inside. Nana might peek when she's cleaning or when she's looking for my plimsolls in the morning and then my goose would be cooked. Only I haven't got a goose. The stone made it like Ali Baba's cave, so I always say, 'Open says me,' when I come to get my treasure, but I whisper it because I mustn't give the game away.

I say, 'Open says me,' now and roll the stone away. There isn't any treasure in it like gold or diamonds or the king's crown, but what's in there is my special treasure. I take a pair of scissors and a knife out of the hole. They're Mother's sewing scissors and taking them means I did two bad things, so I'd have to go to prison if anyone found out. First I stole them from the sewing basket by the fire, which makes me a burglar, and second I'm not allowed to play with scissors, so I'd have to go to Approved School like Dora, who's our cleaning lady's daughter. Dora had to go to Approved School because she had a baby and Mother and Nana did lots of tutting when I saw them talking about it once in the kitchen. They said Dora didn't have a husband. 'She's just a common tart, Eleanor,' Nana said and Mother nodded her head so hard I was scared it'd fall off. I only saw Dora once and she didn't look like a tart to me. She didn't have a hole in the middle filled with jam, but perhaps there are some people who are pies. Or puddings. Sandwiches even. You never know.

The knife is just the right size and I found it in the garden shed, so I think it's Father's because all the tools in there are his, Mother says. That's probably being a burglar too, but because Father's at War, I'll only get into trouble when he gets back. Maybe he won't even notice because he might have gone blind at War. People do. Then it wouldn't matter that I don't know what he looks like now, because he wouldn't know what I look like too. I wrap the scissors and the knife in my pocket-handkerchief, which has lace round the edge and a big blue V in the corner in sewing. If Nana sees me with it, I'll just say, 'Atchoo! Atchoo! Oh, Nana, I've just turned all poorly,' and she'll make me bread and milk and snuggle me up in bed.

I close the hidey-hole and close the cupboard and close the bedroom door as I leave and go back downstairs after I've picked up a damp flannel from the bathroom.

Because it's a hot day the parlour windows are open, so I leave the flannel on the window sill and slide into the garden like a giant snail. Under a plant pot round the corner are the animals me and Ruby found the other day: a butterfly and a spider and a shiny beetle. They're all dead, which is a good thing because if they were alive they'd run away and then where would we be? I put the wrapped-up things in my knickers pocket and don't pick up the animals hardly because I don't want to break them. Back through the window, pick up the flannel and creep, creep, creep to the dining room.

Ruby looks grumpy. 'Where have you been?' she says. 'I was starting to get bored again, so I did some of your sewing.' *Bother. Bother, bother, bother.* She's done all these wonky stitches and the thread's come out of the needle again, but I don't say *Oh, Ruby!* because then she'd go away and I can't do this busy work on my own. I put everything down on the table and pull out my handkerchief and unfold it. Then I lie the scissors and the knife on the top slowly so I don't cut myself. Then I line up the animals like the queue at the baker's when Mr Shepherd's got some bread in. Then I smile at Ruby.

'Well, now. We're all ready-steady-go.' Oh, but I've got one last job. I sit on the floor and wipe my feet with the flannel because they're all mucky from the garden and Nana would know I've been outside if I don't clean them. I put my sandals back on and do up the buckles by myself. Mother patted my head when I did that for the first time and I really liked it even though I'm not a puppy.

Ruby's got the two little pink spots on her cheeks that she gets when she's excited. It makes her look like a clown at the circus and she'd be very, very, very happy if I said that because she likes to be funny like a clown.

We kneel on dining chairs side by side and I say, 'Golly, Dr Ruby, we've got a hard day's work ahead of us – what shall we do first?' I put on the deep voice I use for this game because doctors are men, like Dr Greenaway.

'Oh, this poor spider,' says Ruby in her normal voice but a bit higher, 'it can't fly, Dr Virginia. I think we need to help it fly away, don't you, because otherwise the cat might eat it. Or a monkey.'

'Good idea, Dr Ruby. Shall you take the spider and I'll take the butterfly?'

'Rather! Pick up your scissors and I'll do the counting. One-two-three-five-six-nine-seven.' I pick up the scissors and Ruby picks up the knife and we get to work. I put my face right up close to the butterfly and hold my breath when I snip his wings off. Ruby puts her finger softly on the spider's back to squoosh him flat a bit so his legs stick out sideways and she's cutting each leg off with the knife. We're being so quiet, the tick tock of the clock sounds as loud as the church bells do on Sunday.

When we've finished, we both sit on our heels and look at our busy work.

'Oh, good show, Dr Virginia,' says Ruby. 'Gosh, that was a difficult job but you've done jolly splendidly.'

'Well, Dr Ruby,' I say, 'good show to you too. You have to be ever so clever to do the spider cutting, but there it is – eight perfect legs. Now, shall we help this poor animal to fly?'

'Oh yes, let's!' says Ruby. 'I'll hold him down while you do it.'

I pick up the wings of the butterfly between my thumb and finger and lie them in the palm of my hand like it was Dr Greenaway's tray. Then I lift them off my hand and put them on either side of the spider. I make little humming noises so the spider will know I only want to help him, and when I've finished I say, 'There, little spider, you *shall* fly in the air,' like when the fairy godmother says to Cinderella, 'There, Cinderella, you *shall* go to the ball.' When I do this difficult job, I think I know what Mother means when she says Hard Work Is Its Own Reward. Excepting sometimes she says Virtue Is Its Own Reward.

Our busy work isn't finished yet.

'Shall we clean our hands before we see to the beetle?' I say, thinking it's a good job I fetched the flannel.

'Oh bither-bother-bother!' says Ruby. 'Do we have to?' Ruby likes mucky things.

'Mother says if you don't wash your hands before you eat you'll turn all poorly,' I say, 'and you don't want to make little beetle poorly, do you? We're supposed to be making him better, Dr Ruby, so you just do what you're told.'

Ruby's eyes get smaller and she pushes her mouth together so tightly it looks like a cat's BTM. She reaches over to the beetle, but I grab her hand before she gets there.

'If you don't wash your hands, Dr Ruby,' I say, 'you'll have to leave the doctors' room and go home.' I make my voice go even deeper. 'And you don't want that, do you?'

Ruby growls like the mummy cat when you go near her kittens.

'I'm going to count to three, Ruby – I beg your pardon, Dr Ruby – and if you haven't washed your hands, you know what comes next,

don't you?' I pull my eyebrows down like Mother does. 'One . . .
two . . .'

Ruby sighs and hops down off the chair, swinging her arms crossly
as she goes over to the flannel, which is on the floor. She wipes her
hands and then she suddenly sticks the flannel up under her frock at
the back. 'Ha ha, now I'm going to wipe my bum!' she says and she
looks happy again.

I jump off my chair and race over. I snatch the flannel out of her
hands, which is ever so rude, but sometimes you have to do rude
things. Needs must – that's what Nana says. We stare at each other
quite closely, our noses nearly touching. We're exactly the same
height. The stare goes on for a long, long time, but I'm the winner
because Ruby blinks.

'Righto,' I say. 'It's back to work for us then, Dr Ruby.' Back at the
table we look at the eight spider's legs. 'I think we need to give these
to the beetle, Dr Ruby, don't you?' I say. 'He's not going to get very
far on those tiny pins, is he?'

'Jolly top hole, Dr Virginia,' says Ruby, 'and how about giving the
butterfly the beetle's wings, eh? It'll keep him warm when it's cold.'

'And dry when it's rainy – spiffing idea,' I say. 'I'll guard the legs
while you cut off the wings with the knife, shall you?'

'I certainly shall,' Ruby says. 'Stand well back, Dr Virginia, this
might get mucky.'

I carefully wrap my hands round the spider's legs like a little fence
and watch as Ruby sticks her face really close to the beetle. She waits
for a second, thinking about how to do this job, and then cuts one
of the purply wings off carefully. I don't say, 'Jolly good show,' because
I don't want to make her jump. She puts the knife into the beetle to
cut off the other wing and – *oh no, oh no, oh no* – the knife slips and
it falls on the top of the table and it makes a big scratch and my
tummy starts to hurt.

'Oh my goodness, look what you've done, Ruby,' I whisper. 'What's
Nana going to say?'

Elsie Redford's having a bad day. She's never been a fan of the heat
and today she's roasting like a pig on a spit. She's a big-boned, brawny

17

woman but her skin's as tender as an infant's, and half an hour in the sun makes her look like a radish. She's moving round with uncharacteristic speed, as though she can dodge the sun's rays, but the buggers will keep finding her. On top of the meteorological curse she's pretty certain she's hit the menopause because six or seven times a day this bloody furnace ignites inside her. Her mother was a martyr to her Time of Life, so she supposes she'll be the same. 'Thanks for lumbering me with that, Mam,' she mutters under her breath as her face pebbles with perspiration for the hundredth time since breakfast.

Her days are lumbered enough, what with looking after Albert and the boys and performing the ordinary tasks of the farmer's wife, but that's her cross and she bears it with equanimity. She's Yorkshire after all, and Yorkshire people don't moan. But looking after Virginia is one more task tacked on to an already long list. She knows it's right that Eleanor contributes to the war effort but, truth be told, she'd forgotten what living with a small child's like. It exhausts her sometimes, even though Virginia usually does what she's told. She's like her mother that way, though she's nothing like as pretty.

She fed the chickens and the pigs first thing, before the heat cranked up, and now she's preparing her men's tea. She's made the dumplings already and they're sitting in the larder keeping cool under their net, next to the slabs of beef. She needs carrots and turnips and onions so she ventures out to the kitchen garden. Generations of manure have enriched the soil so her veg is the stuff of local legend. When she can be bothered, she enters the Best Produce competition at the summer fête and feels the envious eyes on her back when she brings them into the tent. She's won so often they've given her the cup, which now sits in the scullery holding the collar studs.

Her nose fills with the loamy scent of the land as she forks enough roots to fill the pot. It's her favourite smell in the world – much more to her taste than the Soir de Paris Albert buys her every Christmas, which just smells to her of city soppiness. From time to time her lower back twinges, but she doesn't stop digging. Hardiness is next to happiness in her book. She didn't even cry when she gave birth to her two sons, and they were giant specimens, both of them.

She sees a hole in the ground at the edge of the garden: them bloody rabbits have been at it again. When she's done for the day she'll fetch the shotgun and lie in wait for the buggers. She tries to remember if she's locked it in its cupboard. It wouldn't do to have Virginia sniffing around. Little fingers on the trigger – doesn't bear thinking about. Once when the kids were little she came across Frank and John sitting in front of Eleanor, holding the gun to her forehead between them. How she walloped them – they couldn't sit down for a week! But then boys are little heathens you've just got to rein in till they can look after their womenfolk in a proper manly way.

When she's washed and chopped and fried and stirred, she stows the stew in the Aga's belly. She sent the boys out with chunks of cheese and home-made bread and pickle this morning, but they'll eat their own arms when they come home if there's nowt on the table. John and Frank have inherited their parents' burliness, though thankfully Albert's ruddy complexion too, and have appetites that need constant stoking. Eleanor's different. Sometimes Elsie thinks she must have been swapped at birth because she's twig thin and toys with her food as though it's dangerous. She was always careful with her weight and her appearance, but when she married William and went to live in Harrogate, she turned into a fashion plate, all crisp and pricey like that Wallis Simpson. She changed her accent too, replacing its Yorkshire vowels with a southerner's yap, and sometimes Elsie has to ask her to repeat what she's said. When they have tea at Bettys Tea Rooms, Elsie wades through chocolate cake or treacle tart or apple pie with lashings of cream and extra sugar while Eleanor sits opposite her slowly stirring her lapsang souchong tea. With a slice of lemon in it. Disgusting. She can tell Virginia's inclined to be a fussy eater too, but she's having none of that.

'You'll eat what you're given and be glad on 't,' she says firmly when she sees the child pushing her carrots to the edge of the plate. 'Plenty of people have nowt on their plates – especially nowadays – so you just be grateful, lass.'

She's grateful now that Virginia's kept quiet so she can get on with her chores without having to run in and out. *She obviously loves sewing*, she thinks – just like Eleanor, who'd sit stitching for a whole afternoon.

She was never interested in helping her father on the farm or her mother in the kitchen, but if you gave her a box of embroidery silks she'd be absorbed for hours. When she was older she offered to do the family's mending which pleased Elsie no end because she was all thumbs with a needle. Accounts for Eleanor's interest in clothes she supposes, though herself she's never seen the point of dressing up except for Christmas and church.

Her daughter's always been mysterious to her. Like trying to see through steam. She was a studious child who'd ask for books on astronomy for Christmas and birthdays, never dollies or teddies like a normal little girl. It was as though she wanted to look away from earthly things, away from her family, live on some distant planet where she could dance alone in the ethereal light of a star. The boys just hit things and kicked things and compared their bumps and bruises, so she rubbed along with them in a way she could never have done with Eleanor.

Once she's put the men's work clothes in the copper to boil and hung the sheets out to dry, it's time to check on the child. Virginia came in twice earlier to have her needle rethreaded which was vexing, but she's not come back again so Elsie supposes she's mastered it. There'll be fruitcake if she's done well.

As she walks into the dining room she sees her granddaughter's face. Virginia is usually inscrutable, but her cheeks are hectic as Elsie looms over her, smelling of laundry and onions. Elsie's mouth flat-lines as she looks down at the table where bits of insect bodies lie in terminal chaos on the Georgian table handed down by her beloved grandfather. Her only family heirloom. For a moment this usually blunt woman is speechless – until she sees the deep cut in the surface. Three inches long in a perfectly straight line. The culprit sits panicky-eyed at the table with a knife in her hand. A pair of scissors lies next to the insects. Elsie makes a primitive sound of outrage that splinters the air. Virginia puts her hands over her eyes and her head on the table.

Elsie grabs her from behind and jerks her off the chair, grazing her shin on the table's edge. Virginia stays still, doesn't wriggle, because she can feel her grandmother's fury against her back. Elsie carries the little girl with beetle wings stuck on her forehead to the end of the hall.

Virginia knows where she's going.

Eleanor parks the car in the drive and walks over to her house without bothering to lock it. Some thief can pinch it. Some meteor can flatten it, she doesn't care. The stone steps feel like swansdown under her feet and she floats through the solemn oak doorway into the hall. She drops her keys on the coat stand and slips out of her skirt at the bottom of the stairs. As she glides over the treads she shrugs off her jacket, slides her blouse down the banisters and weaves to her bedroom in her underwear. She stands in front of the mirror, tracking the traces of the last three days. She looks at her hair, dishevelled by pillows and by fingers; at her belly, mapped and misted by his breath; at her insatiable centre, thrilling now with a desire that buckles her legs. She smiles at this woman she has only lately come to know, this Lazarus woman astonished by life. She takes off her bra and slides her knickers off, as silky as the hands that caress her thighs, ease them apart, open her up to passions in which she gladly drowns. She pops her stockings out of their suspenders and rolls them down her legs. She looks at her skin and feels it struggling to house this new flesh, fruity with sex. She picks up her underwear and crushes it against her nose. She inhales its scent, as frank and earthy as her pleasures. She coils the stockings, folds her lacy traces of underwear and hides them in a pochette at the bottom of her wardrobe. It comforts her to know they are there.

She riffles through her clothes to find something sexless.

Elsie's kneading the dough. She leaves deep knuckle prints in its surface as she punches it over and over. It will forgive her and rise again, unlike Grampy's table. She hears Eleanor's car crunch up the lane and blames her. She's far too kind to the child, far too willing to spare the rod and now the table's spoiled. Well, she'll tell her.

Eleanor stands in the doorway, trim, tailored, immaculate. Her mother pushes a sweaty lock of hair away, leaving a streak of flour on her forehead like a tribal sign.

'That child of yours,' she begins, 'that child is an animal, Eleanor. A wicked little savage. You leave her here, you dump her in my house, you bugger off in your fancy clothes . . .'

'For my war work, Mam, for my work,' says Eleanor evenly.

'For your bloody war work, and I leave her alone for a minute and she's at the table, at Grampy's table, hacking away with her knife till she's dug this bloody great hole in it so deep it's bloody ruined. I don't know what you've done to her – or not done to her, more like – but you've raised a little devil and I'll not be taking care of her again. You'll have to make other arrangements, lass.'

Eleanor feels a sudden rush of panic. She takes a step towards Elsie and tries to look remorseful. 'Oh, Mam, I'm truly sorry,' she says. 'I'm sure she didn't mean to. She's not normally destructive, only a little careless sometimes. Doesn't look what she's doing. I know she wouldn't want to upset you. She loves you to bits. I can hardly get her to sleep when she knows she's coming here. Remember that Christmas card she made you?' Elsie does. She was charmed at the time. 'She didn't make one for William's mother. Just you. *Special Nana*, do you remember? Only she spelled "special" wrong.'

Elsie looks over at the Welsh dresser where the card, heavily decorated with purple and orange rickrack, sits next to her best teapot. 'Well, she'd best make it up to me,' she says. 'She's in 't punishment corner – you know where to find it. She can probably come out now.'

I'm sitting on the floor, leaning up against a lawnmower. Well, I think it's a lawnmower but I can't see anything because Nana's turned the light off. I haven't been crying because if I cry Nana'll leave me down here till I'm all grown up and then I'll starve to death. I hear a horrid rustling noise over there and I get a sort of hiccough in my tummy. I hope it's one of those dear little field mousies, but suppose it's a dragon? Suppose it's been hiding in here for years and years waiting for a yummy little girl to come along? Suppose it burns me till I'm cooked then it gobbles me all up? I try talking like Uncle John does when the cows are scared. I say, 'Shaa now, lass, shaa, shaa, shaa,' lots of times but it doesn't make me not scared. Maybe it's because I'm not a cow. I wouldn't be scared if I had blanky to suck or my flappy book to read. Mind you, then I'd have to be an explorer and find a torch, but when I'd found one, I could look at my book with the cut-up people as long as I liked. I could make a doctor with a butcher's tummy and ostrich legs, or a soldier with a lion's tummy and little girl's legs, and they'd be my friends and we'd all go up a mountain and have a picnic and throw snowballs and laugh a really lot.

Poo! The cellar smells like the lavatory and the chicken shed and the dustbin all pushed together. I try smelling the inside of my arm because arm-smell might get rid of cellar-smell, but it doesn't work. It's very cold down here so I sing a lullaby because then I can fall asleep and not hear the dragon rustling. I sing 'Rock-a-Bye Baby' and 'Hush, Little Baby, Don't Say a Word' and then 'Rock-a-Bye Baby' again, but in a quiet voice so I don't wake myself up if I go to sleep. I'm still awake. I close my eyes and then I open them and I can't tell the difference. I hear voices up above me and one of them sounds like Mother, but it might be witches trying to trick me. Then they'd put a spell on me and magic me away and I'd never see her again. A little crying comes out of my chest.

I hear the cellar door rattle and then it's open, and I see Mother in the doorway with light round her head like Jesus's mummy.

'Mother?' I say, quietly in case it's a witch.

'I hear you've been a very, very naughty girl,' says Mother.

# 1975

Faisal hears the tapping on the bathroom door through the shower's thrum. Labelle's singing on the radio by the sink and he's weaving about, singing along without knowing exactly what it is Lady Marmalade's offering. He calls out, 'Yup, who is it?' and Ismail shouts, 'Me, Daddy!' and changes his tapping to keep time with the music.

'It's OK,' he says, 'door's not locked, you can come in.' His son's silhouette looms against the glass door, his head about knee height.

'Watch this, Daddy,' he says and pushes his face against the glass, inflating his cheeks like a blowfish.

'Aaaagh!' yells Faisal in mock terror. 'It's an alien!' Ismail finds this mighty satisfactory. His fingertips scamper up and down the glass and Faisal gives a little scream, 'Oh my goodness, baby aliens too – help!'

Ismail pulls away and giggles. 'Hah! Had you fooled, eh?' he says.

Faisal stops the shower and steps out. Wrapped in a towel, he squats down and draws his son into a damp embrace, smelling the little-boy excitement in his hair. However much he adores his other two, this child with the saucer eyes will always be his first. 'What's going on, skidoo?' he asks. 'You about ready to rock and roll?'

Ismail started big school two weeks ago, six months after Faisal started at St George's, and he stands there now in his crisp school uniform. When he'd been kitted out, he and his father compared outfits, Faisal's surgical scrubs a pale imitation of Ismail's Sherwood green, and Amina took photos of them larking about in the garden, Faisal pretending to sit on his son's head. Ismail has his father's height and slender grace and his mother's assumption that she'll always be loved, which has made the reception class a piece of cake.

'Have you had breakfast yet?'

'Nope. I was waiting for you.'

'Well, come and talk to me while I get dressed, then we'll eat together. Meal one, here we come!' he says, quoting Ismail's favourite book.

Amina's at the sink when they come into the kitchen, Farah gurgling on her ample hip. Shafiq sits at the table, experimentally pushing toast up his nose.

'Hey, Shaf, how about using your mouth?' says Faisal, moving his hand away, and Amina turns and smiles.

'That'd be another job for Dr Usman, wouldn't it?' she says. 'Remember when Daddy had to get that sweet out of your nose, Ismail? You were crying and crying and he had to use the tweezers.'

'Yes, and he had his doctor tie on – you know, that red one – so he knew what to do. Why haven't you got that tie on now, Daddy? Aren't you going to be a doctor today?'

Faisal had told Ismail that his tie gave him magical doctor powers, so he thinks quickly. 'Well, you know how before your birthday you didn't know how to ride a bike, and after your birthday you did?'

Ismail nods.

'It's a bit like that. Back then, when the sweet mysteriously jumped up your nose, I was just learning how to do doctor things, but now that I've learned, I can wear any old tie. I can even wear no tie at all, like at weekends. I'm still a doctor when we go swimming on Saturdays even though I'm only wearing my trunks. Or when I'm in my overalls, fixing the car.'

'That's when you're being a car doctor, Daddy, isn't it?' says Ismail. 'And when you fixed the shelf by my bed, you were being the book doctor, and when you're digging in the garden, you're the plant doctor.'

'Absolutely,' says Faisal. 'And now I'm going to be the breakfast doctor and fix us some toast using my special doctor powers.'

He is a hero to his son, a Colossus who keeps him safe in a sometimes scary world. When Ismail wakes in the night with a bad dream, it's his father he wants and Faisal can always settle him by cutting the fears down to size.

'So,' he says now, 'what's it to be – Marmite, marmalade or – mmmmm, what else begins with M?'

'Mmmmm – mermaid!' says Ismail. 'I want mermaid on toast!'

'Oh, bother,' says Amina, 'I'm completely out of mermaids.' She looks in the cupboard, shaking her head, 'But I've got plenty of rats, if you want them – fresh from Sainsbury's yesterday – or there's a little snail slime left, if Shafiq hasn't gobbled it all up. Anyone fancy bird dropping?'

'Yucky, yucky, yucky, yuck,' says Ismail. 'Marmite please, Daddy.'

Half an hour later, Faisal drops his son off at school, watching as he springs across the playground greeting other children by name. Two children from his class are wrapped, sobbing, round their mothers' middles as though hunting for a marsupial pouch, and one of the women pulls a rueful face.

'I don't know what your son's on,' she says to Faisal, 'but I'd like some of that, please.'

Ever since Ismail was born, Faisal has worried about how good a father he is. Wondered if he has the necessary patience. He's never forgotten the one time he smacked his son. He'd just come to the end of another hundred-hour week, had killed one of his patients in a fog of fatigue, and Ismail had whined at him once too often. The sharp pain of his hand hitting the little boy's forehead has stayed with him, along with the patient's name. Mary Samuelson. An internal haemorrhage he failed to diagnose. He knows now that doctors sometimes inadvertently kill their patients and has forgiven himself for the mistake, but he's never forgiven himself for losing control with his baby.

He mounts his bicycle and makes his way to the hospital. Amina uses the family Volvo for her work as an educational psychologist and he relishes the freedom of cycling, even through Britain's inclement weather. He never had a bike when he was growing up, though he touched one once. One of the boys from the big house left it propped up against a wall while he played cricket and Faisal dared to put his grubby hand on the saddle. Just for a second it felt like he was borrowing a wisp of the other boy's life.

St George's has been serving this part of South West London with its large Asian population for generations, and when Faisal was appointed senior registrar he told himself he was only taken on because of his background.

'They just want someone brown,' he said to Amina. 'Someone who can talk to the patients in their own language.'

They were in bed at the time, and she kissed his brow and his nose and his mouth. 'When will you realise how good you are?' she asked. 'You must be one of the youngest appointments they've ever made. This is one of the most prestigious teaching hospitals in London, Faisal – they don't employ fools.'

He saw the post advertised and realised it was in Virginia Denham's firm. Applying for the job had felt at once optimistic and impertinent and he procrastinated so long he nearly missed the deadline. She was his heroine. She was the reason he'd specialised in obstetrics and gynaecology and not in neurosurgery as his professor had wished. This queer, gangly figure loped into the lecture theatre at King's College medical school and drew him so completely into her mind that while she was speaking he could only think her thoughts. Other lecturers brought theory, learning, research, instruction, but Virginia brought the women she treated and made them come alive. She loved her patients and made it possible for Faisal to love his own.

When he got the job, he was told he had so far outstripped the previous candidates that the panel was inclined to stop there and send the rest packing. He tries to believe it but the voice in his head tells him that they got the name wrong, that they misread his application form and it's only a matter of time before he's unmasked. Amina doggedly shores him up when he crumbles, but she could be trying to stop a landslide with a toothpick.

Before the morning's ward round, he pops into Champney ward to check on a patient he operated on two days ago. She'd been plagued by massive fibroids and he had his work cut out calming her down in his clinic. She just knew she was bound the same way as her mother, she said, who died on the operating table when she was only forty-five. Same thing, she said. Women's troubles.

As he walks on to the ward, he sees Sue Burlington at the nurses' station. 'Hi, Sue,' he says. 'How did Anthony do in the race yesterday?'

'He did just great,' she says. 'Only came in second, didn't he? I tried not to gloat because one poor little lad was in floods, but I couldn't have been prouder!'

'Brilliant!' says Faisal. 'Send him my congratulations – next stop the Olympics?'

Sue grins. 'Why not?' she says. 'He can only try.'

She knows that Dr Usman doesn't stand on ceremony and that he treats his patients like human beings, not diagnoses. After he's operated he often pops in to see them during the day – 'Just passing by,' he says, as though it were a social call. The night sister told her that he once turned up still with a napkin tucked into his collar to talk to a woman convinced her treatment had made her infertile. Miss Denham is as tender with the patients, but can be brusque if she thinks a member of staff has been less than assiduous, so there's always a touch of trepidation in the air when she's due.

Faisal comes to the side of the bed. 'Hello, Mrs Peck,' he says, 'do you mind if I sit down?'

Mrs Peck's eyes flicker open and she gingerly pushes herself upright. She pats the blanket by her legs.

Faisal sits down, careful not to rock the bed. 'How are you feeling today?' he asks.

Mrs Peck has been busy devising new ways to frighten herself, her medication only one step ahead of the pain, but Faisal's direct gaze soothes her.

'It's all a bit painful, Doctor, to tell you the truth,' she says. 'When I came in I'd only just got over this nasty cough, but my throat's terrible now and when I cough it's like knives in my belly. Is that normal?'

'Yes, but I don't normally let my patients suffer, so why don't I up the painkillers a bit to make you more comfortable?'

'Thank you. I'm not usually a grizzler, but it's all I seem to do since the op. Before the op too, if I'm honest. I hate what this is doing to me – I've turned into a real moaning Minnie and there's plenty worse off than me.' She lowers her voice. 'Like that poor woman over there,' she says. 'You can hardly see her face on the pillow, she's so pale.'

'Well she's not my concern right now, Mrs Peck – you are. We

28

need to get you up and about as soon as we can, so let's concentrate on that, OK?' Mrs Peck nods.

'OK. But you need to tell me one more time – there wasn't anything else in there besides the fibroids, was there?'

Faisal has tried to reassure her before, but he knows that some patients are haunted by what their bodies are harbouring. What monsters are lurking in their ovaries or their uterus or their breasts, biding their time before savaging their host.

'I can promise you, hand on heart, that all I found were the fibroids – entirely benign, as I told you before – and nothing more. I might have to say it again, and that's fine, but there was absolutely nothing sinister in there. Your menstrual cycle should settle down shortly and there'll be no more heavy bleeding and discomfort.'

'That'll be a relief, Doctor. It was crippling me, all that.'

'I know. Now, get some rest and see if you can potter about a bit later – it'll do you good and get things going again.'

Virginia is in surgery all day so Faisal takes the ward round. When he arrives ten minutes early, the registrar is already waiting. Rupert Purkiss is a dapper young man, cheeky with ambition but without the skills to realise it. His bedside manner has all the charm of a used envelope and while Virginia does her best to introduce grace notes of empathy, his attitudes are hard-wired, so she contents herself with growling at him when his inexperience shows.

Faisal's first consultant was of the old school, a man as precious about the pecking order as the corners on his bow tie. He taught his juniors by humiliation and set Faisal and the senior registrar against each other in the ward round week after week. He'd sit back in his seat, his hands steepled on his waistcoat, watching the diagnostic cockfight he'd staged being played out in front of him. Desperate to win the boss's approval, the doctors would scratch the ground and strut and peck and crow and flap, but winning was illusory. The boss always won and he'd shovel them back in their boxes at the end, chastened by what they didn't know. Virginia gives time and space to each member of her team, whatever their rank, and pays their contribution her full attention.

As long as the patient is its heart and soul.

As long as there's nothing personal.

Faisal's clinical excellence is tempered by humility and he encourages the nurses to play a speaking role in the little piece of theatre they perform as they swish round the wards. At the end of the bed, having greeted the patient and examined the charts, he'd first ask her how she was feeling before turning to the nurses for their account of her progress. Purkiss was there to look and learn and listen. He would have had difficulty spelling the word humility. Faisal once overheard him on the labour ward speaking to a midwife as though she were an incompetent porter trolleying a patient down the corridors.

'Dr Purkiss,' he said, 'perhaps we could have a word.' In a side room he gave him a dressing-down that would have withered a more sensitive man.

'You will never, *ever* speak to a midwife like that again,' he said. 'You are to treat them as independent practitioners with more experience of childbirth in their little fingernails than you or I will ever have in our whole bodies. I suggest you sit at their feet and learn from them. They have little to learn from you.' Purkiss managed a flush of contrition which lasted about as long as a hen's sneeze, but Faisal never saw him do it again.

He's beaten Faisal by five minutes today.

'Tsk tsk – late again, Dr Usman? I'll have to mark you down in the late book.'

Faisal gives him a watery smile. He rarely dislikes anyone but Purkiss sticks in his craw. He reminds him of his housemaster at school, who'd look at the wiry brown boy dumped in this British outcrop as if he were a tick on the cheek of a cur. 'Usman!' he'd bark. 'Pick up a brain on your way to the swamp, would you? It might come in handy one day.'

But Faisal has learned how to dissemble, so Purkiss would never know that the cool professional walking towards the nurses' office with him would happily have taken him to the sluice and flushed him.

The nurses compete to make Faisal his tea and when they've brought him up to speed they sally forth on to the maternity ward.

A sweet milky haze hangs in the air, shivering with the wails of babies, the answering coo of their mothers and the emotional busyness of new lives. The first three beds contain women whose labours were textbook smooth, so Faisal has had nothing to do with them, but he stops nonetheless to congratulate them and to dandle their babies. He's refreshed each time he sees a woman open her heart to her child because in his Kashmiri village each new baby seethed with unmeetable needs, and each hungry mouth was a burden.

In the fourth bed a frail Bengali woman lies asleep. After she'd been in fruitless labour for fifteen hours Faisal was called in because she was exhausted and the baby distressed. As he hurried towards the delivery room, an untidy man sprang at him and grabbed his arm with both his hands.

'Doctor,' he said in heavily accented English, 'my wife is long time in this room. I am here long time also. You will kindly help her with my baby.'

'We'll look after her, Mr Khaliq, don't worry. The baby just needs help to come out because Mrs Khaliq's labour's been going on far too long. I'm going to do an emergency Caesarean and you'll meet your baby very soon.'

'Sheezer–?'

'Caesarean. We'll have to operate on your wife and lift the baby out. It's very safe.'

'No!' the man shouted. 'You will not cut with knife! She must have baby natural or . . . It is in God's hands and if He wills it, she must to die.'

'That's not an option, Mr Khaliq. We're going to save the baby's life, and your wife's too. Now please let me go.' He gently prised the man's hands off his arm, noticing the cuts and burns along his fingers. Mr Khaliq slumped against the wall.

'Just a little while, Mr Khaliq, and you can come in and see your baby – it's all going to be fine,' Faisal said as he went into the room.

But it wasn't fine and the corridor was empty when a nurse went to fetch the father. The baby needed urgent attention and the paediatric team worked heroically to revive him from a torpor close to death. When finally he was breathing, albeit fitfully, he was given to his mother swaddled so entirely in white blankets he looked like a currant in a snowdrift. Two nurses had to support her arms so that she could hold him as he jittered and trembled in his cocoon. Faisal knew immediately. The telltale facial features – the folds of skin obscuring the inner corners of the eyes, absent philtrum, narrow receding forehead and underdeveloped lower jaw – were diagnostic neon. Foetal alcohol syndrome. He'd call in Robina, the paediatric consultant, but the symptoms were unmistakable.

He draws the curtains round the bed and maps out the trajectory of the baby's future in a low voice, resting his hand gently on the tiny form in the cot.

'I'm sure you've all noticed this little chap's symptoms,' he says, 'pronounced ataxia, hypotonia and strabismus. Fortunately he's been spared any cardiac malfunction – but there may be renal anomalies, so the prognosis is not good. He'll almost certainly be mentally handicapped, his developmental stages will be delayed – if he reaches them at all – and mother's going to find him difficult to feed from the outset. Has she tried yet, Maureen?'

The nurse shakes her head. 'I sat with her for an hour this morning,' she says, 'but we couldn't get him to latch on. Mum was getting anxious, so we took him down to the nursery and fed him there. The poor little scrap's so floppy it took an hour and a half to get enough down him, but we managed it in the end.'

'Has her husband come to visit her?'

'Nope. Haven't seen hide nor hair of him. Not answering his phone either, though we've tried a dozen times at least. No one else has been in to see her and she doesn't speak any English, so we're doing our best with sign language. We've called the social work department, though, and they're sending Batool down – she's a Bengali speaker.'

'Good. That's excellent. They'll be able to follow this up and give her the support she needs. I'll try and have a quick word with her now, then we'll move on.'

Faisal has taught himself enough Bengali to get by, though his syntactical grip is often limp. Standing by the side of his patient's bed, he looks at her flushed face and wonders if she'll survive the shame. Her husband has already rejected her for failing to give birth naturally and she'll have no sanctuary either here or in Bengal, having so fatally offended Islam by drinking. He bends down to her ear.

'Hello? Mrs Khaliq Begum?' he says in Bengali. 'Can you wake up?'

Her eyelids flutter open and he looks into eyes so fretted with scleral haemorrhages they look like bloody thumbprints. 'I just a word to want with you,' he says. 'Can you me sit down if you allow?'

She nods and he pulls up a chair to the bed.

'My baby?' she says faintly.

'He being looked after by nurses. You are knowing he not good. You are knowing something is very bad when he born. Perhaps you not it know why no good, Mrs Khaliq Begum, but I tell you. I know you and alcohol – I know you drink alcohol, perhaps much, much alcohol, and your baby to take it in his body and is hurt. Bad hurt.'

'But you can make it better, Doctor, you can make him well again. Ibrahim, my son.'

Faisal pauses. 'I sorry,' he says slowly. 'We no can do nothing about Ibrahim – but he can live happy, although some things are bad. He is need you, his mummy. He is need you.'

Mrs Khaliq closes her eyes again and makes a sound that Faisal knows. His skin tightens with the memory of dusty mornings shredded with mothers' voices mourning their children. His own mother and her three. He resists his inclination to hold Mrs Khaliq's hand, piling dishonour on top of grief, but gestures to the ward sister to take his place by the bed. She sits by the diminutive form in the bed and strokes her forehead, crooning to her like an overheated baby.

Faisal moves on to the next bed.

However turgid our schedules, Faisal and I contrive to meet every day once we've ploughed through our clinics and lists and paperwork and meetings. And then meetings about meetings. It's a relief to work with a man whose philosophy so exactly chimes with mine. I'm the only female consultant I know among male peers who see nothing bizarre in pronouncing as though they, too, have a generative space inside them.

'I always tell my patients, when they ask me how much pain they'll feel when they give birth,' one said to me when I was training, '"Don't worry, Mrs So-and-so, it's a bit like banging your shin – only not quite as bad."' The seconds bled by as I battled to articulate my rage. Finally I said, 'Well, yes, Mr Carson, that might be one way of putting it, but only if your shins were being banged by iron poles for ten hours at a time.' With other male colleagues I sometimes feel like I'm speaking Yalunka, but Faisal's different. He understands that most women need to attempt a vaginal birth before the machines take over and the delivery room floods with experts. He knows, too, that if a patient has to put herself in a surgeon's hands to save her baby's life, or her own, she needs reassurance that she hasn't failed.

We sit in the canteen, bandying acronyms across the crusty table. I'm sipping mineral water but Faisal has wolfed down a cheese and pickle sandwich already and is now dipping biscuits into tea that could tar roads. Apart from his extraordinary reputation when he joined me, I know nothing about his background and am incurious. But what I do know is that he has the breadth of mind to imagine what a woman might be feeling, what she might need, and to take it into account.

He tells me about Mrs Khaliq, and I groan.

'Sometimes I think there's something savage at the heart of Islam,' I say, 'and I'm sorry if I'm treading on your cultural toes, Faisal, but I find it hard to stay rational in the face of some Muslim attitudes. I suppose I mean male attitudes, don't I? As though women only mattered for their breeding and feeding capacities. And then they're rejected if they fail to perform, just like your patient. I came across this when I was working in Africa and it never failed to infuriate me. How can that be justified? It's the twentieth century, for heaven's sake, not the eleventh.'

'I wouldn't justify it at all in Judaeo-Christian terms, but they're the wrong terms to use. When Muslim women have been brought up in this country by broad-minded parents – like my wife, for example – their cultural identity includes western ideas of rights, but Mrs Khaliq has brought with her from the subcontinent all the assumptions of her culture. And her class. I suppose if you raise an individual in a cardboard box from birth, that's how they imagine life to be. And of course that's what Mrs Khaliq's done to poor little Ibrahim, isn't it? Her un-Islamic habit's created the box he'll have to live in forever.'

'You've called in Robina, have you?'

'Yes – and the social work department's also been involved. Obviously they'll do what they can for the two of them, but the baby's prognosis is pretty grim. Along with all his physical handicaps he's likely to be severely retarded.'

I grimace. I remember delivering an anencephalic baby – only the second delivery I ever did solo – and the horror of seeing a head with the top third missing emerging from between his mother's legs. The mother – a young girl of sixteen – passed out when she saw the tiny boy, but I held him till he died forty minutes later.

I've never forgotten the guttering candle of a life spent dying.

# 1975

Gilda's alarm clock doesn't waste time. It wrenches her from her dreams with no manners and little ceremony. She smacks it on its idiot head, but even with her eyes closed she knows it's watching her not face the day. She's sluggish as she eventually crawls out of bed, sluggish as she crawls to the bathroom to pee and sluggish as she crawls downstairs to make herself coffee. She pushes the plunger down so fiercely the cafetière spits hot tears on the floor and she fetches kitchen paper to mop up the mess. She feels thrashed, something that rarely happens in her karate class. There she's not defenceless. There she studies the moment between defending herself and giving up. 'Fight or die,' Takeshi says, and she's fucked if she's going to die. But something did die last night. Raymond killed it off, sitting with his hands between his knees as though to stop them reaching out.

'You changed,' he said. 'You were so feisty when we first met. You looked like you took no prisoners, you know? When you walked into the bar that time you looked like you were a woman in control. You didn't need anybody, and I liked that. And I liked that you kept me at arm's length for so long and that I felt I had to earn you in some way. But when I'd done that, when I'd earned you, got close to you, you – I dunno, it was like you got these suckers or something and I . . . I . . .' his hands escaped and sliced the air. 'I can't be everything to you, you know? I can't be your total universe. No one can. Oh, don't do that, Gilda. Please don't cry.'

She wasn't crying, she was leaking.

'I never wanted to hurt you, but it's just too easy and now I have to get out before you suck me dry.'

'But I need you.'

'And that's the trouble. I know you do and you needing me feels like quicksand. It may be me. I may be bad for you or something, I don't know, but the truth is, I can't carry on. There's no future for us like this, Gilda. Perhaps one day you'll know it's for the best and forgive me.'

What is there to forgive? All he's done is repeat what her previous boyfriends have said. All four of them, like ducks quacking their ducky chorus in a ducky row. She allowed herself to imagine that Raymond was The One because he understood something about her that the other three missed. That she's a quick-change artist, a mistress of disguise, but he seemed to spot the hoax and reached his hands underneath to touch her skin. With him it had felt safe to stop playing the roles. Safe to come to him naked. She told him her stories in bed, in the bath, over meals laced with leeks and honey: told him about cooking with Dilys, her mother, and eating with Aaron, her father. About her time on the scene. She thought he knew she was different and would be careful. But here she is, dumped again.

She goes upstairs and pulls the bedding off the bed. She holds her breath so she doesn't have to smell his sweet spiciness on the sheets. She'll overdose it with fabric conditioner. Meadow Flowers, or some such. Tropical Fruit. Maybe Myrrh might be better, to mark the death of another relationship.

Colour. She needs colour today, so she pulls out her cobalt-blue dress with the stitches round the neck like a skinhead tattoo and buckles a red belt round hips no one would call childbearing. The bolshie colour keeps her going as far as the bathroom mirror, but she has to reapply her mascara three times before her eyelashes are dry enough. She finds the lipstick that's as shouty as the belt and slicks her lips with a fat layer of Jezebel. She singles out curls with her fingers and lets them toss their gloss down her back. She squirts herself with the perfume he always said made him feel sick, which today just smells of solitude.

'Spinster of this parish,' she says out loud, wishing spinster didn't sound like a spidery cry for help.

She bangs the bedding in the machine, doubling the amount of conditioner, wishing she could just leave it in there until it mildewed. She could chuck it out then. She says out loud, 'Fuck you, Raymond, you cunt! Cunt you, Raymond, you fuck!' but it gives her only fleeting satisfaction. Raymond was curiously squeamish about swearing and she'd always had to watch her tongue.

She's concealed the smudge of grief under her eyes but puts on her shades as a precaution when she leaves the house. Fortunately there's enough wan sun whimpering through the clouds to make wearing them plausible, but she doesn't mind looking pretentious. Not today anyway. She keeps her head high as she walks to the tube station, like she's scouring the sky for scavengers, but lowers it to look both ways, then both ways again as she crosses at the tube station.

As usual, she's ten minutes early as she arrives at Maxim's salon sitting snug-as-a-bug-in-a-rug in a Regency house behind the Hilton. Samuel, aka Maxim, will have been there for half an hour, giving the equipment an extra polish and bullying the towels into neat stacks. He hears her come in and twirls round prettily.

'Darling!' he trills. 'Ten minutes early. As usual!' He flutters his fingers at her. 'Denise just can't get this right, can she? Never mind, it gives me a reason to get up in the morning – I really should get out more! How's you?' Maxim is camper than a row of tents, which is how their clients like it, but is in fact president of his synagogue and lives with his wife and five children in a part of Ealing that aspires to be thought sylvan. Gilda has worked for him since she qualified and he calls her his Head Prefect despite the fact that Pamela has been there ten years longer. She does her best to conceal her resentment behind the YSL mask but sometimes Gilda finds her equipment rearranged. 'Bloody mice,' Pamela says when she mentions it.

She slips on the white tunic edged with blue she wears for work, which looks comfortingly clinical in this temple of vanity. Its vaguely medical air reassures their clients that what goes on here is less a matter of vapid wanting, more a question of need. They don't call her a beauty therapist for nothing.

She spends the day smoothing and pummelling her clients' skin, the wickedly seductive creams plumping wrinkles and tightening jowls and unknotting backs. She wakes up women who've fallen asleep under her fingers, and keeps safe their confidences in her pocket, along with their generous tips. She hears of infidelities and adventures and more than once of sexual practices at the indelicate end of the spectrum. She calls her friend Karen before she finishes and arranges to meet her in a bar near Grosvenor Square after work.

'Goodie, goodie!' says Karen. 'We can celebrate your liberation – make sure the bastard can hear us from Hampstead! I always thought he was a conceited git – I'm sorry, I know you really liked him and everything, but he never really floated my boat, you know?'

Over a bottle of champagne, they assay Raymond's qualities and, by extension, men's. There isn't much left of them by the time they've finished the bottle and eaten a bowl of elderly peanuts, and Karen suggests maybe they should just fall in love with themselves. 'Or each other,' she says, 'except you might taste funny,' and she cackles.

When Gilda emerges from the tube at the other end and crosses the road, she sees a man on a bike stopped by the lights, his long leg propping him up against the kerb. He's looking at her. She's being looked at. Nothing new there, but as she turns her head slightly she clocks an attractive Asian man in a suit.

Objectively attractive, that is.

Whether it's the champagne or the conversation that lies so morbidly in her stomach, she feels too queasy to eat when she gets home, and spends the evening not contacting Raymond and crying so hard she's surprised the wallpaper doesn't peel.

He's right of course. Graham, her first proper boyfriend, was the first to say it. He'd tentatively introduced her to the scene and was stunned when she took to it like a hound to the chase. But when his mistress turned slave, he'd thrown her over. With rather less courtesy than Raymond, since he was a man for whom disappointment was distasteful. She knew she was doing it with him and with Jock and with Melvyn, but didn't seem able to stop herself. When she was offered even a crumb of affection, she would for a while feign lack of appetite until she thought it safe to be ravenous.

But she's nothing if not a consummate actress, and her girlfriends never know since, after a feast of gossip and calumny, she always bounces back. Life and soul, she is. Never poops a party. She and her posse prowl the city streets like vixens on stilts, ribald and rowdy, dangerously sexy, sniffing the air for prey. Karen wears her Ray-Bans because she says she's channelling Jackie O, but from behind them she marks their impact, collecting boys' stares like scalps. They swoop into clubs fashionably late, catching fame-hungry bands in The Speakeasy and wolfing down steak in the Bag O'Nails. Paul met his Linda in the Bag and there's always a chance that they'll snaffle a star if they make enough noise.

While she revels in her friends' morning-after stories, Gilda always goes home alone. She knows she's too choosy, but it keeps her safe. *Better a book at bedtime than a boy*, she thinks.

# 1938

A crack of thunder loud enough to startle stone wakes Eleanor and she slowly opens her eyes, sticky still with sleep. As usual, William has stolen the blankets and lies with his back to her, a hummock under the counterpane. She hates her husband. He is a liar and a thief. When he said that he loved her two years ago, his grubby fiction stole the last vestige of hope left after Edgar died. She must have been drunk with grief, she thinks, to have accepted the suit of his dull, unreachable brother. She must have thought he'd be Denham enough. Along with the wedding dress made by his mother, she slipped on the career of wife, her future vaporised like an early morning puff of breath. The future she'd imagined ever since she'd known she had one. Two weeks before the wedding, she sat bolt upright in bed at three in the morning. It was as if she'd been looking at the world through a Vaseline smear. As if William could ever be Edgar. She roamed the farmyard shivering, not sure if it was temperature or terror that made her feel so desperate.

She went through with it of course, her options crushed by family expectations. She stood at the altar in flat shoes so she didn't tower over her new husband who is two inches shorter than her, hair coiled at the base of her head to avoid adding more height. Their wedding photographs show a couple posing on a sunny day, but William's dark face is in shadow, as though he's attracted his own little cloud. Eleanor has the kind of stick-on smile usually to be found in a joke shop, her eyes wide open and her head cocked at just the right angle to show the noose of Denham pearls round her neck.

Every day disappointment worms its way further into her guts. She tries not to show it, practises tipping her head to one side and smiling winsomely because unhappiness will carve ugly lines on her face. The first clause in her job description requires her to look good at all times, either on her husband's arm or roaming the town doing wifely things, and she is nothing if not a perfectionist.

He rolled on to her last night and had sex. It was, as it always is, nasty, brutish and short. That phrase rages through her head when his sweat drips down the side of her neck, but she doesn't think whoever said it was talking about sex.

She found out about mating from the farmyard. Her father insisted that she watched the ram tupping the ewes and the stallion pummelling her favourite mare, and jerked her head back when she tried to look away from its mindless urgency. William never asks if he may, which would at least be polite, but lifts up her nightie under the sheets and pounds at her body as though digging a ditch. While he's pounding she sometimes pictures Edgar, wonders how he'd have been as a lover, but it just makes her cry. She stifles the tears because if William saw them she'd have to explain.

She slides out of bed, careful not to tug the blankets and wake him up. She's done that before and he's rolled on again, his ugly morning breath marinating her face. It's chilly and she slips on her woolly dressing gown and slippers, shivering her way to the kitchen to riddle the range. Five steps down the stairs the nausea hits her and she races to the bathroom, clutching her mouth. She vomits so long and so violently she's surprised not to see her intestines looping the mess in the sink. *Food poisoning*, she thinks, when her heart steadies and she stops trembling. She casts her mind back to last night's meal, but there's nothing suspicious. The butcher saves her choice cuts of meat because he's sweet on her and she is always careful to cook the vegetables into despair. She supposes it will pass and cleans up, holding her breath to avoid retching again at the stench. She asks William at breakfast if he's feeling all right. He is. He has the rudest of health. She doesn't tell him she's been sick.

*Must be a bug*, she thinks, as she continues to feel sick all day and chucks up her lunch and her tea and her supper. The next day is the same. As is the next, so it's time to go to the doctor.

Dr Prendergast retired six months ago and she knows that a new doctor has taken over. She isn't sorry to see the back of the old one, who regarded patients as vexatious diversions from his golf and his drinking and had a talent for misdiagnosis. She's heard from her neighbour that Dr Greenaway's a good egg, so she doesn't brace herself as she arrives at the surgery. She's reapplied her make-up after this morning's paroxysms and hopes she won't be sick again in his presence.

As she enters the waiting room she is startled to see a new receptionist, but then remembers Dr Prendergast took the old one with him, since he was married to her.

The woman behind the desk is enormous, as though she has eaten her own body weight in butter. 'Good morning,' she says. 'I don't think I've seen you before, Mrs . . .?'

'Denham. Mrs Denham.'

'Very glad to meet you, Mrs Denham. I'm Annie Greenaway, doctor's wife – but do call me Annie. I don't stand on ceremony. Make yourself comfortable – Harrogate seems to be in fine fettle today, so he'll be with you shortly.'

Eleanor settles herself in the far corner of the room so she can inspect Mrs Greenaway without drawing attention to herself. She thinks she must be in her forties because her hair is turning grey, though her face is unwrinkled. She wears an incongruous bow in her hair, as if she's about to play hopscotch in the playground, but her clothes are those of an elderly woman indifferent to her looks. Her frock bothers neither with fashion nor with form and its sleeves are losing the battle to contain her arms' dimpled flesh. Eleanor has put on her yellow Moygashel frock this morning, topped by a cream tailored jacket and accessorised with amber jewellery and kid shoes. When Annie gets up to go to the filing cabinet, her buttocks swing against the crêpe of her frock like balloons in a breeze and Eleanor can't keep her eyes off her, though she knows it's uncouth. She thinks she could probably fit into Mrs Greenaway's hem without making much of a bulge. A buzzer sounds twice and Annie turns to Eleanor.

'You can go in now,' she says. 'Doctor's free. I expect you know where he is.'

'Yes, I do. Thank you.'

Gerald Greenaway stands as she enters his room, towering over his patient, who is above average height herself. He sees a woman with the pellucid skin of a real redhead, her hair organised in auburn coils on her head, her face tight with anxiety. He has cerulean blue eyes and the sandy colouring of the English, though his brown skin testifies to a love of playing cricket in all weathers. He wears what he always wears for work: brown slacks, cream Viyella shirt, woollen tie and tweed jacket, the elbows reinforced by the leather patches Annie attaches with blanket stitch. He holds out a hand and Eleanor takes it. It is surprisingly soft.

'Dr Greenaway,' he says. 'How do you do, Mrs . . .?'

'Mrs Denham,' she says. 'Eleanor Denham.'

'Do have a seat, Mrs Denham.'

She sits opposite him on the other side of his desk. She can smell him from here. He smells like a man confident of himself and his gifts, unlike William, who smells of treachery.

'So, what can I do for you today?' he begins.

'I've been suffering the most awful sickness, Doctor. At first I thought it must have been something I ate, but Mr Denham was fine and since it's been going on for three days I thought it was time I came. I'm sorry to bother you.'

'Well, you know, if my job bothered me I'd give it up and sell tractors or something. Nothing you say can bother me at all. Do go ahead.'

He takes a history of her illness on a notepad and when she's finished asks her to lie on the couch so he can examine her. He pushes a button on the intercom on his desk and says, 'Annie dear? Would you be kind enough to pop in here for a moment? Thank you. My wife's a nurse,' he says, turning to Eleanor, 'so she's a great help, as you can imagine.' *And chaperone*, thinks Eleanor, who always thought Dr Prendergast stood too close.

Annie smells of Parma violets and is a sympathetic presence. Dr Greenaway examines his patient, apologising when she winces. Her breasts hurt.

'How are your periods, Mrs Denham?' he asks. 'I wonder when you had your last one?'

'It should have been a little while ago – I can't think when exactly because I've never been very regular.' Dr Greenaway puts an arm round her shoulders to help her sit up on the edge of the couch.

'Look, there *is* a tummy bug doing the rounds at the moment, but I don't think you've got it. Is there any chance you might be pregnant, do you think?'

Eleanor turns the colour of bone. She sways slightly.

'Oh dear, oh dear – now just put your head down, low as you can between your knees. Well done, that's grand. Annie, would you be kind enough to get Mrs Denham some water?'

When Eleanor has recovered, she holds the glass of water in hands that have lost their grip.

'Feeling better now?' Gerald asks.

'Yes – yes, I suppose so. I thought I was just coming down with something, that's all. It never occurred to me that I could be . . . could be . . . was maybe . . .'

'Pregnant?'

'Yes.' She blushes. 'I mean, we're very careful if you know what I mean. We use . . . oh, I can't say it. It's too embarrassing.'

Annie pats her arm. 'I know, dear, I know. Do you mean Durex by any chance?'

Eleanor nods.

'There you are then,' says Annie. 'Jolly good. Sometimes it's hard to talk about those things, isn't it?'

'We'll do a test anyway,' says her husband. 'I expect you know the form, do you?'

'No.'

'I'll give you a bottle to take home with you and I want you to collect a urine sample first thing in the morning. Leave the first little bit of the flow and fill the bottle up from the next bit. What we call a mid-flow sample.'

Annie catches the look on Eleanor's face. 'It can be a bit messy, dear,' she says, 'but spread your legs wide and wash your hands afterwards. It's not so bad really.'

Eleanor leaves the surgery, the bottle in her handbag jeering at her. She vomits in a privet hedge on her way home and doesn't bother covering it up with leaves.

★

She is pregnant of course. When Dr Greenaway tells her, she sits taller in the chair as though stretching her neck for the hangman.

He watches the tears course down her face and says, 'It doesn't look as though this is welcome news, Mrs Denham.'

She shakes her head.

'Were you planning to wait a little while before starting a family?'

She shakes her head again.

'Are you worried about the health of the baby – any problems in your family?'

'Not the sort of problems you're referring to, no.' Eleanor sounds like she's speaking through a towel. 'My husband and I . . . my husband . . . my husband isn't what I want, you see, and now there's a baby I'm stuck with him. Can't get out and . . .' she jackknifes forwards, her face in her hands. 'Can't you do something, Doctor?' she says from her lap. 'Can't you take it out of me?'

Gerald has been asked this before and tries not to judge. 'I can't,' he says. 'Not only is it illegal, but I'm a Catholic, you see.' Eleanor sits up and wipes her eyes.

'Yes. Yes, I see,' she says. 'I'm terribly sorry I asked.'

For four months she says nothing to William, nothing to her mother, nothing to her mother-in-law. Dorcas has tried to be subtle about her craving for a grandchild but Eleanor feels inspected every month. Sometimes she's wanted to write a diary of her menstrual cycle and give it to Dorcas to shut her up. 'Here you are, Dorcas – bit of a bedtime read for you.' Now she's inadvertently done the right thing, her mother-in-law's triumph will be unendurable.

She's making suet pastry in the kitchen when she feels a butterfly in her womb. Later that day it flutters more insistently and she sits down heavily on the bed she's making. It's a baby. She's been willing the pregnancy to get better, as though it were some fleeting indisposition, but it seems to have settled in for the duration. Her future's now chronically sick.

She tells William the next morning over breakfast, thinking that once she's said her piece he'll at least go to work. He's never taken a day off in his life so he won't hang around celebrating and she can get back to grieving.

46

'I think you should know, William,' she says stiffly, 'that I am going to have a baby. I'm pregnant.' William's about to take a bite of toast but his hand freezes. He doesn't flush with excitement or leap up shouting hurrah! or race to the other side of the table to embrace his wife, but sits like a petrified tree in his chair. His hand tips and a gobbet of marmalade drops on to his tie.

'Are you sure?' he asks. 'How do you know?'

'I went to the doctor of course, and he did a test. I'm quite sure. The baby's due in August.'

'Well, that's fine then. Will you tell Mummy?'

'Of course. And my parents too. I'm sure they'll be pleased.'

'Good, yes. Oh Lord – look at the time – must dash!' and he gets up and leaves. In the car on his way to the factory he curses Edgar for dying. For condemning him to this job, this woman and now this child.

Eleanor goes to the drinks cabinet in the drawing room and pours herself a cherry brandy before she picks up the phone to spread the tragic news. The sticky boiled-sweet drink relaxes her throat and she pours another to blunt the needles in her head.

Dorcas is predictably ecstatic and insists on coming round in half an hour's time.

'I'll cancel my bridge party,' she says. 'You and I can make a list of everything the baby's going to need. There's an awful lot of things to buy and you won't have thought of them all, so I'll give you some tips. I am an old hand, after all.' *As though having two children gives her a VC in childrearing,* Eleanor thinks sourly. Her mother's pleased too – about as pleased as she would be had Albert come home with a combine harvester he'd won at cards.

'That's grand, lass,' she says. 'At least one of you's doing your bit. John and Frank might get the idea now, though they're showing no signs last time I looked.' She invites her and William for lunch on Sunday – 'Just the usual,' she says. 'Nothing fancy.'

When George finds out from Dorcas that their son has impregnated his wife, he is rueful but relieved. At least William has some spunk in his dunk. But he hopes the young couple don't have any sentimental ideas about naming it after its dead uncle and wonders

47

if he should say something. He does the right thing though, and takes William to the Tap and Spile where he and Albert plough through a bottle of Jameson's. William has a shandy.

Three days later Germany annexes Austria, swallowing it into the Reich's maw like a bedtime snack. William devours the press reports and talks of little else at the factory and at mealtimes and in bed, muttering darkly, 'This doesn't bode well for England, Eleanor. We must steel ourselves. I think war with the Germans is inevitable.' Eleanor has her own wars to wage, what with the baby sapping her strength and causing her skin to erupt and giving her piles so severe the lavatory becomes enemy territory. She goes to see Dr Greenaway every week and he comforts her. She never mentions abortion again, but he understands that, like Austria, she feels consumed.

She discovers that he finds the same succour in music that she does, inclining both to the precision of Bach and the grandeur of Beethoven with a sly fondness for swing. She tells him one day of her love for the cinema – in particular the tip-tapping charms of Fred Astaire and Ginger Rogers.

'I go in the day,' she says, 'on my own. William adores reading but rather despises films.'

'I wish I could go more often,' he replies, 'but Annie doesn't go out.'

Eleanor has never seen his wife about town and has wondered. 'Does she think the cinema is foolish nonsense, like William?' she asks.

'No, no, it's not that she won't go out, it's that she can't. She suffers from agoraphobia, you see, so she's pretty much confined to the house and the surgery.'

Eleanor hasn't noticed she was ill. 'Agoraphobia?' she says. 'Does it hurt?'

Gerald laughs. 'Not physically,' he says, 'but she's prostrated by anxiety if she so much as thinks about going outside and has terrible panic attacks if she actually does, so she stays indoors mostly. We manage.' He looks disconsolate. 'I do rather miss the flicks, though.'

Eleanor feels a question rising in her gorge like another wave of nausea – *Will you come with me then? Please?* – but it wouldn't do. It wouldn't do at all, so she says instead, 'What a pity,' and they talk about her indigestion.

Dorcas has convinced herself that Eleanor's carrying a boy and insists she has the nursery painted blue. She gives her the family cot in which her sons dribbled and cooed, and talks about them compulsively. *She could bore the ears off an elephant*, Eleanor thinks but she nods her head and smiles in the right places.

'They were so different,' Dorcas says. 'Could hardly believe I'd produced them both. I knew right from the start that Edgar was going to be a leader of men. Kicked me like a kangaroo when he was inside, and when he finally shot out, he'd fill that tiny chest like a pair of bellows and howl like a banshee. I always felt he wanted me to know what he needed *right away*. The darling boy was in such a hurry all his life, may he rest in peace. William was quiet from the beginning. The midwife used to say to me, "Be thankful he's such a peaceful little thing, Mrs Denham," and I suppose she was right because Edgar did take up most of my time.' Her face falls. 'You and he would've had your own babies by now, if he'd lived of course. I wonder what they'd have been like?'

*And you think I don't?* thinks Eleanor.

Dorcas recovers herself and continues. 'Terrible what these Nazis are doing in Germany' – she pronounces it 'nayzeyes', as though that way they become comic book characters and she can just turn the page – 'But I'm sure Mr Chamberlain will keep us safe in our beds. Now, you won't be nursing baby, will you? Don't want to spoil your lovely figure . . .'


The baby dawdles when she comes, and Eleanor labours for twenty-seven interminable hours before she finally slips out.

The midwife lifts her up and says, 'Well done, Mrs Denham, it's a beautiful little girl!'

Eleanor is appalled by the blood streaking the baby's face like some Neanderthal rite: it looks like she'll continue to leach her, as though making her bleed through the pregnancy wasn't enough.

She's taken to the hospital nursery and Eleanor is able to sleep at night, but she's brought back during the day and the nurses pester her like tsetse flies with instructions: 'This is the way you feed the baby/wind the baby/bathe the baby.' 'This is the way you change her nappy.' 'Congratulations, Mrs Denham, well done.' William arrives the morning after the birth and Eleanor hears her marriage revving up its engine.

'Well done, old girl,' he says, shifting from foot to foot by the bed. 'Mummy tells me you must have had a hard time because it took so bally long. Poor old thing. And there she is,' he says, glancing at the cot. 'What are you planning to call her?' *Once she's named*, he thinks, *we'll be yoked together like galley slaves*.

'I haven't really thought,' says Eleanor, 'but I'm sure something will crop up.'

'Jolly good. I suppose Mummy might want one of her family names in there – have a word with her, will you? Look, I have to dash. There was a nasty accident yesterday and one of the men is on a ward in the other block – I have to go and see him, poor chap.'

The baby is long and scrawny but seems to understand she's to do what she's told. She takes to the bottle with an air of resignation, sucking so quietly you'd hardly know she'd been hungry.

When Eleanor sees Gerald coming into the ward three days later, the sun splits the storm clouds outside and shines on her alone. He lopes over to her bed.

'Oh, haven't you done well!' he says, his dear eyes crinkling. 'And here's the baby – what a gorgeous little creature! May I hold her for a moment?' He lifts the baby out of Eleanor's arms. 'You know, Mrs Denham . . .'

'Do please call me Eleanor.'

'Eleanor. I think the smell of babies is finer than the most expensive French perfume you can buy. You'd make a fortune if you bottled it, don't you think?'

Eleanor can only smell purgatory, but she smiles. 'I'm so grateful you came,' she says. 'I was hoping you would,' and she pulls herself up in bed, her stitches suddenly forgotten.

When he asks her if the baby's got a name, he makes choosing one sound like an adventure, and they bandy possibilities about. He tells her he had a sister called Virginia who died of scarlet fever when he was ten and she reaches out and touches the hand that's cradling her daughter's head.

'Then that's it,' she says. 'We'll call her Virginia.'

The baby develops eczema three months later, her enraged skin leaking blood and pus over her clothes and her bedding and her mother. Eleanor is up seven, eight times a night, trying to stop her yowling. It feels avaricious, as though she wants more of her mother than there is to give.

Gerald explains that the condition is not uncommon and that she is likely to grow out of it. 'By the time she goes to school, probably,' he says, and Eleanor slumps.

'Is there nothing you can give her?' she asks. 'Surely I don't have to get up to her eight times a night for the next five years, do I, Gerald?'

Gerald leans over and strokes Virginia's blotchy cheek with such tenderness that Eleanor wants to weep. 'Poor little scrap,' he says as the baby twitches in her mother's arms and lets out a squeal, 'she's having a perfectly beastly time of it, isn't she? And I can see you are too.' He pats her hand, and her engagement ring ticks against his palm. 'Look, I can certainly prescribe something to ease her symptoms. It's a bit messy, but all it means is washing day'll take a bit longer – you won't mind that, will you?'

Eleanor's face sets.

'Oh dear,' he says. 'What a clot I am! I'm so sorry – Annie's rather in charge of all that sort of stuff.'

'It's never ending,' Eleanor says desperately. 'I hardly know who I am any more. I look in the mirror and all I see is someone with only the housekeeper to talk to. Someone who watches her wash the bottles and sheets and clothes all day then puts food on the table for Mr Denham when he comes home and washes up afterwards. I never planned to be a drudge when I grew up. Actually what I really wanted to be was an astronomer.'

'Oh, but how fascinating! I had a telescope when I was a boy and was absolutely positive I saw creatures roaming round Saturn once. But then I carried on believing in fairies for far too long – didn't tell anyone of course, because the other boys would probably have put my head down the lavatory if they'd found out.' He glances at his watch. 'Look here, Eleanor, I think you're my last patient today, so why don't I ask Annie to make us a nice cup of tea and we'll drink it while I show you how to deal with Virginia's skin. Is it Virginia, or do you ever call her Ginny?'

'No, never. I rather disapprove of diminutives. I was never Ellie as a child and William has always been William. But was your sister ever called Ginny?'

'No, but she had the brightest red hair, so I used to call her Ginger Nut, like the biscuits. I missed her like stink when she died.'

Annie offers to take the baby out to the waiting room while Gerald and Eleanor drink their tea. 'Oh, what a little cherub!' she says as she lifts the baby out of Eleanor's arms. 'And what a treat to have a bit of a borrow. I expect you'll miss her dreadfully when she's gone, Mummy.'

'Mm,' says Eleanor.

It takes them a while to get round to discussing Virginia's treatment because the air fills with stars and planets and meteors. Gerald tells her how he laughed for weeks when he looked for Uranus, apologising for his ribaldry, and Eleanor turns the colour of carnations when she admits she giggled too. They've been talking for half an hour when Annie taps on the door and brings Virginia in. Eleanor falls out of her orbit round Gerald and takes the baby back.

'She's been so good,' says Annie. 'We've quite set the world to rights, we have – but she told me she needs Mummy now. Do you think maybe it's time for her lunch? It's certainly time for ours.'

'Goodo,' says Gerald. 'I'll come in shortly, thanks,' and Annie goes off in the direction of their house behind the surgery.

When he shows Eleanor what she's to do, she's both appalled and gratified. Appalled because she's to slather a thick layer of ointment on Virginia's body and gratified that she's to bandage her so she won't ooze.

She puts on a pinny when she applies the ointment – sometimes four times a day when Virginia's skin is bad – and washes her hands frantically afterwards, not persuaded the condition isn't contagious. Despite her attention to hygiene, however, the baby develops blisters that march rapidly over her body, and Gerald pays a house call.

'Oh dear, it's terribly badly infected,' he says, and takes them in his car to the hospital, where the baby is immediately admitted.

The four days Virginia's in hospital are heavenly. Eleanor goes in to see her at around teatime, which is her only commitment of the day. She takes leisurely baths, her book propped up on the rack, a cup of lapsang on the floor. She drinks several cups a day, though never in the evening because William says the smell makes him heave.

But she was always going to be forced to bring the baby home, and Gerald makes another house call.

They sit together in the polite drawing room, Virginia asleep in the nursery. The hospital has given Eleanor antihistamine to calm her down at night, so an hour ago she dosed her up to keep this precious time unencumbered. Gerald looks weary. He's been up all night delivering a pair of twins who were disinclined to leave their pod and has been practising geriatric medicine all day, his waiting room abuzz with the thises and thats of old age. Eleanor looks at the fatigue folding his face and longs to stroke it away with her fingertips. Instead she offers him a drink. He has been careful to make this the last house call of the day, so he accepts. He watches as she kicks her shoes off and skips to the drinks cabinet like a seed pod frisking in the wind.

'I've got pretty much everything, I think. Willi– . . . I make sure everyone's tastes are catered for. Gin, sherry, whisky . . .'

'Stop right there,' he says. 'If you had a single malt, you'd make me a very happy man indeed.'

She pours him a wildly generous glass and brings it over. She holds on to it just a shade too long, so his fingers wrap round hers for an instant. Before she sits down with her equally generous sweet sherry, she goes over to the gramophone and riffles the records on the shelves.

'What shall we have?' she asks. 'Anything you want.'

Gerald knows perfectly well what he wants but can't ask for it, so he settles for the *Goldberg Variations* and Eleanor puts it on. She carries herself over like a gift and sits down at the other end of the sofa from him, folding her legs under her. There's a glimpse of lace at the swell of her thigh and he flushes with the effort of staying at his end. He pushes at the cushion next to him to wedge himself in.

It isn't the alcohol speaking – though it helps – it's the feeling between them that they fit, and as they tell their stories they move together like an agile joint.

She tells him of a young girl with mud on her boots and ambition in her head. A changeling child in a family expert in weevils and worms but amateur in raising a daughter. Tells him she imagined looking through a telescope, watching nebulae and planets and stars step out from behind the night's arras. Tells him about Edgar. About their perfect match. About the hole in her life that wasn't William's shape.

He tells her of a little boy who always knew he'd be a doctor. Always knew he'd get married and have children. Tells her that these things were as ordinary as toast – not a matter of wishful thinking, but of certainty. He tells her of his splendid wedding to his sprightly nurse in a cathedral whose grandeur nearly crushed him, where the heady scents of faith and flowers made him reel.

'I loved her, Eleanor, I did,' he says, sounding perfidious to himself, 'and we had such plans. No, they weren't even plans – we never sat down and wrote a list, but I knew she wanted the same things as me without having to spell it out. She stopped working as soon as we married and we waited. We didn't worry for the first year or two because I knew these things sometimes take their time and we were just settling into married life anyway, so we were content. Making a home together, you know, and she's a grand cook, so staying trim was a bit of a struggle.' He pats his front. 'But cricket has always been my passion, so mostly I manage to keep the weight off.'

*But she didn't*, thinks Eleanor.

'But she didn't,' he says. 'When it became clear that she wasn't able to get pregnant – and we never found out why, though she had all the tests – she started eating for two. It was as though if she couldn't fill up with a baby, she'd fill herself up with food. But she won't listen to me, won't listen when I tell her that the diabetes and the hypertension will shorten her life. She's forty-five now, three years older than me, and I doubt she'll see sixty. Fifty-five even.' He drains the last of his whisky. 'Which leaves me looking at a pretty long and solitary retirement.' He puts his hand over his eyes as though to blind himself, so doesn't notice that Eleanor has put down her glass and is sitting at his elbow. She gently peels his hand away.

'I understand,' she says, and he turns his head like a sunflower to the sun. 'My future's a pretty bleak place too,' she says, 'except sometimes I allow myself to see you in it. I don't want to apologise for this, Gerald, even though I know it's wrong, but saying this – saying that I've fallen in love with you – makes me feel more real than I have been for years. Perhaps than I've ever been. This may be a frightful thing for you to hear, but if you push me away, strangely it doesn't matter. It doesn't matter at all because at least I've known what it feels like to love you so completely it takes my breath away.'

Gerald's own lungs have seized. Words fail him.

Eleanor's eyes redden. 'Do you feel the same?' she asks.

He manages to put his glass down and cup the back of her head with his palm. As he leans towards her face, her eyes spill and he kisses each meandering tear away. He pulls back and looks at her, the salty tang of her on his lips. 'I've never . . . not in my life . . . not like this . . .' he begins.

She rests her fingers on his lips. 'Nor have I,' she says, 'and I'd given up hope.'

A car's tyres scramble over the gravel. Eleanor starts. She closes her eyes. 'It must be William,' she says dully. 'He's early. I'll just go to the nursery. You'd better stay here.' She picks up the glasses and leaves the room.

Gerald greets Eleanor's husband as they pass in the hall.

# 1975

Thursday, 5.52 p.m.

Magda has lived in Britain for twenty-five years and only curses in English. She makes her confession to Father Tadeusz at St Andrew Bobola in Polish, so doesn't feel enjoined to mention the words that rattle her speech outside the confessional. When Pete comes home from the garage on Mondays and Thursdays, he knows to expect a barrage, but after twenty-five years of marriage, he also knows to nod and smile and hear nothing.

'She leave her bollocky clothes on ground again!' she says as she crashes pans around in the kitchen. 'I suppose to pick up? Why she no pick up own shitty, hm? She no have arms or leg on body? She no can pick up shitty clothes on ground and walk to bollocky wash machine and put him in wash machine and push fockin' button and wash him? And she bloody doctor and know about keep clean and not bloody sick? Pete, you bloomin' hear what I saying?'

'Yeah, yeah. Awful. Is that golabki you're making?'

Magda's string of South London ladies includes Mrs Finchley, whom she likes. She approves of the way Mrs Finchley's made sure everything matches everything else in her house: the daisies on the three-piece suite and the walls, the fruit on the tea towels and the curtains, and the fishes on the tiles swimming on to the blinds. There are dog hairs on the sofas because her employer is soppy about her snappy spaniel in the way of the English, but that's forgivable because the house is otherwise orderly. Mrs Finchley is a savvy woman and knows that Magda expects sandwiches when she arrives, and that a little light conversation makes her work more palatable. She wasn't meant to be a cleaner, Magda – she finished school and learned typing

56

and shorthand, but jobs were hard to find in war-flattened Gdansk, so she'd hoped meeting the English sailor who wanted to ship her home gave her prospects. But while she learned to swear in English, shorthand defeated her, so she's built up a solid reputation and is passed on by her ladies like a handy hint. It was Mrs Finchley who passed her on to Virginia.

'I don't know her very well,' she said, 'she's only just moved in next door, but she's a doctor at St George's and badly needs a cleaner.'

They met up the next week and Magda asked for, and got, a sum thirty per cent more than she was usually paid. She doesn't think the doctor will waste her great brain gossiping about money, but she might use it as leverage with her other ladies some way down the line.

In nine years she's only met Virginia five times because she's always at work, but she knows a lot about her. The walls and the cupboards and the drawers are incontinent spillers of guts. When they've met, the Good Doctor's been dressed in cagey clothes, but Magda pulls out leather jackets and trousers and sweatshirts from the wardrobe that seem to belong to someone else. She's pretty sure there isn't anyone else – only one side of the bed's ever slept on and there's only one toothbrush and one name on the mail – so the Arab robes are a mystery too. She wonders if they're for fancy-dress parties, though Virginia doesn't look the type to dance on tables looking foolish.

Since there's nothing girly-girly about her employer, she's surprised to find all the perfumes in the bedroom and the lotions and potions in the bathroom. Pretty pricey ones too, so she treats herself to a squirt and a blob when she's finished her day. And Virginia often chucks the containers away before they're empty so Magda's shelves are now stacked with leftovers, which impresses her friends no end.

She never has to do much in the kitchen, which is always immaculate, so she'd be tempted to think that Virginia's too busy to cook if it weren't for the feast and famine she observes in the fridge. One minute it's stuffed to the gills with a huge variety of food and drink and the next it's evacuated, as though it's been fed an emetic. There's not even any bollocky milk, so Magda always brings a container of Marvel for her coffee on Thursdays.

Unlike Mrs Finchley, Virginia clearly neither knows nor cares about classy decor and Magda boggles at the gallimaufry of furnishings as she moves around the house.

'Is a mishy-mash,' she tells Pete, 'like she don't bother with nothing. Like she don't think nice home important.' In common with Mrs Finchley, Magda takes care to make sure that everything accords with everything else in her home, though on a considerably lower budget. Her upholstery matches the Axminster's swirls and her bedroom is a poem in blue next to a bathroom with a nautical theme, which pleases Pete and reminds them both of how they met.

But there's nothing personal in Virginia's house: no family photos, no souvenirs of jolly holidays spent on a beach or up a mountain, no pretty things that might have been for Christmas or a birthday, nothing to hint at a history. The rosewood box, which bafflingly moves between the living room and bathroom, simply reflects what she does for a living and the pictures hanging on the stairs reflect nothing at all.

And then there's the room at the top of the stairs, which Magda has to steel herself to clean. As she goes in, six beady eyes follow her from their frames, a trio of interrogators quite as implacable as the MBP at home, who disappeared four of her friends. The two on the right-hand wall are bad enough, but she has to approach the third with her head turned.

'She has bum stick out!' she tells Pete. 'She don't care who bloomin' see. Stick out her nudey bum in my face! And bollocky cock, Pete – you listening? – bollocky cock flying to bum through air like it going to fock her! She look at me like prozzie, like lady of street, look at me like she say, "Come and do like me, Magda. We make fock together." Why lady doctor have picture of fockin' cock and bum on wall, hm? Why not nice pretty picture of flowers maybe or forest with birdies maybe? You asleep, Pete?'

She rampages through the room using every product at her disposal, wiping skirting boards, brushing down curtains and cleaning the window frantically with vinegar and newspaper as though the glare might blind the pictures' eyes. She turns them to face the wall anyway to stop them bloody looking at her while she cleans.

She hoovers the carpet into submission and gets down on her hands and knees to corral the crafty dust collecting round the edges. She has to move a chest of drawers away from the wall to complete the circuit and by now she knows what to expect, but the first time she hauled it out, she was mystified. Why would anyone want to attach all those things to the wall and then hide them with a piece of furniture? She can't work out what they're for, but she dusts them anyway even though nobody but her sees them.

She always makes sure she closes the door as she leaves, so the pictures don't spook her when she next walks up the stairs.

# 1975

I've got a paper to write for the *Journal*, but Ruby and I have been busy with the rosewood box, so it's pushing midnight by the time I've cleared up and showered. When I'm dry I slather Hartnell In Love on my body and scrub my face. I soothe it with the criminally pricey cream I bought yesterday.

I've always loved Marilyn Monroe's maternal hips and breasts and I sashay like her as I go to my bedroom, the air's cool fingers skimming my flesh. I kick the skirting board as I pass and bump the door frame as I go in: the pain is exquisite. During the quads I make sure there's water in every room, so I go over to the bottle of San Pellegrino sparkling by the window and take a slug. From my wardrobe I pull out one of the djellabas I bought in Fez when I gave a keynote speech, this one made of loosely woven black cotton with gold braid hedging the neck and arms. As I slip it over my head, I feel myself dissolving. In a djellaba – under a djellaba – everything is possible. I can mix and match, pop and slot, change shape as capriciously as smoke on a breeze. I can be doctor-butcher-child, spider-butterfly-shark, crocus-clematis-weed. Anything.

I clump across the landing, the robe clinging to my sticky belly.

My study is designed for a steely mind. The flooring is wipe-clean vinyl of inconsequential colour, the walls are white, the woodwork white, the metal furniture grey. In this frippery-free zone I flex my experience on to the page, passing on what I know. I'm told I have a stellar reputation, but mostly I turn down the invitations to give keynote speeches or address committees or write another book. I enjoy teaching but given a choice I'd spend all my time with my patients. They need me.

They keep me alive.

The paper I'm writing for the *Journal* is on vulvectomy, but as I seek to explain why certain pathologies need unorthodox techniques, Sierra Leonean women noisily, bloodily interrupt.

A year after I qualified, a new junior doctor joined my firm at the Leeds Royal Infirmary. A graceful woman whose hair seemed perpetually on the brink of flight, Kalaitu said nothing during the first three ward rounds, her brown eyes flicking from face to face as each participant competed for that day's Brownie badge. Apart from the dark sheen of her skin she was at first unremarkable, her silence taken for the proper respect a junior doctor owed her seniors, but in the fourth ward round I felt her stiffen next to me as the senior registrar started pontificating about a patient's cervical carcinoma. When he'd rounded up with a triumphant smile, she addressed him in a clear, high voice.

'But you are wrong,' she said. 'You have misdiagnosed this patient. I will tell you what I know.' Every eye in the room turned to her. Deftly she demolished his account, exposing the tunnel vision of his observations, the lacunae in his conclusions. 'I think we will find this patient has a far advanced necrotic sarcoma and will need a hysterectomy. This is a matter of urgency,' she said. 'Of course, should the tumour have spread beyond the uterus, the prognosis is very bad.' The senior registrar blustered, the consultant froze, but she was right. The patient would have died had Kalaitu not got uppity.

I was artless where friends were concerned, but was drawn to Kalaitu in a way that mimicked the manners of friendship. We never met out of work, but at the hospital we'd eat together in the canteen and sit together in the common room and talk together with a fluency that surprised me. Maybe it surprised her too. I don't know. Beyond our work we had little in common. She told me of her family life in the sweaty outskirts of Bo, Sierra Leone's second city. She told me about living in a country trying to build an identity after the British handed it over. A country full of hope in its first three years of independence, now riven by tribalism and corruption under its second prime minister, Albert Margai. A country whose people could barely expect to see their mid-forties, whose children died in droves. She wasn't evangelising and her accounts were pared of hyperbole or rancour, but I found myself listening to accounts of tragedies as ordinary in Sierra Leone as a rainy summer's day in Britain. I had no ties, so by the end of the next year I was on a plane to Freetown.

The irony of the name didn't escape me.

The day after I arrived at my tiny hospital in the south of the country, a harmattan wind blew in from the Sahara and obliterated the settlement's features. The thatched roofs of the houses clotted, dunes rippled up against the walls and scrawny farm animals complained as sand silted their eyes and stifled their babies. When the sky cleared the next day, I watched my new community excavating their lives with a resignation that made the back of my eyes burn.

I was the only doctor. I learned enough Yalunka to get by and was all they had to cure their diseases and deliver their babies and act as a dyke against the swells of death. I was physician and pharmacist and anaesthetist and surgeon. I extemporised with paper clips and staples when supplies stammered to a halt. I cut tumours out of viscera, infants out of their mothers and found little relief in sleep. My dreams were haunted by the days' casualties and I'd wake before the birdy dawn as disturbed as I had fallen asleep.

I lost my first patient to female circumcision three weeks after I arrived. When day broke that morning, I boiled myself a cup of water and opened my door to let in some air. At first I took the red heap by the window to be a jettisoned cloth and went over to pick it up and throw it away. As I drew nearer, I saw the face of a young girl in its folds, hideous with agony. The cloth in which she was wrapped had originally been green but was now saturated with blood. I dropped my cup and threw myself on my knees beside her. The fetid stench of old blood punched me in the temples as I lifted the sodden fabric from her body. She was barely formed, her breasts like peas on her chest, her hips still those of a bony child, her pubic hair wistful on an unripened sex. She'd haemorrhaged from the ragged cuts in her genitals made by knives left unwashed from the previous girl, wielded by the woman whose task it was to mutilate young girls into marriageability. Her pulse barely registered and I yelled for Vitoria, my senior nurse. As we carried the girl into the hospital, I was dimly aware of a woman appearing from behind a rosewood tree and shadowing us.

The girl's clitoris had been removed and her inner and outer labia crudely lopped, mortifying the heart of her femininity. We battled for two hours to save her as the sun steadily punished the air, but she was beyond our skills and slipped without complaint into death. Vitoria went out into the corridor to tell the girl's mother. Her wails buckled the walls.

I stood by the operating table clammy with my patient's dying and my own impotence. I turned away when her family carried her out of the hospital in case I saw their contempt.

Three weeks later, a middle-aged woman came to see me, accompanied by four others in a solemn phalanx behind her. Aminata complained of unslakeable thirst, frequent urination, blurred vision and sudden severe weight loss. The other women squatted around the walls of the room, prepared to leap to her defence should I show any disrespect. I took her blood and explained that I'd need to do a glucose tolerance test the following day. She wasn't happy that this entailed fasting for some hours. She looked exceptionally well fed, despite the weight she said she'd lost.

She left, the other women processing silently behind her in the sun's swelter, and Vitoria came into the room.

'Do you know who she is?' she asked.

'No – is she someone special?'

'Yes. She's the circumciser – you know, the woman who cut the girl who died. She's a very important person in our community.'

And I had to cure her?

I did of course. I prescribed insulin for the diabetes and monitored her blood sugar levels. She was quickly stabilised and I discharged her with instructions and advice. I hoped it was the last I saw of her. It wasn't quite.

I used to find it comforting when I'd finished work to walk away from the hospital and into the bush beyond. The flat-headed trees straggled against an orange shout of evening sky and I was able to collect myself, removed from the everyday failures I was learning to tolerate. Removed from the people I'd failed. I rarely encountered anyone else since the meagre fields lay the other way.

There was a dusty congregation of low-lying bushes gathered round one of the trees, and as I approached I saw a figure slumped among them, her skirt rucked up to the middle of her thighs. It was Aminata.

I squatted in front of her and Ruby squatted by my side in the dust. Her bare feet were filthy, as though she'd walked for miles to reach me. Aminata was pale, her breath shallow, her skin running with sweat: she was comatose. I could revive her. Ruby put her arm round my shoulders.

'Won't take long,' she said. 'Let's wait. Let's watch.'

We waited and we watched as she died. It didn't take long. I put out my hand to pull down her skirt so she had at least some semblance of dignity at the end of her life, but Ruby stopped me. She hoiked her skirt further up so her genitals were on display, their mutilation now withered with age.

'It's only what she deserves,' she said, and took my hand as we stood up. We walked slowly back to the hospital.

In the two years I worked there, I battled daily with the fallout from privation and ignorance. I snatched women from death's thorns, I repaired butchered genitalia, I delivered babies out of bodies raging with septicaemia, I desperately – often fruitlessly – prescribed antibiotics to patients suffering from tetanus. When I had any. I encountered diseases unknown or treatable in the developed world: polio, meningitis, TB, yaws, schistosomiasis, pellagra. And malaria. I watched children die in the pitiless grip of cerebral malaria, knowing that a net would have protected them.

Death threats hovered over the delivery room, so each live baby, each live mother, was a triumph.

I oscillated between anger and despair, knowing that my attentions could only ever be palliative. It felt as though I were scratching a thin line in the sand, briefly leaving a mark before the weight of a dune deleted it. My life since has been dedicated to the unique forms and functions of women's bodies, but whenever I hand a newly delivered

64

baby to its mother I scrutinise her face. I want to see it smudged with love. When occasionally I glimpse something else – rejection, perhaps, or dismay – I want to snatch the baby back, spirit it off to a safe place, settle it on the chest of a woman who knows how to love it. In Africa I met many women who knew how to love their children, but whose hands were tied by custom and belief.

I have never lost my rage at that. It fuels my days.

While I was there, I began to have the symptoms of what I knew to be an early menopause. I was overjoyed. One less distraction. One less choice to make. Liberated from my own fertility I could concentrate on helping other women enjoy theirs.

When I left Africa to come home – though 'home' was a name, not a feeling – the whole community turned out to bid me farewell. They stood together in the red dust in front of my hospital, singing in the kind of African voices, weaving the kind of African harmonies that make western skins tighten, all the pleasure and pain of a continent called out in the key of history. Among them I saw young women leaning on sticks, barely able to walk, who may not have been marriageable but were at least alive. I saw infants and toddlers I'd brought into the world – some of them motherless – flopped on their granny's back or stomping the ground in imitation of their elders. My work there skated along the Möbius strip of life and death, with no intercessor between my patients and me. I could never have subsided into a chair to write about my work as I do this evening. I was too busy spending my medical capital to afford contemplation.

I map out my thesis in the sterile niceties of science. I dictate it into my machine to give to Eileen, my secretary, in the morning. I've beaten the deadline by a fortnight.

Breakfast is porridge and toast and smoked salmon and scrambled eggs, followed by fruit salad and coffee. I put two chocolate croissants and a Danish pastry in my briefcase to take to the hospital, hoping they'll see me through to mid-morning.

When I went off to medical school, I was finally free of Mother's grudging sludge-on-a-plate and could eat how I liked. When I liked, or not at all if I liked. I divided my weeks into three days of stuffing and four days of starving, and once I'd decided on obstetrics it made sense to call them the triplets and the quadruplets, though they quickly became the trips and the quads. Bit of a mouthful otherwise. Choosing to eat like this put me in absolute control and I never had to depend on Mother again for food. I never went hungry for her attention or felt full of her bile. On trip days I stuff myself with the most desirable foods I can imagine – way, way beyond my appetite's outer reaches. Quad days starve me into submission. During the three days of the trips, I can believe myself the most loved woman on earth. The austerity of the following four stops me wanting more.

*It wouldn't do, Virginia, to put your elbows on the table/eat with your mouth open/talk with your mouth full.* It wouldn't do to want more. Ever.

Eileen has been with Virginia for years and is ferociously loyal. On the rare occasion that a doctor or nurse says something critical, she lets rip. She tells them hell would freeze over before they were even a twentieth as good as the boss. She takes no prisoners. Virginia relies on her to juggle her diaries, field telephone calls, remind her of messages and keep her professional life on track. In turn, she never objects if Eileen has to take time off when there's a flap about one of her three children. When Eileen's oldest developed epilepsy, she arranged a private consultation with a senior paediatrician and somehow managed without her during the follow-up appointments. When he took up bunking off school for a living, she found him a psychologist.

Eileen grins when Virginia comes in. 'Morning, boss!' she says. 'You've got a busy day ahead – you ready for a coffee yet?'

'In a minute, Eileen, thanks. How's Simon?'

Eileen grimaces. 'Steve's had to ground him again. He only came home two hours after his curfew covered in that anti-climb stuff, didn't he? Said he'd been going after his ball, but you don't exactly play football after dark, so we had a bit of a go. Don't think he's been out nicking or anything, but those lads he hangs around with are right little tea leaves, so you've got to worry.'

'Oh, I'm really sorry about that. Just when he seemed to have turned a corner. Adolescence can be absolutely bloody, can't it?'

'Yeah, specially for him. It's like he's always got to prove he's the big I Am, on account of the epilepsy and everything. Thinks the other kids'll think he's a bit of a sissy – or a cripple, you know? It's no good really. I mean, you've got to feel sorry for him, but he can't keep staying out all night. We're at our wits' end, to be honest.'

'He's still taking the medication, is he? I know you were worrying about that the other week.'

'I hope so, but I can't stand over him like some little Hitler – which he calls me, by the way – he's got to take responsibility for himself. I mean, I suppose we'd know if he'd bollocksed it – excuse my French – because he'd be jerking around on the floor, wouldn't he?'

'Well, it wouldn't be the best way to test it, but it would be a bit of a giveaway. Look, I'd love that coffee now actually – will you come into my office when it's ready?'

'Coming right up.'

Virginia's room overlooks one of the car parks, which even at this time of the morning is teeming. It gives nothing away about its occupant save for a small object on top of one of the filing cabinets. It has no obvious function, so Eileen supposes it's Art of some sort and that it has some personal significance because it's the only thing in the room not associated with work. It consists of a stack of nuts and bolts, some glued together, some on swivels, with a skirt of screws suspended from the top by chains. If it's twirled, the skirt flares out like a fairground ride and clacks a merry taradiddle. Eileen tried it once when Virginia was away, but it clearly involved some special technique because she got a nasty scratch on the back of her hand which became infected. It migrates round the filing cabinets' surfaces, sometimes at the back of the scientific papers, sometimes at the side of the research materials, sometimes – less often – on Virginia's desk, but it's always well dusted. She's never asked what it is because it would feel like prying. Given the absence of baby photos, she's assumed Virginia's childless but she's wondered about her partner. If she has one. Probably someone very clever. Maybe a professor or something. Or a philosopher, one of those guys too busy sorting out the meaning of life to bother much about their appearance. Like Virginia, who today is wearing an algae-green jacket, shit-brown trousers and battered Birkenstocks. Sometimes her clothes sport food stains, as though she's been too distracted by important thoughts to find her mouth. Like her Simon, who always eats as though this might be his last meal ever. Once Miss Denham turned up with bright blue paint under her finger-nails and when Eileen remarked on it, she said she'd been painting her spare bedroom late last night and had run out of white spirit. She seemed to do a lot of home decorating because after that Eileen noticed purple, red and yellow paint under her fingernails.

When Eileen comes into her office with her coffee and diary, Virginia can only nod and grunt, her cheeks stuffed with the pastry.

'Sorry, Eileen,' she says finally, 'I was starving. What's on the menu today then?'

There's too much in my day, as ever, but that's how I like it. I pick up a bacon and egg sandwich from the canteen on my way to my first clinic. I've finished it by the time I've gone down three floors and two corridors and am still not quite full.

I never weary of my work, even when a clinic presents nothing out of the ordinary, but this morning I encounter more clinical riddles than usual. I've always avoided sweeping into rooms with a fawning entourage in my wake, like some I know – I just amble in, take a seat and start chatting. Patients don't need technical terms, they need the doctor to know what's wrong and how to make it right. I eat two packets of all-butter shortbread biscuits while I read the history that sister's taken of my last patient, a 35-year-old woman who's having difficulty conceiving. She's presenting with often acute abdominal pain, irregular periods, pain on intercourse and intermittent post-coital bleeding. She's been trying for a baby since she married five years ago, has a normal, regular sex life and has had no previous pregnancies or abortions. She has never taken the pill, having relied on barrier methods since becoming sexually active at seventeen.

When I go in, she's sitting there in a starchy hospital gown. Her fingers are twisting in her lap like mad snakes.

I plonk myself on a chair. 'So, you've been trying to have a baby,' I say. 'It's tough when it doesn't happen, isn't it?'

'Dreadful. It's like climbing mountains, you know? Every month I get my hopes up, then my period comes along and I'm tumbling down the other side again. I wish there was some way of cutting the hoping bit out of me so I didn't spend a day sobbing every month, but I don't suppose you can do that, can you?'

'Well, we may have very sophisticated surgical techniques nowadays, but I've yet to find a way of removing hope. What would we call that, I wonder? Hmm, a hopectomy probably.'

The patient stills.

'Look, sister's given me a jolly good account of what's been going on, so why don't you pop up on the couch and we'll make a start. Have you ever had an internal examination before?'

'Yes, I have, several times – I hated it.'

'I know, I know. It's horribly intrusive, isn't it? But I'll be as gentle as I can.' While she settles, I run my hands and the speculum under the hot-water tap to warm them up. I go over to the couch and pat her on the shin.

'Here we go then,' I say. 'Let's have a look at what's going on down there.'

When the examination is finished, I turn my back while she covers herself. When I sit back down beside her, I cross my legs gingerly because of the infected cut at the top of my thigh.

'Look, there are some polyps on your cervix, which probably accounts for the post-coital bleeding, and it's possible you have a retroverted uterus.'

'What's that?'

'It means your uterus is tilted backwards in your pelvis. It's usually congenital, not at all serious and by itself doesn't cause any problems, but it can be significant of other conditions, so I'd like to have a closer look.'

'What other conditions?'

'Fibroids maybe, or endometriosis is another possibility, which is when tissue that by rights belongs inside your womb develops outside it, often resulting in what we call adhesions.'

'That sounds nasty.'

'It's not nice, no. Webs of tissue form and stick the ovaries to the side of the pelvis for example, or the fallopian tubes to the womb – it's certainly painful, but fortunately quite treatable.'

The patient's face clouds.

'I don't think it's cancer,' I say, 'if that's what you're thinking. But we need to identify quite what's going on. I'll book you in for an ultrasound, after which I'd like to examine your pelvis with a laparoscope, just to be sure.'

'That means an operation, doesn't it?'

'Yes, but it's a very minor one. You'll have two tiny nicks in your abdomen, which'll heal in no time at all. Does that bother you?'

'Not the cutting, no – I'm not squeamish about blood – but anaesthetics terrify me. I like to be in control, you see.'

'I quite understand. I do too. You'll have to trust me, which can be a big thing.'

'I think I do, Miss Denham. I don't seem to have any choice, do I?'

Clinic over, I stop off at the canteen for a sickly slice of gateau before I go up to my office. I ask Eileen to get Faisal on the phone.

# 1975

Amina is grumpy – no, scrub that, she passed grumpy around lunch-time and is now well into furious. She's spent the greater part of today locking horns with a school that's hell-bent on expelling one of her clients. She's explained and she's rationalised and she's argued and finally she explodes.

'You're not listening!' she says, aware that she's raising her voice.

'I've spent the last hour listening, Amina,' says the head, 'just as I've listened to Cara's form teacher and her year head and her science teacher. For heaven's sake, he was off for three weeks after she attacked him. I absolutely *won't* tolerate violence of any sort in my school and it was a particularly nasty assault. My staff are as much my responsibility as the students and while I hear what you're saying about Cara's dysfunctional family, I'm the one who has to pick up the pieces when she disrupts her classes. Think of the other students . . .'

'I *am* thinking of the other students! Of course I'm bloody thinking about them! What else was I talking about in those staff sessions last term? Look, I know I'm repeating myself, but Cara is definitely on the autistic spectrum and we're just waiting for a referral to . . .'

'Well, we can't wait any longer. Sorry to be so blunt, but she'll be better off in the unit and, who knows, maybe they'll find her a place in a special school. We just can't have her here.'

'But . . .'

'That's it I'm afraid. I honestly think we've discussed it long enough and while I admire your passionate defence of this girl, I'm just as passionate in defending my staff and the other students. Is there anything else?'

*Yes, there is something else,* she thinks, as she reverses rather suddenly out of the school car park. *You haven't got the sense god gave bloody mushrooms, and this poor kid's going to suffer as a result.*

She's aware of her reputation. Aware that her feistiness borders on the volatile, but the head's intransigence makes her blood boil. She doesn't see the Belisha beacons up ahead and hits the brakes to avoid the giggle of girls on the crossing. 'Shit!' she says aloud. 'Shit, shit, *shit!*' and waves an apology to the girls. Their language is stronger.

She wishes she could temper her temper with her mother's calm authority. Aarya never backed down either at school or at home, but her opponents would adopt her ideas and congratulate themselves later for their cleverness. Her father always agreed with Amina when she railed at injustice, but it was Aarya who helped her set up Scotland's first school council and who tried to teach her diplomacy. It was only intermittently successful.

Amina has the patience of a host of saints when she's working with a client, but her fuse tends to shorten as she leaves the session. At least she can let off steam to Faisal when she gets home, she thinks. He's had the afternoon off and promised to see to the kids and get some food in for dinner.

She's startled when she lets herself in and sees Mary ready to catch Shafiq as he jumps off the stairs.

'Hi, Mary,' she says, 'what's going on? Where's Faisal? Hi, Shafiq – don't jump for a minute, hen.'

'He gone to the hospital,' says Mary. 'He call me, say him boss want him and he go. He come back later. 'S OK.'

Amina's fists ball. 'I'm really sorry, Mary. He's got to stop doing this all the time – it's driving me nuts. All she has to do is jerk the chain and . . .' she stops herself in time. 'But I *am* sorry – hope it wasn't too inconvenient.'

'No problem y'know – no problem at all. G'wan now, Shafiq.'

The little boy launches himself into her arms and she hands him over to his mother. He pretends to bite Amina's neck. 'Hungry, Mummy – starving!'

'Ow – careful! Stop it – you'll just have to wait a second. You're OK for tomorrow, though, Mary, are you? At eight? You know I have to get off early.'

'I'll be here.'

'Please don't be late again.'

'Don't you worry.'

Mary goes off to kiss the other children before she leaves. She has a knack of going through the food cupboards and finding unlikely combinations to make what she calls her 'concoctions'. She always cooks enough for everybody, even though she bears responsibility only for the children, so Amina sits down with them to a plate of Chinese rice noodles and an assortment of vegetables tasting of the Caribbean.

She's simmering as she baths the children, simmering as she settles them in bed and fuming by the time she sits alone in the kitchen.

She loves her husband dearly, but his gentleness is veined with a passivity in which she sometimes finds herself mired. When something's wrong with his food in a restaurant, *she* complains; when a shop assistant is surly to him, *she* speaks to the manager – and given half a chance she'd remonstrate with Virginia too when she exploits his compliance. He is endlessly at the hospital and while she respects his work and his devotion to it, its embrace is more importunate than a lover's. She sometimes thinks ruefully that if he were having an affair, at least guilt might drive him back to her from time to time.

She knows – of course she knows – that his docility is driven by fear. That he's terrified to raise his head above the parapet in case it gets blown off. That if he makes waves, refuses an order, questions an authority, he's convinced he'll be robbed of his uncertain place, but it's sometimes hard to gag the part of her that wishes he'd get a grip, wishes he'd stop being such a wimp, wishes he'd *do* something. She's never said any of that to him and never will because she understands that often he stands upright only because his hands are on her shoulders. That her understanding helps him – sometimes – believe in himself. That what has felt like a flimsy disguise is now a thing of substance.

Yelling at him doesn't achieve anything, since he's never learned how to yell back. She's neither afraid of her own anger nor of anyone else's, but she knows that for him it feels catastrophic.

And yet.

73

She watched him play squash once, took Ismail to sit behind the glass to see Daddy play this noisy game for grown-ups, and was astonished. Her tender husband, his affectionate father, was hitting the ball as if he wanted to kill it. Ismail was terrified and she tried to reassure him that Daddy didn't want to hurt the other player. 'It's just a game, hen,' she said, 'you know, like when you kick a football really hard.' He wasn't mollified, so she took him to the club's café and fed him distracting ice cream. She said nothing to Faisal, happy that he'd finally found an outlet for his aggression, but she kept it in mind.

She does yell at him when he comes back of course – she can't help it. He does the maddening gesture with the shrugged shoulders and the upturned hands – he can't help it either.

'Just say no sometimes!' she rages. 'Just refuse, can't you? I bet some people would.'

'I can't – no, really I can't. I have to be there, Amina. What kind of doctor would I be if I didn't show up when I was needed? Not the kind of doctor you'd respect anyway. I made a commitment to the job . . .'

'. . . and to me. And to the kids – if you can bring yourself to remember that.'

'I know, I know – of course I know. And I'm sorry. I'm really sorry this happened today.'

'And it'll happen again and again and again if you don't put your foot down. You don't have to be so bloody *good* all the time, you know? The sky won't fall on your head if you break out occasionally.'

But he does have to be so bloody good. All the time. To dodge the falling sky, and as they trudge in uncompanionable silence up to bed, Amina knows she can neither rewrite his history nor lend him hers.

Faisal's growing up was as arid as the land his father worked in their Kashmiri backwater, each day driven by the effort of not dying. There were nine mouths to feed and six dowries to find, so Omar's only son knew that his place was in his father's shadow until he was old enough to cast his own on his sons behind him. Until Choudry Akbar Khan intervened. He was the zamindar, the local squire, alerted by the schoolmaster to the quiet little boy at the back of the class whose intellect ran like a cheetah, devouring information as though he'd never eat again. When he wasn't falling asleep over his books. The zamindar consulted with the panchayat, the village elders, and they announced their decision on the eve of Muharram. Faisal was to be sent to Murree. To Dickens Academy, an English boarding school, where he'd be taught maths and manners. Murree could have been a distant planet, but the zamindar willed it, paid for it, so Omar bent his head.

When Faisal went to the zamindar's house to take his leave, Choudry was reclining on a day bed under a rheumatic ceiling fan.

'Stand there, boy,' he said, indicating a place in front of his knees, and Faisal's sandals ferlap-ferlap-ferlapped across the tiles.

'I am not sending you to Murree for a holiday,' Choudry said, 'nor am I a whimsical man. I am sending you because an educated man is of value. An educated man will return home and use his learning to improve the lives of his people. This is your task, Faisal, and your duty. You will not fail me.'

'No, Saab.'

'You will not shame your family.'

'No, Saab.'

'You will bear this conversation in your heart.'

'Yes, Saab.'

'Then you go with my blessing.'

Sitting in the back of the cart taking him to the station, he looked back at his family shading their eyes from the sun. Except for Omar, who stood two paces apart. His father's eyes picked at him like a vulture at carrion. Pinning him to his history. Blaming him for his future.

When he returned at the end of his schooling, the sight of his village appalled him. As he breasted the hill overlooking his birth-place, the whine of poverty insulted sensibilities now translated into English. His mother was pleased to see him, as were his sisters, but his father barely acknowledged him when he trudged in at the end of the day. Omar didn't know how to forgive.

He visited the zamindar at the appointed hour and found him in

75

the garden instructing the gardener. Faisal had shot up like a beanstalk while he was away and Choudry, who'd seemed so monumental a figure before, now looked like a squat, weary old man in crumpled clothes. He drew Faisal over to two chairs under a pomegranate tree, where a small pile of documents lay on a table. Faisal listened as his benefactor lifted each document from the pile and read its contents out aloud. They were his school reports. He had been lauded by teacher after teacher, commended for his diligence, his curiosity, his obedience, but each year the housemaster had added the same comment: *Faisal has failed to join with the other pupils in the life of the house. He needs to show more interest.*

It was less lack of interest that kept Faisal away from the everyday scrums, more self-preservation.

Choudry sat back in his chair and turned to the slender young man inspecting his feet.

'So, Faisal,' he said, 'what now?'

'Well, Saab,' said Faisal, keeping his eyes dropped, 'Mr Templeton, my headmaster, is very keen for me to study medicine. His brother is the principal of King's College medical school in London, which he says is one of the best in the country. He says he can arrange for me to be offered a place. Probably with a scholarship, Saab, but it would still be a frightfully expensive affair, and you've been so generous already . . .'

'Do you remember what I told you when you went off to Dickens Academy?'

'Saab?'

'Perhaps my words were of no consequence to you?'

'No, Saab. I'm sorry, Saab, I mean no disrespect.'

'Perhaps you need reminding. When you return as a qualified doctor, you will repay me a hundredfold. I have it in mind to build a hospital over the hill to serve Jugnuwalla and the other villages in the valley, and you will be its medical director. I might even let you look after me.' He snorted. 'It will certainly be cheaper than travelling overnight to see my doctors, as I am forced to do now. Do we understand each other?'

'Yes, Saab. And I must tell you how grateful . . .'

'Gratitude doesn't heal the sick, Faisal. Skill does. Western medicine and drugs do. Bring them back to us when you've acquired them.'

But even after thirteen years in England armed with the habits and mannerisms he adopted at school, Faisal retains the wariness of a cat burglar slinking through stolen rooms. He has been guided by Amina, Glaswegian to her Asian core, but still wakes in the night from dreams where he's been dumped, naked, on a Kashmiri hillside. Where he doesn't understand what white people are saying. Where all he hears is derision.

Mahmood, her cousin, had mentioned her when he and Faisal came out of a particularly dreary lecture at medical school.

'You'll like Amina,' he said. 'She's got interviews at three different colleges down here – she's incredibly bright – and we said we'd meet up for dinner tonight. Why don't you join us?'

Faisal arrived before the others and was studying the menu as they approached the table.

'Here we are then,' Mahmood said and Faisal temporarily lost the use of his limbs as he looked up at his friend's cousin. She was luscious and curvy with a mischievous grin and a reckless knot of hair at the back of her head. She put out a hand to Faisal. He blinked in surprise. Clumsily he stood and took it, wondering if that was what she meant him to do, worried that he may have misread the gesture and was about to insult her. She smiled at him and squeezed his hand briefly. He was disinclined to let hers go, but minded his manners, released it, and waited for her to fold into her chair before sitting back down himself. Mahmood told him afterwards that he'd looked like a starving goldfish all evening, but that mysteriously Amina hadn't been put off.

'She really liked you,' he said. 'Said if she comes to London for her degree she hopes you'll meet up again.'

She had and they did, discovering a shared love for obscure foreign films, Italian food and political debate into the morning's first blush, Tamla Motown strutting on the tape deck.

At school, Faisal had attracted the attention of several older boys, but had reached this point in his twenties untroubled either by sexual experience or expectation. Amina taught him. She taught him how to read the cadences of her body and his own, taught him that tongues could shape other things than words.

He was an eager student.

Amina knows now that when Faisal tells her his stories, he longs for them to become as remote from him as they are from her. That he longs to borrow her certainties, to shrug on her fearlessness and her sense of belonging. She was born to parents who left Pakistan when it exploded out of India's guts. Who prospered in Scotland and never looked back. Her father was invited to stand for parliament, but demurred. 'Not yet,' he said. 'Scotland isn't ready for someone like me,' and he was right. Three years later, Enoch Powell conjured up a chimerical Britain flooded with immigrants and rivers of blood and his supporters lurched out of the walls. For a while the family felt eyes following them down the street and kept themselves to themselves for fear of becoming a target.

While her parents' marriage had been arranged, Amina was expected to choose for herself, so she was undaunted when she and Faisal went north for the first time. Faisal was terrified. Perpetually perched on the flimsiest of twigs braced for an impetuous wind, he wasn't convinced the Iftikhar family would let him join. He might have been dressed like an English professional, but he felt it was only a matter of time before someone tugged at his hem and exposed the village boy squatting in the dust sorting grain.

When he accepted the Iftikhars' our-family-is-your-family invitation, it felt treacherous, as though by brushing his history's dust off his jacket his family became inconsequential motes. He has sent them money every month since he's been in England, and offered to pay for plane tickets when it came to his wedding. He was unsurprised when they refused. Shame has been his constant companion since he left home to go to school, and tightened its grip when he reneged on his promise to the zamindar.

After he qualified, there was no question of returning to Kashmir, though sometimes he thought he heard the sounds of suffering borne on the wind. He told himself Amina would never have gone, though he never asked her. He told himself his children would never have survived the cultural leap, though he had. Choudry wrote to him twice a year, asking when he planned to come home and he wrote back promptly, pledging his fealty and explaining that he had one more step in his training, one more skill to acquire, before he could return. It was a relief when the old man died. He had no sons, so a nephew took over the property and the position, but not the biannual appeals to Faisal's honour.

He wrote long letters to his mother once a month, which the schoolteacher read to her. She replied rarely and curtly, news of his sisters itemised like a shopping list. When his sister Rana developed severe gynaecological problems in her late teens, Faisal tried to persuade his mother to bring her to Britain for treatment. He had to write three letters before she replied. *Rana will be well treated here*, she wrote, *insha'allah. Don't worry about us, my son. We are safe in the hands of God.*

Over the years, Amina has encouraged him to tell their children about his growing up, but he could have been speaking Mandarin. His children bear his name, but they're Iftikhar through and through and he is relieved. They belong in a way he never will.

# 1944

Ruby and me are sitting in Mother's wardrobe. Before we got in, I had a good look at the shoes sitting on the bottom with the metal things in them. Mother calls them trees, but they haven't got any leaves and you can't sit under them when it's hot and you can't climb up them, so it's jolly funny to call them trees. But grown-ups can call things what they like, not like children who must Learn. 'Oh, why won't you ever learn?' Mother says when I've forgotten to roll my socks up before I get into bed, and I always say sorry but it doesn't usually make her not cross.

I look at the shoes because I have to remember which ones are next to which ones so that when I move them to make a space I can put them back in the same line. Like three little pretty maids all in a row. I'd like to be a pretty maid but I don't know how. When I'm on my own, I only have to move six shoes to make room for my BTM and I sit very still because if I didn't sit very still one might jump out and make a big noise. When Ruby's in here with me, like today, I have to count out twelve shoes and then three more for luck because she's like a wriggly worm. I always tell her not to wriggle but she likes to be a bit wormy, Ruby does.

We've been playing sniffing Mother's shoes to see if daytime shoes smell different from night-time ones, when Ruby rocks back suddenly and makes a coat fall off its hanger.

'Oh, pooey!' she says. 'I'm bored! We'd better do something else or I'm going to run away with the raggle-taggle gypsies-o and then where would you be? I know! I know! Let's be explorers and travel all over the world and see new places and make discoveries and things. You have to be ever so brave if you're an explorer because you never

80

know what you might find up a mountain or somewhere where it's chilly, like where there are those pole things. Or in a jungle with coloured people swinging through trees.'

We climb out of the wardrobe and I hope that Mother will think that the coat dropped off the hanger all by itself. Like when things drop out of my hands. I put the shoes back and I hear a noise behind me. Ruby's feet are sticking out from under the counterpane and she's patting the floor under the bed with her gloves.

'Shh, Ruby, shh!' I whisper, scared that Mother will run into the room.

'There's nothing here,' says Ruby in a too-loud voice and she crawls out the other side. 'Nothing to discover. Oh, but let's have a look in here.' She tugs at the drawer in Mother's bedside table. I tiptoe over.

'What's this?' says Ruby. 'Hmm, could be pirate treasure – let's have a look inside.' She puts the little box she's found on the bed and we climb up next to it. It doesn't look a lot like a treasure chest because there's no shiny bits on the corners but you might find treasure in all sorts of things you don't see in books, you never know.

'Probably we need a good spell to open it,' says Ruby. 'I bet Mother's put a bad spell on it to keep us from seeing inside. I bet it's some big giant jewel or something.'

'Or maybe a magic ring that could make you invisible and you could go everywhere and look at everybody even when they're bare,' I say. 'That would be super!'

Ruby rolls her eyes back in her head and starts saying stuff. Her voice sounds like it's coming out of a cave. 'Oh wally-waller-woom-wom-wah-wah-wah,' she says. 'Oh smoo-smoo-smoo. May-our-magic-powers-unlock-this-box-and-show-the-treasure-that-lies-inside-only-to-our-eyes. If-you-let-us-see-oh-mighty-bloomer-bloom-we-will-never-never-never-be-naughty-again.'

Mother says you should never make promises you can't keep, but I close my eyes and make swimmy movements with my hands over where the box should be.

'Open says me!' Ruby says. 'Oh.'

I open my eyes. 'What is it?' I say.

'I don't know,' says Ruby. 'Do you think it's for eating custard in?

Like if you wanted not very much custard. Or maybe ice cream.'
She's holding a small rubber bowl with a thick top.

'Perhaps it's a swimming hat for someone quite little,' I say, 'like
a guinea pig or something.'

Ruby puts it on her head. 'Well, they'd have to be teeny-tiny, wouldn't
they? Even if it is quite stretchy.' She pulls it between her hands. It snaps
back and bounces on to the floor. 'Let's see what else she's hiding,' she
says and lies on her tummy so she can dig around some more.

The things in the drawer are quite boring. There aren't any
diamonds or biscuits or spell books, just a comb and a hairnet and a
needle and thread. Ruby's quiet for a moment. Sometimes I think I
can hear her head ticking.

'Aha!' she says suddenly. 'I know! Let's see if we can make a strainer
for cooking little yummy puds for our tea. Get the rubber thingy,
Virginia. It's time to be inventors.'

We slide off the bed and sit on the floor, our legs sticking out in
front of us, four white ankle socks in a row. Ruby's got the needle
and she takes off her gloves and pokes it into her palm.

'Ow!' she says. 'Well, that's sharp enough then. Hold out the bowl
thing, Professor Virginia, we've got inventing to do.'

I hold the rubber bowl between my thumb and the pointing finger
of both hands and put it near Ruby. She carefully pricks tiny holes at
the bottom of the bowl, counting as she goes. When she's counted
to ten, she drops the needle on the floor and grabs the bowl.

'It's rude to snatch, Ruby – Professor Ruby,' I say, but she's jumped
up.

'Professor Virginia!' she says. 'Time to test the strainer with a
'speriment!' and she races out of the room, down the corridor and
into the bathroom.

By the time I've made the counterpane flat again and put the
needle back in the drawer and gone to the bathroom, Ruby has
already done her 'speriment and is standing by the sink looking sad.

'It doesn't work, Professor Virginia,' she says. 'I filled it with water
two times but it doesn't come through, so we're not very good at
inventing today. Bother.'

'Let me try,' I say, and I take the rubber thing out of her hands.

There's a rattle and a bang from downstairs. Mother's coming in from the garden.

'Oh cripes!' says Ruby. 'Time to go – bye!' but I'm running down the corridor, drying the not-very-good strainer on my skirt.

Now it's lots of weeks later and I'm in the wardrobe by myself. I'm sitting on the this-hand-side so I can lean against the wall. I'm underneath Mother's frocks, which are all soft and floaty, and when I put my face up into them, they tickle my chin like buttercups except they don't make it shiny, so I can't tell if I like butter. At the other end are her suits, which are a bit scratchy. The cupboard smells like Mother, like flowers and soap and sometimes even like strawberries.

If I've been a good girl, Mother lets me be in the bathroom when she's making herself smell nice in the morning. I sit on the laundry basket and I have to not bang my feet because she sends me away if I'm noisy. She's got loads and loads of creamy stuff in bottles and jars which don't look a bit like the jars in the kitchen that have got the sugar and the rice and the flour in: Mother's jars are little and pretty and when she opens the lids, it smells like you've raced into the garden on a summer's day. She gets this dreamy look when she's putting the creams on her face and on her neck and on her hands and on her arms and even down nearly at her bosom. I'd like to look dreamy too but I don't dare ask if I can try the creams because they might be dangerous for little girls. They might set me on fire or something. Maybe turn me into a frog. When I'm a lady I'm going to have loads of jars as well and I'll put the creams all over me. I'll get bare and put them everywhere. Even where I go to the lavatory. When I'm a lady I can do what I like without being ticked off, which would be super.

Sometimes I stand up in the wardrobe and put my head inside one of the frocks because then it feels like Mother's cuddling me. I do it now. I stand inside my best frock, which has got frilly things at the bottom and red splodges all over like when you drop jam on the floor. I stroke it with my very clean hands. I always wash them before I come in here so I don't make the clothes mucky. One time when it got very hot in the wardrobe, Ruby's hands were wet and she left this mark on Mother's blue jacket. I said, 'Crumbs, Ruby, look what you've gone and done now,' and Ruby gave me a wink. Mother says it's rude to wink, it's what scruffy people do, but Ruby never cares and she does it all the time. Wink, wink, wink. After she left, I crept back to the wardrobe and looked at the jacket and hooray, hurrah, the mark had gone, but I jolly learned my lesson and now I make sure Ruby always wears her gloves when she comes in here with me. Even though she says in a complainy voice, 'But it's not winter. Why do I have to wear my gloves?'

I just look at her and say, 'Because,' which is what Mother says.

Mother's cooking in the kitchen now, so I can stay in here for a long, long time. She's having one of her supper parties tonight, though it never looks much like a party to me. There's never any cakes with candles and they don't play games like ring-a-ring o' roses or blind man's buff and they don't sing songs but, oh well, that's just grown-ups for you. She's been a bit grumpy this week, Mother has, and I think she's been eating too much cakes because her tummy's getting a bit fat. I haven't seen any cakes, but there might be a rainbow fairy who brings Mother secret cakes in the night and she eats them in bed, then the fairy clears up all the crumbs. I'm not allowed to eat in my bed except when I'm poorly because Mother says that's mucky, and anyway Cleanliness Is Next To Godliness.

Lots of days before this day I got quite bothered because I heard Mother getting poorly in the bathroom. I heard her getting poorly in the bathroom every morning. There was a horrid sound like coughing and once I saw her when she came out and she was all white and sweating and she was holding on to her fat tummy. But at lunchtime she wasn't poorly any more so she must have got better. I said to her, 'Oh, Mother, perhaps you should go and see Dr Greenaway because you're quite poorly really,' and she said, 'No, I don't need to do that,' and she smiled, which was funny because you don't usually smile when you're poorly.

Dr Greenaway's coming to the party tonight, Mother says, but Mrs Greenaway isn't because she likes to stay at home. Perhaps she stays there to cook yummy things and then scoffs it all herself because she's quite a fat lady, except you must never say that because it's a Personal Remark. The food Mother makes for me is all mushy except for the meat which I have to chew and chew probably a hundred times – maybe even fivety hundred – before I can swallow it. I have to sit at the dining-room table until I've finished chewing because Mother says, 'There are plenty of children who would be grateful for your tea, Virginia, so you'll stay there, if you please, until I can see a clean plate.' Mother comes in and out like a cuckoo clock just to check that I'm still chewing.

One time, Ruby said, 'Ugh! This is so yucky-yuck – let's go and play robbers in the garden,' but Mother came in and saw me standing by the door and tied me with some of her pretty scarves so I couldn't get off the chair. I jolly learned my lesson and next time Ruby said the same thing I blocked my ears and hummed, which made it quite difficult to eat.

Even in the wardrobe with the door nearly closed I can hear the wireless in the kitchen playing music and Mother's singing sometimes, but not all the time. At breakfast, she brought her little box of cards to the table and she said, 'Hm, now what did I make for Dr Greenaway last time?' She's got other people coming to the party, but she doesn't look them up on the cards. Just Dr Greenaway. Probably he's her best friend because he's very kind. I haven't got a best friend, but I know what they look like because some girls put their arms through some other girls' arms and then they go into corners and whisper secrets. Ruby's my best friend but she doesn't come to school, which makes me sad because if she did I'd have someone to play with. It's lucky that there's this big long wall round the playground so I can sit on it at playtime when the other girls are running around, laughing and telling secrets and things. I always look at the wall very closely and scratch it with my fingers so the others will think I've got something ever so interesting and clever to do and not make fun of me because I'm quite lonely really. I wish Dr Greenaway could be my best friend except he's a grown-up and I'm only a little girl and anyway he might only have room for one best friend and that's Mother of course. When I go to see him in his sugary, he puts the smelly cream stuff on my itchy bits in a really nice way, like he doesn't want to hurt me, and he always gives me a pear drop at the end. I like the way the pear drop makes my mouth feel all sort of empty.

I'm allowed to stay up in my best frock when the people come for parties and Dr Greenaway always strokes me on the head and calls me Bubbles because my hair's very curly. Mother doesn't like it because it's quite difficult to comb. She tugs and it hurts, but there's no use saying ouch because she doesn't stop combing even though I've said ouch. I always say sorry because it's probably my fault for making it all tangly except I don't know how I do it.

My new best frock is lying on my bed right now like a giant dolly. It's dark blue and hasn't got any frills on it like Mother's frocks because she says, 'You'll just spoil it, Virginia, with all your spilling and everything.' I don't tell her it's Ruby jogging my arm because Mother's never met Ruby and she'd say I was fibbing. All of my clothes are dark colours because I'm such a mucky pup, but I like it here in the wardrobe with the purples and the creams and the pinks. There's one frock that's just as blue as the sky is in the summertime and it looks like Dr Greenaway's eyes. He always looks like he's smiling the sky at me. Mother's eyes are green, which might mean she's the Green-Eyed Monster that I have to beware of.

I've got lots of hidey-holes and I'm very glad when I find another one. I found a new one last week in the dining room, behind the screen thing in the corner that's made of stuff like a basket. I know Mother won't look there because she puts the gumboots behind it when she has her parties. 'So people won't trip up when they come in through the door' – that's what she says.

Ruby made one of her plans when we were behind the screen. 'I know what,' she said, 'let's hide here when Mother has a party and then we can spy on the grown-ups and see if they really do play games or maybe throw bread rolls at each other or spill the gravy on the carpet or speak with their mouths full. Come on, Virginia, it'll be jolly fun!'

I wasn't sure at first, but Ruby went on and on like she does sometimes, so we decided to do it this evening.

I climb out of the wardrobe carefully and put the six shoes back: the cream ones with high heels and the black ones with a buckle and the little brown boots that only come up to your ankle. They wouldn't be much good for slooshing through a puddle because you'd get your socks wet. Or your nylons if you were a lady who's allowed to sloosh through puddles. I walk downstairs to the kitchen, holding tightly to the banisters. I'd like to slide down the stairs on my tummy like a snail but I'd spoil my clothes.

There are three dishes on the kitchen table and I go up to them, quiet as a caterpillar. If I stand on tiptoes I can look at the top of the table, so I lift my heels and see some chicken with creamy stuff on it on one of the dishes. It's all shiny and I put out a finger to touch it to see if it feels as shiny as it looks. My elbow knocks a spoon off the table and it bangs on the floor, making a loud noise. Mother turns round from the Aga really quickly, like a firework's gone off on top of her head even though it's not Guy Fawkes day.

'Oh, what have you done now?' she says. 'Look at the floor! As if I didn't have enough to do.'

I didn't see that the spoon was on a plate of green bits and some of it has fallen on the floor too. 'Sorry, Mother, I didn't see it. I'll clear it up, though,' I say, hoping Mother will be glad I'm being a helpful girl and maybe even give me some of the creamy chicken as a prize. I run to the broom cupboard and get the dustpan and brush and I'm very happy when I come in the kitchen and see Mother smiling. Hurrah, hooray. And she's wearing her best pinny too.

'Well done, Virginia. Good girl,' she says. 'It's only a little mess after all. Nothing can spoil today for me, nothing at all.' She goes back to singing and stirring whatever's in the saucepan.

When the people come for the party, I stand up very straight in the hall with Mother to say hello. I'm pretending I'm a sentry on guard to keep out the robbers. When the visitors have all arrived and Dr Greenaway has called me Bubbles, they go into the drawing room and Mother says, 'Now say goodnight to everyone, Virginia, and take yourself up to bed. I'll pop up and see you later.' She always says this when people are here but she never does pop, so Ruby's plan is going to work. Goody goody gumdrops.

I walk round the room. 'Goodnight, Mrs Russell – goodnight, Mr Peters – goodnight, Mr Russell – goodnight, Mrs Peters – goodnight, Dr Greenaway,' I say, and Dr Greenaway holds me by the shoulders.

'Goodnight, Bubbles,' he says, 'sleep tight,' and he bends over and kisses me on my head.

He kisses me. A real kiss. That bit of my head feels hot, like it's suddenly turned into a tiny oven. I wish I could put a lid on it to keep it warm. I put my finger on the hot spot as I go upstairs so I don't lose it, which makes me wobble a bit.

As I close my bedroom door, Ruby slides out from under the bed. 'What're you doing with your head?' she says. 'You look like a loony.' Her finger makes a screwy shape in the air.

'It's a special Dr Greenaway spot and I don't want to lose it. And I *don't* look like a loony anyway – oh, don't do that!'

Ruby's jogged my elbow and I've lost the spot.

'That was really horrid of you, Ruby – now I'll never ever find it again.'

'It's only a stupid bit of hair, Virginia. C'mon, we've got busy work to do, spying on the grown-ups.'

'Well, you'll just have to wait till I've taken off my frock, that's all.'

Ruby's looking really excited, like she's going to the seaside or something. She gets noisy when she's excited, so I put my finger on her lips and say, 'Sh, Ruby, we've got to be as quiet as a fish.'

'Spoilsport!' Ruby says, but she says it in a whisper.

When I've changed into my nightie, we creep downstairs to the dining room without Mother rushing out and giving us a flea in the ear, which wouldn't be nice because it would bounce around and bite you. We can hear lots of talking from the drawing room and every now and again Mother's laughing jumps out really loudly.

Ruby's very clever at arranging things and she puts the tops of the gumboots into each other and lies them on their sides so they won't fall over. When I sit down, I feel something wet on my BTM and I stand up quickly in case I've squished a snail or something. Ruby's got her hand over her mouth so she doesn't laugh out loud and she's pointing to the back of my nightie with the other hand. *Bother. Bother, bother, bother.* I've sat too close to the gumboots from when I was playing in the garden today and now there's some mud and squashed berries on my nightie. Ruby's looking really cheerful and I frown at her. I don't say anything, but what I'm thinking is, *It's not very best friendy to be glad I'm going to get into trouble, Ruby.*

The drawing-room door clicks open and there's the sound of

voices coming closer. We can see through the gaps in the basket-screen and Mother comes in, her flowery frock swooshing round her like a waterfall.

'You'll find your names on the cards,' she says. 'Gerald, you're over there. Perhaps you'd be good enough to charge everyone's glasses while I go and get the first course.'

'Anything for you, Duchess,' says Dr Greenaway, and he bows like Mother's a very important lady. Like a queen or something, and she does this little curtsey and they both do a big giant smile.

The room gets very hot and I'd really like to take my nightie off but then I'd be bare and if Mother found me bare, who knows what she'd do? I let the sweat dribble down my chest and my legs even though it feels like creepy-crawlies.

From where I'm hiding I can see Mother sitting at the this-hand-side of Dr Greenaway, who's at the top of the table. I've never seen Mother looking like she's looking and I wonder if maybe a fairy's flown in and put a magic wand on her face because she looks really, really happy. Like she's been told she can eat nothing but ice cream for the rest of her life and she can walk around bare if she likes and make lots of noise and even break things without someone putting fleas in her ear. She's leaning over to Dr Greenaway and her cheeks look like mine do when I'm all poorly and hot. She turns her face to the rest of the table and says something in a very fast way so I don't understand and everyone laughs a lot.

Mrs Russell's sitting at the end of the table just next to the screen and when she's had her chicken, she gets up and leaves the room. Perhaps she needs to go to the lavatory, even though she's not jiggling. Now I can see right to the end of the table underneath and I see Mother's foot sitting on Dr Greenaway's shoe. She's taken her shoes off, the pink ones with jewels, and her toes are curling round as she moves her foot up and down. As I watch, her foot pushes up inside Dr Greenaway's trousers and rests there. It's so hot in the dining room she can't be trying to warm her tootsies like I do at the fire when it's winter, but I can't think of any other reason why Mother's foot would climb up his trousers like that. I look at Ruby, but Ruby's looking straight ahead like her eyes have got glued.

Mrs Russell comes back and gets in the way again.

When all the food is finished and the grown-ups have had so many cigarettes the room's all foggy, Mr Peters stands up and says, 'Well, Eleanor, you have done us proud. What a feast! Thank you so much for inviting us. Sandra, I think it's time we pushed off.'

It's like someone's blown the whistle for playtime and everyone else stands up and says it's time they pushed off too. They trot out of the room in a queue with Mother and Dr Greenaway at the end. Just as they're about to go out of the door, Dr Greenaway does this really funny thing. He puts his hand out and lies it on Mother's tummy. He gives it three little pats and two little strokes. I've never seen anyone do that before. It's what you'd do to a baby rabbit. Or a kitten.

Mother switches off the lights and closes the door. When I've heard the front door stop opening and closing, I creep back up to my bedroom. I worry about the squished berries on my nightie for a little bit before I fall asleep.

# 1975

Smells always do it for Gilda. When she had her kitchen installed, the sweet smell of wood made her weep and she took herself off so the fitter wouldn't see. Her father used to let her sit under his workbench when she was small and she'd make complicated villages with the wood curls that fell from his plane. She knew they were fragile so she handled them gently, building houses and tents and trees by a pond. Her villagers were a cheery lot who sang hymns a great deal and Aaron joined in from above, helping her when she forgot the words.

And a whiff of cinnamon puts her back in the kitchen, her finger in the mix when her mother's back was turned. *Teisen mel* was Gilda's favourite, a honeycake with peaky meringue topping, which Dilys told her looked like the Black Mountains of her childhood. Told her stories of growing up one of the small dark people from the west. Told her never to use the word Taffy. When she left home, Gilda learned other ways with honey and with lamb and with leeks to make them her own. Now when she stirs saffron into a sauce it feels like a defiance.

She's had no appetite in the last few weeks and thinks she's probably just pining for Raymond – or maybe it's a bug, though she hasn't lost weight. She lost twenty pounds when her mother disappeared, though nobody noticed. The amorphous lines of her frocks hid everything anyway. She probably could have hidden a fridge up there. A pregnancy even.

*Fuck.*
*How long's it been?*

*Five weeks? Six weeks – seven maybe?*
*Oh fuck-fuck-fuck.*

She begins to feel shifty, as though there's something not-her inside.

She dithers. Could be indigestion that's turning her skin the colour of dust, she thinks. Or stress. The constant, draining lethargy she puts down to this year's eccentric summer, but it could be low blood sugar or something. She should probably go to the doctor. She does a bit more dithering. But when she's certain she must have missed two periods at least, she goes to a chemist in Islington and buys two tests. One to make sure and the other to apologise to the god she can't quite silence. She puts them on the floor in the bathroom because she doesn't know what she'll feel when she sees the result, so she'd better be sitting down.

They agree. She is.
Pregnant.
With child.
Up the duff.

What she feels is so primitive there are no words for it. Only a sound would do. The sound of tectonic plates shifting, for example. An iceberg cracking. A tsunami's roar.

Someone of her own. Unconditionally. Hers, just as she'd be his.
She knows he's a boy.

She gets up in the morning pregnant. Gets on the tube pregnant, holding her bag across her belly. She's pregnant when she sees to her clients, stifling a smile when they talk of their babies. She's pregnant on the way home and is affronted when she's not offered a seat. The world is suddenly full of pregnant women in shops and in cinemas and sitting in parks. She's secretly joined a sorority. She stops drinking when she goes out with friends. 'Bit of a spring clean,' she says. 'My body is a temple and all that crap.' One of her friends tries it too, but gives up in a week. 'Christ, you've got an iron will,' she says, and Gilda says, 'Yup.' Her home looks different, pregnant. She imagines its clean lines cluttered with primary-coloured plastic. She imagines the equipment:

the baby monitor, the bottle sterilizer, the gently mouldering nappy bin by the table. She imagines reading him stories about clowns and then, when he's older, the racy adventures of gangs. *Swallows and Amazons* – that'd do.

The Brethren forbade reading fiction, so when Aaron found the pills and threw her out, she gorged herself. She read her way through the stacks in her local library with such avidity, the kindly librarian took her for a university student and suggested more books, from Austen to Zamyatin. She filled notebooks with the new words she learned, though most of the time she was too timid to use them. She made notes and asked one of the other girls in the hostel to test her.

The second bedroom in her home has been her reading room but her son needs it now. She puts up shelves in the hall for her books, gratefully running her fingers along their spines before bringing them downstairs. She wants to mix them up like at a good party, so she lets Roth sidle up to Brontë and smiles as Orwell flirts with Atwood who, on the next shelf down, is haranguing Waugh. She settles the heavy art books on a shelf by themselves like a blue plaque to Graham, who'd taken her education in hand, appalled by her ignorance. John Singer Sargent's women look from their sculpted taffeta at Hodgkin's exuberance and wish they could bust out of their corsets too.

She has painted her house the colours of peace, but suspects her baby needs something more boisterous, so she goes for red and blue. *Trains*, she thinks. *And boats. Planes*, she thinks, because he'll be a boy who goes far, so she stencils the walls with the transport they'll use when they travel the world. When they walk the Himalayas. When they see Machu Picchu's altar blush at dawn. When they turn to each other in wonder.

There'll come a time when she's forced to tell people that she's pregnant, but not yet. She begins to live a sequestered life and fibs to her friends: *I'm really knackered – busy day; terrible leak in the bathroom – just clearing up; you know the bug that's going round? Yep – me too.* She's routinely lied about herself over the years – or edited the truth anyway – but she'll be honest with her son.

# 1975

Monday, 6.09 p.m.

It's light when I get home, the air still gravid with the day's heat. I go to the kitchen, pour myself a stiff glass of Evian and take it into the hall. After a day pleated by my patients' needs, an evening with my roses usually straightens me out and today I need them badly. I change into the striated overalls hanging in the cupboard and go to the shed for the secateurs and the knives and the twine and the tape.

I stand in the middle of my lawn, framed by a pandemonium of blooms, their scent rushing to my head like laughing gas. When I bought the house, the outgoing owners took a tearful leave of the garden as though it were a beloved child whom they were handing over for adoption. They were moving abroad, so couldn't take their plants with them but gave cuttings to their friends to root in the corner of a foreign field that is forever Tooting. I ripped it all up: ripped up their twenty-five years of persuading acers to arch over hellebores, of cultivating cobalt drifts of delphiniums and struts of torch lilies, and cremated the lot.

I stood at the kitchen door, looking at the denuded garden, its soil shivering in the ashy air. Now it was mine.

I love the irony of roses, the contradiction of thorns and petals, and plant only old varieties. Nothing later than the turn of the century. If a plant's persisted for a hundred years it has the instincts of a survivor, which I admire. Charles de Mills has been doing his maroon mooch since 1746, his flowers looking like a deranged horticulturalist scythed their tops off in the grip of a full moon. Baron Girod de l'Ain is a late-nineteenth-century arriviste and flexes his pink bolshiness round a romantic heart. Sombreuil started its social mountaineering thirteen years after Victoria's accession and now

94

casts its tea scents into the city murk from the top of the trellis. Its flowers glow in the dark on summer evenings, and on trip days I settle in my deckchair under their creamy white flow, prosecco popping against my glass. I know my roses more intimately than my neighbours, with whom I'm on a nodding I'm-away-for-a-week-please-watch-out-for-burglars acquaintance. I know that General Jacqueminot, old warhorse though he is, has a certain *faiblesse* where greenfly are concerned and that Reine des Violettes' ebullience needs pitiless pruning in spring or she sulks. Mutabilis is a ditherer who changes his mind from yellow to orange to pink to crimson, often picking up mildew on the way as though all those decisions have quite worn the poor dear out. My horticultural pharmacy treats greenfly and whitefly and mildew and root rot and I have remedies for ailments my hypochondriacal plants have yet to imagine.

I dose and sprinkle and scatter and spray, my diagnostic nose as sensitive in the garden as it is in the clinic. I find the chemical sting of the sprays bracing and allow them to settle on my skin long enough to hurt before I wash them off. I've tried creating my own hybrids, but whatever I do the hosts always reject the grafts. I go over now to my latest attempt, but despite having bribed the native with extra feed it's wilfully starving the migrant, who's losing the will to live. I'll give it another week then lop it off.

I move round the garden for the next two hours, browsing like a boll weevil in cotton. I examine every stem, tying back renegades and scouting out pests, before making another circuit to do the deadhead-ing. Decapitating the dead and the dying always maps my mood, and tonight I slash at them so vindictively I realise I'm furious. The mael-strom of Sierra Leonean customs and beliefs often tossed women at my hospital wild-eyed and starving after months of exile. I discovered there that ostracism kills as surely as any parasite. As implacably as any bullet. Faisal told me today that Mrs Khaliq's baby has been taken into care because she's had a psychotic breakdown and I feel enraged all over again. She didn't survive the transplant from her native soil and she'll now live the rest of her life beyond the pale.

I chop at a heavy cluster of browning blooms and catch the side of my thumb. Bleeding copiously, I drop the knife and reach into my back pocket where I keep the antiseptic wipes and dressings. The blood drips another layer on to the injuries documented on the overalls, written on my skin, which I sometimes read like a good novel.

I leave the garden preening itself and pour myself another glass of water in the kitchen, sparkling this time. During the quads I drink only mineral water. Bottles of every variety hunker down in the cellar next to my wines and I ring the changes hour by hour, day by day, as though working my way through a tasting menu. It's Badoit today, its salty tang hailing from the same region as my beloved Pouilly-Fumés and Sancerres and Saumurs. As I trudge upstairs, sipping at the water's meek bubbles, I can almost imagine it's Saumur Crémant de Loire. The damn pictures are farting about again, so I prod them back into place on the wall. I've considered junking them before now but their anonymity suits me, so I let them hang. For the moment. I go into the room at the top of the stairs. Magda's been in today and rarely puts things back in the right place. She's taken a dislike to this room for some reason.

I flick on a light as I go in and see that the pictures have their faces to the wall like naughty schoolchildren. I go to flip each one over, beginning with the two poster-sized Magritte prints I've hung on the right-hand wall. *L'Evidence Eternelle* stretches itself in a falling cadence, five irregular-sized canvasses of a woman's naked body interrogated by blank spaces. Magritte painted his wife's head, her torso, genitals, knees and feet, her body's continuity interrupted by the gaps between the canvasses. He forces me to speculate about the absent links between her parts and to wonder what she'd look like whole. Why he needed to disarm her. Mrs Magritte looks not at all bothered she's been fragmented. Her half-smile invites me to agree: *Just look what my René's done – isn't he brilliant?*

*L'Importance des Merveilles* hanging next to it shows another disassembled woman, this time consisting of mismatched parts stacked like so many plant pots. Her tiny head emerges from her chimney-like neck and her weedy arms pop out of holes in her torso, which sits in the next pot, her belly, which in turn nestles in her giant haunches. No hollow aspect of the woman accords with the next, which may have been marvellous to Magritte, but to me it's a painful depiction of incongruity that I recognise.

I meet Magda rarely, but whenever I do she is vitriolic about the Dali on the opposite wall above a chest of drawers. My favourite. She tells me it affronts her every time she sees it. She asks me why I don't have pretty pictures in here, like the watercolours on the stairs. She gave me a calendar from Poland one year for Christmas, full of Disney-eyed animals, and her card said: *Put him on wall of bad room please Doktor.* Magda's standards of cleaning waver in the rest of the house, but she maniacally wipes and polishes and hoovers in here, leaving the air heavy with cleaning smells. As though the bluebells and the lilacs might harbinger redemption for this benighted soul.

Dali's subversion of a 1930s porn image is an audacious slap in the face and, like the other two, hangs from an industrial bolt. *Young Virgin Auto-sodomised By Her Own Virginity* shows a saucy young woman's body ruptured by erotic excitement, punished for her chastity by a zooming prick. I call it *Who Gives A Flying Fuck*.

I walk over and turn the picture outwards again so I can see it whenever I pass the open door. Its violence is in tension with its dulcet colours, like the pain and delight at the heart of a life. I can feel my earlier rage subsiding as I stand in front of this woman who looks so aroused by her abasement.

I'm jerked out of my reverie by the phone shrilling. It's Faisal.

'Virginia, hi. How are you?'

'I'm fine. A bit pooped, but I've been pottering in my garden, so I'm OK now.'

'Good. Look, Amina and I are having some friends round for dinner on the sixth and we wondered if you'd like to join us. The others are mostly psychologists and Amina's a terrific cook.'

I calculate. It's a Saturday. 'That would be great, Faisal, thanks. How kind of you to ask me. What sort of time?'

'Oh, eightish? The kids should be in bed by then, so we'll be ready for some adult conversation.'

'I'll be there. Lovely. See you tomorrow.'

Amina has met Virginia a few times at the hospital since Faisal took up the post and thought her pleasant but unknowable. She listened to Faisal's accounts of her clinical manner and was intrigued by how

97

such an illegible woman could read her patients so empathically. She wondered if she might be different – more accessible perhaps – when she shrugged off her professional persona, so suggested to Faisal they have her over.

She's always teased Faisal that he never brings anyone home. 'What am I, some sort of Cyclops?' she says, but it's less his monstrous wife, more that until they got married Faisal had never had a home to bring anyone to. Nor the leisure to make friends, so their guests are usually Amina's friends from work or the kind of comrades parents meet at the school gates.

But he has for once invited someone, Anna Ashton, who took up a senior registrar post in a parallel firm six months ago. He came across her in a meeting with a hospital big cheese, who was set on revolutionising the department and had called the doctors together to sock it to them. Streamlining, he called it, but it felt more like amputation. Virginia was away and Faisal found himself sitting next to a small woman wearing Mr Magoo glasses whom he hadn't seen before. The meeting was going badly, the doctors confounded by the welter of figures being chucked around like knives, when Anna coughed and got to her feet. Blushing furiously, she delivered a halting disquisition that fatally undermined the big cheese's argument. What her address lacked in oratorical skills, it possessed in intensity and no one in the room could have doubted her conviction.

The cheese retreated to regroup, Faisal congratulated Anna and they had a cup of tea together in the staff room. When he told her he worked with Virginia, her face lit up like a stage-door Johnny catching sight of the star.

'Oh, how I envy you – she's completely brilliant!' she said. 'I can't think of anyone else like her – she just knows her patients inside out, doesn't she? Just knows what a woman feels about her body. I think I must have read everything she's ever written and I've heard her speak at conferences several times. She knocks spots off everyone else because you know she's got the patient in mind as much as the pathology. I'd love to observe her in surgery sometime.'

'I'm sure I could arrange that – she's always very happy to pass on what she knows.'

'Oh, I'd be so grateful! I'm probably sounding like some creepy stalker or something, but I'd love to sort of sit at her feet. Please let me know if it's possible.'

He fixed it up for her, since when they've got together from time to time to drink the hospital's execrable coffee and talk about work. When Amina suggested inviting Virginia for dinner, Faisal thought Anna might like to meet her heroine off duty, so he invited her too. When he told her who else was coming, she embarrassed them both by flinging her arms round his neck.

She pulled herself away, blushing. 'Oh God, sorry, Faisal,' she said, 'that was a bit much. But I can't tell you how excited I am – can't wait to meet her properly!'

On his way home that evening, Faisal stopped at the traffic lights by the tube station and watched pedestrians swarm away from the Northern Line hellhole. He saw a young woman among them who took his breath away. Other women were clunking along in wedge-heeled ankle-killers and embroidered jeans, but she was a picture of understated elegance. Her black hair was so heavy it seemed to bounce in slow motion against the back of her cobalt-blue frock, which was tight enough to hint at full breasts and loose enough not to boast. He wasn't in the habit of ogling women and fortunately she was looking straight ahead, but he glanced at his watch and wondered if she passed his way every evening. After a little while, he noticed the pregnancy.

He's just settled the last child in bed when the doorbell rings. Amina's having a flurried last-minute shower, so he goes downstairs and opens the front door. Anna's standing there and for a startled moment he thinks she has glitter in her hair. It's only raindrops, but she's sparkling like a Christmas decoration. She can barely contain herself.

'Oh, I've really been looking forward to this,' she says as she comes into the hall. 'Edward and I don't get out much, what with work and the children and everything, so it's such a treat coming here for dinner. Thanks so much for inviting me.'

Faisal looks down the garden path. 'Is Edward . . .?'

'No, no – sorry, Faisal, I should have said. The poor chap's had to stay behind because the babysitter cancelled. He's terribly disappointed. She says she's got flu, but I bet it's more like a last-minute party invitation – you know how teenagers are. God, I'm dreading my two getting there – all those surging hormones! Is Virginia here?' She's looking into the living room.

'Not yet, no – you're the first. But what a shame Edward can't come – I was looking forward to meeting him and I know Amina wanted to pick his brains.'

'He's probably better off at home, actually.' She waves a dismissive hand. 'He's got loads of work to do and he's exhausted anyway. Virginia *is* coming, though, isn't she?'

'Absolutely – unless she's had a better offer. Come and have a drink.'

When she's settled on the sofa with a glass of wine, Faisal realises what's different about her. She's wearing make-up. She's taken her glasses off and applied it like a six-year-old at her mother's dressing table. Her eyes look like a tropical fish with the parrot-green shadow and spiky mascara and her cheeks blush with an ill-advised apricot. Her mask-like foundation, three shades too dark, ends abruptly at her chin, as though you could tuck your fingers under it and peel it off. She's wearing a frock with sequins round the neck, two strings of pearls and shoes with heels that are pockmarking the floorboards already. Every time the doorbell rings, she sits bolt upright. She's polite to the other guests when they arrive, but distracted.

When Virginia shows up – late, apologetic, bearing a huge bunch of roses – she too has dressed for the occasion. She's wearing a black velvet evening skirt, a shrunken tartan sweatshirt and green Birkenstocks. Faisal blinks. At the hospital he's only ever seen her in sludge-coloured clothes in which she could be anybody.

Anna sits opposite Virginia in the living room, leaning forwards as though she might otherwise miss some pearl. Virginia drinks three glasses of wine before dinner and inhales the bowls of South Asian snacks, which Amina replenishes twice. The other guests talk about their children, the sclerotic state of the tube and the recent murderous attack on a woman in Bradford, but Virginia talks between mouthfuls only about work and the hospital. Amina's spent the day cooking and loads a side table in the dining room with dishes on plate warmers that cloud the air with coriander, with cumin, with methi, cardamom and ginger. She cuts the stems of Virginia's bunch of roses and arranges them in a vase next to the food.

When dinner's announced, Virginia goes ahead of the others as if on roller skates. At the side table she fills her plate with something from every dish, takes two stuffed parathas and carries it all to the table, spilling a gloop of dahl on the way.

'Oh crikey,' she says, 'sorry,' but is in too much of a hurry to help Amina clear it up.

The conversation over dinner is mercurial and Virginia says very little, except when Faisal mentions community service cuts in Wandsworth. With her mouth full, she scatters words and rice over the table like bullets, inveighing against a government depriving a population already hanging off the bottom of the food chain. When someone else takes up the subject, she wipes her plate with the remains of the paratha and goes back for more. And then for more. To Amina's keen eye, there's something raw about Virginia's hunt for fullness that's painful to watch, but when she mentions it to Faisal later, he brushes it aside.

'She works longer hours at a greater intensity than anyone I've ever known,' he says, 'so no wonder she's hungry. You're over-interpreting again, Mrs Psycho – relax! Sometimes things really are as they seem.'

Amina struggles sometimes to keep her professional mind quiet when going about her ordinary life, but Virginia's insatiable appetite stays with her and she wonders what it means.

Wonders what she's really hungry for.

Edward isn't unhappy about staying at home to look after the children. He has some papers to read and he's anyway not the most sociable of men. He's impatient with chat, which he regards as so much mental lint, though he understands that others find it entertaining. He understands people for a living and is now a consultant psychiatrist in the drug addiction clinic at Friern Barnet hospital. His family brings him great joy but he is happiest when he's rooting around in patients' minds to discover the reasons why. When he's engaged in the archeological dig for meaning. He has a pharmacological cornucopia at his elbow but is much persuaded by the tenets of psychoanalysis and gives his patients' unconscious his fine-tuned attention. It makes his days longer but their recovery shorter, and he has written about this, though he's aware that as a writer he's no great shakes. He sometimes thinks that the hospital's corridor – the longest in Britain – is a useful symbol of the journey into a patient's history, with its closed doors and cupboards and tributaries full of questions, but has yet to insinuate it into one of his papers.

He is a thin, nervy man, whose fingers are in constant motion but he has a way of staying calm in the presence of turbulence that's beguiling. He feels privileged to have his patients teach him the geography of the human mind, which he learns to map so he can help them out of their dead ends. Guide them past their No Entry signs.

The only reason he might have been keen to go tonight would have been to meet Virginia. Or, more truthfully, meet her again. He hasn't been entirely truthful with Anna because he didn't want to contaminate her feelings about this woman who has become so pre-eminent in her field. Famous even. Infamous, he understands, in some circles for her conviction that women are entitled to make choices – even in extremis, when most doctors insist they know best. He is proud of his wife, though realistic. She is less an original thinker, more a faithful disciple who needs the inspirational leadership she tells him Virginia provides.

When she found the advertisement in the *BMJ* for the senior registrar post at St George's, she became almost ecstatic. He was impressed by that. And curious.

'I telephoned the hospital to get some details and they told me it was in Virginia Denham's firm! Virginia *Denham*, Edward! I feel a bit light-headed actually. Suppose they appoint me? Suppose I get to work with her? It'd be all my dreams come true.'

She worked the whole of one weekend on her application while he took the children swimming and to the park and out for lunch and out for dinner, but by Sunday evening, she was despondent.

'I can't possibly get it,' she said, her hair fussed about by anxious fingers. 'She's such a phenomenon, the world and its auntie'll be applying and my CV doesn't look anything like good enough.' He reassured her of course, pointed out her fine, fine qualities, but he braced himself to understand her disappointment when it came.

He didn't tell her what he knew of Virginia. What he remembered, though the memories flooded back when he heard her name.

Anyone seeing them at medical school together in Leeds would have taken them for friends, though it was less a friendship, more a needful cleaving. He would in those days not have been able to articulate it, but looking back now he realises that they were linked not only by their dedication to the learning but also by the alienation that hung round them like fumes. His growing up in a Northumbrian mining village would have marked him out as an interloper had he been willing to tell anyone. Truth be told, his training alienated him from his family too, which caused him some disquiet, but he thought it was probably inevitable. Virginia was one of only five women in their year, and was certainly not woman enough for her peers. She seemed unable – or unwilling – either to flirt or to comport herself prettily like the other female students, and appeared to find puzzling the ribaldry most of the male students deployed. Neither of them participated in Rag Week, despising the tipsy puerility of young people letting off steam after precociously facing death. While the others were partying, they'd be in the library together, or meeting up in her room or in his to talk about their studies and offer each other pointers. There was nothing else on offer. He had no sexual interest in her and she evinced none in him. He noticed that sometimes she ate huge amounts of food and at other times nothing at all – sometimes for days – and wondered if her thyroid was out of sorts. It was always such a joy to come across symptomatology on legs.

From the outset she told him she wanted to be a surgeon. She'd bought herself some textbooks and would list the names and the shapes and the functions of scalpels in the way someone else might quote poetry. She'd talk about the magic of healing the wound you've just caused and while he understood her excitement, he was becoming more interested in healing the psychic wounds someone else had caused. Now when he looks at surgeons he sees the madness of cutting into a live body to make it well and wonders about their pathology, but then all he saw was the art of precision and the science of systems.

Virginia was the only woman among them as they trooped into their first dissection class. When he saw the shrouded figures laid out in ranks like victims of a terrible disaster, he was sure he heard the sound of twenty pulses racing. They were assigned their tables and he and Virginia stood opposite each other, together with two hearty men who were more famous for rugby than their studies. The tutor stood behind the desk and asked them to uncover their bodies, which they knew now to call cadavers, were relieved to call cadavers, because that way they were stripped of their humanity. Edward unpeeled the shroud, revealing the waxen body of a middle-aged woman. The reek of formaldehyde was brutal and it was all he could do to stop himself covering his nose with his handkerchief. He saw his burly neighbour blench, sway and fall heavily to the ground. On the other side of the room, another man stopped himself falling by gripping the table's edge. A fellow student put his hand on the cadaver to steady it.

'Always happens,' said the tutor cheerfully. 'There's water over there on the bench.'

When the students took their shamefaced places back at the tables, the class was asked to bring out their instruments and the books that were to be their constant companions over the next year. Along with *Cunningham's Textbook of Anatomy* they'd each bought an eighteen-inch canvas roll tied up with tapes which, when unrolled, revealed the instruments lying cosily in their berths. Edward was conscious of standing in a live body amid the malodorous evidence of death and while he'd seen dead bodies before – mining has its perils, after all – these bodies looked like the plasticine he'd played with as a boy, their flesh the sort of yellowy grey that plasticine goes when the colours are kneaded together. But when he tentatively touched his cadaver for the first time, his fingers warm against its glassy chill, it had none of the give of plasticine. Tough as old boots it was. Stiff as pickled leather.

Edward glanced at Virginia to check she wasn't distressed – must be difficult, he thought, to be chopping up a body so like your own – but she simply looked spellbound.

Textbook in hand, he later made his first incision through flesh that resisted his knife, as though determined to hang on to its secrets.

The book spilled the beans in its own arid language but the cadaver would tell him about its organs and systems and bones. About its pathology and oddities and health.

As they left the room, the other students began joshing each other, already revving up the comedy that would sustain them through the shocks.

'Why d'you think they do it? Donate their bodies, I mean?' one asked the other.

'Some men'd do anything to get away from the wife,' the other man said and they fell about laughing. Neither Edward nor Virginia found any of it funny. They were both too awed by what they'd just seen.

Bent over *Gray's Anatomy* that evening, he suddenly realised what he'd been afraid of. 'You know,' he said to her, 'just before I pulled the cloth off the cadaver, I was quite filled with anxiety – suppose she'd been someone I know? Suppose my mother'd died and no one had told me?'

'That hadn't occurred to me,' she said calmly, 'but it would have been jolly strange, I must say.'

As the term drew on, the class began to seethe with stories at the tables and in the breaks, stories that the teller swore to god were true.

'There was this American student who smuggled an arm out of the hospital,' said one. 'Toll collector nearly had a coronary when he took the money from a severed hand.'

'Friend of mine knew this bloke in London,' said another, 'sent someone who'd bullied him at Wellington a heart in the post with a stake through it. Bloke had a breakdown on the spot.'

The stories helped defuse the tensions that built up as they dug deeper into the bodies, and were especially useful when it came to the genitals.

Especially when they came to the genitals.

He'd raced through an electric storm one morning on his way to the class, reminded of the moment when lightning animates Frankenstein's patchwork man. They'd been taking it in turns to uncover their cadavers and today it was Virginia's turn. As her hand went towards the cloth, one of the men around the table snorted, which he tried to turn into a sneeze. She was standing by the dead woman's hips and leaned over to unroll the cloth. There was a palpable air of anticipation all round the room as she slowly uncovered their excavations.

She came to the woman's crotch. She unveiled the vulva. She unveiled the vagina, which was no longer a void. It was stuffed.

With a severed penis.

The room erupted as sniggers turned into hoots and the rest of the class gathered around the table, foolish with glee. The tutor wandered over to see what the fuss was about.

'Oh dear, someone's been a very, very naughty boy,' he said when he'd seen. 'Hands up whoever's responsible. I may have to stand you in the naughty-boy corner for the rest of the class,' and he smiled.

Edward wasn't laughing and neither was Virginia. She stood by the table with the cloth in her hands and he saw a rage in her eyes that he's never forgotten. They were alight with it. Shot through with it like Frankenstein's monster with the lightning, and her hands were wringing the cloth like a neck. Then, he'd never seen anger so violent before. Now, he's come across it in the seriously ill, when voices urge a paranoid schizophrenic to kill.

She wouldn't talk about it afterwards and Edward was too fearful to insist. At least, he told himself he didn't insist because he was a sensitive man, but later he realised he'd been silenced by the look on her face. He might have said she looked like a killer, but that would have been fanciful.

But there was one other time when he caught sight of something in her so unhinged it was an effort to remember she was a student, not a slasher.

He'd turned up early for class, his alarm having gone off prematurely. He thought he might as well steal a little extra time before the others turned up because he wanted to check something in the pancreas he thought he'd missed the time before. His mum used to call him the panther when he was young because he could steal up on her unawares, so he made no sound as he came into the dissection room. Virginia wouldn't have heard him anyway, because every one of her senses was pinned to what she was doing. She'd uncovered their cadaver and lifted out its uterus. It lay in her palm, shrunk to the size of a pear. She was holding it in her left hand in front of her lower abdomen. She was rapt. He froze, not sure what he was watching. She lifted her right hand and he saw she was holding a scalpel, but not in any way a surgeon might. She held it in her fist, her knuckles pushing against the skin. She held it like a stiletto. She twitched the knife upwards and she smiled. He saw her fist begin to plunge and he shouted.

'No!' he shouted. 'Stop!' She did stop, but didn't look startled. She gazed at him as he walked towards her, no curiosity on her face. He took the knife out of her hand, which she left in the air. He lifted the uterus, dense with death, out of her other hand and laid it back in its proper place. He put his hand on her shoulder. She seemed slowly to wake up.

'What were you doing?' he said, trying not to sound desperate.

'Caesarean section,' she said. 'Just giving it a whirl. Decided on obstetrics.'

The rest of the class clattered in at that point, but Edward didn't know how to ask her anything else. He was paralysed by his natural reserve – and she hadn't done anything, had she? Absolutely understandable, he told himself, that someone interested in obstetrics would investigate a woman's plumbing. That's all he saw, he told himself, her interest. He was fascinated by a person's psychic plumbing after all. And anyway he had no one to tell.

But it created a distance between them and he began to study alone, late into the night, driven by his raging ambition. She didn't seem to notice.

He watched her walk off with all the prizes when they qualified, and buried what he'd seen that morning. She was clearly a shooting star in the medical firmament, whom he quite forgot when he went to London to study psychiatry – until Anna reminded him.

And just as he told no one else then, he thought it a matter of simple discretion when he told Anna none of this now. She was so thrilled to be applying to join Virginia. So overjoyed to be shortlisted. So crushed when she wasn't appointed. They know now that Faisal was, and he admires his wife for bearing him no animus. Three months later she applied for, and got, a post in another firm at St George's and seemed happy enough just to be under the same aegis as her heroine.

He'll get Anna's take on Virginia when she comes back at the end of the evening. Interesting to compare impressions, then and now. He hears *Match of the Day* calling to him, which drowns out the moan of work in the study.

He settles down to watch Newcastle trounce Chelsea.

The young woman comes into the room. She's dripping. Her mac's dripping, her plastic hood's dripping, her galoshes are dribbling on the scabby floorboards. She puts her shopping bag carefully, almost reverentially, on the desk and switches on the standard lamp that stands on its right-hand side. It lost its hold on the perpendicular some time ago. She goes over to the gas fire and tries to light it. The rain drips off her sleeves and puts the match out three times. Still crouching, she slips off her mac and lights the spill. The gas pops and the fire begins the arduous task of heating the room. The woman hangs her mac in the wardrobe, takes off her hood and snaps it back into its folds. She undoes her galoshes and kicks them off. One of them has developed a hole and as she pads over to the desk her right foot leaves prints behind her. She goes to open the shopping bag but decides to wash her hands first in the sink by the window. She dries them carefully. She wishes she had anti-bacterial soap, but she forgot to sneak some out of the operating theatre. When she's sitting at the desk, she takes a deep breath. Out of the shopping bag she takes four packets of crisps, a large wedge of Cheddar cheese in greaseproof paper, a jar of pickled eggs, three floury baps and a bottle of Cyprus sherry. She sets them up in a row at the back of the desk, against the wall, where there are already greasy marks on the wallpaper. The cheese will add a few more. She puts her hand back in the bag and draws out the real treasure. The reason there's been a spring in her step. Jaunty, she's been, on her way back to her digs. It's a surgery textbook, its blue cloth cover fraying slightly at the edges, its gold lettering almost illegible. She puts it on the desk and opens it. Sebastian Fergus, it says in expensively educated handwriting, x.ix.lii. Leeds. Before she goes any further, she opens the packets of crisps, locates their blue twists of salt, dumps them in, shakes the bags and puts them back in line. She has a sudden thought and goes to the sink to fetch the towel so she can wipe her hands between mouthfuls. So she doesn't dirty the pages. She settles down to her feast. Mouthful of crisps, bite of cheese, nibble of egg. Gulp of sherry. Wipe hands. Big bite of bap, half an egg, four crisps. Gulp *of sherry. Wipe hands. She opens the book. She traces the scalpels' outlines on the pages, returning to her favourites from time to time like visiting a close friend. A bosom buddy. She's a third of the way through the book and all the way through the food when the smell of gravy creeps under the door.* Bisto – Browns, Seasons And Thickens In One. *She hears the gong from down-stairs and carries on reading. She's prepared for the knock on the door. There it is.* Miss Denham? *says her landlady,* I've banged the gong for tea. Thank you, Mrs Churchill, *she says,* I'm not hungry actually – I had some fish and chips on my way back from the hospital. But I've done a roast specially, *says Mrs Churchill,* with gravy and Yorkshires and everything. I'm really fine, *she says.* Honestly. Suit yourself, *says Mrs Churchill huffily. The footsteps recede. She knows Mrs Churchill's roasts. You could build houses with them. She stands up and pulls a red book off the bookshelf above the desk. She sits down and opens it to a photograph. It's a photograph of an operation. A hysterectomy. She looks from the text she bought today in the second-hand bookshop, then at the photograph, then back again, matching the tools to the task.*

Womb with a view? *I say.*

Ovary funny, *she says and laughs.*

Get ova it, *I say and laugh too.*

Oh, sperm me the jokes, *she says and we're both rocking. Then I stop laughing.*

That was strange today, *I say.*

Wasn't strange at all. Didn't hear him come in. Bugger crept up like some big cat. Suddenly there. Ruby was furious.

D'you think he believed you?

Why wouldn't he? It's the truth. I *am* going to specialise.

In women?

You bet. You bet I'm going to specialise in women. And girls. Babies too. Make them better. Put them in charge. Make them strong.

Makes you strong too.

Certainly does.

Won't be bullied again.

Certainly won't.

Stay one step ahead.

Always.

What about him?

Who?

Him. You know – your friend.

Not a friend. Just a colleague, that's all. Don't need friends.

You don't?

I don't. Got Ruby. Ruby's got me. We're a team. She knows me.

Yes.

She sees me.

Yes.

She hears me.

Yes.

She loves me.

# 1944

Eleanor's supper parties are looser affairs since William went away and this one goes down especially well – everyone says she's the hostess with the mostest. After she's cleared up, she lies in bed, contentment spreadeagling her limbs. The baby's always frisky at night, as though it knows it's alone with its mother. It's dancing now to her heartsong and she circles it tenderly with her arms. Last weekend she parcelled Virginia off to the farm and she and Gerald slipped away to York. She slides her fingers now between her legs, remembering his body bristling against her back.

When they stay at the Bideawee guest house, they are Mr and Mrs Astaire, a respectable married couple from Pontefract – 'Just taking a break from the children,' they say. 'You know how it is.' But he is Fred in bed and as his tongue slides round her mouth and down her belly and into her centre, he calls her Ginger.

They have a favourite table at Bettys Tea Rooms, which has opened a branch in the city, and if they find it occupied by another couple or a bunch of boisterous Canadians, they wait by the door until they can slip into the still-warm seats and sit knee to knee, his tweed fidgeting against her silk.

It was Bert, the genial barman at Bettys, who showed them the mirror behind the bar where homesick Canadian airmen have scratched their names into the back. *Wing Ding Sgt Brullinger*, they read; *J. N. Fletcher RCAF Vancouver BC*; *61SQ77 RCAF W. Quilley*, and they wondered how many of them were dead. Bert took a shine to the couple and invited them to add their names.

'You might as well,' he said. 'At least you've got a future, unlike them poor lads.'

They scraped their names in the mirror's silvered back with the diamond in Eleanor's engagement ring. *Eleanor and Gerald*, they wrote, *1944 and forever*.

They were scrupulous about using French letters, which Gerald picked up in a town some distance away where he wouldn't be recognised. He muted the guilt by telling himself he wouldn't be buying them for him and Annie anyway, since they long ago stopped making love. He had muted his Catholic conscience some time before. He's been to confession less since he fell in love and tells lies when he does. He confesses that to Eleanor when they meet. She absolves him.

At the guest house, Eleanor would reach into his breast pocket when they locked the bedroom door and pull the sheaths out like chocolates. She loved rolling them down the shaft with her fingers or her mouth but she knew he found them tiresome and she too longed to feel the soft infant skin of his penis inside her. On their third trip to Bideawee they were kissing by the bed, still in their coats, when she reached into her handbag.

'I've got a surprise,' she said, 'something we both want,' and she drew out the diaphragm she'd been fitted for a few weeks before. It was a bit of a faff to use, but their lovemaking became all the more abandoned once they were liberated from the condoms. On their way to York once, her hand was resting on his thigh as he drove, the car speeding up as though it, too, couldn't wait, and her fingers crept slyly upwards until they cupped his balls. He was hardly able to park the car in a field and they raced up an incline to a copse, hobbling with excitement. Under the sturdy shelter of an oak, she rolled up her skirt, he slid down her knickers and lifted her against the tree trunk, their tongues romping, their breath clotting. She hung from his neck, her thighs gripping his hips as he slid into her, desire gasping from them both like steam. She came as she'd never come before, came as though a hurricane raged through her belly, her groin, her thighs, and he called out so passionately the trees barely held on to their leaves.

Later, as she undressed for her bath, he saw the angry grazes on her back where the oak had fought back.

'Oh, darling,' he said, 'I've hurt you. I'm so sorry.'

She turned to him, bewildered.

'Your back,' he said, and showed her the marks with the aid of her hand mirror and the dressing table.

'I wish they would never heal,' she said. 'I wish I could wear you like a blaze down my back forever,' and the bath was forgotten.

She laughed when Gerald confirmed the pregnancy, and then she cried. They clung to each other in the surgery, the baby mysterious between them.

It took two weeks for reality to kick in and one week more to confront it.

'I can't leave her, darling,' he said desperately, 'she's a good woman – she doesn't deserve it. But at the same time staying with her feels like committing suicide. Like committing a slow suicide every day for the rest of my life. She has utter faith in me . . .'

'So do I,' she said, 'but I love you more.'

'I don't want to quantify this, Eleanor. It's not fair on her. You'd win every time. Loving you feels like a sort of incandescence inside me – as though I've only been fully alive since I fell in love with you. If only I'd met you first.'

'I can never wish away our meeting, Gerald. I can never wish away this baby. Whatever happens, I want to know that it – he, she, it doesn't matter – is living and thriving somewhere. Having a life and a future that our circumstances deny us.'

They had both wept, Eleanor astonished that a man could be so unguarded.

They made plans.

As her body changed, she adjusted her wardrobe. When she'd carried Virginia, her belly had swollen immediately, as though asserting itself. *Ready or not, here I come . . .* This time the baby nestled deep inside her, knowing that it needed to hide, keeping as close to its mother as it could. As a child she was known for her sewing, so she deftly constructed frocks and jackets designed to dissemble. She was frequently complimented on how well she was looking and coyly attributed her glow to the food from the farm. 'I count my blessings,' she said, 'especially when I think of the starving children in Europe.' Virginia was another matter. She kept pestering her to go to the doctor – if only she knew she was under the doctor already! – and Eleanor worried that she might say something awkward in public, so when she'd stopped vomiting in the morning she began groaning exaggeratedly after she'd eaten something. 'Oh no, I've eaten too much again!' she'd cry, 'What a greedy pig I am! I'm getting so horribly fat!' Fortunately, six-year-olds are gullible little creatures.

Last weekend as they lay in the guest-house bed, Gerald rested his head on her belly, listening to their baby somersaulting.

'It knows nothing but perfect happiness,' he said. 'It's able to be absolutely fearless because it's never known any danger. If only we could stay in that state of grace. If only we could hang on to the peace I feel with you, with it, right here. Right now.'

'I thought we'd banned "if onlys", Gerald. Agreed to stick with what's happening now. What we've made together. This will never not have happened to us. We'll never not have known this heaven. Sometimes I feel all I consist of is love – for you and for our baby.'

They made love again with the slow ease of two people who complete each other.

As she rolls over now, her belly tightens and a hint of pain claws at her. She's been having painless contractions for some weeks but she knows it's just her body cranking up for the main event. This one hurts and she lies still, ready for the next. It comes ten minutes later and she telephones him.

'Gerald, I think it's time,' she says. 'It won't take me more than an hour to drop Virginia off at the farm, so please come over then. I'll be ready for you.' She hears him turn to Annie lying next to him.

'It's Mrs Denham,' he says. 'Poor thing, she's getting frightful pains in her lower abdomen.'

Annie murmurs sympathetically.

'Look, Mrs Denham,' he says, 'it may well be your appendix having a little grumble, so why don't you monitor it over the next hour or so, and I'll pop over if it doesn't go away. Don't worry. I'm sure it'll all be fine . . .'

She telephones the farmhouse.

'Mam,' she says as her mother answers, her voice blurry with sleep,

'I've just been telephoned by the bureau. Something rather big has come up and they need me there now. I'm sorry, I know it's all rather sudden, but can I bring Virginia over? I'm afraid they think this one might take some time, so I'll bring enough clothes for a week, just in case.'

When she nudges Virginia awake, the little girl lifts her arms as though expecting a hug. She puts them down when she opens her eyes.

'You have to go to Nana's,' her mother says, 'because I've got to go and do my War Work for a little while. Rise and shine now.'

Having installed Virginia at the farm, Eleanor sits in the drawing room, her pink case at her feet. It has been lying, packed, under her bed for a month now. She has doubled everything on the list the nuns gave her, because what do nuns know? She has eight nighties in her suitcase, three bed jackets and enough toiletries for a small village. Her belly is contracting more insistently and she holds it, willing the baby to stay put. If it stays put, she can believe in a future for her and Gerald. If it is born, her life will stand still.

When Gerald arrives, he holds her close, leaning back against the front door with her head against his chest. Suddenly she gasps.

'Oh God, I think my waters have broken,' she cries and she pulls away, warm swill bucketing down her legs.

'Heavens above!' he says. 'I think we may not get there in time.'

She snaps forwards as a bolt of pain shoots through her belly, then looks up at him, terrified. 'I don't think it's going to wait,' she says. 'Whatever shall we do?'

He races upstairs for an eiderdown and two towels and carries her to the car, laying her down on the back seat. He does the only reasonable thing and drives her to the surgery. The labour lasts four hours and he delivers the baby – their daughter – on to her chest. Gently, he unbuttons Eleanor's silk blouse, eases up her bra and puts the baby's mouth to her breast. As the tiny lips flutter, then pull, Eleanor feels a geyser blow at her centre and she bursts into tears.

'Shh, darling. Shh, shh, shh. It's all right. Everything's all right,' Gerald murmurs and leans over to gather them both into his arms.

They lie on the couch for as long as they dare, dreaming the same dream. When dawn comes, he wraps the two of them up and drives them the fifty miles to the Home.

Five days later, Eleanor's arms are empty.

# 1976

Gilda had thought she'd known about Dilys, but she'd been wrong. She'd thought she'd known about Dilys and Aaron's marriage, but she'd been wrong there too. The three of them spent all their spare time together, much of it among the Brethren. Aaron worked exclusively for other members of the Assembly, and the greater part of every weekend was spent at the Ebenezer Hall. In the hall, among the other believers, Gilda inhabited a world of certainty that came as a relief after her life at school among the other girls. Not that she was among them exactly because her beliefs set her apart, but she peeked at their pleasures from her place in the margins. She prayed for them earnestly, but fruitlessly, since she knew they were already damned.

But at the hall and at home, she belonged. At prayer times and at mealtimes, she and her parents fitted together like fingers. And as she grew up, Dilys explained what would happen to her body. Told her to expect lumps and bumps and hairiness, strange turbulences, wild thoughts and blood as she slid into her woman's body. Told her that when the time came, she'd find a boy in the Assembly who would give her babies, just as she'd done with Aaron. Then left before she knew enough. Took up with a fancy man, not of their kind. Disappeared from Gilda's life, leaving her with a father in mourning. Who looked at Gilda and saw her mother. Who turned away.

She watches her belly in the bath, hoping to catch it curve as it makes room for her fatherless baby. Tobias. As a child she was entranced by the story of Tobias and the angel and now she imagines her son with a wise guardian by his side. She looks at her swelling breasts, traces the veiny delta under her skin, runs the tips of her fingers round the darkening areolae. She imagines a tiny mouth round the nipple, needing what she has to give. Giving her what she needs.

She finds herself picking up the phone sometimes and touching the numbers that would connect her to Aaron. If she turned the dial. She'd have to remember to call herself Rebecca of course, because he wouldn't know who Gilda was. Would be bewildered by Rebecca's voice introducing herself as a stranger. He'd told her that the Rebecca in the Bible was a strong woman, a resourceful and hard-working woman, who only wanted the best for her child. Who loved her husband faithfully. 'Remind you of anyone?' he said, looking over the table at his soon-to-be-faithless wife.

They'd read the Bible together but Gilda had her own copy by her bed that flopped open to stories of love when she picked it up. When she discovered *The Song of Songs*, the tastes and smells of desire made her giddy. She had no idea what pomegranates were, or how calamus or spikenard or myrrh smelled, but she knew about thighs and bellies and breasts, though hers didn't look much like the young roes of the beloved. Despite being in the holy book she wasn't sure that the words were quite proper, but she imagined her lover's head lying between her breasts and wondered how he knew that the roof of her mouth tasted of wine.

She never went that far with the boy she'd met in the park. Never went much further than closed-mouth kissing, though she imagined him naked. Dilys had taught her caution, so the pills were in her bedside table just in case, but Aaron didn't know that and roared. He said she was just like her mother, so she packed everything she had into a small bag and left. Took everything with her but the Bible and the frocks.

When she goes to her wardrobe in the mornings, she's artful in her choices. For the moment she dresses to keep herself to herself and buys shirts she can wear over skirts and trousers that hug her belly.

She looks at the clothes hanging together at the left-hand side of the wardrobe, their rubber and leather reminders of something she once needed, but not now.

Not now there's a baby.

When her tunic starts to strain, she tells Maxim one evening when everyone else has gone home.

'Darling!' he says. 'What a clever girl you are – mazel tov!' and throws his arms round her. He doesn't ask who the father is, but begs to be godfather when the baby's born. 'Whatever god you like,' he says. 'Just tell me so I know what to wear.'

The day after she's broken the news, Maxim's wife turns up to take her to lunch. Over lox and cream cheese bagels, she tells Gilda what to expect and what to eat. What to do and not to do. 'You must stop your karate at once,' she says. 'Also running for buses.' She asks if the grandparents-to-be are excited and shuts up when Gilda tells her. She forbears to ask about the father because she knows times have changed. She makes a new tunic for her, which she says she'll alter as she gets bigger, and sends Maxim in with salt beef sandwiches and gefilte fish for her lunches.

Pamela is delighted too, but Gilda knows she's planning her coup when she goes on maternity leave. She couldn't give a fuck.

It's time to tell her friends. She's the first in their circle to get pregnant and the broodiness proves viral. They want all the details all the time and say she's doing a practice run for them until they find the right guy. 'If there's any out there,' they say, shrugging.

But Gilda's found the right guy. Doesn't need another one.

# 1976

Wednesday, 6.23 a.m.

William leaves for work earlier than usual. There's a problem with Germany bubbling under and he needs to see to it today. Philip could deal with it, but every time he hands something over to his senior manager, it feels like another stitch in his shroud. Another reminder that he's retiring next week. Along with the job, his identity's beginning to fade.

He gets into William Denham's car, drives it to William Denham's factory, uses William Denham's key to open William Denham's office and drinks William Denham's coffee standing at William Denham's window. His father would have stood at this window with Edgar, his hand on his shoulder. *One day, my son, all this will be yours* – isn't that the standard line? Edgar would have cracked his famous grin, allowing the old man his day before his own sun rose. They were manly men, these two. Men fierce with muscle and gristle and bone. Men without doubt or dither.

William stands at the window alone. His daughter is thirty-eight and has been a consultant for some time. Precociously, he understands. When she phones or comes to their house to visit, they are all terribly well mannered. Eleanor walks her round the garden, he talks about the exigencies of manufacturing, Virginia gives disquisitions on this or that medical phenomenon and washes up with her mother while he retreats to his study. He and Eleanor have never been to visit her in London and see no need to press for an invitation. None of them regard this as odd. They meet in Harrogate because Hanover House is where they once lived together in what someone else might call the family home.

He wakes every day with the charred taste of hopelessness in his mouth. Every day's a struggle to retrieve memories of when he'd been able to hope. He keeps them in his mind like rough diamonds in a pouch and is pleased when he can locate it, undo the cord round its neck, tumble the gems on to the baize of his day.

The hope stayed alive as long as Edgar was at the window with their father and had a brief efflorescence in France. The two of them standing with their backs to William made it possible for him to seek out like-minded people and talk about things his father and brother would see as the certain marks of a queer. While Edgar was still dazzling his way through life, William was free to follow his passion for poetry and music and art, which his father overlooked as long as his elder son was so convincing a real man. He wasn't so much the black sheep in a family of white, more an orchid growing in sedge, but he was native in the world of the arts. Edgar's accident hustled him into dead man's shoes, where he's had to learn the factory's ways like a prisoner banged up with a stranger.

Over the years, the comradeship at Denham's Tractors has kept him afloat. His foremen and his workers greet him fondly as he moves through the factory amid the din and the grit and the smells of industry. They know him as a fair man, a listening man: a leader, not a despot. His business acumen has surprised him – and his father and his mother and his wife – and the factory has prospered in his hands. He wants to believe that Philip will follow in his footsteps, but sometimes in the night he despairs. He is selling Denham Tractors to a consortium, but Philip will run the place. Once William closes the doors behind him for the last time, he will become ancient history, written out of the factory's future and into his solitary retirement.

He has ordered a new garden shed that will be installed next week. It is vast and sophisticated and will be situated as far away from the house as possible. Far away from the kitchen, which is Eleanor's domain. It is to replace a smaller version where he keeps his armies of supplies, his platoons of plastics and solvents and lacquers, in ship-shape, tip-top, parade-ground order. He makes automata, which he stands on shelves, lifting down this one or that one according to his mood. He oils and polishes and talks to them and moves them around to meet each other: the parrots and the people and the children and the fish. In his new shed he'll have room to make large pieces – life-size even – and plans to see out his days at his bench, peopling his space with machines that are more animated to him than his wife.

The phone on his desk rings and he puts his coffee cup down and goes over. Bound to be the Germans, they're always prompt.

I've spent the evening at a fund-raising dinner for a new neonatal unit that the flagging NHS claims it can't afford. I've had to sit next to people who could bore for Britain, but whose pockets are elastic, so I've bent their ears and bearded them and nailed their pledges to the wall. The Tory bore sitting to my right at dinner could have clotted custard with his opinions and I have to grab the table leg to stop myself from belting him when he tells me he'd never employ young women of childbearing age because all they'd do is breed. 'And ruin the year's profits,' he says, 'let alone company morale with all that sobbing in the Ladies.'

I belt my dashboard instead as I drive away from the dinner, resisting the temptation to rear-end his car as I see him get behind the wheel. But I make a note of his registration number and call the police on my way home because I've seen how much alcohol he's downed. It doesn't quite compensate me for the precious hours I've spent doused in his Neanderthal views, but it gives me some small satisfaction.

When I get home, I make myself a salmon and cream cheese sandwich with dill mayonnaise and take it up to bed with a glass of Benedictine. As I go into my bedroom, the phone rings. I put the plate and glass down and sit on the bed to answer it.

'Virginia Denham,' I say.

'Virginia? It's me.'

'Oh, hello, Mother, how are you? I was going to telephone you tomorrow as usual. How are the bones?'

'They've been twingeing a little lately, but nothing more than I can manage. I usually find a hot bath does the trick. Radox helps sometimes.'

'Well, I did speak to the rheumatologist up there, you know, and he'll be happy to see you whenever you like. Have you been in contact with him?'

'No – no, I haven't yet. What with the WI and the charity I'm kept pretty busy, so most of the time it doesn't bother me. It comes on a bit in the evenings when I stop and sit down after supper, but I can't exactly telephone the consultant then, can I? I just take some tablets with a mug of hot milk and I'm usually fine. Fine enough anyway. I don't like to complain.'

'Well, it's absolutely up to you. It's been several months since I spoke to Parkinson, so if you leave it very much longer I'll have to remind him about you. And after all, the hospital's only just up the road, so you haven't got far . . .'

'I've just come from the hospital, actually.'

I'm shocked. Mother *never* interrupts. 'Oh, something up?'

'Not with me, no. It's Father. He's dead, I'm afraid. A couple of hours ago. Very sad. I've called Dorcas and the funeral directors, but I thought I'd tell you straight away too . . . Virginia? Virginia? Are you there? Did you hear what I said?'

I've fallen back across the bed. I can hear the receiver squawking but feel too weary to lift it to my ear. After a little while, the dialling tone kicks in.

I last saw Father three months ago, awash with champagne and cheers at his retirement party. The people who spoke called him Bill or Will – one even called him Billy – and I was momentarily bewildered. Father has always been William, from the artful italic handwriting in his school poetry books to Mother's way of saying his name in different degrees of frost. I never dared call him William to his face, although I experimented with it in my head, imagining I'd joined Aurora's family. When Aurora arrived at Highfield Prep with a twiddle and a twirl, she was conker brown from life in the tropics. The other girls said her family had gone native, which was why she called her parents by their names.

'But it's what they're called,' she explained, 'so why shouldn't I? They call me Aurora, for pity's sake, not "daughter" or "child" or anything like that – it just makes sense, doesn't it? After all, that's my name.'

Only in my wildest dreams. Sometimes I imagined sailing across the South Seas in a tall masted ship, the wind rebuilding Mother's don't-give-the-game-away hair in a mass of lunatic curls. I imagined her skipping barefoot down the deck, scooping me – her pretty, pretty daughter – into her arms. I imagined her crying, 'Call me Eleanor, Ginny! After all, that's my name!'

Unlikely, I told myself, and anyway I couldn't exactly see Mother in a sarong.

But even on a tropical island, even catching our dinner from the ocean and eating it without napkins or saying grace, I could never imagine calling Father Bill. Or Daddy. Sometimes, after I'd left home, I wondered if it wouldn't have been better to call him Mr Denham, as our cleaners did. At least you know where you are with formality.

I sit up and dial Mother's number.

She answers my questions as though speaking in headlines. Cancer, she says. Riddled with it, she says. Consultant said he must have been in agony for months. Never went to see Dr Strange. Never mentioned it to her. Found him doubled over in the bathroom. Called 999. Got him dressed. Ambulance to Casualty. X-rays, scans, diagnosis. Prognosis. Morphine. Death. She was in the lavatory when it happened, she says, almost as if he'd planned it. She supposes it made sense to him to die alone.

Father's timing is terrible. I'm due to fly out to New York tomorrow to present a paper, so I make phone calls. 'I'm sorry for your loss,' successive Americans say, as though they were personally responsible. I speak to Faisal, explaining that I'll have to take compassionate leave. 'No more than three or four days,' I say, 'though I suppose I'll have to go back up for the funeral.'

*I'm leaving the firm in good hands*, I think as I put the phone down. My previous senior registrar was hopeless. The words 'piss-up' and 'brewery' come to mind.

I pick up the phone again and book a ticket on the first train up to Harrogate in the morning.

I never quite know where the fatted South ends and the bleak North begins, as though there should be a border with guards and suspicious dogs. Cattle prods maybe. But there's a shift in tone beyond a certain point of the journey, when the city bricks are redder, the fields smaller and new passengers greet the old as though they're friends. In a field behind a fistful of council houses I see a young man playing with two small children. He lifts the girl in the air, swings her over the boy's head and they all fall to the ground in a giggly heap. They're heedlessly, gloriously, hilariously covered in mud. I never rolled on the ground with Father. Never laughed until my sides hurt.

We pull out of Horsforth and plunge into a long tunnel. I catch sight of my face in the window, a familiar blend of no one I know. I used to steal glimpses of Father when he came back from the war, trying to see myself in this starving cousin of the groom in their wedding photo. I sometimes thought I might have had his eyes, but they never settled on me long enough to check. Mother had kept her genes to herself.

The train hoots out of the tunnel and the land rolls away from the track, teeming hedgerows edging fields dimpled with cows and sheep and horses and the occasional fleet hare. A havoc of starlings scratches across the lowering sky, wheeling in concert to the east when they hit the horizon. Grey stone farmhouses squat at the hub of their lands, their dense walls marked by the weather cycles tyrannising farming life up here.

As the train slows, I see Mother's silver Volvo in the station car park. She'll be sitting behind the wheel listening to classical music on the radio. She never stands at the end of the platform grinning foolishly when she sees me getting off the train. Never links arms with me as we swing through the station hall, chattering like magpies. When I see mothers and daughters doing that, I wonder how on earth they coordinate their feet. Mother neither does embraces nor chatter, but she does do punctuality, so she's probably been parked there for nine and a half minutes already.

I check her powdery face when I slide into the passenger seat, but it is unfussed by tears. When she moves off and changes gear, I notice that her wedding ring isn't on her finger and that there's an angry rash where it should have been. Our conversation on the way to the house steps back and forth over the viewing at the funeral home, the meeting with the priest, the writing of the eulogy – perhaps an obituary in the local – the pallbearers, the order of service and refreshments back at the house. Amontillado sherry, Mother thinks, for the ladies and a good single malt for the men. She has already placed an announcement in the local papers and is having invitations printed. Good card, black border, embossed lettering in purple. We pass the Old Swan Hotel where Agatha Christie hid in 1926 to escape an unhappy marriage, and drive up the slope to Hanover House.

Mother is expert in organising social events and a funeral's just another event, after all. She has always been as punctilious about the seating at her suppers as she is about the menu. She has noted the details of every supper and every luncheon she's given in the card index next to the cookery books. Date, time of day, names of guests and menu are recorded in her tidy hand so that she never cooks her guests the same thing twice. On the back of the card are individual preferences and allergies. Offal is rarely served.

The index is her guide when she comes to compile the guest list for Father's obsequies. Over the years, everyone of any importance has been invited to the house for drinks (cocktails, champagne or punch); garden parties (marquee in case of inclement weather); luncheons (emphasis on Sunday after church, but sometimes Bank Holidays); and suppers (regular, occasional and celebratory – their Coronation party was the talk of the town). Sheriffs hobnobbed with judges over roasts, generals reminisced with colonels over cigars while the ladies sat in the drawing room talking of pretty things. Lightly, tinklingly, fetchingly. The weather was frequently mentioned. They all danced the social round, steering clear of controversy, inclining their heads this way and that. Thank-you cards were penned and sent the following day. Always.

I see Mother sitting with the card index at her desk and wonder what it would take to walk across the Persian rug. What it would take to stand her up to face me. What it would take to hold her, gather her to my chest, feel some thrill of shared grief pass between us.

Only fools believe in miracles.

'Just off to see Father,' I say from the door.

'Fine,' says Mother, turning slightly. 'I'll have finished by the time you get back. Hope it goes well,' and she turns back to her task.

I walk into town to inspect the body. When I arrive at the grand-but-sombre offices of Farnham and Sons, I tug fruitlessly at the front door before noticing the sign saying *PUSH*. By this time a young man has appeared and he pulls from the other side. When the door jerks open, I fall against him, embarrassing us both. He is wearing too much aftershave, as though trying to hijack grief's stench.

'I'm so sorry,' he says as I steady myself.

'No, no, no – entirely my fault. Stupid of me not to see the sign. I'm Virginia Denham,' I say. 'Come to see my father.'

'I'm Felix Farnham, Dr Denham,' he says, smiling just enough. 'We were expecting you. May I offer you my deepest sympathy?'

'Thanks. Yes, it was very sudden.'

'He was much admired in the town, as you know – far too young to be taken from us.'

I want to say: *He wasn't taken from me. I never had him*, but I nod instead.

'I wonder if I could offer you some tea or coffee.'

'Not now, thanks.'

'Then I'll take you to your father – please follow me.'

As though he were just down the hall in his office. Just dashing off a few letters, looking at his secretary's legs.

Felix takes me through to the back and escorts me down the corridor. He opens the last door at the end and syrupy organ music spills out.

'Mr Denham is in here,' he says. 'Please take as much time as you need. You'll not be disturbed.' He leaves the room silently.

It's like stepping into a furnace. As though cooking the living might assuage the rawness of death. I take off my coat as I approach Father's coffin, a grandiose maple affair resting on velvet. On the wall behind there's a blown-up photograph of a beach with palm trees mid-sway, pacific waters beyond and a bird's silhouette against the azure sky. Father hated holidays, so the clumsy backdrop makes me smile.

His face pokes out of a mania of ruffles. His curly hair, still dark at sixty-five, has been tamed into a helmet as though he were still dodging bullets, and his eyebrows have been given a quizzical arch by the same hand. I suppose some people might say the unsayable at this point. I suppose I could, but what would I say, for god's sake? *Why couldn't you love me, Daddy? Why wouldn't you see me?* Pathetic.

Making my peace with him requires a magnanimity that's too painful to evoke. Reaching out to him would flay me of the skins I've grown over the years. Death has never frightened me: I remember my fellow medical students fainting at the sight of the cadavers laid out for dissection, but for me they were simply fleshy histories to be excavated, pathology to be logged. It's easier to see Father as just another specimen on a slab than to feel anything about him. As I look at his tarted-up face, I remember the smell of his study, my hiding place under the table, the day he kicked me. His anguish.

I turn on my heel and leave him to it.

# 1944

Edith's legs are throbbing and her back's killing her, but she doesn't care. She's been behind the bar of the *Café des Anges* since eight this morning and hasn't stopped smiling once. She wonders if Paul, *le patron*, will bother closing tonight because no one seems inclined to go home and one day's celebration might as well rock into the next. She thanks God that they're drinking to life and not death. It could so easily have been death. By the front window there's a pile of rollicking British soldiers, drinking anything that's put in front of them. She thinks they're probably drunk enough to swallow bleach, providing it came in a bottle or a glass, so she keeps a weather eye on them. They've just rescued Caen from the Germans so they've a right to be pissed, and while she doesn't understand everything they say, it doesn't sound polite.

Halfway through the evening an altercation breaks out between two of the soldiers and a scrawny young man jumps to his feet, waving a broken bottle. His face is grotesque with rage and he flails wildly, cutting the cheek of a Frenchman behind him. The French-man pulls a knife but a small dark man leaps up and grabs his wrist – talking, talking in an awkward mixture of French and English. He says something snappish to the other soldiers and one of them disarms the man with the bottle and drags him back to his seat. The dark man fishes a handkerchief from his pocket and pushes it against the Frenchman's cheek. He leads him to the *pissoir* at the back of the bar. When they emerge some time later, the Frenchman has his arm round the Englishman's shoulders and is telling him an extravagantly scatological joke. The Englishman is ashen.

The easy bonhomie of the bar is restored, and towards midnight the soldiers lurch to their feet one by one. They lean into each other, apparently declaring undying love: *Forever, mate. Forever and forever and forever, amen*. They yodel off into the unleavened dark, but the small man, who Edith now sees is an officer, stays behind, his head in his hands among the dead bottles. Edith remembers Philippe sitting in her kitchen like that just before he left, his fingers mining his dense curls. She doesn't know if he's still alive, but his silence is killing her.

The locals drift off, some staggering, some marching, all noisy, their footsteps lighter now that the enemy has been routed. Edith collects the glasses and the bottles, wipes down the bar and the tables, rights the toppled chairs, all the time aware of the Englishman sitting there still as a plank. She's at the sink when she hears a sound. It's either a sob or a mirthless laugh, she can't tell. He's lifted his head and is staring out of the window, his fisted hands resting on the table. She goes over. She touches his shoulder.

William turns at her touch and looks up at her. Her thighs are pushed against the table's edge, the beer spills dampening her felted skirt. In this light she could be anything from twenty to forty, her face artfully painted to cover the tracks of her life. She has daubed pink circles on her cheeks beneath emphatically lined eyes with peacock-blue lids. When she pulls back her brilliant lips to smile, a row of teeth appear which stop behind her canines as though she could only afford half a mouth. Her hair is cut like an ancient Egyptian princess and a silk flower over her ear makes a purple stab at gaiety.

'*M'sieur*,' she says. 'I think you are not happy. What arrives?'

There's a long pause. He is shaking his head, apparently unable to speak. He looks down again. She rests her hand on one of his and it unfolds.

'So much killing,' he says eventually. 'Too much. So much death.'

She pulls out a chair and sits opposite him. 'But you stop a death tonight,' she says. 'It was brave what you do. The soldier with the bottle, it was not . . . it was danger, *n'est-ce-pas*? But you stop it.'

'My men have learned how to kill, you know? I mean, killing before they're killed themselves, though they've seen their comrades die. Blown to pieces, some of them. Bits of their bodies stuck to their friends' sleeves. In their hair. They've seen such things . . . such . . .

things, and they don't know how to turn it off. Turn off the violence. Andrews is no different from any other soldier. We all stink of death.'

'But you are kill to bring us *la paix*. You are fight to give to us our *libération*, no? It is a good fight. It is a *nécessité* for France, for your country too, that you come with your gun and your . . . your . . . how you say it? Your *avions*.'

'Planes.'

'Yes, your planes.'

'Our planes that have flattened your beautiful city? Those ones? Our planes that have slaughtered your citizens?'

'Your planes that have saved us.'

'Sometimes the contradictions scramble my brains. I try to understand. I try to remember that I joined up to preserve something. To rid the world of the infernal Nazis, but when I see the destruction, when I know that I've done it – *me* – I don't recognise myself.'

'What is reconeye?'

'I don't know who I am. I mean, of course I know who I *am* – I can tell you my name, my rank, my number, all that bilge, but inside I . . . I feel like a foreigner to myself. As though I've gone through some terrible transformation. As though I'm as monstrous as Jerry.'

'Don't say that. Never say that. You are different.'

He looks up at her. He is fierce. 'I. Am. No. Different,' he says deliberately. 'Don't you see? All this killing makes me the same as the enemy. My hands are dripping with blood.'

Paul comes up from the cellar.

'Go home now, Edith,' he says in French. 'I'll close up. *M'sieur*,' he says, coming over to the table, 'not only have you saved our city, you are pulling France out from under the jackboot. We owe you our future and you have our gratitude. You'll always be welcome here at my bar, now and when the war's finally over.'

He is talking in typewriter patter. William is bewildered.

'He says thank you,' says Edith. 'And I do too.'

They leave the bar together and walk down the street past buildings pockmarked from the shelling, past churches whose faces have fallen, past rats fat on the scum of war. Edith is William's height and their shoulders bump as they walk. He moves away but they bump again. He grabs her hand as she stumbles over a car's back axle and she doesn't let go. He is surprised.

They walk along the canal and he's surprised again. He finds himself talking about his life. War has untethered him from his English restraint and the proprieties he knows to observe. From a gentleman's tact towards a lady.

He tells her, as though he's telling himself, about living in the luminous wake of his brother. Edgar George, first and most beloved son of George Edgar. Edgar the hero. Edgar, whose tragedy completed his beatification. Edgar, whose role as heir to their father's factory freed William to go to Oxford. Edgar, whose engagement to Eleanor was fitting. He tells her how proposing to his dead brother's fiancée made sense at the time, but that he'd wake in the nights running up to the wedding, wondering what he'd done. How to undo it.

Edith doesn't understand all the words, but the pain and the rage are palpable. She knows about pain and rage. When he's finished, she tells him about finding her family in their flattened farmhouse. Finding bits of her small brother up a tree. Her mother's hands in a mixing bowl. Just her hands. She tells him that she wanted to die too, but wouldn't give the Germans the satisfaction. Tells him that she wants babies – lots of French babies – whom she'll teach how to hate.

'I learn to hate, you know? I don't know before. But now I hate in all the day, in all the night, and it make me happy. It give me a reason for wake up. Before, I have a future who is like my past, but now I have a new *histoire* and I must to try to live this life the war has give me.'

War speeds up the ordinary gestures of intimacy. The slow, tentative hands-along-the-wall creep towards revelation. The pulling back before reaching out. Instead there's a cut to the chase, and William feels Edith's suspenders pressing against his thigh as they sit on a wall, watching the moon crawl out from behind a cloud. A sudden breeze fractures its reflection in the canal and he watches the light jig about like a dancing puzzle. Just for a moment he can find beauty in something and his spirits rise. Edith has pulled a piece of paper from her shoulder bag and is writing something with a stubby pencil.

'Tomorrow,' she says. 'You can come. I am there at centre of the night – hmm, at *minuit*. You must to come.'

He stands now on the corner of the street, a soft summer drizzle frizzing his hair, the piece of paper in his hand. He's looked at it so often he's surprised his eyes haven't worn the words away, but they're still there, bold as frogs, in Edith's curvy hand. *35 bis, rue de la Paix. Blue door.*

He has learned how to love since joining up. He loves his men and they love him, though they'd repudiate the word, meant as it is for the mysterious bodies of women. But loving has made him brave. His men follow him on the battlefield and turn to him in the night when their minds flood with the day's detritus. He's been known to hold a soldier to his chest when he weeps, but never publicly because wartime shame is lethal. He does it all gladly, finding a place to belong for the first time since coming down from university. Eleanor and Virginia rarely cross his mind, even when the guns are silent and he lies under the stars with his heart thrashing in his ears. To say he loved them would be heretical.

Edith has given him directions, but the street name has either fallen off or been taken down to confuse the Germans and he fears rousing someone unready for him. Only supposing she is ready for him. He's suddenly overcome by the strangeness of all of this. It's as though he's been dropped into the Steppes and told to navigate his way to Honolulu. Until joining up he'd never been out of England. He'd planned to travel after Oxford, to smell Scott Fitzgerald's Riviera, Barrett Browning's Florence, but his brother's death put paid to that. He doesn't know what Edith's invitation means. Whether all she's offering is a faltering conversation, an amiable *bonsoir* and *au revoir*, perhaps a quick drink. He can hardly ask her, can hardly say, 'Good evening, Edith. What will you do for me? Shall we go to bed now?' in case he is humiliated by his impudence and her outrage. He's inclined to turn on his heels and return to camp. To the certainties of rank. But there's a sound, a low whistle, and she's standing in the doorway of a house halfway down the dead-end street.

'*Guillaume*,' she whispers, '*Viens ici.*'

He walks up the rackety stairs behind her, trying not to look up her skirt. She leads him into a room under the eaves, candles in jam jars crouching on the cross beams, stacks of wood against the walls, here a table leg, there a window frame and, bizarrely, a pile of shoe lasts standing on each other's toes by the bed. A fire burns in the grate, in front of which stands a clothes horse festooned with underwear steaming lavender into the air. He stands in the middle of the room, wringing his hands. He's dumbstruck. She's not, and when she's put the lantern on the dining table she comes over, undoes his hands and pulls gently at his arm.

'Here,' she says, 'come and sit by my fire.'

He lets himself be led to an armchair covered in chenille tablecloths. She strokes his face, and points. He eases himself into the chair, which puffs out a sweet fusty dustiness, and watches her as she goes across the room. She is bending over a cabinet by the bed and he looks at her fruity buttocks against her skirt. He is famished for this, for this feeling of difference, for the way a woman's flesh yields to a man's importunity, but he sits helplessly in the chenille welter, waiting for Edith to declare herself. She turns and he sees she has a dark bottle and two glasses in her hands. She sets them down on a packing case by his chair and smiles.

'For this time,' she says, 'to warm your – how to say it in English? – to warm your cocks.'

'Cockles,' he says, embarrassed by her mistake. 'Shellfish from the sea.'

'But why?' she asks. 'It is strange that the English must make warm the *coquilles* in the body, but at the end we are different, *n'est-ce-pas?* We are the same only to fighting *ces espèces de con*. Here is for you,' she indicates the bottle, 'and I will have some also because this night is special, no?' She pours two glasses of caramel-coloured liquor, gives one to him, takes a sip from hers and turns to set a kettle on a small stove. The Calvados seeps into William's joints and he lays his head against the chair, watching her move around the room humming. She smoothes the bed's covers, plumps up the pillows, finds a towel in a cupboard and some soap by the sink. She's like a puppy spiralling round her patch before settling, and it feels like an invitation. When the kettle has boiled she tips the water into a rose-sprigged bowl and adds some cold water from the tap. She brings it over to him, the towel over her arm, the soap in her skirt pocket. She settles the bowl by his feet and kneels in front of him.

'*Alors*,' she says, 'now it is time to take from you *les odeurs de la guerre*.'

She rests her hands at the top of his thighs and he stiffens. She draws her hands down his legs, pausing to massage his calves gently, all the time holding his gaze with eyes that suck him in. Eleanor never touches him or traces his skin with her fingers and she endures his kisses like flies on her face. Edith toys with his laces as though they are parts of his body then unties them, slipping off his boots and his socks. She holds his feet in her hands. Their stench fills the air and he says, 'I'm so sorry. I apologise. I'm sorry. It hasn't been easy to wash . . .' and she shakes her head.

'But I am to wash you,' she says, 'I will to make you clean.'

She rolls up his trousers, puts his feet in water the temperature of blood, and it feels like he has already entered her. As her hands stroke his calluses and his blisters, he knows he's about to weep and tries swallowing. But the grief will out and soon he is shaking with sobs. Edith dries his feet, kisses each of his toes, drawing the smallest ones into her mouth as she passes, then sits on the chair circling his head with her arm. Pulled into her chest, he forgets that this is weakness and that tears are the natural preserve of girls.

When he's stopped weeping, she goes over to the bed and pulls the covers back, laying a larger towel on the sheet.

'*Viens, chéri*,' she says, and he understands that the towel is for him.

He lets her unbuckle him and unbutton him and push him on to the bed. She refills the bowl and she washes him, her fingers sliding round his contours, slipping soapy hands round his dick like cream. When she's rinsed him, she steps back to admire her handiwork and his excitement. She is pleased. She takes her clothes off and folds them on a stool. Her full breasts are at odds with her emaciated body and William can count each one of her ribs and knobbed vertebrae.

She sees him looking. 'Sometimes it is difficult to find food,' she says. 'And when there is some, sometimes it is difficult to eat.' She climbs into bed beside him.

William glides into a world with no proscriptions, where the hours stop pacing: he is unbound. She wraps him round her, slides over his body like oil, takes him into her mouth, her tongue lapping the shaft, the tip, until he teeters on the brink of flying away. She straddles him, her pale thighs gripping his hips with surprising authority and pauses until she knows he can wait no longer. She draws him into her, slides him out, draws him in and he loses himself.

He sleeps, her head on his shoulder, her hand on his belly, till he feels her unpeel herself and leave the bed. His flank cools where she was lying. He can hardly bear to open his eyes to the grit of the everyday, but slowly, slowly, he surfaces. He's done enough fucking to know that he's just made love for the first time, so he tells her.

'This is my first time,' he says.

She looks puzzled. 'You are *vierge?*' she says.

'No, no – I mean, I've been to bed with women before,' he flushes, 'I've – well, I've had sex and everything, but this is different. You're different, Edith. I want to stay here. With you. Not now exactly because of the war, but I'll come back. I'll find you. Don't go away. Please. I need to know you're still here – please wait for me.' He wipes his eyes on the pillowcase. 'Oh I'm so sorry, this is fearfully weak of me. I only meant . . .'

She's there beside him and he clings to her. She gasps as the urgency in his arms drives the breath from her lungs.

'Oh I'm so sorry. I'm sorry. I didn't meant to hurt you,' he says, and pulls away. 'I'm such a beast.'

'You are not a beast, *mon amour.* You are a man.'

And truthfully he feels like a man as he dresses and leaves. As he tells her he'll be back. When they've finished fighting, he tells her, he'll be on her doorstep. They'll make a life. He doesn't mention uncoupling himself first. She watches him from her window as he marches down the street. He doesn't look back.

In the dream, he knows he's dreaming as the smiling woman walks towards him along the canal. As she approaches, he sees that it's Edith. She has filled out and her hips sway as she walks, her breasts delectable against her blouse. He puts out his arms to her and is filled with longing.

She looks quizzically at him. 'Why?' she says, and her voice is Eleanor's.

'I'm dreaming,' he says, and she vanishes.

He wakes with tears chilling on his cheeks. Sitting on the edge of his camp bed drinking tinny water from his canteen, he is suddenly sweltering with rage. He remembers the porter banging on the door of his Oxford rooms. He remembers the sight of his own hand trembling as he took the telegram. His future vaporised in eight words. *Terrible accident. Edgar dead. Come home immediately. Father.*

By blowing himself and seven workers up at the factory, Edgar's negligence created the vortex into which William was sucked, always a feeble substitute. His brother was his father's son, a man well versed in ribaldry and charm, in saloon bars and sex, who took up his role as their father's lieutenant as of right. He was tall, handsome, sporty: all the things William wasn't. All the things that William was, marked him out as a changeling.

When he came home and walked into the drawing room, no one looked up. His usually immaculate mother sat in an armchair, her hair mad with shock, as speechless as the cushions stacked on either side of her keeping her upright. His father paced from one window to the other, back and forth, back and forth, as though if he could but discover a different route across the carpet his son might be revived.

Grief's acuity plundered their waking hours and their sleep in the following months, but the dull thump of mourning accompanied all three for the rest of their lives. Dorcas and George were reminded, every time they looked at their bookish younger son, of what splendour they had been deprived. In death, Edgar's heroism became his life's refrain, his lapses – and there were many besides his failure to check the factory's boiler – buried along with his body. The dead workers' families were handsomely paid off and his reputation for wit, for business and romance waxed in the posthumous years. William shrugged on Edgar's ill-fitting mantle and joined his father at the factory. No one ever said, 'Oxford's over now, lad, your place is here. You owe it us.' But they all knew. He'd been entombed in his family's ambition, and getting married was part of the deal. Without Edgar to pass his brilliance on, the Denhams were forced to rely on

William to produce the next generation. He could do that at least. Boys, naturally. Dorcas read up on genetics and convinced herself that with the right marriage, William could produce an Edgar clone, whom she'd teach the swagger of his uncle.

Eleanor Redford fitted the bill and was now tragically available. She had those two hearty brothers so her genes would beef up William's weediness and Albert, her father, was the factory's best customer. Albert and George had their own table at the Tap and Spile and would sit there, drunk as skunks, hearkening back to the old days and deploring as many things as they could remember. Each had built an empire and, like all emperors, expected obedience from their subjects. And anyway, William showed no signs of having a girlfriend, so marrying Eleanor was as logical as starving wages to fatten profits. The two men set in train the moves necessary to effect the union, which happened two years after Edgar's death.

William knew little about wooing, so his approaches were uncertain, but he knew enough of what to say from his reading. Eleanor was a pretty girl and well turned out, and was, he suspected, brainy, though reluctant to talk of clever things. She was so eviscerated by the loss of Edgar that his small dark brother temporarily filled the hole. He said all the right things, seemed to understand her grief – was grieving himself for his brother she supposed – and was to take over the factory when George retired. She'd seen herself as the boss's wife for so long, if she squinted hard enough she could almost imagine the original plan hadn't died with Edgar. Family obligations were background noise for both of them.

*You owe it us, lad.*
  *You owe it us, lass.*

William has managed not to go back to Harrogate on any of his home leaves, volunteering for special duties or holing up in guest houses in London where he spends his days in libraries and his evenings in taverns. Eleanor was unavoidably recorded as his next of kin but she is a matter of fact to him, not interest. He sees little point in spoiling the respite from the war by visiting himself on her or her on him. He is uninquisitive about Virginia, who was experimenting with walking when he left, though he is not unmoved by children. He has seen too many dead children since going to war and his guts shift when he comes upon another tiny body crushed like a bird's egg. He allows himself a moment in the velvety belly of the night to mourn their murdered futures.

He commits an account of the war to his journals, which he wraps in sackcloth and sends to his new friend Stephen's family when they are finished. Stephen has written to his mother and assures William she will keep the packages safe – and unopened – until the war is over. He doesn't write to Eleanor, or she to him, which surprises neither. He is a single man here in the army, although linked in a primeval way with the other soldiers. He observes the state of play between his men so is able to gauge whom to comfort, how to comfort, when one of them is killed. When he discovered the metaphysical poets at Oxford he felt understood, as though Donne were stretching his hand out across four centuries to cup the back of his head. He has his collected works in his kitbag and 'any man's death diminishes me' resonates along the bleak hours following a soldier's loss as he waits for the bell to toll for him.

He has never known this intimacy before, has never felt the trust that arises from your next breath depending on your companion's grip. He is thriving, discovering aspects of himself that were until now unknown.

He wishes the war would never end.

# 1976

I see little point in staying in Harrogate, and it's a relief to be able to work for a bit until I have to go back up for the funeral. Purkiss has contracted some mysterious bug so the firm's more pushed than usual and I feel gluey with a fatigue I can't fight off. At least I think it's fatigue, though sometimes I have the feeling I'm looking for something I've lost.

There must be something in the water because there's a sudden demographic blip in this part of South London and my obstetric clinics are packed. Women sit on orange plastic chairs in the waiting room and along the corridor, waiting to meet their doctor today and their babies in five months', four months', two weeks' time. They learn to be patient, though there are those who never want the pregnancy to end. Never want to face the pain of separation once the baby's born. Never want to give up this unique link. I keep a particular eye on them. When the baby is born they sometimes resent it for leaving them, as though it has committed an act of egregious infidelity.

Walking into the clinic one day, I see Faisal ambling along up ahead, talking to a nurse. As he passes by the rows of patient women, his head suddenly ticks to the right. I follow his gaze. A young woman sits there, probably in her third trimester. She doesn't return Faisal's gaze because her mind is elsewhere. Some women rest their hands on their bump, some stroke it, others keep their arms well away as though disowning it, but she has her arms round it, hugging it to her tightly. She's smiling to herself, absolutely at one with the baby inside her – a sight that never fails to move me. She is anyway a beautiful woman, with dewy skin and a mass of curly black hair down her back, and while I've never thought of Faisal as a flirty man, I can see why she's turned his head.

Her pregnancy must be going well because she's not on my list, but she comes to mind as I leave the hospital. She looked like a woman in love.

I feel drained as I drive home, hoping Magda's remembered to put the oven on. Before I left this morning, I prepared a haunch of venison that needs hours of slow cooking or I might as well use it to pave the garden. I've got a back-up if Magda's forgotten, but wild salmon isn't what I fancy tonight. The rule on trip days is that I eat *exactly* what I want *exactly* when I want it, and on the rare occasion I fail, the day loses its taste. I feel invisible again. Inaudible. As I turn my key in the front door and go in, I realise I've been holding my breath and tentatively inhale. My nose is flooded by the meat's lusty smell and my shoulders relax. I drop my bag at the door and walk quickly to the kitchen.

Father's customers used frequently to bring him game they'd snared or shot, which Mother hung in the back pantry until it was practically maggoty. I knew that if you did lots of cutting or chopping or walking in ill-fitting shoes, you got calluses on your hands or feet, so I'd go into the back pantry when I was feeling scared. I thought that if I kept looking at things that frightened me I might get braver, as though my fear would grow calluses and I'd toughen up. There was no light in the pantry, so I'd get a candle – I could only do this when Mother was out because I wasn't allowed to play with fire – and walk fearfully through the door. When the draught caught the flame, the light jerked around the twitchy undead swaying on their hooks. The pheasants' eyes needled me from behind their bandit masks, the quails hung about like a gang of thugs and the hares swung slooooowly round, though I couldn't see their heads because they were in bags to collect the blood. I'd slide down the wall and sit on the floor as still as I could because I knew they'd jump on me if I jiggled. I'd force myself to stay put, nearly weeping with the effort, looking and looking and looking at beaks that could pin my eyes like onions on cocktail sticks and claws that could shred my flesh. It took time – once I was in there for an hour – but eventually my heart would calm down and I'd breathe evenly again.

Mother never cooked any of that meat for me because it was only for grown-ups, but even after I became one, I've never been able to eat game. It would feel like swallowing a bag of nightmares.

But Father never came home with venison, so it's safe to make it my own, to cook it in red wine and juniper berries, polishing the juices with redcurrant jelly just before serving.

I need Ruby badly. Need her to unlock my back, rigid with the day's demands. I lay a place for her and kiss the back of her chair. 'I love you, Ruby,' I say to the air. 'You're the only one.' I light the candles and go into the kitchen.

I've opened the Château de la Chaize Brouilly and I'm about to slide the honeyed vegetables into the oven when I feel a movement to my right. I clatter the pan on to the rack, heedless of the courgette renegades escaping the flames. I slam the oven door shut and stand with my back against it, feeling the heat begin to punish my spine.

Ruby is unsmiling, her fiery red curls icy on her head.

'Oh, Ruby,' I say, 'thank goodness you're here. You've been away so long, I thought maybe I'd said something wrong.'

'You're always wrong.'

'I know. I know I'm always wrong. You need to remind me I'm wrong because sometimes I forget.'

'You sent me away.'

'I didn't. I didn't send . . .'

She's glowering now.

'Of course I did,' I say hastily. 'I did send you away. I must have gone mad. Sudden rush of blood to the head or something.'

'And there *will* be blood.'

'Yes. Yes, there will be blood.' I try not to grin. 'Tonight,' I say, 'after I've fed us.'

'Well, give me the wine then and I'll decide if I want to forgive you.'

I give her the opened bottle and a goblet. 'It won't be quite ready yet,' I say. 'Have a sherry or something while it breathes.'

'Fuck that for a game of soldiers!' she says. 'Sherry's for ninnies and I want a drink *now!*' and she swishes out of the room.

I am beside myself. I take a glass of Fino upstairs with me to sip while I dress for dinner. *Leather for tonight*, I think. It makes sense. I have another glass of sherry while I finish cooking, and when it's ready I carry the food into the dining room, the venison under a metal dome for that 'ta-daa' moment of revelation. I open a bottle of Mercurey Clos L'Evêque and sit it on the sideboard. Ruby's singing hymns in the living room, which is a good sign. She only sings hymns when she's feeling merry. I call to her and she comes in, stamping her feet like a flamenco dancer, twitching imaginary castanets above her head.

She grins. 'I had words with myself,' she says, 'and we decided to forgive you. Especially since that grub smells divine. Yum, yum – is that pig's bum?' She goes over to the dome and sniffs like a truffle hound.

'No, it's venison.'

'Oh rats – yuck yuck yuck! I'm not going to eat Bambi! Find me some nice juicy beef, Virginia – right now – or I'm going to leave. I'm going to count to ten: one . . . two . . . three . . . four . . .'

She always does this. She always wants *exactly* what she wants *exactly* when she wants it.

'Well, you'll have to wait a moment – no, don't look like that, I'll do it, OK? Sit down in your chair and I'll pour you a nice glass of wine and go and get something else. Something you'll *really* like.'

Ruby pulls a face like an angry question mark, but that means she'll probably do what she's told. She's wearing her long frock with beads round the bottom the colour of slaughter and deliberately swishes it over the table as she goes to her chair, knocking over one of the candelabra.

I leap forwards and catch it. 'Oh, Ruby! You could have set us on fire and then where would we be?'

'Guy Fawkes day, that's where we'd be – we'd be sitting on this huge enormous bonfire and there'd be baked potatoes and sausages and fireworks and everything. It'd be topping!'

'But then we'd be dead too and I'm not ready to die yet, thank you very much, so you just sit there and behave.' I pour her a glass of wine and bustle into the kitchen.

Fortunately I have some frozen slices of beef that I forgot to give to next door's dog, so I bang them in the microwave to defrost. I'll slather it with venison juices to make its rare heart race – Ruby won't notice. By the time I come in with the steaming plate, she's knocked over her glass of wine and the tablecloth looks like it's bleeding. I give her a look and she looks right back, not a bit chastened.

'So what?' she says. 'It was just me doing a scientific 'speriment. I proved that wine on the table is bigger than wine in the glass. Bet you didn't know that. You think you're so bloomin' brainy but you're just a big fat bossy boots. Ooh – that looks scrumptious! Is that all for me?'

When she's in a good mood, Ruby could eat a horse – though I've never tried her on horsemeat – and she wolfs down the beef before slyly hoiking a chunk of venison on to her plate.

'I'm just going to do another 'speriment,' she says, 'to see if this makes me chuck up. I may be going to chuck up all over the table, all over the floor and all over you – ha ha!'

She takes a bite. And then another. Before long, she's devoured the lot and has licked both the dish and the plate clean. Fortunately there are two tumescent crème caramels in the fridge and wedges of Roquefort and Epoisses.

'There!' Ruby says, 'aren't you glad I came? Now you don't have to wash up these stupid old dishes. Say thank you nicely, Virginia – where's your manners?'

'Thank you nicely. Now sit still till I come back with pudding.'

When the meal is over – the dog will go hungry tomorrow – I take the plates into the kitchen, singing as I stack the dishwasher. In the dining room Ruby is singing too, but with burps. She's a champion burper and with a following wind can do the whole of the first verse of 'God Save The Queen' on one burp.

The evening is ripening.

I know there's no point in hurrying Ruby because she'll only go off in a huff, so when I've cleared up I call out to her to come to the living room for liqueurs. She makes a beeline for the 1960s egg chair hanging from the ceiling. She looks over at me and narrows her eyes.

'Look at me!' she says. 'I'm a big red India rubber ball!' and she begins bouncing in the chair, flinging her legs up so high she flashes her underwear. It's as blood red as her frock. I put the drinks down on the coffee table and march over, grabbing the chair firmly with both hands.

'You stop that,' I say. 'You'll bring the ceiling down, and the bathroom floor as well and then where will we be? We won't be able to play up there later.'

Ruby groans. 'Oh, all right then, Mrs Spoilsport. But I need to keep my strength up – give me a drink right now!'

'Please, Ruby. Say please.'

'Pleeeeeeeeease!' she says through a letter-box mouth.

My groin is throbbing. I cross my legs, which only intensifies the sensation. Ruby takes her time over a large glass of Cointreau and eleven truffles and is finally satisfied.

'Righto then,' she says, 'time to have fun – hurrah, hooray!'

She jumps out of the chair and races upstairs, lifting her frock so she doesn't trip. I clear the drink things and follow her up, collecting the rosewood box from the console table on the way. By the time I get to the bathroom, Ruby's tugged the black towels and the plastic sheets out of the locked cupboard in the Dali room and the cotton wool and the first-aid kit from the bathroom cabinet. She's sitting on the toilet lid, kicking the bath.

'Crumbs, Virginia, you're such an old slowcoach,' she says. 'Hurry up and get ready – I've been waiting for ages and ages.'

I put the box on the cistern behind her and lay the plastic sheets on the floor and over the edge of the bath and the sink. I cover them with towels and go to my bedroom to change.

The red djellaba is only ever used for this and I always make sure it's clean and pressed, just in case. I take off my shoes, my leather trousers, my swimsuit and my underwear and leave them in a heap on the floor. I slip the djellaba over my head and go back to the bathroom. I stand in the doorway with my head bowed.

'Are you ready?' asks Ruby. 'Really, truly ready?'

'Yes, I am.'

'Then you may enter.'

I sit on the edge of the bath, my feet chilling on the enamel, my heart threatening to crash through my ribs.

'You may disrobe,' says Ruby.

I pull at the robe, trying to take it off gracefully, but my hands are trembling with excitement and for a moment I lose my way inside it. Ruby stands up and rescues me from its folds, dropping it on the floor behind me when it's off. She picks up the box from the cistern. On its lid there is a brass shield. On the shield it says: *The Middlesex Hospital Governor's Prize. Awarded to Mr Sidney Fenton Plover. Session 1867–1868.* She turns the box to face me and opens it. On a velvet bed, a row of ivory-handled scalpels and bistouries and needle threaders and tenaculum hooks nestle together like thighs in the night. I furrow my brow as my fingers pass up and down the line, inspecting the troops. I lift out the scalpel with the shortest blade, the steel a lighter grey at the edge from a hundred years of sharpening.

The blade winks in the fierce blue light as it turns in my fingers. Its edge is as fine as a split hair. Its handle presses urgently into my palm. Its heft is perfect. I hold it in my right hand as I open my legs and the tops of my thighs bulge against the bath. I run my hand along the left bulge and settle it on the skin slipping idly over the musculature below. I select a spot at the top of my thigh where a few cowed pubic hairs are straying. I can tease out this whiff of anticipation almost infinitely and I've hovered, knife in hand, for minutes before now like a falcon frozen on a thermal, waiting . . . waiting . . . for the twitch of its prey in the scrub below. I bend closer so I can watch every marvellous change. My left thumb splays along the curvature to hold the flesh still as I inhale so slowly someone watching would be hard pressed to say whether I breathed at all. But there is only me and Ruby here. Me and Ruby and the knife. I lower my hand in slow motion and push the blade against the flesh. The tiny pop of entry makes me smile.

*Here we go.*

My left hand tightens its grip as I draw the knife down, the metal's glissade buttery smooth through the skin's minute follicular pocks. I lift it away and wait, every sense suspended. The cut blushes and crimson petals creep out from under its lips, shivering in the chill of the air. They pause, wax and slip gravidly down my leg, dripping off the curve on to the towel below.

I make nine more cuts of diminishing length.

I throw the scalpel down in the bath, its tinny impact vibrating against the backs of my legs, and watch as my blood gathers and falls. Every drop is a shout of triumph. Every cut is a decision to stay alive for another day. My sites – round my nipples, my vulva, my inner thighs and my arms – are places of beauty to me, their fine tracery of scars as precious as a gold filigree necklace. I flirt with death as ferociously as another woman might with a handsome man at a party, each scalpel stroke like a suitor's tongue on the nape of my neck. Each time I cut into the crook of my arm, I choose to avoid the radial artery lolling close to the surface, daring me to die.

Each incision is a victory.

Ruby shifts on the seat and I turn my head through glue to look at her. She's smiling like a painter teasing the last speck of paint on to a canvas she knows is her masterpiece.

She closes the box of instruments and puts it on the floor next to my feet. 'That's all for today,' she says quietly. 'We'll do it again soon.' She slips out of the room.

I draw out the remaining minutes until it's time to close the cuts. I run the shower over my leg, red clouds swirling in the cold water, and pat the wounds dry. I saturate cotton wool with povidone iodine and I dab them, its sweet sting deep as a kiss. I draw the edges of the two largest cuts together with butterfly sutures. As I cover the site with gauze and seal it with tape, I hum a lullaby. I soothe the wounds like a mother kneeling by the bed of her daughter shocked awake by a nightmare.

I console them.

# 1976

Ten days later, Virginia's back in Harrogate for the funeral. Eleanor could have organised Nuremburg II in her lunch hour, so everyone who should have been invited has been, and everyone who should be there will be. An hour before the hearse and limousine are due to arrive, a Jaguar growls up the drive and a uniformed driver opens the door to help his passenger out. Virginia and Eleanor watch from the drawing-room window as an elderly woman emerges, tentatively bending each limb to check its joints still hinge. The driver reaches into the back and hands her two walking sticks, one of lignum vitae, the other ebony, both with ivory handles. She takes the sticks and adjusts her pillbox hat so that its veil covers her eyes and nose. It is, like everything else she's wearing, black.

Eleanor glances at Virginia and goes to the front door. The glance is one of a small repertoire of signals she uses to save herself talking. As though to speak would be unthrifty. Profligate even. The glance means *Come along*, a hand over the mouth means *Be silent*, a tiny wave over the belly *Guests eat first* and a flick of the right forefinger *Leave the room*. There are others. Virginia follows her mother out of the house and down the steps.

'Dorcas!' says Eleanor as she reaches the old woman. 'Bang on time as usual. Now, let's give you a hand.'

Virginia bends over awkwardly and kisses the visitor on the cheek. The veil claws at her eye. 'Hello, Granny,' she says. 'What a sad day this is!'

Dorcas Denham lifts her veil so she can inspect her granddaughter with her avian eyes. She's looking for something. It's not there, so she twitches the veil back into place and raises her elbows for support.

The tinkle of the teacups and the scrape of the spoons is a welcome cover for Eleanor and Virginia's grieflessness. Dorcas is propped like a plumped cushion in William's wing chair, looking neither at her daughter-in-law nor at her granddaughter. Her eyes are fixed on her tea, as if she's expecting her son's face to appear on the surface like some crazed Turin shroud. She's been in widow's weeds for some time and William's death just adds one more black hat to the flock in her wardrobe. She thinks her life has gone on quite long enough but her death is cruelly dragging its heels. Eleanor's wondering if the caterers have wrapped the food well enough. Curly sandwiches are anathema, especially on so solemn an occasion. Virginia's considering an offer from Harvard for a semester's teaching. She's tempted – there are two well-funded research programmes that fascinate her – but thinks probably she'll turn it down. She's also hungry and is wondering if she could smuggle some biscuits into church. She could have a little chocolate-chip communion of her own while the others go up to snack on their Christ's body.

The three of them make constipated conversation but it's a relief when the limousine arrives and they can slip into the creamy interior and their roles as principal mourners. There's a job to do.

Virginia and Eleanor sandwich Dorcas down St Wilfred's aisle to the front pew, Virginia carrying her grandmother's sticks. What remains of Eleanor's family are already there, her brothers standing broad and straight in their badly ironed suits. Neither could be bothered to get married so both the Denham and the Redford lines end with Virginia. It's not something that keeps her awake at night. Five minutes later, a weeping organ plays Handel's *Largo* as six of William's colleagues – one the union shop steward – carry his coffin into the nave. A faint hiccough of grief shakes Dorcas's shoulders and she leans forwards on her sticks, her head cocked, to watch her son's arrival through the lattice of her veil. Virginia watches too, but the coffin can't tell her anything about her father now. It's just a heavy box carrying an enigma into the grave.

It's settled on trestles, the wreath of Agatha Christie roses that Virginia chose on the lid – it seemed appropriate – and the vicar gathers the deceased in. As he recommends William's soul to Eleanor's

God, Virginia sees a small woman across the aisle sobbing as though her world has collapsed. She wears a showy floral hat quite at odds with the occasion and a suit that's not tactful about her shape. Eleanor glances over too and Virginia catches a look on her mother's face that startles her. It is venomous.

William's death has simply continued his habit of necrotic indifference towards his wife and child, but there was a William – there was a Will, a Bill, a Billy – who so touched some of the congregants that they mind that he died. They mind that he is no longer there to listen to them, to joke with them; they mind that some beat no longer ticks in their lives. Virginia lifts her eyes to the Christ topping the Great Rood, flanked by Mary, John and two seraphim. Every Sunday morning she'd sit bolt upright next to her mother, making up stories to keep herself awake.

*Our Lady's front is all red because she's had a nosebleed and she's used her frock to mop it up. She knows it's naughty, but she hasn't got a handkerchief and it would be worser to bleed on the floor. Or on Reverend Wilson's head, except that would be funny. But you mustn't laugh in church, oh no.*

*It looks like St John's holding a book, but really he's hiding a cricket ball and he's looking over there to choose which window he's going to smash. Perhaps the big one with the man in a funny hat holding a church. He must be ever so strong to carry a church. Probably he could even carry our house.*

*The angels are crossing their wings because they've weed themselves and they haven't got any legs to cross. Angels have feathers instead of legs so they can fly better.*

Religious knowledge has never made faith any more palatable to her as an adult than in growing up and she's never known if Eleanor truly believes or if it's just another formal requirement in a life shaped by required formalities. She could never have asked. Had she been in charge of the arrangements, she'd have paid a van driver to take the body away in a cardboard box and bury it in a forest, but she understands that today's pomp and ritual are indicators of status.

There are two readings – one given by William's factory manager and the other by an old university friend – and psalms 38 and 6, which feature much groaning and stinking and sinning. Virginia listens to psalm 38 with relish: *For my loins are filled with a loathsome disease: and there is no soundness in my flesh.* She'd fix that in an instant with heavy-duty Amoxicillin, she thinks, and covers her smile with a hand.

Uncle Stephen is to deliver the eulogy and he makes his way to the pulpit, grief dogging his steps as he prepares to speak of the friend he met in the war. As a small child Virginia used to hear Father laughing when the two men retreated into the study, and she'd wonder if Uncle Stephen was a wizard because only someone in a starry robe and pointy hat could have turned her father into a light-hearted man. The father she knew seemed to have mislaid his laugh in the war.

Like William, Stephen has just reached retirement age, but there's a vigour about his trim figure in the bespoke suit that belies his years. He felt William's death like a solar-plexus blow. He'd suggested a golfing weekend on the Isle of Wight only a few days before his old friend died, and noticed William's grimace. *Must have known he was ill,* he thought later – *why didn't he tell me?*

As he mounts the steps to the pulpit, he has to silence the part of him that wants to speak the undercover truth about William. That he was a man whose sun rose on disappointment every day. That his creativity was traduced and his ambitions snubbed. Instead he speaks eloquently, movingly, about the William the mourners knew. He speaks of his sterling qualities: his leadership of men in battle and in industry, his concern for others and his integrity. He speaks of his civic pride, how being a son of Harrogate ran down his centre – 'Like a message down a stick of rock,' he says, permitting his audience a timid smile. He speaks of his love of painting and poetry, especially the Romantics, his knowledge of Baroque music and of Gilbert and Sullivan and his deft construction of automata in his large garden shed. He speaks of Dorcas, of the tragedy of losing her second son; of the boys' late father, George Edgar, who's been spared this second tragedy; of how William will now rest in peace under an ancient yew next to his brother, Edgar George.

'And of course he leaves behind a wife and daughter. Eleanor and Virginia,' he says, not looking at them.

Leaving their pew, Virginia looks down the aisle to the baptistery. In the centre of a stepped plinth is the square font of Verona marble where she was received into the church. At the other end of the nave, Eleanor and William were married before the high altar with its massed candles and complicated lights. Edgar and his father and now William have been dispatched from this graceful space, and she supposes her last visits here will be to see Eleanor and Dorcas off to whatever fairyland they believe in. Virginia has made it clear in her will that she wants no religious flimflam when she dies, but that her ashes are to be strewn over the rose garden on Streatham Common from which she has occasionally filched cuttings. *Give something back,* she thinks. *Virginia-mulch.*

As the limousines draw up outside the church, she sees the weeping woman from the service being led away by a stooped man. Virginia asks Mother who she is.

'She's French,' says Eleanor, as though that answers the question.

'But why is she so upset?'

'No idea. Some solicitor's wife, I think.'

It begins raining when the funeral cortège arrives at the cemetery, which turns to hail as the hearse is opened. The mourners gather round the sodden hole in the ground, the hailstones tapping on William's coffin like impatient fingers. Virginia thinks the vicar is rather gabbling the words, as though he's realised she's about to start nibbling her neighbour if she isn't fed soon, and she's grateful for his haste. She'll hoover her way through the mimsy little sandwiches and quiches Mother has ordered for the wake and accept whatever condolences are offered before going out for dinner on her own. *Indian,* she thinks. *Maybe Chinese.* Harrogate doesn't run to much else.

As ashes are added to ashes and dust to dust, she looks across the grave to Uncle Stephen who is standing to attention, saluting his friend, tears chasing tears down his cheeks.

I make twice-weekly telephone contact with Mother after Father's funeral but know I'll have to go back up at some point to help her clear his stuff out of the house. She vaguely mentions moving, as though a new address would better suit a widow, but I am discouraging.

'Never a good idea to make major decisions so soon after a death,' I say. 'Grief can skew things for a while.'

But Mother mentions Father only in connection with throwing things away. Like his pewter tankard in the kitchen and his keys on the hall stand. His old-fashioned cut-throat razor and strap in the bathroom she never uses. There's a Bank Holiday coming up, so I arrange for Magda to water the garden and drive up. I don't think there'll be anything of Father's I want but I empty the boot just in case.

We jumble his clothes into plastic bags for charity. The suits give little away save that a moneyed man bought them and his ties are anonymous silk streaks except for the one bearing his regimental insignia. His bedroom reverts to the spare room it was when he took it over and Mother wonders aloud what colour to paint it.

'Maybe a nice lilac on the walls and a Liberty print for the curtains and bedspread – what do you think? I've seen some lovely linen with lilac sprigs all over it and once I've bought some new furniture and bedding, this could be a very pretty room.'

'Good idea,' I say, my head in a wardrobe smelling of solitude. 'Nice to make a change.'

His study is dismembered just as ruthlessly, rendering it to Mother like a libation.

'I could probably store the lawn mower in here,' she says, 'and the garden tools. It'll be super to take down that beastly shed. I always thought it was an abomination. I could get the builder to open up the window and make a door into the garden so the tools wouldn't be traipsed through the house. Could store the potting compost over there. Put some deep shelves up.' She waves her hand at Father's bookshelves. 'We need to box these up too. He spent a fortune on these art books so they'll bring in a nice little profit for Oxfam. Bound to be someone else in town who's interested in that sort of stuff. Oh, but not that one!' Her voice is suddenly sharp.

'What one?' I ask.

Mother pulls a book called *L'Aube de la Renaissance* off the shelf. 'Must be from the tart,' she says, and throws it in a bin bag with some violence.

'Sorry, what do you mean?'

'Nothing. Nothing of any consequence at all. Forget that I said it,' and she turns away from me to open the window. 'Let's have some air in the room, for heaven's sake.'

When it comes to the desk, my finger strokes the box with the brass corners, tarnishing now in death's wake. I consider taking it, but Ruby is firm. *Don't leave clues, Colonel Virginia*, she mutters in my ear. *Never let them know.*

Mother is kneeling on a gardening pad, turning out the desk drawers. 'Ugh! It stinks of whisky,' she says, and pulls a face as she rests the half-empty bottle on top of the papers in the rubbish bag. 'He was practically an alcoholic, you know.'

I don't know and think I'd have recognised the bulbous nose and broken veins and blurry eyes, but while his skin became crackle-thin with age, I never saw it hectic with alcohol.

'Oh, and there's these,' Mother says, pushing herself up and lifting a Sainsbury's carrier bag off a nearby bookshelf. 'Uncle Stephen gave them to me the week after the funeral. Said they're Father's wartime journals or something. Shall we send them to Oxfam as well? Or perhaps we should burn them, come to think of it. They might be the kind of thing you don't want strangers to read.'

'Can I have a look?'

'Yes – do take them. Dispose of them as you will.'

History's heft fills the bag and I peep inside at the books wrapped inexpertly in tatty sackcloth. There are six of them and I lift the cover of the top one to see Father's faded handwriting pirouetting across the page.

*Father's secrets, Colonel Virginia*, Ruby whispers. *Take them. There may be clues, you never know.*

'Perhaps I will take these, Mother. Might be interesting to read about Father's war. Never heard him talk about it.'

'Please take whatever you want. I have no use for them.'

I lay the bag in the boot of my car and tuck it up with a blanket.

The next day the removal van takes the furniture, some of it to the auction house, the rest to the dump. I stand watching from the door as Father's life bounces down the drive. It wouldn't do to wave goodbye, so I bow my head slightly as though just checking that my shoes are on the right feet.

When the van has gone, I wander round the garden to see how Mother's landscaping is coming on. She's spending a fortune on having an elaborate water feature installed which will, when finished, flood the spot where Father's shed now stands. As I approach the shed, I remember the fork in the ancient rhododendron where I used to sit and watch him, the branches' knuckles digging into my bum, the twigs scratching my thighs. Afterwards, although I knew it was naughty, I'd pull my knickers down and twist round in front of my bedroom mirror to count the red marks on my cheeks and on my legs. If there were more than seven, I knew Father really, *really* loved me: any fewer was a disappointment. And a confirmation.

From my bower I saw his hands hold his tools as he sawed and hammered and drilled. I saw his muscles flex as his creatures took shape. I saw him blow the dust from their heads, stroke the sides of their faces, sit them on the bench to paint them, grinning like a man watching his children growing into fine human beings. When he wound them up for the first time, he appeared to hold his breath, but when they clapped or tumbled or nodded at him, his shoulders dropped and he clapped and nodded back. The sharp planes of his face creased into such joy I'd wonder who he was for a moment and it was as much as I could do to stay put and not rush in and introduce myself.

I open the door and the tart smells of varnish and paint and the balmy scents of oils flood my nose. I turn on the light. Every trace of Father has been extirpated. No nut or bolt or delinquent screw has escaped Mother's attentions. The shelves on which the automata once milled are empty, swept clean even of the dust that gathered round their feet. The tool racks hang like memento mori of his fertile imagination.

I find myself standing at another grave's edge and back away before death becomes contagious.

# 1945

William's legless for five days when the Germans surrender, every day as incoherent as a howl. He and Stephen drink together, piss together, doze together, wake together in ditches and in doorways and in uniform. Stephen and the others find life hilarious, but for William it feels more like standing on a frozen pond, the ice zigzag-snapping beneath his feet. He can't go back. Not to Harrogate anyway. He writes to Eleanor. It takes seven tries because he wants to tell her the truth. Wants to write: *Dear Eleanor, I don't love you. You don't love me. I will give you grounds for divorce. I will send photographs and a legal document handing over my property to you and the child. We never have to meet again.* But the habit of untruth is too hard to kick, so he tells her he's joined a specialist team resettling the human flotsam of the war. *I don't know how long it will take*, he writes, *but I know you will manage well, as always.* Never having written to her before, he doesn't quite know how to end it. *Love, William* is out of the question, *yours sincerely* too businesslike, even though theirs is a businesslike marriage, and *Cheerio* too – well, too cheery, he thinks. He settles on *with best regards*, which he thinks he can afford.

But he tells Stephen the truth, their friendship flayed by the war into a candour that shocks them both.

'I can't go back, Stephen – d'you see? I've learned things about myself in these last years that make going back unthinkable. I can't spend the rest of my days walking around like a living corpse. Don't think too badly of me.'

'I don't.'

'Most people would. My parents will. My wife's family will too. But at the moment I don't care. Going back would be an act of such rampant dishonesty, I couldn't look at myself in the mirror.'

When he sees Stephen off in a truck with a bevy of bellowing soldiers, his eyes prick. He feels the camaraderie of the past six years choking in the clouds of dust.

He turns and goes to pack his kitbag.

Three days later, he bounces into Caen on the back of a hay wain, his shiny suit busy with barn-dancing insects. The buildings are still maimed, the local church still faceless, but flags flap their red, white and blue from every window. He doesn't think it would be proper to go and see her looking like this, so he asks the farmer driving the cart where he can get a room.

'You could knock on any door, *m'sieur*. There is no one in Caen – no one in the whole of France – who would refuse you a bed.'

'But I must to pay,' says William in his halting French. 'There is no inn where I could stay? I will to pay the money of course.'

'Then there is the *Café des Anges*, *m'sieur*. You will find a welcome there.'

William considers this for a moment, then remembers Edith washing his feet. She'll take him as he is, he thinks, and makes his way to the square.

The café is heaving, its blue bentwood chairs massing in the square and under the awning and around the bar in the cheery disorder of victory. William wades through the Gauloise pall inside and when he opens his mouth to ask for a room, there's a ripple, then a wave, then a collective halloo. Paul rushes from behind the bar and pulls his arm into the air like a triumphant boxer. Chairs are pushed back and glasses are raised and he's carried round the café like a leaf on a column of ants, his cheeks burning with kisses. He can't see Edith and doesn't like to ask. *She must have the evening off*, he thinks. He'll go and find her at home later. When eventually he makes it up to his room, tipsy with French gratitude, he goes to the washstand to freshen up. In the mirror he sees a palimpsest, the last six years scraping his skin clear of his boyhood, his marriage, his compliance, telling the wartime tale in bold, spare strokes. Death has its own economy and since joining up he's lived every day on its bottom line.

He steels himself and goes back downstairs. The café erupts when he appears, as though theatre curtains have swished back to reveal the leading man at centre stage. He is called to every table but smiles and shakes his head and refuses.

'I want your beautiful town to see,' he says. 'I want to have the memories.'

'Then we will wait for you,' says a lush middle-aged woman, putting her hand on his shoulder. 'When you come back we will celebrate again,' and her musky breath dampens his ear as she leans in. 'I will be waiting,' she says.

*Rue de la Paix* looks no different in peacetime than in war, its walls and windows surly with neglect. The blue door is still there but the upstairs window is dark. He rings the bell. He rings again. She's asleep maybe. Has maybe popped out for bread. He just needs to wait. He just needs to watch, to listen for the clack of her heels down the street. He waits and he watches and he listens as the town falls asleep, flinching each time the *mairie* clock chimes. He resolves to come back every day at different times, as though he can surprise her back into his life. He puts the flat of his hand on the door to give it a fare-well pat. It eases open.

Forgetting his manners, he goes in and climbs the rickety stairs, his Zippo lighter showing the way. The room is still there. The bed is still there. The chair where he wept is still there. He wants to lie on the bed, but not alone, so he stands by it like a supplicant at a church door, silently begging Edith to appear.

Minutes pass.

The sound of a rat gnawing at something in the corner startles him and he makes his way slowly back downstairs. As he reaches the street, a window opens in the next-door house and an elderly woman beckons to him.

'You are looking for Edith, *m'sieur.*'

'Yes.'

'She doesn't live here any more. She was a good neighbour to me and I miss her, but Philippe came back for her – as if from the dead. They've gone to Paris to make a new life together. I'm happy for her of course, but I miss her badly.'

'Philippe?'

'Her fiancé. You didn't know him? He's a fine young man and was courageous in battle, so they say. They've known each other since they were children, but she thought he was dead. You should have seen her face when he came back – the years just fell away and she looked young and beautiful again!'

When William opens the door to his room, the woman from the café is asleep in his bed.

Her eyes flicker open.

'You see?' she says. 'I waited.'

He joins her.

He tries to stay, tries to become part of the town, tries to grow a provincial French skin, but he is always, inevitably, *l'étranger*. He takes what work is available – in the fields, behind the bar, clearing the garbage of war – but he knows all he's doing is delaying his return.

He grows his hair, grows a beard, learns better French, misses Edith.

He loses hope.

He shaves off his beard and tells the barber to cut his hair. He watches his face become Mr William Denham of Denham's Tractors again. He disgusts himself. He visits all his usual haunts and thanks everyone for the food and drink – especially the drink – and they thank him again for what he and his compatriots have done for France.

'Come back with your family next time,' they say, and he tells them he's not a family man.

He writes to Eleanor. *Back on October 5th*, he says.

# 1945

Monday, 4.34 p.m.

I ask Mother why I haven't seen Father since he's been at War and she says, 'Special Operations,' in a funny way. I know that doctors do operations, so that must mean he's making people better when they've got hurt. When he comes back, I'll give him a big giant cuddle and say, 'Thank you for making people better, Father,' because he must be very kind, like Dr Greenaway.

One afternoon, I look out of my bedroom window and see a man standing in front of the house. His eyes jump around all the windows and over the roof and stop at the porch. I think he's probably trying to bust the front door down with his iron will, so I tiptoe downstairs to Mother, who's reading the paper in the drawing room.

'Excuse me, Mother,' I say, trying not to squeak, 'there's a robber outside – I think he's come to murder us in our beds!'

Mother looks over the paper. 'Don't be foolish, Virginia. What kind of robber would come round in broad daylight?'

'But he's just standing there staring. I think he's working out how to get in. He's probably got an axe or something. Or even a giant stone so he can smash it on our heads till they get all bloody and . . .'

'Virginia! I'll thank you not to use that word.'

'But I didn't mean bloody, I just meant . . .'

'Stop that right now, young lady, or you'll go to your room.'

My mouth twitches.

Mother folds the paper with a snap. 'If I find you've been telling fibs,' she says, 'you'll go to your room *and* get a smack,' and she goes over to the window in a huff. She looks out at the front drive and her very straight back bends. 'Oh,' she says. 'He's early. Come with me, please.'

I follow her to the front door and stop by the elephant foot, trying to look like an umbrella. When Mother opens the door, the man is at the bottom of the steps.

'Hello,' says Mother, 'are you coming in?'

The man nods slowly and walks up to the door.

'Virginia,' says Mother, 'say good afternoon, please. This is Father.'

The house changes after Father comes home, like he's moved the air around. For a while there's something funny about his voice, as if he doesn't like speaking English very much, but I expect he's just been speaking in a special war way because of killing people and things. Or maybe making them better.

The first time I hear him in the bathroom when I'm waiting outside, I wonder why he's sweeping the floor. Perhaps he drops things like me. Breaks them, then has to say sorry to Mother. That would make us the same, which would be super. When he comes out, I say, 'Good morning, Father,' and creep into the bathroom through his sticky hair smell. There's a belt thing hanging by the sink which is quite scratchy when I touch it, and a sort of penknife by the soap. I check the door is closed – not locked, I'm not supposed to lock it – before I pick it up. It's heavy, with a handle that's so smooth I want to lick it. I open it. First it makes a V, like for Virginia, and then it opens up completely like a number 1. The knife bit that comes out of the handle is very pretty and very shiny. I can just about see my eye and a piece of my nose if I hold it up to my face, and if I hold it the other way I can see both my eyes, as if I'm looking through the letter box. I touch the edge of the knife very carefully. *Ouch. Ouch, ouch, bothery ouch*. It's made a cut down the top of my finger, which sends out a bloop of blood, then another, till there's all blood down my finger and down my hand and when I hold it out, it drips into the sink like big fat raindrops. I run my finger under the cold tap and I close the penknife and I run to the bedroom and I drop my water glass on the floor. I'll have to say sorry for breaking it again, but I can pretend I've cut my finger trying to clear up the bits, so it'll look like I was being a helpful girl.

After that, I notice Father sometimes has little bits of paper with

162

blood on stuck to his face when he comes out of the bathroom, so when I cut myself or prick myself with a needle, I put bits of tracing paper on the blood. It's like saying, 'Look, I'm just like you. Welcome home, Father.'

I look at Mother and Father, but I don't stare because it's rude. They don't talk much to each other but then they've both got lots to do, what with Father going to the factory every day and Mother busy in the kitchen and at the shops. I try and think how to make them talk to each other, but I'm not very clever and I'm quite little really. I've got this storybook called *Miranda's Happy Day* which is my very favourite because Miranda's mummy and daddy have got kind faces even though the daddy goes off to work in the morning like Father. In the book he comes home in the evening with a cake and when he brings it into the dining room with the candles all lit up, the mummy says to Miranda, 'Surprise, surprise, dear!' The mummy and the daddy stand really close together when Miranda blows out the candles and they're both smiling. Maybe Mother and Father smile at each other in their bedroom or at night-time when I'm asleep.

One Saturday afternoon, when Father has gone out somewhere and Mother is somewhere else, Ruby and me are playing with my dollies.

'I know,' I say, 'let's play *Miranda's Happy Day*,' and we dress up one dolly in her best party frock and put a scarf round Edward Teddy's neck so he can be Daddy. My walkie-talkie dolly with the hair you can brush is Mummy and in the game she takes Miranda to the park and to swimming and to the cake shop and gives her big hugs all the time. Ruby's doing the Daddy and when Miranda and Mummy come home and tell jokes in the kitchen, she walks Edward Teddy across the floor.

'Hello my little loves,' she says in a deep voice, 'have you had a lovely day?'

'Oh yes, Daddy,' I say in a jolly voice, 'me and Mummy have been playing games all day and we had a picnic in the park. Have you got a present for me even though it's not my birthday?'

'Come over here, Miranda,' says Daddy, 'and come over here too, Mummy. See what I've got for you!'

As I bounce the walkie-talkie dolly and the Miranda dolly over to Teddy, Ruby jumps up and laughs in a horrid way.

'Ho ho, ha ha!' she says, forgetting to do the deep voice. 'This is what I've got for you!' and she bashes the two dollies lots of times with Teddy until they're lying flat on the floor, then she takes off his scarf and ties it really tightly round Mummy's neck.

'Hah!' says Ruby very loudly. 'Now I can go off and do what I want and spend all my money and go to lots of parties you can't come to and then I'll eat all the sweets in the world!'

We don't play that game any more because I know Ruby would just do that again and it makes me sad when the daddy's so horrid to the mummy and Miranda.

When he's home, Father goes into his study a lot, so I don't see him very much. Ruby says, 'I bet he's a magician making spells to stop people fighting and being rude and things, or maybe he's magicked all the sweets and all the gold in the world into the cellar and it's up to us to be brave like the Famous Five and go and find them.' She tells me to borrow the cellar key – well, pinch it really – so we can go and have a look, but I say I'm not going to because there'll be spiders down there as big as moles and they're bound to have eaten all the toffees anyway. Toffee is Ruby's favourite. But when Father's in the study, sometimes I sit scrunched up against the grandfather clock in the hall. I just want to hear what sounds he makes when he's doing his spells. He might be singing hymns, for instance. Or doing that funny dancing coloured people in Africa do – I saw that in a newsreel once and Granny and Papa tutted at each other over my head.

There's no sounds, so probably Father's put an invisible wall round the study so no one can know what he's up to. One day, I have to write a story at school called 'My Father', and the other girls write things like: *Daddy is very kind to me and my hamster. He gives money to poor people a lot because he's very kind.* Or: *My dad likes to tell jokes and laugh very loud. He makes me laugh as well, but not as loud as him because I'm only seven.* But all I can write is: *Father is quite tall and has dark crinkly hair and brown eyes. He works very hard at his work.* I don't know if he gives money to poor people or is kind to hamsters, though I'm pretty sure he tells jokes because of him laughing with Uncle Stephen when he's there.

Ruby says I should find a hidey-hole in the study and then I'd be inside his wall and I'd hear his magic words. I might even see a spell happening, which would be super. I say no for a long time, but then I start thinking it'd be quite exciting really, except it's a bit bothering as well. It'd be as naughty as hiding in Mother's wardrobe, but at least I know what Mother'd do if she found me. She'd smack my bottom probably and not let me have pudding for a week. Father's different. I don't know what he'd do, and because he's been away at War, I think he might have a gun in there, you never know.

When I tell Ruby that I'm scared Father might shoot me, she snorts like a horse. 'Oh, don't be such a chump,' she says. 'Fathers never, *ever* murder their daughters! If they did, God would send down angel tigers from heaven to gobble them up and then they'd be sorry.'

I'm not so sure, but Ruby tells me that if I find a hidey-hole I'll be really important, like a spy. Like that lady we saw at the flicks. Martha Harry.

Father often doesn't come to supper when Mother bangs the little gong, so she sighs and sends me to say the food's getting cold and he'd better come right now. If you please. When I stand in the door-way saying the message, I whoosh my eyes around the room trying to remember where everything is, like being a map-drawing person, which is part of being a spy. I can see his big leather chairs with sticky-out bits at the top and loads of books on loads of shelves and even another little bookcase as well. There are three tables in the room – well, one's a desk but it's quite like a table because you can see his feet underneath, and the other two are next to the chairs. The desk sits in front of the window. Father usually has the curtains shut, so it's very dark in there apart from a green lamp on his desk and the standing-up lamps by the chairs. Ruby says that probably means Father's a vampire, but when I say I'd better not hide in there then, she says, 'No, I bet it's just his eyes've been hurt by being at War so he can't let the daylight in or he'll go blind.'

When I come back from my visits to the study – recces, Ruby calls them – we have meetings to talk about what I've seen. Ruby says that only very important people have meetings, like kings and queens and princesses, so I feel quite puffed up.

'Well, Colonel Virginia,' Ruby says at our last meeting, putting a pencil behind her ear, 'I think it's plain which way the land lies, don't you know? Which way the wind blows. Shall we make a plan?'

I do a little cough, which is what people do when they're going to say something very special. 'Indeed so, Colonel Ruby,' I say, hoping my voice sounds a bit like my headmistress, 'indeed so. Hidey-hole number 4A33R in the M65L shall be used by our special spy on the 999.' Then I start whispering. 'It's code, Colonel Ruby,' I say. 'What it means is, I'll hide under the table on the this-hand-side,' I flap my arm, 'on Wednesday evening because Mother's going to a meeting about girls who have babies when they don't have a husband, so I bet Father will be in the study all evening.' I cough again and talk in my headmistress voice. 'The plan will begin at 06.00 hours and end when it's my bedtime. Over and out. God save the King.'

Ruby jumps to her feet and salutes. She clicks her heels in that way I can't do and bows so low she looks like a broken lolly stick. 'Yes, sir, my leader girl,' she says, all ratatatat like a gun. 'Good luck, old thing, and remember – don't leave any clues. You're doing a brave, brave thing for England.'

All day at school that Wednesday, I have this lump of scaredness in my chest like I haven't swallowed something properly. Martha Harry in the film looked beautiful in her posh frocks and it makes me wonder if spies have to dress up to do their job. When I get home, I look at my special-occasion frocks in the wardrobe and think about which one to wear. The tartan one is quite new and a bit itchy, the navy-blue one is older but made of a thin stuff which would tear very easily and the purple one is too short and too tight. None of them look like spy frocks, and anyway if I'm caught in Father's study I'll get into trouble for two things, hiding and spoiling my clothes, so I decide to put on the old clothes I wear when I go to the farm.

As I go into the kitchen, Mother looks at me and frowns. 'What on earth are you doing in those clothes, Virginia? Are you proposing to dig in the garden?'

'No, Mother, but they're very comfy and I want to practise something we did today in PE. Sort of backward somersaults. Miss Gibson said practice makes perfect.'

'Well, please yourself then, but put them in the washing basket when you've finished.' Mother puts a plate of grey food on the table. 'Sit down now and say grace, please,' she says and turns back to the stove.

I eat my food and I'm specially careful not to make a mess because Mother's been quite quiet and quite sad lately. I don't know how to buck her up, so I just try not to do anything that would make her more sad.

After Mother has gone to the meeting, I sit on my bed with my heart pitter-pattering. I can tell the time now, so I know I have half an hour before Father comes home to his supper in the oven. Half an hour to sneak into my hidey-hole and do my spying. The thoughts in my head tick and tock from side to side like the thing in the grand-father clock. *Be a spy? – yes. Get in trouble? – no. Spy? – yes. Trouble? – no. Spy?* . . . I can hear Ruby in my ears. It *is* a brave, brave thing I'm doing for England. If Father's a wicked magician then I'll save the whole of Harrogate – the whole world even – from a fate worse than death. He may not look like one – for one thing I've never caught him wearing his pointy hat – but behind the closed door of his study, who knows? And then I think that even if I die in the end, like Martha Harry, I'll be everybody's best hero so it doesn't really matter. They'll probably put a statue of me in the park.

I stand up and catch sight of myself in the mirror. I look very white, like I do when I've been sick. 'Chin up,' I say to my reflection. 'Every man has to do his duty. King and country and all that. Tally ho, Martha,' and I pull my shoulders back and quick-march out of the room.

Father's study smells different from the rest of the house, which is probably because of the sparks the spells make, and as I close the door behind me I look from side to side and up and down to make sure there aren't any leftovers hanging around. I don't want to be turned into a beetle. Or magicked away to chinky-China.

The curtains are pulled open so I can see there isn't any magician stuff, but I go over to the desk just to check if there's any jars of potions or powders behind Father's chair. I've never been this far into the room before and it feels dreadfully naughty, like trying to sit on his knee or something, but I imagine what Ruby would say if I turned back now. She'd call me a chickeny-scaredy-cat and pull that face like she'd just smelled a really nasty pong like pig poo. Pig Number Twos.

There are two boxes on the desk, one quite fancy with metal bits at the corners and the other with words on the top. I open that one first. I lift the lid slowly in case there's a bomb inside, and crinkle my face up waiting for the bang. Inside there's a row of sausagey cigars with pretty paper band things round one end. I didn't know he smoked. I lean over and take a deep breath, sniffing the warm smell into my nose. I stroke my middle finger along the cigar tops and they jiggle against each other like piglets drinking from their mummy. I close the box – *don't leave clues, Colonel Virginia* – and open the other one. I've got a sort of fizzing noise in my head. Just because one box didn't explode doesn't mean the other one won't. It squeaks and I hold my breath in case this is where he keeps his wands. He's probably got some for bad spells and some for good spells and some for killing spies. The window lights up the box and for a moment I think it *is* lots of wands and my heart jumps around in my chest, making it quite hard to breathe.

I squeeze my eyes, thinking one's going to pop out and do the beetle spell on me, but I open them wide again when I see they're only Father's pens. He's got loads. Black ones and red ones and ones like the back of a tortoise, skinny ones and fat ones, all in neat rows ready for writing. He must do really a lot of writing, probably when he puts his spells in spell books or writes lists of things to buy for making potions. I lift one out and take off the top. It makes a plopping noise. It's quite heavy and I shake it up and down a bit to feel how much it weighs, but it slips out of my fingers and lands on its nib on the blotting paper pad. *Oh no oh no oh no*. A puddle of red leaks out all round it like it's been stabbed and some crying crackles at the back of my throat. I pick the pen up and look at the nib. The end has bent in two, like tiny legs, and I try pushing them back together but I'm not strong enough and now it looks like I've cut myself. What should I do? What would Martha do? She wouldn't leave any clues, that's what, so I put the top back on the pen and slip it into the pocket of my trews. The red stain is the only mark on the blotter, which means Father will know what I've done as soon as he sits down, so I carefully take off the top layer and scrunch it up. *Cripes.* There's a pink mark on the next sheet too, so I scrunch that one up and stuff both pieces up my jumper, where they scratch against my collywobbly tummy.

I'd better not touch anything else – and anyway it's time to hide.

Hidey-hole number 4A33R is under the table near one of the armchairs. It's a very tight squeeze and I have to lie on my front and push backwards to get underneath. I bend my legs when I reach the wall because I'd stick out otherwise and Father would see me straight away. Nowadays Mother often says, 'Oh Lord, you're growing too fast, Virginia,' as if she's ticking me off. I don't think I can help it. Not even if I stopped eating, which I've tried sometimes, but the food just makes my pockets smelly.

Just as I've settled in, I hear Father's car crunch up the drive, so I was just in time. I think he'll stop off in the kitchen for his supper, but he comes straight in and drops his briefcase on the other chair with a plunk. He swishes the curtains shut, clicks on the light and takes out a bottle and a glass from his desk.

He makes a sighing noise like a kettle when he sits down and pours himself a drink. If I twist my head really, really slowly to one side I can just about see him above the desk. I hope he won't hear the scrabbly noise my hair makes in my head, but it doesn't look like he has.

He looks different in here. For the first time ever I think he's rather handsome. Not quite handsome-prince handsome, but someone a lady might fall in love with. Like when Mother fell in love with him in the olden days. He sips his drink slowly, his other hand stroking the desk like it's a hamster. I'm worried that he might be going to write something so I'm jolly happy when he reaches over to a shelf and pulls down a big book with pictures on the front. He opens it and looks at a page, going so still he might have suddenly turned to ice. I didn't see what the front picture was, but what if it's a spell book and the first spell shows all the spies in the room?

After ages and ages, Father looking at the page, me waiting to be shown, he pours himself another drink and sits back in his chair with a little smile on his face. He looks so kind it makes me wonder if he does give money to poor people, which might explain why he's out at work all the time, but I can't exactly ask him from my hidey-hole.

He sits like that and sits like that and sits like that for so long, I get a bit bored and even though I've got little pains in my legs from the bending, I begin to feel sleepy. I pull myself awake several times but I can't stop my eyes closing.

I'm in a waterfall in my dream, the water raining down on me like soft blue diamonds, when I'm suddenly jerked awake by a pain in my head and a loud clomp. When I open my eyes, I see that I've slid out from under the table in my sleep and that the clomping noise was Father falling on his knees on the carpet. I think he may have kicked me, but I'm sure he didn't mean to. I pull myself out from the hidey-hole, getting ready for a big giant ticking-off and preparing to say sorry a lot a lot. But Father isn't looking at me. He has his hands over his eyes and his mouth is doing this opening and closing thing like a trout. He's making a sort of moany noise and he's rocking backwards and forwards on his knees. He stays doing the same thing when I stand up, my hurt head banging, so he isn't going to tell me off – not now anyway – and I tip-toe to the door. I keep my eyes on him as I slowly turn the doorknob and slide out into the hall. He's still making the moany noise when I close it behind me.

He never says anything to me the next day, and when Mother feels the bump on my head as she's doing my hair, she just says, 'Oh Lord, you have been in the wars,' and carries on plaiting. I'm quite glad she doesn't ask me where the bump came from because it means Father and me've got a secret like friends do. I'd like to have a friend who is always there. Sometimes being lonely makes me cry.

*I see the girl in the room. I can't see her face because her hands are in the way. But I can see her tears. On the backs of her fingers. Dark stains on her blouse. She's sitting up against the headboard, her knees drawn up. One sock has slipped down and wrinkles round her ankle like an old man's neck. There's a thread hanging down from the bottom of her gymslip. Just a little tug and the hem will give up. Then she'll be in trouble again. Her hair hangs over the still-painful bump in unlovely hanks, tangled with misery and sweat. Her sobs are silent. Practice makes perfect. She takes her hands away and wipes them on the eiderdown. Front. Back. Front again. She looks closely at the eiderdown. Looks at the clusters of tiny flowers on the fabric, checking for stains. She knows it's only water, knows from experience it'll dry, but she has to check. Just in case one day she weeps something else. Blood maybe. Yellow end-of-a-cold snot perhaps. Her lips are moving. Purse, stretch . . . Purse, stretch . . . Purse, stretch. It's only a whisper, but I can hear it. Of course I can hear.* Ruby . . . Ruby . . . Ruby.

She won't come, *I say.*

She might.

Not when you call her. Only when she wants.

She might.

You have to stop wishing. Stop thinking it'll be different.

But things change sometimes. They do. I've seen them.

What things?

. . .

What things?

. . .

You can't change it. You're too little. Only big people can change things.

Like Mother?

Yes.

And Father, I suppose.

171

Yes.

And Hitler. He changed things.

Yes.

And fairy godmothers. That's how Cinderella changed. She changed into a girl who was so pretty she married a prince. I wish I had one.

I said stop wishing.

But if I had one, she'd make Ruby come. She would. She'd just wave her wand and there she'd be. She'd sit on the wall next to me in the playground. When Linda points at me and says *Oh look, there's the stupid stick insect*, Ruby'd stop her. She'd say rude words and probably hit Linda. Not badly. Not to make her bleed or anything, but just to stop her pointing and laughing. Then she'd play with me, Ruby would. We'd play together in the middle of the playground so everyone would see. All the girls. Then they'd want to be my friend and tell me secrets. They'd say *Oh, come to my party, Virginia. Come and eat some cake. As much as you like. No one's going to tick you off.*

Then you'd be sick.

But it wouldn't matter. It wouldn't matter a bit. I could make all the mess I liked. I could smash the plates and everyone would laugh because you have fun at parties. I'm nearly sure you have fun at parties.

*The drawing-room door opens. It squeaks helpfully like a warning bell. Like an air-raid siren.*

*Take cover.*

*Bombs ahoy.*

*The girl scrambles off the bed. She pats the pillow in the middle, where there's a dent. A her-shaped dent. She tugs at the eiderdown to straighten it and puts her teddy in the wet patch. He's big enough to cover it if she lays him on his back. As though he's just having a little rest. A snooze. She realises only one sock is pulled up and quickly pulls the other one up to match. She goes over to the desk and opens up a book. Just in time.*

*The door opens suddenly.*

# 1976

Saturday is a trip day, so I join the queue at Camisa's in Old Compton Street, each shuffle forwards bringing me closer to the salamis hanging from the ceiling like peppery stalactites, the olives dawdling in garlic and in herbs and in chilli and the Parmesan wedges massing by the door. When the next customer leaves the tiny shop, I trail my fingers along the glass of the chiller as I move up a place. A sticky brick of taleggio, perhaps. Maybe bresaola and those artichokes marinating next to the bocconcini. Maybe pecorino. Maybe Dolcelatte. Maybe both. Maybe pasta. The trips are prodigal.

Signor Camisa grins at me as my turn comes.

'*Ciao, bella! Come stai?*' He towers over the women buzzing back and forth behind the counter, taking his time with the female customers in the way of roguish bossmen everywhere.

'*Bene, grazie,*' I say. 'I fancy some pappardelle today – have you got any?'

'For you, *signora*, of course,' and he calls down the stairs, '*Pappardelle, Emilia, pronto!*'

A few moments later, a young girl brings up a tray of wide pasta ribbons tossed in semolina.

'How many for?' he asks.

'Four people,' I say. 'For dinner tonight.'

'Lucky people,' he says. 'Today we have hare sauce – look.' He gestures to a bowl on the counter. 'A little of that, some Parmesan, and *ecco*! A feast for a king.'

'And they're hungry friends,' I say, 'so be generous with the sauce.' For my second course tonight I choose squid ink ravioli, sinister on the tray, seductive on the palate, and some cannoli to bring up the rear after the cheese. I buy vongole for tomorrow, porcini for a risotto, the chilli olives that could peel paint, grilled courgettes, the artichokes and six inches of Sopressa Veneta shaved into coins by the electric slicer at the end of the counter. Parmesan, taleggio, bocconcini, focaccia and I'm done. The pecorino and bresaola can wait.

I leave the shop and hear *'Ciao, bella'* behind me as the next customer takes her turn. Camisa's is only the first stop on today's Grand Tour. Berwick Street market next for fruit and vegetables – maybe some venison sausages from the butcher. Maybe sea bass from the fish stall.

I pull a second bag out of my basket.

Gilda hasn't been feeling well for a couple of weeks. She's been getting headaches so severe she retreats to bed with the curtains drawn. She won't take painkillers because she doesn't want to bewilder Tobias and anyway they go away eventually. But sometimes it feels like she's fallen into a trance and she finds herself talking nonsense when she comes round, like scribble on a blackboard. Her fingers are swelling too and she can't get her rings on any more, but that's no great hardship – there's no place for fripperies now. Six more weeks and three days. She wishes she could calculate the minutes and seconds. She drifts into his bedroom several times a day, checking the stacks of nappies, the tiny Babygros and the bedding jolly with clowns. It always cheers her up.

But today she feels sick as well and her eyesight's gone wonky. It's quite warm outside, so she puts on her mouldy old tracksuit bottoms and a giant sweatshirt and takes herself off to the Common for some fresh air. At the door, she checks her handbag for her keys. Recently she had to rely on Stephanie next door to let her in with the spare set three days running. Memory's shot to pieces too. *They don't tell you that one*, she thinks. Or did they?

Her legs are unsteady as she weaves up the street and her head feels like it's being hit by a million hammers. If she can just make it to the Common, she'll find her favourite bench and have a rest – catch a few rays even.

\*

174

I'm salivating as I drive back, planning what to eat first. I'll roll the courgettes round the bocconcini and drizzle a little chilli oil over them to nibble while I cook, but I can't decide whether I'm inclining more to the fish than the ravioli for my main course. Nearing home, I turn a corner and see a small woman staggering slightly as she walks towards the Common. I wonder idly if she's drunk, but as I pass her, she suddenly keels over backwards. Her legs splay as she lands, her trousers' crotch so soaked with blood she could have been stabbed. I jam on the brakes, jump out of the car and race over to the woman who is, I see now, pregnant. She's babbling as though speaking in tongues and as I kneel beside her, she suddenly vomits. I clear her airways, turn her on her side and take her pulse. It's dangerously fast. I go to the car, push the passenger seat back as far as it will go and return for the woman, who is twitching slightly. I carry her to the car and lay her on her side in the front, locking the seatbelt round her tightly.

I drive to the hospital with the heel of my palm jammed on the horn. As I pull into the ambulance bay, I lean out of the window and bark, 'Stretcher!' at two paramedics smoking by the door. I tell a nurse to phone ahead for an operating theatre and run beside the trolley down the maze of corridors. Emergencies preclude manners and when we arrive, I bellow at the staff to get into theatre. *Now.* Someone – I think it's Meadows – offers to take over, since he's on duty, but I say, 'No, thanks, this one's mine.' I slip off my blood- and vomit-spattered clothes, tug on my gown and cap and when I've scrubbed up, crash into the theatre. It's heaving with medical and nursing staff as I swiftly cut a severely distressed infant out of his mother, whose pre-eclampsia has caused a placental abruption. The baby boy takes a while to breathe and the paediatric team fight to keep him alive as I do the same with his mother, who is haemorrhaging. I work to stop the bleeding and avoid performing a hysterectomy on this young woman so perilously close to death. It takes all my energies but I manage to preserve her uterus and keep her alive.

Mother and baby are whisked off to their respective ICUs.

I stick around until midnight, when it becomes plain that the patient's out of danger – as is her son, who's recovering from the hypoxia that took his breath away.

When I get into my car I could be back in Camisa's, the air rich with the smells of overheated Italian food and the fish from the market, which may not have survived the wait. I'm still up at two o'clock, eating till I'm full and then eating some more just to make sure. I call the hospital twice to check on the patient who, according to her driving licence, is called Gilda Francis and lives two streets away from me. When I saw her in ICU, I thought she looked vaguely familiar, but I couldn't quite place her.

Twenty-four hours later, Gilda is trying to swim towards the light through water the colour of dung. As her head breaks the surface someone says, 'All right, love? You coming back to us?' It's her mother, the Welsh lilt in her voice unmistakable, and Gilda feels long dry fingers on her forehead as she sinks back into the murk.

When she wakes fully, Dilys has gone. She tries to move her hand to feel her belly, but it's attached to something. For a moment she panics that she's gone mad and been strapped to the bed, till her eyes manage to focus on the drip and the panoply of machines standing like sentinels around her bed. Her other arm is free, so she moves it under the waffle blanket to where her son should be. And isn't.

He's gone.
    Left her like everyone else.
    *Oh.*
    *Oh, oh, oh, oh.*

Her throat balloons and she tries not to cry, but tears creep out and stroll down her cheeks to her ears. She squeezes her eyes tight shut so she doesn't have to see the truth. She hears the door open and the rustle of someone's bustle across the room.
    'You awake, love?'
    'No, I'm not,' she says, 'I'm asleep.'
    There's a deep-throated chuckle. 'I'm in your dreams then, am I?'
    She opens her eyes wearily. She can at least be civil. The sturdy nurse who pretended to be Dilys is standing by the bed.

'Sorry,' Gilda says. There's nothing else to say. If she says anything else, she'll ask for her son.

'What you sorry for?'

'Causing you so much trouble. I can't remember much. What happened?' (*Where's my son?*)

'You nearly died is what happened. We nearly lost you. C'mon now, let's sit you up.' The nurse slips her arm under Gilda's shoulders and gently lifts her off the pillows, which she plumps up behind her.

There is broken glass in her belly. The nurse is speaking, but she's not sure if it's meant for her. She hears the word 'baby' and puts her hands over her ears.

(*Where's my son?*)

'Your ears hurting you, Gilda?'

She can't block her out. She shakes her head.

(*Where's my son?*)

'Your head hurting then?'

She shakes her head again and hears her brain rattle against her skull. The bed rocks as the nurse sits by her legs and puts her hands over Gilda's. Her long dry fingers draw Gilda's will out of her and she drops her arms on the bed.

The nurse picks up her hands as though they're friable. 'I was just telling you about your baby. Your son.'

'I don't have a son.'

'Yes, you do. A beautiful little boy. He's going to be fine.'

Gilda's eyes fill again. 'Why're you doing this? Can't you leave me alone? Let me go home. I won't make a fuss.'

The nurse looks puzzled. 'Maybe you're a bit confused, my love. He's not very far away. When doctor's seen you, I'll take you to see him in ICU.'

The door opens and a tall woman steps into the room. The nurse quickly takes herself off the bed and stands to attention.

'Good morning, Miss Francis,' says the tall woman. 'I'm Virginia Denham. How are you feeling?'

'Miss Denham,' the nurse says, 'saved your life.'

'You certainly weren't very well when I found you,' says Virginia, 'but you're looking a bit better now.' She checks the chart at the bottom of Gilda's bed. 'Good,' she says, 'blood pressure's coming down. Not quite normal yet, but it's going in the right direction.' She sits down carefully on the spot the nurse has just vacated and Gilda notices her skin, whose creaminess belies her age. Virginia smiles, revealing crooked teeth. 'Your son is quite lovely,' she says. 'He's a valiant little chap and you can have him with you very soon, but tell me first how *you're* feeling.'

'I'm – I don't know how I'm feeling. My tummy's really sore and – well, that's it really. How should I be feeling?'

'No should about it. You feel how you feel. You've had a thoroughly rotten time and we'll have to keep you – well, both of you – in for a little bit, but we'll get you home as soon as possible. Nurse, can you rustle up a wheelchair for us, do you think? How about going to see your baby, Miss Francis?'

Gilda doesn't answer.

One of the chair's wheels is loose and it squeals down the corridor as though warning the baby she's on her way. She doesn't want him to know. Wants to creep up on him, take a look and go back to bed. Her own bed at home with its frills and feathers and safety. As Virginia pushes her through the door of the neonatal ICU, Gilda's hand grips the drip stand trundling beside her more tightly. She's wheeled up to an incubator where a wrinkly baby lies asleep, wearing only an over-sized nappy that makes him look like a boiled egg in a cup.

'There he is,' says Virginia. 'Have you got a name for him yet?'

'No. No, I haven't got that far yet.'

'Very wise. You probably want to get to know him first, don't you? See what name suits him.'

But this isn't Tobias. Not the Tobias she's been talking to for the last seven and a half months. Not the baby growing inside her like a bud. This baby's a stranger, and as she watches him, he yells, his whole body yells, his arms and legs flailing in the plastic-coated air. He knows she's there. She looks away, afraid of what she might see in his eyes.

Virginia bends over her shoulder. 'I expect you'd like to hold him, wouldn't you? I'm sure you can. Let's ask the nurses.'

(*No. No, no, no, no. I'll hurt him.*)

'*No!*' she says with more vehemence than she means to. 'Not yet.

Not till he's better. I'm sure they're looking after him really well. I think that's enough, thank you. I'm not feeling so good. Can I go back now?'

Virginia looks at her when she's back in bed. She looks like a crushed flower on a highway. *Need to keep an eye on this one*, she thinks.

A few days later, the baby's brought into the side room to which Gilda's been moved, his cot pushed up against her bed as though he's still attached. He does nothing but cry, his features smudging in his purply-red face, his limbs panicking against the blanket. A nurse comes in and shows her how to hold him while he's feeding, but he turns his head from her breast and she's glad. This isn't what her breasts are for. Breasts are for sex, for the hot breath of a man, not the gummy claim of an infant. He's taken away from her and she summons up the courage to tell the nurse that she'd rather bottle feed him, thank you. There's a flash of disapproval in the nurse's eyes, but she brings a bottle of formula, puts the enraged bundle in Gilda's arms and shows her how to tilt it so he doesn't get too windy.

Virginia comes in and notices how far away from her body she's holding him.

Faisal's on his way to the ward round when he passes one of the side rooms. He glances through the window in the door and is transfixed. Virginia is sitting on the bed, her arm round a woman holding a baby, an empty bottle in her hand. The patient's head is resting back on Virginia's shoulder and her eyes are closed. He's seen Virginia with patients many times before of course, has seen how adept she is in helping them understand what's going on, but he's never seen her look like this. She looks – well, *happy* is what he thinks. And the patient looks familiar, though she's not one of his. Then he remembers the woman he looks out for on his way to and from work. Whose pregnancy he's been monitoring from a distance. Whom he saw in the antenatal clinic. He's about to go in and congratulate her but stops himself intruding.

He steps away and goes towards the nurses' station.

Despite my being more than usually busy, Gilda Francis rather preoccupies me. I remembered that I'd seen her before in the antenatal clinic, that time when she turned Faisal's head. I check in on her each time I'm on the ward and often find myself making a detour when I'm on my way to somewhere else. The nurses tell me she's had no visitors, despite having been so ill, so I stop and chat to her from time to time, making sure I say nothing alarming. I don't pry, but when I ask casually one day if her family is excited about the baby, she turns her head away from me and looks pointlessly out of the window. She's pulled her hair back in an elastic band, but I can see that it hasn't been brushed for some time – or washed for that matter – and that the neck of her nightgown is seamy. Her fingernails are beautifully manicured but grubby and her cuticles are ragged where she's been picking at them. I know the difference between privacy and isolation so I say nothing, but I start wondering what I can do to help her. She doesn't appear to be known to the authorities, so once she's discharged I can't be sure she'll have anyone keeping an eye on her. *I could pop in*, I think; *she only lives round the corner*. It's not something I would usually do, but her desolation is palpable and I'm concerned for the baby. All it would take is one phone call from a vigilant neighbour and she'd be sucked into a system whose hold is sometimes mighty.

One morning, as I come into her room, I see the baby lying right at the edge of the bed. The poor little creature's beside himself. Gilda sits like a bookend up against the pillows with a bottle dribbling listlessly into her gown.

She doesn't look at me as I rescue the bottle and the hysterical baby, and says nothing as I lay him in her arms. I put the bottle in her other hand and wrap my own round it as together we feed the baby. The room fills with the sound of greedy sucking and she closes her eyes and begins silently to weep. When the baby's fed, I sit on the bed and put my arm round her shoulders. She rests against me, exhausted and damp like a toddler who doesn't know how to stop.

A couple of days later, I'm taking a break from the wall-to-wall crises I've been fielding all day. I'm lying on the banquette in the staff room with my feet on the arm, the sugary traces of three doughnuts on the table at my head. I feel myself drifting, but the beeper on my belt shakes me awake.

Back to the fray.

As I hurry towards the delivery room, I see Purkiss talking to a smartly dressed man in the corridor outside.

'Hello, Miss Denham,' says Purkiss, 'you'd probably better be introduced. This is Paul . . .?'

'Paul Rogers,' the man says, holding out his hand, 'Wandsworth Social Services.'

I shake his hand. 'You're involved with this patient, are you?' I ask.

'Yes. For quite some time actually. We've already had to take Annette's first three children into care – they've been adopted now, thankfully – and I'm afraid I'm here with a Place Of Safety Order for this next little one. She's got a substantial history with us. In and out of care herself, self-harming . . .'

'I don't need to know the detail, Mr Rogers. You've got your job to do and so do I. I'll have someone tell you when the baby's been delivered.'

As I approach the table, the woman's smell makes me reel. The room's clinical air curdles with the reek of poverty and neglect and too many cigarettes smoked in shuttered rooms. Annette's body is clumsy with malnourishment and her pasty face is blotched with pain.

She sees me approach. 'Oi!' she yells. 'You the doctor? Get this fuckin' baby out of me, will ya? Place is full of fuckin' idiots – oww!'

The midwife turns to me. 'It's babies actually, Doctor. Annette's having twins, both breech. She came in already well into the third stage and the first baby's got stuck.'

'Why wasn't this picked up before she went into labour?'

'She hasn't been attending the antenatal clinic, unfortunately, so . . .'

'Fuckin' butchers!' Annette shouts, trying to sit up. 'Stickin' their fuckin' hands up yer cunt – course I didn't fuckin' go! Just get this baby out, will ya? For fuck's sake!'

I can feel the first baby's bottom. It's an extended breech, its legs straight up round its ears. The foetal monitor is showing signs of distress and the amniotic fluid is stained with meconium. The babies need to be delivered fast. Annette has her eyes closed and is whipping her head from side to side, moaning.

'Annette,' I say, 'Annette, listen to me. I'm going to have to deliver the babies with forceps. Do you know what that means?'

'Don't care what it fuckin' means! Just do yer fuckin' job!'

'I don't want you to tear, Annette, so I'm going to make a cut down here so we can get them out quickly.'

'Noo . . . o! They done that to me last time. Don't want no cut, d'ya hear me? You come near me with your knife and I'll fuckin' kill ya, swear to God!' She starts to thrash on the table, but her legs are in stirrups and she can't get down. 'Lemme go!' she screams. 'Lemme fuckin' go! I'll fuckin' get it out myself, ya stupid cunt!'

'Nurse, would you help Annette stay still, please? Annette, you need to lie as still as you can while I'm doing this.'

Two nurses position themselves at the patient's shoulders, holding her down firmly. I prepare the syringe of pudendal anaesthesia. I bend over and inject Annette's perineum.

Ruby's at my shoulder, her white coat crackling with venom. 'Waste of space,' she says, her wasp voice buzzing in my ear. 'Tub of lard. All she's ever done is fuck and breed, Virginia, fuck and breed. Stop her now. Stop her breeding more vermin. You know what you have to do.'

I pick up the scissors. Ruby's hands wrap themselves round mine, tentacle-tight.

'Spoil her,' she says. 'Spoil her fun. Make sure she never fucks again.'

She guides my fingers to the patient's groin, where a clumsy snip will ruin her pleasures. Put her out of the baby business. I hesitate. I slip my finger into the birth canal. I position the scissors. I know what I have to do.

I make a perfect medio-lateral cut.

'Coward!' Ruby hisses as she leaves.

Every time I hold a woman's womb in my hands, I struggle not to destroy it. I hold in my hands the part of her that defines her womanliness. That makes her not a man. The part where she grows new life, and I want to wrench it out of her. I want to smash it. I can. I have the power to kill it off and the skill to cover my tracks. No one would ever know. Sometimes the temptation startles my fingers and makes my vision fierce and fills me with a certainty that I rarely otherwise feel. Ruby is under my scrubs, pressed up against my wild heart, her arms snaking down my sleeves, her voice roaring, roaring in my ears, her will sapping mine and I teeter . . . I flail . . . I feel myself falling as she sucks the good out of me, leaving me a danger no longer to myself, but to another woman. She was there the first time I touched one. When I put my hands in the cadaver's guts and lifted it out, its cold dead history weighty in my palm. This is where you start, *she said.* Power of life and death, *she said.* This is where you choose, Virginia. Where you do what you do because you can. *I was poised to do it. I was. Her hand round mine, round the knife, was tender and firm. She loved me. I'd have done anything for her.*

But he stopped me. He saw me and he stopped me. He stopped me because he thought I was about to do something bad. He didn't realise it was love.

# 1976

Fortunately the pet shop keeps long hours and I stop by on my way home. The owner beams at me as I come in.

'Evening, Doc,' he says. 'What about that news then?'

'What news?'

'You haven't heard? That bloke – you know, that billionaire bloke, Howard Hughes – he just pegged it. On a plane going somewhere. Bloody weirdo, he was. Used to prance around naked because he was terrified of germs.'

'Not sure I know much about him, but it's a not uncommon phobia actually.'

'Bit difficult to have one of those if you've got dogs though, eh? How's Bugsy?'

'Gorgeous as ever,' I reply. 'Keeping me fit.'

'They take a lot of walking, Weimaraners, don't they? Bloke round the corner takes his two with him when he's training for the marathon. Says they can outrun him any old day. You've probably seen them on the Common – most people have. He puts them in these little vests the same colour as his. Dead cute, they are.'

'I think I did see him once, yes, but I expect he keeps different hours from me. I take Bugsy out very early before I go off to the hospital, and then again late at night when I'm back. Dog walker does the rest. But I'll keep an eye open for them next time I'm out.'

'What can I do you for today then?'

'Oh, he's been at it again. Slipped his collar off and chewed it to bits like he did before. D'you remember?'

'The little tinker! D'you want the same one again?'

'The black leather one with the studs – yes, please. Goes with his colouring.'

As I drive home along the seemly Tooting streets, the collar nudges the Dictaphone in my briefcase. It's bidding for the evening.

Over my dinner of Perrier with a Crystal Fall chaser, having cleared up a vase I smashed in the hall earlier, I plan the work I've brought home. I'm trying – and failing – to stifle my yearning. Ruby some-times remains incommunicado for months, never relating where she's been, who she's seen, what she's done, toying with me like a malevolent cat: *Now you see me, now you don't . . . see . . . don't . . . see . . . don't.* I stack the glasses and turn to go upstairs. Ruby's standing in the kitchen doorway looking furious. Her black hair is cut in a bob as glossy as the rubber catsuit she's wearing under thigh boots with shark's-teeth toes. She glares at me.

'Virginia!' she growls. 'You've been a bad, bad girl today. I'm very angry. You told me you'd mend your ways and do what you're told, but here I am, having to come back and discipline you again. Why won't you learn to follow orders?'

I shake my head.

'And what happens to naughty girls?'

I say nothing.

Ruby clacks closer on her spiky heels. She puts her face right up to mine, her acid breath burning my cheek. 'I asked you a question, bitch! What happens to bad girls?'

'They get punished,' I say, my voice reedy. 'They get hurt.'

'And they deserve it.'

'Yes, I deserve it.'

'Then get the ice cubes. Get them, I say! We have work to do, you and I. And you'd better be quick – I haven't got all night.' She stalks down the hall.

By the time I've put the ice cubes in a sock, dropped my clothes on the hall floor and walked upstairs, Ruby has readied the room. The new collar lies on the floor, two wristbands nesting in its coil, and a tribe of belts gathers nearby. The Dali has been taken off its bolt, from which chains now dangle above a studded plank on the floor. The chest of drawers has been shunted to the other side of the room, revealing the array of rings and hooks on the wall. An open pot of paint – daffodil yellow – gleams in a corner and Ruby stands in the middle of the floor, swinging two sets of keys from her black lacquered fingertips.

'You dare to stand?' she snaps. 'Dare to hold your head up? On your knees, dog – on the ground with you!'

I drop on to all fours.

'You know where to go. Take your place!'

I crawl across the floor, dragging my knees as heavily as I can across the jute flooring. I sit on the plank, the studs mobbing my buttocks, my back against the wall. Ruby straddles my legs and I look up at her towering above me.

'What shall I do with you?' she says. 'I can do anything I choose. Anything! What should I do to a girl who has been so, so bad? The baddest girl I've ever known.'

'I need to be punished, Ruby . . .'

Ruby bends down and jabs the points of the keys into my chest.

'Never, *never* call me Ruby,' she snarls. 'Did I give you permission to use my name?'

'No, Mistress. Sorry, Mistress.'

'Not sorry enough,' says Ruby. 'You can never be sorry enough. But you can be punished enough. You can be punished enough so you never do bad things again. Do you hear me?'

'Yes. I hear you, Mistress, and I'll never do bad things again.'

Ruby buckles the dog collar round my neck and I inhale the tart smell of new leather. I watch her beautiful hands with their oval nails strap the leather bands round my wrists and attach the chains to them with cleats. She runs her fingertips inside the bands to check on their tightness and I'm flooded with love. I'm safe. She runs the chains through the loops on the wall, padlocking the ends below the bolt. She straps belts in tight parallels down my body, along my legs, pinioning my bottom half like a mermaid's tail. A rubber gag holds a dog's ball in my mouth, wax plugs dull my hearing and my eyes look at nothing from behind the blindfold.

'I'm going to leave you now, bitch,' Ruby says. 'You'll stay there till you decide to be good.'

I nod and grunt. I know that she'll be dropping one set of keys into the paint pot now, and settling the other key ring round the ice-filled sock hanging from a hook on the wall to my left. She kicks my leg. The pain is beautiful. She loves me too.

'By the end of this evening,' she says, 'you're to be the best-behaved girl in the whole world. Do you understand? I'm leaving now and I won't be back. You can call out all you like, but no one will help you. You're alone, do you see? Alone with your wickedness, taking your punishment like the wretch you are.'

She slams the door as she leaves.

I descend into a place where there is no other consideration than what I feel. What I need. What I desire. Everything else drifts away like feathers from the mute-blind void in which I've been sealed by Ruby's trusted hand.

Here my impotence is mighty.

Bound like this I am free.

My thoughts melt into incoherent bliss. My identity crazes and shatters. No thinking, only feeling. No demands, only surrender. No one else. No loss, no insult, no longing. Only me.

Who knows how long it lasts?

Even through the earplugs I can hear the padlock keys falling on the floor as the ice melts and they drop off the sock. I reluctantly begin to surface, my body tingling, my mind flexing, the outside world impinging.

I slip my legs sideways and edge myself crampily to the left. A sigh as long as a death rattle escapes my chest. The keys lie in the damp patch left by the melted ice cubes. I pick them up with the tips of my fingers and raise my arms above my head, fumbling in the air until I find the padlock. Unbuckling myself is more painful than any whip-lash, since it returns me to my unattended life. I unmask myself and free my mouth and unplug my ears.

Ruby has placed the paint pot by my thigh. The keys are there at the bottom in case I can't wait for the others to drop off the sock. If I had to stick my hand in the pot and retrieve them it would be a messy admission of failure and I've never, ever failed. I can always wait. I roll up the belts and the collar and lock them in the top drawer of the chest, which I push back into its usual place. The young virgin goes back on the wall until Magda banishes her again. I throw the sock in the washing basket, slip on a robe and take the paint pot and a colander outside. My nipples harden in the evening chill and my feet leave prints in the frozen lawn as I go to the end of the garden. Behind the shed there's a hole covered with a dustbin lid, which I remove. I tip the paint through the colander and the yellow joins the maroon and the green and the violet looping round each other in the pit. The spare keys lie in the bowl, spitefully dripping paint down my robe. I keep white spirit in a half-gallon can in the shed, so I retrieve the container and go back into the house.

# 1976

Eleanor tidies the kitchen and stacks the sink. Mrs Bailey's coming today, so all she needs to do is a little light wiping. She leaves a note on the kitchen table to remind her to wash and iron the sheets and make a start on cleaning the house's extensive woodwork. She walks upstairs, spraying Lily of the Valley air freshener behind her as she goes, thinking about the busy day ahead. Yesterday she finished organising this season's talks for the WI, a role she has performed for the last seven years. She has transformed the programme from meetings where members bored everyone silly with their this-is-me-on-the-Acropolis slideshows, recruiting speakers to talk about current affairs and architecture, archaeology and astronomy. Jam is seldom mentioned. She has also sat on the committee of the local branch of the NSPCC for years, rising two years ago to chairman, voted in unanimously. She has insisted on being called chairman, eschewing the idiotic feminist term 'chair', because she's not a piece of furniture. Anyway she thinks chairman sounds more authoritative than chairwoman.

She has taken over the top floor of the house, her study window overlooking the back garden and her sewing room giving an uninterrupted view of the Royal Baths enthroned at the heart of the town. Some time ago she installed a bathroom on the landing between the two rooms, which is hers alone. William never set foot in it, though he'd paid the bills without demur, but had he ever entered, used the toilet perhaps, she would have locked it up and lobbed the key down the drain.

She goes in, as she does every morning, to dust and adjust the bottles and jars on the shelves, each one holding a creamy promise of youth. She dabs herself with a little extra Lanvin and pats her hair into place before going into her study.

This room is more her home than any other part of the house. Mrs Bailey doesn't venture this far because Eleanor told her she has particular ways of cleaning up here, so she should stop at the floor below. It suits Mrs Bailey well since it saves her rheumatic bones one more flight of stairs. On each side wall hangs a large framed picture of the infinite worlds beyond the earth, the planets sidling round the universe in one, and in the other the major constellations visible in the northern sky. By Eleanor's desk is a small but expertly engineered telescope, pointing towards the skylight. On a bank of shelves on the other side of the desk there are books on astronomy, more than in most libraries: one more and they'll start to colonise the rest of the room.

Apart from a cloisonné vase containing pencils and pens her desktop is clear, so when she's sat down she reaches into the drawer to pull out her materials. Today she begins the business of organising a fund-raising auction for the society and she spends a happy couple of hours making lists of possible donors and venues and printers, each detail checked and rechecked, cross-referenced where appropriate and alphabetised in clothbound notebooks. She hears the back door open and grudgingly goes downstairs to make Mrs Bailey a cup of tea. Not one of her special teas, which her cleaning lady reckons taste like talcum powder, but ordinary, mahogany-coloured tea with four sugars. Always with biscuits, because tea without biscuits is like a careless remark. With biscuits it's a conversation.

Mrs Bailey has her overall on and is scrubbing the Aga plates.

'Morning, Mrs D,' she says. 'Nice day for it, isn't it?'

'It's lovely, Mrs Bailey, yes. How's your elbow?'

'Mustn't complain. Doctor gave me some of those anti-inflammatory thingies and it's a bit easier today, but there'll be something else tomorrow.' There always is. Mrs Bailey has a compendious medical history and is at her most spirited when she is listing her complaints and her diagnoses and her treatments. Her day is made when she contracts something rare. Her favourite place in the world is under the doctor.

'Oh, don't be so pessimistic. You might even wake up healthy one day,' says Eleanor and makes Mrs Bailey's brew, leaving it on the table to cool along with three Scottish shortbread biscuits on a plate. She makes a cafetière of Costa Rican coffee for herself and sets it on a tray with a jug of milk and a bone china cup and saucer. No biscuits for her. As she leaves the room she says, 'Please don't forget the sheets, Mrs Bailey – they're in the laundry on the machine – and perhaps you'd be good enough to do the skirting boards today.'

'I saw your note, Mrs D. Last time I looked, my reading was coming along nicely.'

'Sorry – just wanted to make sure. I'm going to be up in my study – very busy day ahead – so do come and say goodbye when you've finished.'

'Okey-doke. Post came. It's on the hall table.'

Eleanor puts the tray on the floor as she looks through the small pile. She told everybody in William's life about his death but he still gets mail, which is vexing. There are people out there determined to remind her that she spent nearly forty years trapped in her iceberg marriage spinning fictions. Seeing Agnès around town reminds her. Every time she sees her silly mournful face she wants to smack it, but then people would know what had gone on and she'd have to endure the whispers.

William seems to have been on seventy per cent of the nation's mailing lists, so she leaves the offers of thermal underwear and surgical trusses on the hall table. She'll throw them away later.

She has three letters, two of which look official – the bank, probably – and one personal. This last one's in an envelope with a local postmark and is addressed to her in slightly untidy handwriting. She's intrigued. She rests them on the edge of her tray and goes upstairs.

Once she's poured her coffee, she opens the official letters, which are from the bank telling her of a) another hike in their charges and b) a gold credit card opportunity. She leaves the best till last.

There's no return address on the back of the envelope, so she's left guessing until she pulls out the letter, written on light blue Basildon Bond notepaper. She opens it up.

*Dear Mrs Denham*, it says, *I believe you are my mother.*

Words that could quicken the dead. Her vision blurs for a second. She checks that the door is closed and the window's secure.

This will come as a terrible shock to you, and of course you're free to bin the letter when you've read it, but I implore you to hear me out before you decide what to do. Give me a chance.

My name is Hermia Reynolds and I was born on 25th October 1944 in the home run by the Sisters of Mercy in Bletherington and adopted five days later by Sarah and Francis Marshall. A year later, they adopted my brother Benedict who, like me, was the result of a wartime liaison.

I was brought up in Leeds, where Sarah teaches English at the university and Francis writes and directs plays. For the last five years I've been Team Leader in the Fostering and Adoption team here in Harrogate, which probably won't come as a huge surprise.

Everybody I know claims to have had a happy family – it feels a bit rude to say anything else, doesn't it? – but mine really was and I never felt unloved. <u>Never.</u> Because Sarah's sandy and quite tall, people used to say I looked just like her. Strangely, even when they found out I was adopted they carried on saying it, as though that might wipe out the fact that my biological parents discarded me. Or couldn't keep me – perhaps that's closer to the mark. I don't want to offend you.

I wonder how you've thought about me over the years? Did you imagine me the same as you or very different? But perhaps you didn't imagine me at all. Maybe you've gone on to make a happy family of your own and put me out of your mind. If that's the case, I'm sorry. Actually, I'm sorry every which way. Sorry if you've been caused pain over the years since you gave me up, sorry that conceiving me was such a shameful thing and sorry if this letter hits you with it all over again.

Four years ago I married Jonathan, and two years later I had our first baby, Saskia. Jonathan wanted to call her something ordinary-with-a-twist, like Jayne or Karyn, but I put my foot down. I'm quite strong-minded really. As you'll see when we meet. If you'll meet me. Please.

Please write back. Or phone, if you can bear it. My address and phone number are at the top of this letter, but here they are again at the bottom.

Can I say 'with love'?

Hermia

Gerald's been dead for years, but she feels him walking into the room. Feels him standing behind her. Bending to kiss her temple. He straightens up and together they gaze at the letter. Hermia's parents read the letter again and again, its words curling round their memories like incense. The three of them dovetail into the family they could have been, Hermia the evidence of the desire that tilted Eleanor's world.

She puts the letter down and opens a drawer in the desk. She takes out writing paper and envelopes and stamps. She selects her finest fountain pen. Her hand hovers over the paper.

*Darling Hermia*, she writes.

# 1976

Every time the baby cries, Gilda knows he hates her. He turns his head away because she's the enemy. He closes his eyes so he doesn't have to see her. He pulls his knees into his chest to stop her changing his nappy. He cries when she picks him up, cries when she puts him down, pulls his mouth off the bottle to cry, is inconsolable at bath time. She goes to the toilet: he cries. She brushes her teeth: he cries. She puts on her clothes: he cries. He cries when she takes her clothes off. Sometimes when he's yowling in his cot, she lies on the floor of his perky room crying along with him. It's the only thing they share. She didn't buy any 'how-to' books because she thought she'd know how. But she's discovered she's got no idea. That she never did. She wasn't good enough/pretty enough/clever enough to keep Dilys at home and she's not good enough for the baby now. In the maddening hours just before dawn, she considers parcelling him up and popping him in the post for Mummy: *Dilys Francis, Wales, Special Delivery.*

Let her take over. She used to know how.

Her friends come round as often as she lets them to do all the gooing and ahhing babies are supposed to need. She doesn't tell them he hates her of course, and explains that he yells because he's got pyloric stenosis and will need an operation. She overheard two nurses on the ward talking about another baby and hopes it'll evoke sympathy, as much for her as for him. It does. 'Poor love!' they say and hug her. She looks brave and stoical and gets more hugs.

But when Karen cancels a visit, she knows it's not because she's got a cold and doesn't want to infect the baby, she knows it's because she's seen her with the baby and can tell he hates her. Now Karen hates her too.

She does her best to get her figure back because she wants to destroy the evidence. Fortunately Miss Denham's an excellent seamstress and the scar will be a reprimand visible only to her and her bikini. She last saw Miss Denham a week ago at the hospital and has been signed off. When the doctor reached over to the desk to pick up a file, she saw the silver tracery of scars on her arm and wondered. Miss Denham's a bit funny-looking – nothing that a good haircut and a bit of mascara wouldn't fix – but seems to understand that having babies isn't a cakewalk. Gilda didn't tell her how frightened she is, but she remembers her arm round her that time she couldn't get the baby to feed. She smelled good, the doctor: Gilda could have been dozing in a bubble bath against her shoulder. When she was asked at the last appointment how things were going, she thought she said 'awesome', but Miss Denham looked at her strangely, as though she'd said 'awful'. She didn't think she had, but nowadays there are times she doesn't know what she's said as fatigue and fear and failure wind round her head and suck her thoughts right out.

The baby's cried himself to sleep upstairs and she sits in the kitchen with a cup of black tea – all she's allowing herself today in penance for eating a whole steak pie last night in the despair that midnight brings. The doorbell chimes. She's tempted not to answer it because her hair's hauled back in a ponytail and she hasn't bothered to put a face on, but she's not expecting anyone and it might be the postman. She keeps thinking Dilys is going to write to her.

'Oh, I'm so sorry,' Miss Denham says when Gilda opens the door. 'Have I come at an inconvenient time?'

'No . . . well, I . . . no. Really. No.'

'I think I told you the other day that I live round the corner, so we're practically neighbours. After I'd finished work this morning, I was just picking up a cheesecake in the Polish deli and thought I'd pop in to see if you'd like to share it with me – there's far too much for one person. And to see your lovely baby of course.'

'That's very kind of you, but . . .'

There's a howl from upstairs.

'Oh god. Oh god. Oh Christ – he's off again.' She slumps against the wall, her hand over her eyes.

Miss Denham's inside. She's shutting the door. She's walking with her to the kitchen, her arm round her shoulders.

Gilda's sitting on a stool at the breakfast bar. She doesn't know how she got here. There's a slice of cheesecake in front of her but she can't reach for it because her hands are over her ears. Trying to shut out the racket. The baby's clamour shoots through her fingers, straight into her head and splinters against her skull. Miss Denham's saying something to him upstairs in a gentle voice but all Gilda can hear is his need and her terror moiling round her head.

He's here. Oh god, he's here. Miss Denham's brought him down. She clamps her eyes shut. She knows he'll be squirming, his back and legs strong enough to throw himself out of stupid arms. Maybe Miss Denham's here to take him away. Report her to the authorities. She hears the blame in the baby's voice. He's telling Miss Denham everything so she can rescue him from her stupid arms. Find him a proper mother.

She pushes her hands more fiercely against her head and all she can hear is silence. They've gone. She can open her eyes. She can lower her hands.

But they're still here. The baby's in Miss Denham's arms, his black hair fussed up against her jacket. He's sucking contentedly on the bottle she's holding in his mouth at just the right angle. In this battle-ground house where she's assassin and target all at once. Miss Denham's smiling. At him, then at her, as though they're related.

'There,' she's saying, 'he was a hungry little chap.'

Gilda's empty too. Like there's this big fat hopeless space inside her.

The baby takes the bottle. All of it. The baby lies over Miss Denham's shoulder and gives a big wet burp. Milky goo spurts down her jacket. 'Oops!' she says, as though it's nothing. As though he isn't chucking back what she's given him because it's toxic. She finds a piece of kitchen paper and dabs the goo off her shoulder. The baby's fallen asleep, his features clear now in his face. Gilda's only ever seen them folded in rage and accusation.

'Why don't you hold him now?' Miss Denham's saying, and she's bringing him over to her side of the breakfast bar. Miss Denham's holding him out to her, but she can't move her arms. Panic's pounding her ribs.

'I can't,' she says, 'he doesn't want me.'

'There's no one he wants more,' says Miss Denham, smiling at Gilda as though she's his mother. As though she loves him and he loves her right back. She unfolds her rusty arms. She's holding the baby. He's beautiful. The corners of his generous mouth are twitching upwards. 'He's smiling,' she says.

She's crying. 'He's smiling at me?'

'Of course. He looks very happy there in your arms. You both look happy.'

She does?

The baby twitches.

'Oh no,' she says, 'he's off again.'

His eyes open and he begins to wriggle in her arms. His mouth opens and he bleats. Just a little bleat, but the yelling comes next.

'What does he want?' she says. 'What does he want from me? I don't know what he wants!'

'Well, I think I heard a bit of a rumble down below when I was winding him. Probably a good idea to check his nappy. Where do you usually change him?'

Gilda jerks her head upwards.

'Jolly good. Let's go up there then, shall we?'

Miss Denham walks upstairs behind her. As though Gilda's the queen. As though she's in charge. But perhaps she's just there to catch her when she falls.

When she lays him on the changing mat, he stops wriggling. It's a miracle. He keeps his legs down when she takes off the eggy nappy. Another miracle. When she's wiped him and creamed him and put the new nappy underneath him, he pees. It's not a denunciation, it's a pee.

'Little monkey,' Miss Denham says. 'Just testing Mum, are you?'

'He does that all the time.'

'Has he ever peed in his own face?' Miss Denham asks. 'Little boys do that sometimes. It gives them a terrible shock.' She laughs.

'He's only ever peed on me.'

'Just you wait. It'll happen.'

When he's got his clothes back on, he falls asleep over her shoulder. She feels his belly's warmth, his breath's flutter. 'What should I do now?' she asks.

'Well, he's had his food, so it's our turn now, I think. Why don't you settle him in his cot and I'll go and make us some coffee.'

She's alone with him now, in this room where she's never felt more alone. But he's on her shoulder like he's rooted into her. She almost doesn't want to put him down, but Miss Denham's downstairs waiting. She holds her breath as she lays him in the cot on his tummy and stiffens when he peeps. But it's a going-to-sleep peep and he lies still on the stripy sheet, full and satisfied and dreaming.

The kitchen's rich with the smell of coffee. She thought she'd run out of the ground stuff, but the cafetière is sitting in its cosy on the worktop.

'I picked up some lovely Honduran coffee from Whittard's on my travels today. Have you ever tried it?'

Gilda shakes her head.

'Well, it's enough to make grown men crumble – but then we tend to be the stronger sex, don't we?'

'I don't feel very strong, to tell you the truth. Having the baby's sort of knocked the stuffing out of me. Ever since I left home I've been in control of my own life, you know? I've made my own decisions, done everything my own way, but he just makes me feel out of control. Like *I'm* the baby again. When he kicks his legs in the air and screams like that, I want to lie on the floor and do it too. I do sometimes, actually. Must look ridiculous, but I feel better afterwards. Thank Christ I don't live with anyone – they'd think I'd gone awol.'

'Is his dad not around?'

'His dad doesn't know he's a dad. And his granddad doesn't know he's a granddad either. And I'm not about to tell him. The Brethren wouldn't exactly approve.'

'Brethren?'

'Plymouth Brethren – nutters.'

'How about your mum? Are you in touch with her?'

There's a long pause.

Virginia waits.

Gilda looks as bleak as she did when Virginia arrived. 'No,' she says finally. 'I'm not in touch with her. She tried to be in touch with me, but . . . I don't want to talk about it, OK? Sorry to be rude.'

'Not rude at all. Sorry to have been intrusive.'

They finish the cafetière and work their way through the cheesecake. Gilda manages two generous slices and watches Miss Denham finish the rest. *She must be hungry,* she thinks, but there's something frantic in the way she stuffs it into her mouth that reminds her of the baby.

The following Saturday is uncharacteristically warm and Gilda decides to go out for a walk. Maxim phoned her last night and she's feeling pressurised.

'Just checking, sweetie,' he said. 'We miss you horribly. Pamela's been doing your ladies, but I've had complaints. Had to redo a tan myself the other day – lady looked like a plate of streaky bacon, and I had to refund her the money. D'you know when you're coming back? Make it soon, please. Pretty, pretty please?'

'Give me three months, Maxim. That should do it. Have to find a nursery that fits in with work but there's not many of them about and they're bloody expensive.'

'Then we'll talk about money, darling. I'm not stupid. I know what little ones cost.'

A bit of fresh air might help her think. The baby's had his first snuffle and he's hoiked her out of bed four or five times a night, three nights running. In the lonely early hours she tried to resist the feeling that it was deliberate, but found herself giving him a resentful shove when she put him back in the cot. One time his moaning seeped under her skin and she felt a tingle rush across her palms. She put him down carefully and took herself as far away from him as she could. Standing in the garden, every part of her body was trembling and it wasn't the cold. If she hadn't put him down, she'd have hit him.

She's sombre now as she zips up the baby's coat and puts him in his pram. He has Raymond's round face and short fingers, but he has her light eyes. His vulnerability terrifies her. Since he's been born, the world's become a dangerous place and she sometimes has to tell herself out loud that the Yorkshire Ripper isn't coming for her. Unless he fucks up again and mistakes her for a whore.

As she's leaving the house, she sees Miss Denham walking towards her. She's only seen her in work clothes before and is startled to see her wearing a huge jumper with cherries on the front and jeans with zips at the hems that stop suddenly above her ankles. She's wearing the kind of sandals that beardy men who like folk songs and fell walking wear with amusing socks.

'Miss Denham!' she says. 'How lovely to see you.'

'I'm off duty now, Gilda. Try calling me Virginia. Thought I'd just pop round and see how you were, but you look like you're on your way out.'

'Just to the Common. Needed some fresh air – clear the cobwebs, you know?'

'D'you fancy company?'

'Oh yes please. Haven't had a proper conversation in days.'

Walking down the street together they make an odd couple. Gilda's dainty as a doily in her lavender trench coat and tight fawn boots and Virginia stoop-clomps beside her, nearly a foot taller, but someone seeing them together might have taken them for friends.

By the time they've done two circuits of the Common they're not yet friends, but they know each other better. Virginia knows that Gilda was raised in Birmingham, which accounts for the occasional adenoidal vowel, and Gilda knows that Virginia decided to be a doctor when she was very young and has no children of her own. 'But one of the great thrills of my job is helping other women have theirs,' she says, 'especially when there've been difficulties.'

It's lunchtime by the time they get back to Gilda's house and the baby's rowdy with hunger.

Virginia sees Gilda's face and says, 'It really gets to you when he fusses, doesn't it?'

'It just throws a switch somewhere, if you want the truth. Makes me feel helpless.'

'I quite understand. Terrifying to be in someone else's grip. Do you want a hand feeding him? I've got nothing else planned.'

Gilda's relief feels like a sudden hot wind. 'Would you?' she says. 'I could offer you lunch.'

There's a meteorological shift in the house with Virginia there, and when the baby's been fed and rocked to sleep in his bouncy chair, the two women retire to the kitchen. Gilda goes towards the fridge, Virginia insists that she sits down while she pillages the cupboards to make minestrone soup and bread and cheese and baked bananas and cream. They eat slowly, talking fast, Virginia's eyes constantly flicking back to the cupboards. Gilda stops eating several plates ahead of her friend, who gets up to make coffee when she's finished. She finds a bag of ancient macaroons behind the bread bin and carries them to the table triumphantly. 'Always room for more!' she says.

Over the following weeks, Gilda learns about the baby. And herself. She learns that there are moments when he's just out of sorts, despite being clean and dry and full. That she's not at fault. That there'll come a time when he has words to tell her what he's feeling, but that right now her job is to listen and imagine. She learns that the passions he arouses are more sublime and more crushing than any she's ever felt before. She learns that this is the love affair she's been waiting for.

Virginia's learning too. There's something she recognises about Gilda, as though she's looking in the mirror and seeing two faces instead of one. One evening as she's getting out of the bath she says aloud, 'Gilda is my friend,' and it's like rolling a gobstopper round her mouth: awkward, rattly, but impossibly sweet. She's stepping over the line between doctor and patient, but it doesn't feel wrong. She practises saying 'friend'. She says it over and over till it sounds like gibberish. There's no history to call on, apart from Aurora, no previous convictions for intimacy, but spending time with Gilda, and her son, doesn't feel like a decision. It feels like something she needs.

The two women meet regularly and it's always a pleasure. That's what they say when they part, and it's not a vapid social tic. Usually they stay at Gilda's house or go to the Common, but one Saturday, a month after she's gone back to work, she suggests going to the

Hayward Gallery to see a Magritte exhibition. He was Graham's favourite, but she's never seen the paintings in the flesh.

'What a good idea,' Virginia says. 'It's something I always mean to do but never quite manage. Laziness probably. But I do like Magritte, what little I've seen of him.'

The two women go round the exhibition at their own speed, Virginia charging through the galleries as if she badly needs to pee, Gilda at a more leisurely pace. Having been brought up in a community where all forms of art, even the sacred, were regarded as profane, she's had to teach herself to stay with a painting long enough to refract it through her own internal prism. She's becoming increasingly disturbed by the feelings of alienation and loss and grief that the paintings evoke in her and by the time she reaches the last gallery she's quietly in tears. Virginia has finally stopped running and is standing rapt in front of a descending series of small canvases, each one depicting a portion of a woman's body. She has her hands clasped at the back of her head, as though to stop it rocking off her neck.

Gilda moves to her side.

'I can't believe it's here,' Virginia says. 'That I'm really seeing it. I love this painting. I saw a reproduction once in a magazine a patient left behind and tracked down a print. It's always seemed to me to speak volumes about how women experience themselves in a man's world. Don't you think?' When Gilda doesn't answer, Virginia looks at her properly. 'Oh Lord, I'm sorry,' she says, 'have I upset you?'

'Not you, no,' Gilda says, her voice thickening as she tries to stifle a sob. 'Just what these paintings are doing to me. I . . . I think I have to leave, if you don't mind.'

They go to a café in The Cut, which is full of enough conversation to cover the sound of weeping, and Virginia comes back to their corner table with three doorstep sandwiches and a pot of tea.

'Cheese and pickle and ham and chicken,' she says. 'Take your pick. I can always get more.'

Gilda wants to tell Virginia about herself but she feels like a feathery moth emerging from its pupa, its wings untried and folded. She holds her breath for a moment, and begins.

It's too risky to look her friend in the eye while she's talking, so she examines the tabletop intently. What she says temporarily stops Virginia eating. She tells her of a girl sitting alone in cabbagey class-rooms while the other girls read or sketched or played games. Tells her of a girl in formless frocks and knee-length socks adrift in a flurry of circular skirts and paper nylon petticoats. Tells her of the rows of women in the Assembly, each one wearing a blue headscarf, their hair uncut and pulled back, their heads bowed. Tells her of the injunc-tion to women to Submit And Be Silent.

'But that was OK,' she says, 'they were my people, after all, and I felt more at home at Ebenezer Hall than I ever did at school. I suppose I felt chosen in some way, you know? My mother always said she and Daddy'd chosen to have an only child, but I was never quite sure about that because everyone else had loads. Then she fucked off. Told me all that crap about finding a boy among the Brethren, then she found the next-door neighbour. He was a fucking atheist too. Didn't say anything – or not to me anyway – just disappeared over the horizon. At least if she'd killed herself she'd have left a note. Don't know where she went either, though I suppose it was probably Wales. All these Brethren and Sistern came round to support my father – they did lots of praying and singing hymns and stuff – but no one seemed to notice she'd left me too. She wrote me letters after a few months. No return address of course – strange that. Sent them to a friend of hers who wasn't one of the Sistern. Her friend waited for me by the school gates and gave me the first one. I told her I didn't want it, but she came back every week with another one. I told her that I didn't have a mother. That she'd died and gone to hell. "She'll send for you," the friend said, "when she's settled," but she never did. I used to think she'd probably had another baby and forgotten me, because the letters dried up after a bit.

'I was called Rebecca then, but when Daddy slung me out, I changed my name because I wanted to take charge of my own life. He didn't want anything to do with me and I didn't want him right back. I saw the film *Gilda* on Sunday afternoon telly when I was staying at the hostel. I love Rita Hayworth in that scene where she peels off her glove and chucks it at the men – and then her necklace. She just knows what she wants and goes ahead and gets it. I wanted to be like that. Live by my own rules. It's kind of why I got into karate. To be able to defend myself, you know? And I'm good. Takeshi – that's my teacher – says I'm the best girl in the class. Actually I'm the only girl in the class, so that's not so hard, but I'm a brown belt now and I can beat most men. At the dojo anyway. In my life? Not so much. It's like that old thing – you know: "You start off sinking into his arms and you end up with your arms in his sink." That'll be me. Every time.'

The baby's sleeping in his buggy and she bends down to stroke his thistledown hair. He stirs and she takes her hand away quickly. She sits up and braves what she'll see on Virginia's face. What she sees is compassion.

'I'm sorry to rabbit on like this,' she says, 'but I've only ever told little bits of this before – and only to Raymond before he fucked off too. Never felt I could trust anyone – well, until Graham introduced me to the scene anyway. Then I learned what trust really was. Like putting yourself in someone's hands because you know they won't let you die. D'you know what I mean?'

'Not exactly. What do you mean by the scene?'

The baby interrupts.

Gilda picks him up. 'I'll tell you,' she says. 'Perhaps not here, though. Don't want to shock the baby. I've decided what to call him by the way. Now I've got to know him better.' She holds him up and he gives her a gummy grin. 'Tobias, meet Virginia.' She waves his hand and speaks in a squeaky voice. 'Hi, Virginia, my name's Tobias, and I'm going to live to a hundred and two.' She grins. 'I know that's a bit of a stretch, but Tobias in the Bible made it. Must've been all that guardian angel stuff.' She nuzzles the baby in the neck and he squirms with pleasure. 'I'm going to keep you safe, baby. Forever and ever, amen.' She leans over and takes half a sandwich. 'I'm hungry now,' she says. 'All this talking and everything.'

Gilda's noticed that sometimes Virginia doesn't eat, but when she invited her to dinner after the gallery, she insisted on bringing a contribution. 'I like to cook,' she said. 'Especially for friends.' When she arrived, she brought with her a salmon roulade and a bowl of ceviche and a chocolate and brandy mousse. 'Just a little something,' she said. 'To top and tail the meal.'

When they get back, Gilda makes the chicken casserole that she'd planned and the roast potatoes, but she reduces the quantities and hopes she's got enough Tupperware for the leftovers. After he's been fed, Virginia takes the newly named baby upstairs to bath him and Gilda hears her singing nursery rhymes in a tuneless crack of a voice.

Virginia's brought wine too – three bottles, two white and one red – and she's poured herself a hefty glass by the time Gilda comes down from putting Tobias to bed. From the look of the bottle it isn't her first. They talk freely as they eat the meal, but there's a hint of something that's biding its time.

There are no leftovers and Gilda stands up to make coffee. When she turns back to the table, Virginia's gulping cream straight from the carton.

'Just finishing the dregs,' she says, 'can't bear waste,' and she wipes the white moustache from her lip with her sleeve.

Gilda's living room is a graceful space, with low-slung furniture in creams and yellows and a taupe carpet. As they sit down with their coffees, Virginia's arm suddenly jerks and the contents of her cup spill on the floor. She is devastated, Gilda phlegmatic.

'Oh, don't worry about it,' she says as she mops up the mess, 'really, Virginia. I'm going to have to replace all this stuff soon anyway when Tobias gets more mobile. Look, he's stained the sofa here already – and here too – with his chuck-ups, and I'm not so sure Ribena and cream wool is such a great combination.' She brings Virginia another cup and sits down opposite her.

'Look, you were asking me about the scene earlier and I said I'd tell you about it. It's not for everyone, but it was where I truly belonged for a while. My first boyfriend when I came to London came from this really posh background. You know, boarding school and all that, and he was my teacher in all sorts of ways. Introduced me to books and films and art and stuff and I really looked up to him. Too much probably. So when he told me he went to these parties and asked if I wanted to go, of course I said yes. All he said was that they were gatherings of people who liked the same things, and I'm thinking he must mean the arts, so the first time I go's a bit of a shock. I'm all tarted up for a regular party and when I walk in there's all these people in the room and they're dressed up in rubber and leather and there's whips and chains and canes and gags and things and they're doing stuff to each other I can't believe. Like hurting each other deliberately. And when Graham takes his raincoat off, he's dressed the same and it's like someone's turned him into a frog, except frogs don't tend to have pierced nipples. Well, maybe I haven't met enough frogs. He sees my face and he tries to make it OK, but I'm trembling all over. Like in shock, you know? And there's this guy in a mask that's tied to a cross and this girl's hitting him with a cane and his head's going from side to side and he's moaning and she's carrying on and I say to Graham, "Stop her, Gra', for Christ's sake – she's hurting him." He gives me this big hug and he says, "It's OK, love, it's OK. No one does anything to anyone here that they don't want. If he can't take it any longer, he just says the safe word and she stops. Just like that." And that's the thing, Virginia. When you're playing – that's what it's called – you've got to trust your partner with your life, because what she's doing could kill you. I don't find it easy to trust people mostly, but I trusted Graham – and my other two boyfriends from the scene – more than I've trusted anyone ever. *Ever!* Do you see?'

Virginia sees almost too clearly. She tries to nod her head. Tries to remain impassive.

'Probably straight people think it's disgusting or just for perverts or funny or something – or that it's something only tarts do. There's this woman over in Streatham who's doing it for a living – funnily enough, her name's Cynthia Payne – but that's different. I mean that's more of a brothel thing, not a bunch of like-minded people getting together to play. Graham was amazing – he was really gentle with me and never pushed me to do anything I wasn't comfortable with. I started off as a sub but once I'd learned the ropes' – she giggles – 'I found I was better at being a top. Suited all three of my boyfriends anyway. I know it seems like a weird thing to be into, but you'd be surprised, there's plenty of people who're interested – who fantasise about it, you know? – but they don't dare get involved because it scares the shit out of them. Scares them to imagine trusting anybody that much.'

She has her eyes on Virginia's face. She takes a deep breath. 'Look,

Virginia, I've got a feeling you may be one of them. I've seen the cuts on your arm . . .'

'Gardening probably.' Virginia clears her throat. 'Roses sometimes object when you prune them.'

'. . . And bruises on your wrists. You don't have to answer me now. I'm just sort of sowing the seeds. You know, just in case. I was on the scene for eight years – Raymond was my only boyfriend from what we called the vanilla world – and when he fucked off, I was all for going back because truly it's the safest place I know. But the baby's changed all that. I don't need it any more. But if you want, I'll introduce you. You'll find yourself with people who share something with you at the deepest level you've ever known. You've done so much for me and I'd really like to do something for you in return. Give you something back, you know? Look, can I show you something? Upstairs? Just so you get a feel for it?'

Virginia's head is melting.

Gilda puts her cup down and stands up. She holds out her hand and Virginia takes it. She follows Gilda upstairs, moving stiffly, as though she's been nailed to a plank.

Gilda leads the way into her bedroom, which eschews the elegance of downstairs. The room smells of roses and is a riot of femininity: wherever it's possible to fix a flounce or a frill or a furbelow, several have been fixed. They have clearly been breeding.

'Why don't you sit there?' says Gilda, gesturing to the bed, and Virginia sits at the end, on the edge, to stop herself falling in.

Gilda opens her wardrobe. 'Have a look at these,' she says, and unhooks the last seven hangers from the bar. When she's laid them on the bed behind Virginia, she stands back.

She watches.

It takes five minutes. Virginia's eyes are closed when finally she turns. She opens them and rocks back as though she's been hit. She puts out a tentative hand and runs it across the studs on a red leather bustier. She picks up a latex gown and drapes it over her arm, where it hangs like an eviscerated body. She pats a pile of belts, metal rings loitering on the leather, and a pair of PVC leggings.

'Try something, why don't you?' Gilda says softly. 'Just to see what it feels like. Here, how about one of these?' She finds a pair of latex gloves and holds them out. 'Not sure shocking pink's quite your colour, but you'll love how tight they are. Like a second skin.'

Virginia takes a glove and holds it firmly between thumb and fore-finger as though it might otherwise vaporise. She stiffens her left hand and slides her bunched fingers into the glove, feeling the powdery insides slip like baby skin over her flesh. She pushes her fingers further in, thumb first, then the other four. The glove resists and she pushes harder, tugging at the wrist. She grinds her teeth as she pushes, her hand sweating now, her fear rising now. She tries to weasel her fingers in, but the rubber's not having it. She tugs and shoves one last time and her fingers slowly, stickily, reach the glove's tips. Except for her middle finger, which pushes through the split it's made.

'Oh,' she says. 'Oh.'

'I'm so sorry,' says Gilda, coming over, 'it must have perished. I haven't worn them for such a long time – maybe I didn't powder them properly when I put them away. Let me . . .' she puts her hand out to help her take it off.

But Virginia's on her feet, tearing at it as though it's singed her skin. 'No,' she says, 'no. This is all wrong. You're wrong. Couldn't be more wrong, as a matter of fact. Maybe if you're into this sort of thing you see it everywhere, Gilda, but not in me, OK? It doesn't suit me at all, OK? You go ahead and do it – go right ahead, but count me out.'

'I didn't want to shock you . . .'

'Not shocked. I'm *not* shocked, OK? I'm sorry I split your glove. Tell me where they came from and I'll get another pair. Good Lord, is that the time? I'd better go now. Better go. It's been a great day. Really great, thanks a lot. I'll pick the dishes up next time we meet. See you soon then. Sleep well. Going now. Bye!'

She clumps down the stairs and out of the house.


It begins to rain as I hurry back home. Of course it didn't fit. *I* don't fit. I remember standing shivering among the prattle of girls on the sports field when the captains chose their teams. I was always the booby prize because I'd drop the ball or break my racquet or trip over my boots, so mostly I loafed on the sidelines while the others played the game. I'd halloo along with the rest of them, but the victory was never mine. Gilda's trying to pull me out of the ranks, but the risk unsteadies me. I so badly want some of that. Some of the world she's offering me. I long for the affinity that comes with the exchange. With the bold, bare fact of the other.

But joining them means losing my self.

I close the door behind me as I step into my morgue-quiet home. I stand in the hall. I'm sitting outside the study in the house of deaf ears, straining to hear the sounds of Father's life. I'm in Mother's wardrobe, her frocks stroking my cheek. I'm on the playground wall, watching the other girls skipping and singing. My legs aren't working. My arms aren't working. It feels too hopeful to stay standing, so I sit on the floor and slump against the wall, the skirting board pressing into my back. I press back. The pain is a blessed relief.

But I have to do something. Keep moving. I think maybe I'll do some work but the study feels airless and claustrophobic. I can't be bothered to run a bath. Sorting something is often soothing, so I go to the understairs cupboard to check through my dusters, but Magda is punctilious and there's nothing to chuck out or fold.

I'm pinging like a pinball from room to room and when I ping into the living room for the fourth time, Ruby's at the window with her back to me. She's wearing an emerald shot-silk frock and when she turns round, she fixes me with her green eyes, luminous as spotlights. I look away and walk over to the chesterfield. The silk rustles as she comes to stand behind me, so close I can feel the warmth of her thighs on the back of my head. She says nothing. I say nothing. It's less that there's nothing to say, more that what would be said would be incendiary. The longer I sit trying not to turn round, the more my neck goes into spasm and my head starts to twitch.

She speaks, her words coming from the centre of the earth. 'I. Have. The. Box,' she says.

'Please, Ruby,' I say, 'don't. I don't want to. Not now. I want . . . I want . . . I want . . . I don't know what I want – just not that.' I'm flapping like a dying flounder.

'You never do. But I *always* do. I always give you what you want. *Exactly* what you want.'

'You do – you do. But suppose Gilda can too? Suppose she knows what I want too? Suppose . . . please come and sit down. I need to see you.'

She's on the sofa next to me, pushed so tightly against my body we could be the same person. We both look straight ahead and see nothing. I don't know where to put myself.

'I don't know where to put myself,' I say. 'Don't know what to think. She wants me to join them. She knows who I am, don't you see? She could tell just by looking at me – like I'm made of glass. No one's ever seen that before and it's terrifying. Or thrilling. That's what it is – it's thrilling.'

'Go and jump off the hospital roof if you want thrills. Go and stand on the wing of an aeroplane. It's safer than going off with a stranger. A *patient*, for Christ's sake, Virginia? Why do you think I jogged your elbow at her house?'

I stand up. I walk round the room. Ruby dogs my footsteps. What the fuck am I doing?

'What the fuck am I doing?' I say. 'I want to go to her, Ruby. She's offering me something . . . something . . . She's the same as me . . .'

'. . . And I'm not?'

'Of course you are. You've always been the same as me. I'm safe with you. I love you, Ruby – you know that. When you're here, I'm all of me at once. I'm not alone any more because you feel my feelings. You think my thoughts. But there are other people like me. Gilda's one of them. Others. I'm one of them. Maybe I can t– . . . I can tr– . . . I can . . .' The word is monumental. The word swells in my throat. The word stops my breath. Ruby is in front of me, her face pressed into mine. I can see my eyes in hers. I am sinking into her.

'*Trusssst?*' she says. Her breath smells of arsenic, '*Trusssst?* Trust will flay you, Virginia. Trust kills.' She's holding my hands, pinning my arms to my sides. Her hands are icy. 'Come upstairs,' she says, 'to the bathroom. You need me. Now.'

I'm weeping. Quietly at first, but then loudly, wildly, as though there are centuries of tears backed up in me. Her face contorts. She bares her teeth. I think she's going to bite me.

'You are *nothing* without me,' she says. 'Without me you live a half-life. If you go to her, you'll hang from her like a puppet. If you go to her, I'll leave you.'

We go to the bathroom.

Gilda's wondered why she's never been invited to Virginia's house, but has assumed it's because Virginia knows it's easier for them to meet at hers, what with Tobias and everything. She knows her house number though, and on her way to the corner shop the next morning she stops outside number 96. The house looks like its neighbours, but is mysterious, as though it has turned its face from the road.

She takes a pale blue envelope out of the nappy bag, slips it through the letter box and walks on.

The letter lies under a pile of circulars and local rags when I get home. I put it next to the rosewood box and go to the kitchen to fetch wine and pitta bread and nuts and taramasalata and cornichons. I drop a glass on the kitchen tiles and cut two of my fingers clearing up the debris. I close the wounds as expertly as I do at work and take the meal's preamble to the living room. The Médoc needs time to breathe, but I can't wait. I fetch another bottle from the cellar – a Puligny-Montrachet, good vintage – and pop it in the fridge to chill.

I'm intrigued by the envelope since I rarely receive personal letters and never write them. At the hospital I have a file in my desk of letters from grateful patients, but they belong at work. They're testimonials, not love letters.

I select three cashews and four almonds, a macadamia nut and two hazelnuts and stuff them in my mouth. I slit open the blue envelope carefully with my thumb, trying to avoid a paper cut. I look at the signature first. Her handwriting jives across the page.

Dear Virginia,
I think this friendship has been unexpected for both of us. I've never been friends with a doctor before, though I've come across

several in the world I told you about last night. But unexpected doesn't mean unwanted. I desperately want Tobias to know his own mind as I've come to know mine – though I thought I was losing it when he was first born. The simple fact that I'm sitting here peacefully with him peacefully asleep next door is down to you. What you saw going on between him and me. What you know about me.

And now you know more. I'd like to know more about you too, but I can wait for you to tell me. I'm good at waiting.

I'll leave it to you to decide when we meet again, but I really hope it's soon. I can hear my baby chirruping in his sleep. He must be having a happy dream.

Lots of love,

Gilda xxx


I go to the study and find the postcard I bought in the Paracas museum in Lima. I took time away from the conference and went to see the strange deformed skulls of pre-Incan people who strapped their babies' heads to planks to elongate them. To bring them into the tribe or mark them out as royalty. No one would take me for a queen but I am a pointed head in the land of the round.

Gilda has a pointed head too.

I turn it over and write. *I'll be over on Sunday*, I say, *bright and early*. I don't sign it. She'll know. I address it and stick a stamp on it and leave it on the hall table for posting tomorrow.

I go on Sunday, but we don't mention the glove. Or what it means. But what we know about each other subtitles our friendship from then on.

# 1949

Eleanor sits at her dressing table, daubing cold cream on her face. She's managed to get through today by sheer force of will, just like every other day in the last four years. Since Gerald died of a heart attack six months after William came back, she has woken every morning outraged that she's still alive. Her God refuses her the relief of suicide and He and Gerald have walked off arm in arm without a backward glance at the smoking pyre of her life. For a while she was furious with Gerald for dying, as though he'd deferred to William out of some misplaced gentlemanliness, but she's beyond that now and feels only grief. Dragging, relentless grief whose undertow threatens to drown her.

She went back to York six weeks after his funeral. She stood outside the tea rooms' door for so long, a waitress came out to ask her if she was feeling ill. She said she was fine, thanks all the same. Just waiting for a friend, she said, and the girl retreated. But there's no waiting for the dead, so she finally had to go inside. A young couple were just leaving her and Gerald's table and she hovered round it for a moment before sitting down in what had been his chair. The debris on the table – the half-drunk cup of tea, the flakes of pastry, the paper case smeared with chocolate – felt like a ruination. She surprised the waitress who came to clear the table by saying she'd rather drink her tea with the table still mucky, thank you. 'I know it's mad,' she said. 'Humour me.'

When she went to the Bideawee, its sign said No Vacancies. Someone else was making love in their bed. Someone else with a future. She sat numbly on the grassy verge, careless of the stains on her skirt. She stayed there until nightfall, then went back to the house she kept ruthlessly clean.

Virginia had a birthday party today, her eleventh, though 'party' hardly describes the small gathering at the farm. She invited that rather suspect girl Aurora, whose parents turn up at school events looking like gypsies despite being stinking rich, and two other mousy classmates, Beryl and Marian, who are dreadfully clever but dreadfully dull.

Elsie put on a feast for the girls. Ever since rationing came in she's found ways of circumventing the rules, so Eleanor's larder is always amply stocked. Her body discovered its curves when Gerald was alive, but since he died she's become so thin she can do without a waspie for Dior's New Look. Virginia's shooting up so she supposes she should take her shopping for clothes, but it's a dreary business because nothing suits her. Eleanor hasn't had the birds and bees talk with her yet. *But there'll come a time*, she thinks, and sighs. What if Virginia stumbles on the passion that she found and lost with Gerald? It makes her feel murderous just contemplating it.

Tomorrow she and William have a garden party to go to and they'll arrive, stay and leave in the guise of a respectable married couple. He's in his study now and she heard the sound of a bottle clinking against a glass as she went past the door earlier. She has no idea what he does in there besides drinking, but it keeps him away from her.

She finishes her toilette and gets into bed.

The next morning she takes her time titivating. Walter and Harriet Maplin's annual summer party is eagerly awaited by their guests. The firm of solicitors he founded thirty years ago has devoured all but one of his rivals in town, so his hospitality is always a lavish affair. Dressmakers from Harrogate to Leeds find themselves besieged as the ladies look for just the right frock to enhance their husbands' status. And trounce the other ladies of course.

Eleanor has bought a silk frock whose green printed tendrils draw attention to what Gerald used to call her cat's eyes, its embroidered belt a joyless simulacrum of his hands round her waist. She slides it over her head now and its profligate yards of fabric flutter and swoop on their way down to the stiff net underskirt. She straightens the seams of her stockings, checks them with her hand mirror and puts on the emeralds Dorcas gave her for her thirtieth birthday three years ago.

She glides downstairs, painted, powdered and perfumed, and checks her hair again in the hall mirror. She taps on the door of the study.

'Ready, William. Let's go. I have the car keys.' He will drive them there, as always. She will drive them back, as always. She doesn't drink at parties. She hopes he doesn't fall asleep again as he did last time they were out together. Snoring like a dog on the sofa. She'd grimaced and said, 'Oh dear, there he goes again – the poor man's exhausted. Wake up, dear, let's get you tucked up in bed.' She'd railed at him in the car but they both knew it was pointless. Nothing could survive the wasteland between them.

They drive in silence to the party.

The sun is radiant in a cloudless sky, so the guests drink their cocktails on the terrace overlooking the garden and the lake. Eleanor's frock is admired (and envied) and she is talking to Miss Pearse, Virginia's headmistress, when the last couple arrive. She's a pretty little thing, although there's something odd about her even at this distance. He looks dusty, as though he's crawled out of his troglodyte cave for the day. He has his arm round his wife's shoulders. He is apologetic.

'Car broke down,' he says to Walter. 'Couldn't get the mechanic out. Had to fix it myself. So sorry.'

Walter nods benignly. 'Don't worry at all, old chap,' he says, 'could happen to anyone. Harriet, here they are at last.' His wife joins him and together they draw the couple over, decanting them into their separate vessels. Walter takes the man over to the left side of the terrace where William is talking to Dr Strange, Gerald's replacement, and Harriet brings the woman over to the right, where the ladies are convening.

'This is Agnès Taylor,' she says, 'Martin Taylor's wife. He's just joined Walter's conveyancing department and is doing frightfully well.' Agnès is introduced around the group, holding out a plump little hand to each lady. She does the right thing and admires Eleanor's frock, in the process revealing what is odd about her. She is French. She explains that she came to England to work as an *assistante* in a local school and met Martin when he turned up to visit his younger brother.

'*Franchement*, his brother may not have the gift perhaps of languages, but he gives us to each other, so he has one talent at least!' She giggles, keeping her eyes open. She has obviously used this line before.

Agnès is folded into the conversation but she is as exotic as a cockatiel in the company of wrens. Her fair hair is cut like an ancient Egyptian princess, an insouciant toss away from her companions' orderly coiffures, and her face is made up with look-at-me colours. Her cheeks are rouged into shiny pink globes, her somnolent eyelids are peacock blue and her mouth looks like she's been eating blackberries. Rather carelessly. Her frock is struggling to contain her, its neck so low her breasts can be seen larking with each other in their undergarment. She speaks with an assertiveness that's not quite proper. *But she'll learn*, Eleanor thinks, *if she wants her husband to get on.*

As the sun climbs higher in the sky, the company makes its way into the marquee where a lavish spread is laid out on trestles. The sexes pick and mix over cold salmon and salads and Eleanor, trapped with a pompous judge from Leeds, notices William deep in conversation with Agnès. He almost never talks to the ladies at parties, but she's incurious about what so animates them both. It's unlikely to be cooking or children. Thankfully the judge's wife drifts over to join her husband. She is eloquent on the subject of hats.

While there has been no stipulation on the invitation, common consensus regards five o'clock as the proper hour for departure, tea and scones having been served in the conservatory. Eleanor looks around for William and is dismayed when she can't see him. *Probably sleeping it off in the library*, she thinks, *pink-cheeked and grunting. How shaming.* She puts her cup down, preparing to go in search, and is surprised to see him emerging from the wooded area behind the lake. He is brushing himself down. When he comes into the house, he doesn't seem drunk, just a little tipsy, and there are grubby marks on the knees of his trousers.

They circulate around the party until they have bid farewell to everyone, and are standing with Walter and Harriet at the door when

Eleanor sees Agnès strolling out of the woods. She is patting her hair, which is even more dishevelled than when she arrived, and licking her lips. Her step is sprightly as she walks across the lawn.

I stay at Nana's after my birthday because Mother and Father are going somewhere the next day. I'm pleased with the way the day goes, though I know it's not like other girls' parties. Not that I go to them much, but I hear playground gossip. Aurora doesn't go to them much either because the other girls think she's a bit queer, having lived abroad until she turned up for school smelling still of the sea. I invite Beryl and Marian, not because they're special friends, but two girls isn't a party and having them there makes us nearly a gang. Not quite the Secret Seven or the Famous Five, but I suppose we could be the Famous Four and have ripping adventures. We're too old for games now we're eleven, but Grandpa said we could ride the horses, so I told Aurora and the other two to come in their old clothes. I'm already quite a good rider – though I've fallen off a few times – but the others are beginners, so Grandpa leads them round the paddock on long lead reins. Aurora is a natural so I'll invite her over to ride again – perhaps we can learn how to jump together.

When we've had our tea and I've blown out my candles, Grandpa puts his head round the dining-room door. 'Now, lasses,' he says, 'when you've finished your tea, I've got a birthday treat for you. Come out in 't yard after.'

When we come out, he's at the stable door talking to Misty, his grey mare. There's a horsebox in the drive and a ferretty man's leaning against it, smoking. Grandpa sees us coming out and waves. 'Over here, Virginia! Come and help me bring Misty out. Today's her lucky day.'

Misty's my favourite – she's all long legs and shiny coat and doesn't put up with nonsense. You can't put one over on Misty, and I love her for it. Grandpa gives me the bridle and I fit it over her head, adjusting the bit tenderly. I've often wondered what it might feel like to have something in your mouth like that. What it might feel like to be controlled. If it would hurt. I lead her to the centre of the yard and stand there. I glance over at the girls and they're looking at me

217

in this really admiring way. I can feel myself blushing. Grandpa calls over to the man by the horsebox. 'Hey, Eddie, she's ready for you now!'

Eddie crushes his cigarette under a muddy boot and goes to the back of the vehicle. 'Steady boy, steady,' he says as the box rocks. He opens the door gingerly.

He leads out the largest horse I've ever seen, coal black and glossy, his eyes rolling, his head tossing, his tail whipping from side to side.

'This is Crow,' Grandpa says. 'He's been looking forward to this. Champing at the bit, he's been.'

My shoulders go stiff as the stallion is led into the yard. He rears slightly when he sees Misty. It looks like he's grinning.

'Off you go now, lass,' says Grandpa, 'you'll not be able to keep a hold of her and I want you to get a good look.' He waves at where Aurora and the other two are leaning against a fence. 'Stick your arse over there.'

I stand next to Aurora, daring to lean sideways so our arms touch. Grandpa holds Misty's head firmly so she can't see Crow come up behind her. 'Ready for you now, Ed,' he calls and Eddie brings the harrumphing stallion forwards to Misty's rump. Suddenly this long red thing slides out under his belly, all wet and glistening.

We all jump and Aurora grabs my hand. 'What's that?' she whispers.

'I don't know. Please don't let him hurt her. Please God, don't let him hurt her.'

Crow rears and drops on to Misty's back. She whinnies as he shoves the red thing up her bottom. She's trapped by the giant horse pounding at her tail, but I'm too small to pull him off, too young to tell Grandpa to stop him. It seems to go on for a week, but Crow suddenly snorts and jiggles and pulls himself off, stamping his hooves in triumph. The red thing hangs down like it's lost its stuffing and Grandpa turns to us.

'See that, lasses?' he cackles. 'Now you know you'd best be good, or you know what's coming to you.'

Before she goes home, Aurora takes me into the bathroom and tells me that ladies and men do what we've just seen in the yard. 'Men have got one of those red things,' she whispers, 'and they put it in ladies, just like that.'

'What, in their bottoms?' I ask, horrified.

'I don't know exactly,' says Aurora, 'but down there somewhere. Your parents did that to make you – can you believe it? – and mine have done it three times to make Hera and Sandro and me. It makes me sick just to think about it.'

I feel sick too. If Father's done that to Mother no wonder she doesn't seem to like him very much. I imagine her on all fours with Father ramming himself into her, and wonder how she can sleep in the same bed as him. Suppose he did it again? It doesn't bear thinking about.

I'm too big now to hide in Mother's wardrobe, but I wish I could eat or drink something like Alice in Wonderland to make myself small enough to sit among the shoes. I could guard the bedroom, and if Father tried any more funny business I could burst out and stop him. Save Mother. She'd be grateful then.

When my friends have gone, I creep out to the stable to comfort Misty, though I don't exactly know what to say. I expect I'll find her lying crumpled on the straw, but she shakes her head when she sees me and whinnies. She doesn't seem bothered by what Crow did to her and takes the carrot I've pinched from the pantry and nuzzles my face. I wonder if maybe horses have shorter memories than people because I'm never going to forget what I saw this afternoon.

Mother seems particularly tense when she arrives on the dot of seven. She refuses Nana's offer of a cup of tea, saying that she has a terrible headache and needs to go home and lie down, but thanks her for doing the party food anyway.

'And what do you say, Virginia?'

'Thank you for having me, Nana. And thank you for my lovely party.'

Mother tries to chat on the drive home, but then she stops and the car goes quiet. I look out of the window, trying to take my mind off the fact that she once behaved like a horse.

*

Lying in bed later on, the windows rattling with the coming storm, I suddenly remember Crow's red thing and I see him pounding at Misty again. It goes on for longer than it took in real life and I get this funny feeling down where I do Number Ones. Without thinking, my hand slips down and I pat at the feeling, which gets stronger with each pat. I see Misty's head held firmly in place by the bridle, Grandpa's hands gripping the reins, and my hand rubs up and down, faster and faster, and Down There starts to twitch and gets hot and I feel something in the pit of my belly that swooshes down and my hips push up into my hand for a moment before dropping back on the mattress.

My heart's jumping around my chest like billy-o. Whatever that was felt really super. I don't know if it's allowed, but since Mother has never actually said don't, it can be my secret. But, golly, if that's the way to make babies, I just won't have any, that's all. I know that some ladies like having babies but since there's only one of me, I think Mother probably isn't one of them. I fall asleep quickly.

I'm woken up by bangs and thumps and I look over at the window: it's still dark outside and there's no sign of the storm. The sounds are coming from the spare room next to my bedroom, which is never used because no one ever stays with us. Maybe it's a burglar. Or a murderer and we'll all be found dead in our beds tomorrow, the sheets bright red and dripping. I should probably go and warn Mother and Father but then the murderer will see me and I'll be the first one to die and maybe that'll be enough for him and he'll run away leaving Mother without anyone to protect her and that would be dreadful. I stay put, praying for the intruder to go away. He does. The sounds stop and the sliver of light under the door vanishes as the hall light is switched off. I toss and turn for a bit, worrying that the murderer might realise he's forgotten to kill me and come back, but next thing I know is it's morning.

Father has already gone to work when I get up, and Mother is more than usually bustly in the kitchen. I escape upstairs to get my swimming things as soon as breakfast is over and I notice the spare-room door is ajar. I give it a little push and look in. The room is rather boring to look at usually, but it looks jollier this morning. I see why. The bedding has slipped halfway off the bed and the chair is piled high with men's clothes in a higgledy-piggledy mess. There's a heap of shoes at the foot of the bed and ties curling round each other on the dressing table. I race downstairs.

'Mother! Mother! I heard dreadful noises in the night and I was too frightened to come and tell you but there's been a burglar in the spare room and he's left a terrible mess and I'm really sorry I didn't wake you up and . . .'

'Calm down, Virginia,' says Mother, still bending over the sink. 'There are going to be a few changes around here, that's all. Father needs his own room because he snores so dreadfully – you must have heard him – so we decided it's best that he takes over the spare room from now on. Nothing to worry about.' She clatters a plate on to the draining board with some force. 'Nothing to worry about at all.'

On my way to the baths, I think that while I've never heard Father snoring, at least the move means I don't have to do guard duty.

## 1977

The Usman family spends the afternoon at Tooting Bec lido under the tetchy sun of a midsummer's day, which nips in and out like a celestial tease. At seven and five, Ismail and Shafiq are already confident swimmers but Farah's afraid of water, so she putters about in giant armbands, claiming to be a very hungry butterfly. Faisal and Amina take turns shadowing her as she goes in search of her flowery lunch, flapping her arms and buzzing like an unhinged bee. When Faisal comes round the pool behind her for what feels like the ninetieth time, he catches sight of his wife at the far end as though through the eyes of a stranger. Her casual voluptuousness as she rests back on her elbows, her legs crossed at the ankles, stops him in his tracks. His mother would have been a beautiful woman too, had privation not pillaged her life, but Amina is free to be beautiful and he floods with love as he comes towards her. He hands Farah over and smells his wife's floral sweetness as he kisses her head before dive-bombing the boys in the pool.

By the end of the afternoon everyone's starving, so they decide to catch an early dinner at their favourite restaurant, the Sri Krishna. On their way to the car Shafiq starts goading Ismail, who tries to rise above it but finally snaps and punches his brother in the face. Holding a nose pouring with blood, Shafiq kicks out at Ismail's shins and he yelps and falls to his knees. A teenager riding his bicycle on the pavement appears from round the corner, heading straight for Ismail's back. Forgetting he's holding Farah's hand, Faisal leaps forwards and grabs the bike's handlebars, pushing it sideways into a hedge. Amina is bending over, trying to staunch Shafiq's nosebleed and in that infinitesimal moment of distraction, Farah sees a squirrel in the road and runs to catch it. There's a screech of brakes and they all whip round to see a small figure bouncing off a bumper and slamming into a lamp post. The street is eerily silent for a millisecond before it churns with screams.

Amina gets to Farah first.

'Don't move her!' Faisal shouts. 'Wait!' As he reaches his daughter's oddly angled body, he thinks for a moment she's already dead, but when he takes her pulse, swallowing his sobs, he feels a feeble flutter.

Faisal goes in the ambulance with Farah and Amina follows in the family car, not certain she still knows how to drive. The paramedics decide to go straight to Great Ormond Street, where there's a specialist neurosurgery team, and London's traffic Red Sea parts as they speed north.

Faisal watches the ICU team hook his daughter up to tubes and pumps and monitors and his hands twitch. He's not a doctor here, just a distraught father in shorts watching white coats swarm around the bed where death's toying with his baby. Brothers in guilt, Shafiq and Ismail stand silently in the corridor outside with their mother, all of them paralysed by the not-knowing. Ismail badly wants to believe that his father can make Farah better even if he's not wearing his red doctor tie, but the gravity of the accident is pushing him back into his little-boy myths. Amina is standing as close to the door of her daughter's room as she dares, as though her body's warmth can shimmy through the wood. As though a mother's love trumps medical science every time.

An agonising forty minutes – forty minutes and twenty-four seconds – later, Faisal emerges. Amina scans his face for clues. He pulls her to his chest. She feels him shaking.

'Daddy?' says Shafiq in a tiny voice. 'Is Farah OK? Is she, Daddy? Can we go and get her some sweeties now, please? Please can we, Mummy?'

Faisal collects himself. 'She's not very well at the moment,' he says, 'but the doctors here are really, really good and they'll absolutely make her better soon. When she's well, you can bring her all the sweets you like. Hang on there just a second, boys.' He walks Amina down the corridor with his arm round her shoulders, explaining as best as he can what's going to happen to Farah.

The next twenty-four hours are critical. Spinal injuries of this severity frequently result in paraplegia – if she survives at all, that is – and even if she battles through this first day, there'll be days to come when the arc of her barely begun life will dip.

They can't keep the boys at the hospital forever, so Faisal takes them home and Amina begins her vigil. Farah looks like a peanut in the hospital bed with a tentacular system of tubes perforating her body, willing her to stay alive. The only sounds in the room are the machines' beeps and whirrs as they assume her body's functions and the squeak of nurses' shoes as they come in and out to check them. Amina is terrified of turning her head to speak to a nurse, of scratching an itch, of reaching for something – blinking even – in case in that split second Farah dies because her attention flagged. She sits so motionless in her chair that her back goes into spasm and her legs numb. She wishes she could numb her mind too, but it persists in feeling the razor-slashes of an agony so acute it seems to be shredding. She rests her hand on the only part of Farah's body not compromised by tubes, holding her thigh over the blanket. Flesh of her flesh. There's nothing she can give her, not a heart or a liver or a kidney or a spine, and a refrain is weaving wildly through her head: *Bad mother, bad mother, bad-bad-bad. Bad mother, bad mother* . . . She's failed to keep her daughter safe, and if Farah dies she knows that her own heart will stop.

Extremity slackens inhibitions and she's anyway too tired to fend off the unbidden thoughts. He did this. Faisal. He's responsible for the broken child in the bed next to her. Not quite alive. Not quite dead. He put the boys first. Perhaps he always has. Perhaps she just never noticed before. When the chips were down, he chose his own kind and now all Farah has is this mother who fell short.

When Faisal comes to relieve her in the morning, she doesn't look at him. She can't – won't – leave her chair. She doesn't open her mouth to speak, knowing that if she did she'd curse him. But in the end she can't spare the energy for anger as she watches Farah's face for a sign. Some magic sign that she's coming back. Mary's at home, fielding the fits of grief and accusation that ricochet between the boys, so Faisal silently stays all day with his silent wife. They're both blaming him as they watch their silent child.

*

224

A week later, Amina is still there, her eyes bloodshot with the effort of keeping her daughter alive. The doctors are talking cautiously of possible treatments should Farah hack her way out of the coma, and Faisal relays the gist of their discussions to his wife. She's taking none of it in. He can talk to them all he likes but she has a job to do and prognostic ambling will only waylay her.

On the eighth day, just after a nurse has checked the machines and her vital signs, Farah's left eye blinks and flutters open.

Amina jolts upright. 'Nurse! Nurse!' she shouts. 'She's awake! She's coming round!' By the time the nurse arrives back at the bed, Farah's eye has closed again, but Amina knows what she's seen.

Three hours later, both eyelids flicker open and Farah makes a sound that would have been 'Mummy' had a tube not been down her throat. Her eyes roll from side to side till she finds Amina sitting there with a lunatic grin on her face, tears dripping down her cheeks and off her nose and off her chin. But even a crying mummy is better than no mummy at all and Farah keeps her eyes glued to her in case she goes away.

There's a sudden froth of busyness around the bed and Amina goes into the corridor to call Faisal. It's too soon to celebrate, but they can stand by her bed watching life beginning to dance on her face. They can begin to hope.

In that first week, Faisal goes to work when he can, but Virginia makes it clear that his duties are to be kept as undemanding as possible. She tries to persuade him to take compassionate leave, but he demurs.

'At least I can be of use here,' he says. 'At least when I'm with a patient, I feel there's something I can do. Some skill I have to offer. When I'm at Great Ormond Street, it's like I'm a snail without its shell. It's not only that it's not my field, it's way beyond my competence. I let go of her, Virginia. I dropped her hand and it dogs me, it dogs my every second, day and night. It's like some terrible heresy – I became a doctor to save lives, to heal people, and here I am guilty of doing something that nearly killed my daughter. My *daughter*!' He pushes his palms into his eyes. 'Actually, sometimes I think I just should give it all up – chuck it in, you know? In case I start killing my patients.'

Virginia surprises him – and herself – by putting her hand on his arm. 'You won't do your patients any good if you do,' she says. 'Or Farah for that matter. You're a fine, fine doctor, Faisal, and we can't afford to lose what you bring to the work. I won't let you throw in the towel.'

There are daily gestures of compassion – of love – from the staff who know him and even from those who know of him only by the quicksilver gossip that slicks down hospital corridors. Special cups of coffee made, paperwork whisked away and completed, board games for two boys with absent-minded parents, chocolates for him and bath oils for Amina.

One evening when the boys are in bed, Faisal pours himself a generous glass of the whisky Purkiss gave him and sits in the living room next to the phone. He's three-quarters of the way down and contemplating a top-up when it rings. His heart jerks. Phone calls are never innocent nowadays.

'Faisal? How are you?'

'Oh, hi, Virginia. I'm OK – well, you know, hanging on.' He tries not to slur. 'I thought you might be Amina.'

'Look, I was thinking about what you said today about the surgery Great Ormond Street's suggesting. I want you to know I'm absolutely not casting aspersions on their competence – Fitch is very well thought of and I know several others in his firm who are terrific surgeons – but I wanted to run something by you. Just so you have a choice.'

'There aren't many choices available right now, so thank you. What were you thinking?'

'There's a neurosurgeon at Ninewells in Dundee whom I've known for years. Brilliant, brilliant clinician. Name's Farooqi. She's developed ways of operating on neural damage that most surgeons would give their eye teeth for. Published extensively. Sadly, the techniques are so sophisticated most people aren't up to it yet. I could call her. See what she'd be willing to do. Probably best not to move Farah I'd have thought, so she'd better come here, hadn't she?'

'If she would.'

'She may not be able to of course – she's always frantically busy, but she'd be upfront about that. Ask around, if you like. You'll find her reputation is extraordinary.'

'Don't think I need to do that. I trust your judgement absolutely.'

'I'll call her tonight. Let you know tomorrow. Strangely, her name's Farah too.'

Farah Farooqi arrives five days later. She is a rotund woman with a balletic grace at odds with her size and no time for niceties. In consultation she is brusque, as though being spare with words will conserve her energies for more important tasks.

She meets with Faisal and Amina the day she arrives. She seems to have swallowed Farah's notes whole. 'I'm promising nothing,' she says. 'You'll understand the odds against repairing such extensive damage, Dr Usman, but when I operated last year on a 26-year-old biker with similar injuries, he was walking in a month.'

Amina leans forwards. 'I'm not a medic, Miss Farooqi, so I know nothing about the technicalities. Faisal does. All I know is that Farah's alive, and even if the operation doesn't succeed, that's all that matters. If she has to spend the rest of her life in a wheelchair, we'll adapt, that's all. Just keep her alive.'

The day the surgery is scheduled, Faisal arrives at the hospital at half past five in the morning, Amina's clean clothes in a carrier bag. Mary has ironed the salwar kameez expertly, flicking scented water on the silk as she smoothed its creases. Amina usually wears traditional clothes only on special family occasions but this, bizarrely, feels like one.

When Farah wakes, her head flips to where her mother always sits.

'Good morning, hen,' says Amina, 'how are you feeling today?'

'I'm thirsty, Mummy. Can I have some squash?'

'Not now. Do you remember how today's a special day and you've got to pretend you're like Beetlebunny in your book? Remember how he had to go across a desert to save the little girl and he couldn't find anything to drink but he walked and walked under the hot sun, getting stronger and stronger?'

'And he made the baddies go away and it was funny, Mummy, wasn't it? Then they all fell in the water and they had to swim across the sea.'

'That's right – that bit does make us laugh – remember the baddie with the helmet on and when his helmet falls off you can see he's got no hair?'

'And he looks just like a football, doesn't he? But I'm still thirsty. Can't I have a drink before I turn into Beetlebunny?'

Amina glances at the sign above her daughter's bed. *Nil By Mouth*. 'No, hen, you can't. If you had a drink, you couldn't turn into him and then the little girl would have to stay with the baddies. That would be awful. I think she's relying on you to be really strong, so after you've been asleep – remember, I told you you were going to have a looo-ong sleep today? – we'll see about some squash.'

Faisal sees Amina's face reddening and he strokes Farah's hair. 'D'you know what I've got in my bag?' he says.

Farah shakes her head.

'I brought all your best books with me and I'm going to read you every single one. Then when I've finished, we'll start again from the very beginning. We're going to read and read till it's time to go to sleep. How about that then?'

Farah smiles happily. 'Can we start with *The Cat in the Hat*?' she asks.

Amina and Faisal walk to the operating theatre with their hands on the trolley to steady themselves. Farah is sleepy from the pre-med, but as the anaesthetist prepares to slide the canula into her hand, she blinks her eyes wide open and says, 'Beetlebunny away!' before slipping into unconsciousness.

It's too much like watching her daughter dying and Amina teeters. Faisal grabs her round the shoulders and moves her towards the door.

'Don't worry, we'll take good care of her, Mrs Usman,' the anaesthetist says. 'She's in brilliant hands.'

Faisal can't read Dr Seuss to his wife or tell her a story or sing her a song to distract her from what's being done to Farah only a few yards away. He's buffered by his profession only until the theatre doors banish him, along with his wife, to the layman's agnostic limbo. They sit in a waiting room decked out in bogglingly bright colours.

They do what you do in a waiting room. They wait.

Seven hours later, Farah Farooqi comes into the room in her scrubs. 'I think we may have done it,' she says. 'Actually the neural damage was less extensive than I thought, and while there were some interesting problems, I think we managed to repair it. Time will tell. Farah's in recovery now. You can go and see her.'

A week later, Faisal looks up from the finger puppet show he's putting on for Farah and sees an angular figure in the doorway.

'Virginia,' he says, 'how lovely to see you. Farah, do you remember Miss Denham?'

'Virginia, Faisal, please.'

'OK. Do you remember Virginia?'

Farah looks doubtful.

'Is she a teacher at Ismail's school?'

'No, she's not. She's a doctor like me, but she's a very special doctor because she helped to make you better.'

'Do I have to say thank you then?'

'Well . . .' Virginia cuts in. 'No need to thank me, Farah. I'm very happy to see you looking so well. I've brought you a special present – look! I used to have one of these when I was a little girl. It was my absolute favourite.' She holds out a paper bag, but it slips from her hands. 'Oops, butterfingers!' she says, picking it up. 'What a silly billy I am. I'm always dropping things.'

Farah pulls a book from its bag and opens it up. She looks mystified. 'It's all torn up,' she says. 'Did it get torn when it fell down?'

Virginia laughs. 'No, that's just how it's supposed to be,' she says. 'Look, you can make all sorts of funny people,' and she shows Farah how it works.

Farah lies on her bed chortling as she gives chicken legs to a podgy policeman, while Virginia and Faisal talk by the window. London fizzes its business three floors below, but it could be Kazakhstan as far as Faisal is concerned. Since the accident he's been moving from his house cocoon in his car cocoon to the hospital cocoon and back again, his mind running on a single track. Then Virginia insisted on extended compassionate leave, so he begins with that.

'I'm so grateful to you, Virginia – I barely know where to start actually, but it was absolutely essential to have this time off – both for me and for my family.'

'But I didn't do anything. You were entitled to it. Take as long as you need.'

'I'll come out of this tunnel sometime, but I couldn't do the job right now. I'd be a danger to my patients.'

'Of course not. Look, Farooqi called me when she got back up there. She's absolutely delighted with Farah's progress, but I'm sure she's told you that. Actually she says she's never seen such a speedy recovery. You've probably realised she doesn't waste words or chuck empty promises around, so if she says she's satisfied, the prognosis is good. Excellent even. But you look exhausted, Faisal. I want you to take an extra week on top of whatever's needed for Farah so you can get your own strength back. I won't let you back until you do.'

Faisal nods.

'Thank you, Virginia. I know you're right.'

A squeak comes from the bed. 'Daddy, Daddy – look what I made! It's a fairy rhino!'

As he goes over to his daughter, Virginia slips away quietly. At the door she looks back at him sitting on the bed next to Farah, twisting her hair round his forefinger as they make strange creatures together. *She's a lucky girl*, she thinks.

# 1977

I have the next day off and force myself to stay in bed until eight o'clock. I'm exhausted. To avoid shipping in locums I've picked up most of Faisal's sessions, delegating the routine matters to Purkiss, whom I monitor closely. There's always a chance he'll grow into the role, but since he has the subtlety of a swede I'm not laying bets.

I pick the *Guardian* off the mat on my way to the kitchen and read it at the table as I eat my kedgeree, eggy bread and cornflakes, Italian coffee and custard. Proper custard that is, stirred slowly in a double boiler until the eggs thicken the milk. Vanilla sugar. The Bird's fake-yolk-yellow stuff offends me.

I can only do this – read the paper from cover to cover – on my days off, and while it smacks of indulgence, I stay at the table till I've worked my way through the national and international news, the op-ed pages, the sport and the Women's Page. Jill Tweedie's on splendid form. When I was growing up, Father's relationship with the *Times* was the nearest thing to a love affair going on at Hanover House, his blackened fingers as he emerged from his study the only evidence of congress.

Gilda has the afternoon off today and I promised I'd go over after lunch to work on her garden, which is becoming wayward. I spend the morning baking, and by lunchtime a Sachertorte, a ginger peach cake, some flapjacks and a slab of shortbread gather sweetly at the end of the worktop. They've decimated my sugar stock, so I nip out to the High Street to replenish it.

On my way, I stop off at Green Fingers. I try to limit my visits here by taking alternative routes, but when I pass by, it entices me in like a seedy Soho cinema. It's a gardening pornucopia – every variety of tool, accessory, powder and pellet on offer, every practice and position available – at a price. They know me well and keep back new products, stashing them under the counter to seduce me when I next show up.

Judy looks over and smiles as I come into the shop. 'How's it going?' she asks. 'Did that stuff get rid of the wretched bugs OK?'

'Really powerful,' I say. 'They didn't know what hit them.'

'Bit pungent, though, isn't it? One of my customers said she felt like she'd been gassed.'

'Oh, I didn't mind it actually. It's only doing its job, after all.'

'True enough, but then none of those pongs bother you, do they?'

'I suppose I'm just more interested in whether it works than its smell.'

She knows of my passion for roses, but we talk about her wisteria for a while, which has been especially abundant this year, and the subtleties of pruning. But it's like small talk at a party and I know there's bigger talk to come. It comes.

'I kept this back for you,' she says, reaching under the counter. 'We only ordered two because they're pretty special and I'm not sure Tooting's ready for them yet. Bit pricey, but I know you of all people know that quality doesn't come cheap.'

She lays the knife on the counter, snug in a leather sheath embossed with gold script.

'It's called a Hori Hori knife,' she says. 'From Japan. Officially it's for weeding but I reckon you could use it for loads of other things, providing you take care of the blade.'

I slide my fingers down the wooden handle, which already has the patina of age. There's a strap with a tiny popper holding the knife in place and my forefinger circles it for a moment before pushing at it.

*Pop.*

Judy and I are both holding our breaths as I draw it out of its sheath. It's beautiful.

'It's beautiful,' I say, and Judy nods. Its blade is double-sided, one side all steely-blue edginess, the other a toothsome saw.

'Look,' says Judy, 'it's got this dip for scooping too, so you can cut

232

and saw *and* dig. Apparently the Japs use it for collecting bonsai specimens, but you'll find your own ways of using it, I bet.'

I hold it in my palm. I'm rapt. 'It's perfect,' I say eventually. 'I love
it. Really beautiful – thank you, Judy.'

We maintain a reverent silence as I pay and leave the shop, the
knife crouching in its paper bag in my satchel.

I buy the sugar – and some *bacalao* from the market and some
mangos for Tobias – and set off home, past the Portuguese coffee
shop. Suddenly the door slams open and a red-haired woman storms
out, dragging a small girl behind her. She is furious. She pushes the
child up against the estate agents' window and bends over her.

'Don't you *dare* do that again!' she says, stabbing the girl's shoulder
with her finger. 'Don't you ever, *ever* show me up like that again!
You're a naughty, bad, horrible little girl and I'm ashamed to be seen
with you. I *hate* being your mummy!'

The little girl, already blotchy and tear-stained, struggles not to
weep. 'I'm sorry, Mummy,' she says. 'I'm sorry. Don't hit me again
– please, I'm sorry.'

The woman grabs her and shakes her so violently her head nods
in lunatic agreement: *I am a naughty, bad, horrible little girl. I am!*

'Just you wait,' her mother hisses, 'just you wait till we get home.
Just you wait till Daddy comes home this evening.'

The little girl loses control and begins to wail, her eyes shut tight
against her mother's rage.

I take a step forwards as the woman raises her hand, but then she
lowers it and grabs the child's forearm, holding it in the air like some
futile cry for help. She marches her down the street, her shapely legs
flashing through the slit in her skirt.

Ruby's hand slides into my satchel and finds the knife. She draws
it out of its paper bag. 'Judy said there were loads of uses for this,'
she whispers, and I take it and unpop the strap, keeping my hand in
the bag. We follow the mother and child through the backstreets,
past the workers' cottages and the houses of the bourgeoisie, towards
the grand houses on the Common, built for splendour and servants.
We stop at the postbox on the corner and mark which house they go
into, the child now frozen into silence.

Ruby's shoulder presses against mine. 'We'll see to her,' she says. 'No one'll ever know. Burglary gone wrong. Happens all the time.'

I nod.

'But wait a bit,' she says. 'You need to look like a passer-by.'

We walk along the Common for ten minutes, Ruby issuing instructions. 'Cut her, Virginia. Cut out her heart. Chuck it away. She doesn't deserve to be a mother.' Her hand grips mine so tightly I feel the blood stopping.

As we approach the house, we see the child sitting in the window, her cheek flattened against the pane. She's slumped like an unstitched rag doll. She doesn't look at us as we walk up the garden path past the prim shrubs, and registers nothing as we ring the bell. Her mother takes her time, so we ring again.

She's standing there, a well-groomed woman in her early thirties, who's switched on her smile before she opened the door. She smells expensive.

'Yes?' she says. 'How can I help you?'

'I was just passing by,' I say, 'and happened to see the little girl in the window – your daughter, is it? She looked as if she was about to fall off the seat and I was worried.'

'Oh, how sweet of you! I was just getting changed upstairs so I didn't see.' She comes out and stands so she can see her daughter.

'Oh Charlotte, don't be sad, darling – ooh, and do be careful! Don't want you falling off and banging your head again. Poor lamb,' she says, 'now I feel awful I didn't hear her crying. But I know what'll cheer her up.' She fetches keys from inside and goes to a substantial BMW crouching at the kerb. 'She's probably just realised she left Robbie in the car this morning.' As she comes back to the house, she waves a battered soft toy at the window. 'Look, darling, look! Here's Robbie rabbit – he's been all alone in the car and he's missed you terribly!'

As she goes past, Ruby whispers, '*Now!* Follow her in, Virginia,' and she moves my hand and the knife in the satchel.

The woman turns at the door. She flinches, as though she's seen something in my face. 'Thank you so much – most kind,' she says, and she's gone.

We go across the road to the Common, my ear burning with

Ruby's vitriol. She accuses me of failing the child, of turning my face, of betraying her. 'Did you see her at all? Did you see how she lives? You've got the sensitivity of a gnat, Virginia – you could have rescued her and you just walked off the fucking job!'

She's right. I did. I try to go home but I'm stopped by what I've seen. I stay on the Common behind a large horse chestnut until I see the woman leaving the house again, her daughter walking behind her as though attached by an invisible hawser.

'At least see to the car,' says Ruby. 'Can you at least do that?'

I cross the road and bend over by the car, pretending to do up my shoe. I pull out the knife and stab the nearest tyre four times. I stand, undo the petrol cap and tip the sugar into the tank. I brush stray crystals off the car's bodywork, screw the cap back on and walk smartly back home.

I take the peach cake and the flapjacks round to Gilda, explaining that I think I'm running a fever so I'll have to see to her garden another time. 'But I've got a lovely new gardening tool,' I say, 'which seems to sort everything.'

She's sympathetic and says she'll call me tomorrow to see how I am.

# 1977

The woman lies on the ground, chunks of rubble pressing into her back. Between the allotments and the cemetery. She looks surprised, as though her last thought was *Oh my God – why me?* She takes pride in her appearance, attends to her grooming, makes sure her red hair is cut and coloured, her eyebrows plucked and her nails polished. Pearlised pink today. She's wearing a pencil skirt in black wool, with braiding and a cheeky slit up the back. Was wearing. The skirt lies on a sad patch of grass a little way away, next to a photograph of a small girl. It is already swarming with ants hunting for crumbs. Her knickers and tights tangle nearby but are, for the moment, insect-free.

Her legs are akimbo. She could be a frog pinned to a board, waiting for a class of appalled adolescents to dissect her. Her arms are semaphoring above her head: H . . . E . . . L . . . P M . . . E. H . . . E . . . L . . . P M . . . E. H . . . E . . . L . . . P. No one saw. No one heard anything – that's what they'll say later, stunned by what they missed. Her blouse has been torn open and her bra has been slit. A lacy cup lies on either side of her breasts. She's proud of her breasts and never minded when men looked at them. They're full and perky. Were.

The blood stopped spilling some time ago and is now enriching the soil. If the allotments expand, if the rocks were cleared, you could plant parsnips here. Dahlias maybe. After they've taken her away of course. After they've taken photographs. Put pegs in the ground. Patted the leaves with their gloved hands, looking for clues. Strung the blue and white plastic tape between the trees to keep the prurient and the horror-hounds at bay.

When they've examined her under unforgiving lights, they'll list her wounds. They'll use dry language to describe the sites and the damage done. The stab wounds in all her female parts. They'll be circumspect when they speak to the public. It's enough to know that a woman has been murdered this close to where people live: no point in unsettling the neighbours further.

But she has to be found first. Has to become the nightmare that rattles around the head of the dog walker who finds her. She's been missed, but her husband thought maybe he'd forgotten. Maybe it was tonight she was staying with a friend.

And when she's found, when the news breaks that the Ripper's killed again, how will he tell her daughter?

# 1977

Saturday, 12.05 a.m.

I eat the Sachertorte and the shortcake and run a bath. I'm aching all over. I sprinkle jasmine bath oil into it and sit on the edge when it's run. The water is too hot to get into straight away, so I wait. I have before now scalded myself by being too eager and it hurt for days. Accidental pain is a waste of time.

When the water is the right temperature, I slide in, closing my eyes and drifting till my skin puckers.

I towel myself fiercely and get out the Elizabeth Arden. I put my foot on the edge of the bath and lob a fistful at my thigh. Most of it sticks, though a delinquent gloop plops on the bathmat. The rest sits there, looking like whipped cream on prawns. It feels delicious and I'm almost tempted to lick it off, but instead I rub it in with long firm strokes until it's absorbed.

Perversely, the bath has woken me up, so I put on a robe and go to the study to catch up on the piled accusation of journals. As I sit down at the desk, I remember that last tableau at the hospital. The hum of love between Faisal and Farah is something I hear on wards and in cafés and at school gates as I pass, but describing it would be like trying to make a flat-pack bed without instructions.

I rest against my chair and it eases backwards. My eyes lift to the top shelf where my student textbooks from twenty-one years ago loll lazily against each other. *Gray's Anatomy* is the bossy head prefect bringing up the rear, but a carrier bag nudging its flank is making it look foolish. Maybe Magda's left her cleaning stuff up there – it wouldn't be the first time. I'm forever finding scrubbers in the laundry basket and polish in the fruit bowl – once, mysteriously, scissors in my sock drawer – but then I remember Father's journals.

It feels both audacious and necessary to read them, but the risks are great. I no longer believe he was a magician but for all I know he might have been an empathic man, a wistful man, a man of honour or courage or spite. It was never safe to be curious. I wheel my chair to the shelves and step on to it, unfolding carefully up the stacks of books. As my head reaches the top shelf, the chair rolls sideways but I manage to grab the bag before I crash to the ground, knocking my knee on a shelf and biting my lip as I fall.

I move the journals, put my pens and papers on the filing cabinet and rest Mr Sainsbury's incendiary cargo on the desktop. It seems to growl like a slumbering beast about to awake and I take an involuntary step backwards. There's no point in enlisting Ruby, even if she'd come when I called. She'd race over to the bag, rip it open, pull the sackcloth off the books and read them from first page to last, smacking her lips with glee. I try talking to myself in Nana's voice. *Don't be such a mouse, Virginia, it's just pieces of paper – what's it going to do to you? Sit down and read it, for pity's sake. And when you're done, wash your hands before tea.* None of it works.

Over the years, I've learned how to walk into a room full of strangers, using my size and my status as ballast. By sitting down, which I do, and opening the bag, which I do, and piling the unwrapped books in front of me, which I do, I'm walking towards a single giant stranger. Unarmed.

I want to dash randomly into this one or that one, as though that way I could catch Father unawares, but it makes more sense to read them in chronological order so I open the first one, dated December 1939.

I've seen the photograph of him in uniform as he set off in the early days of the war. It sat in its carved wooden frame next to Granny Denham's recipe books in her kitchen. His face looked eager and shiny and smooth under his cap, as though he were just off to a party. Granny said she was proud Father'd enlisted, but that for six years Adolf wasn't the only enemy. She'd watch the telegram man walk up other people's paths, she said, and hope it was his only delivery that day.

I meet my 29-year-old father on the first page, his new uniform box-fresh.

It felt like a million termites on my skin and my boots felt like bricks, but I'm happy. I'm doing what I've chosen to do for the first time in years. Yesterday in training I met Stephen Keen, who's a solicitor from Bradford, and we got on like a house on fire. In the Officers' Mess this evening the other chaps were getting as drunk as lords, but over a beer he and I spoke of how we felt about the war. We know you're supposed to be awfully gung-ho when you talk about the enemy, but he and I talked differently, though quietly in case we were overheard. We talked about how we both felt that we were carrying something into battle for our families but how terrified we were that we'd drop it. Let them down.

He's a great admirer of the World War I poets and we speculated about what kind of writers would emerge at the end of all this. We agreed to meet after the war is over and discuss who'd best represented the conflict. If we survive, I suppose. Life is suddenly being lived in capital letters and without punctuation, each second a moment of high drama that might presage your death. Somehow Stephen and I agreeing to meet after the war to talk about poetry is like a talisman that will keep us alive. As though making a plan gives us a future.

As the war jittered around him, Father seemed to know instinctively how to calm his men's nerves. He knew it was terror that made them vomit in the troopship, but sympathised instead with their seasickness. He held their shoulders as they retched so their uniforms wouldn't stink of the fear that's only a white-feathered step away from cowardice.

When they got to France, he thought it prudent not to record where they were in case the diary fell into enemy hands. Of course if Jerry were reading it, he wrote, he'd probably be dead.

Moved forwards today past the hamlets in H . . . The gardens had been stripped of anything edible and the naked stalks looked pitiful, as though trying to hold on to their dignity in the bitter wind. There was a high-backed sofa in the middle of the road as we passed a house with a china-blue shutter hanging recklessly off a single hinge. It had been slashed by a knife or a bayonet and its springs were already starting to rust. I imagined what it might have looked like in its prime, where it might once have sat – maybe by the fire in the living room – and what had happened on it. A couple spooning perhaps; a sick child propped up on pillows; a grandfather telling tall tales. Perhaps a fierce row, ending with one party sitting glumly on its paisley seat, the other clattering upstairs to bed.

But it doesn't do to let my mind run away with me because my job is to protect my men. Thinking of these things must be confined to these relatively quiet moments at the end of an action when I am free to write, though I am frequently interrupted by one soldier or another needing to talk.

Whenever he encountered a dead body – sometimes a pile of bodies – his words hiccough across the pages, some of them savagely crossed out as he struggled to explain to himself how it felt.

Jerry was well dug in in A . . ., but finally after three days we silenced their guns and they retreated. I sent my men out in groups of five to rout any stragglers. I took the four men whom I have seen falter in battle – Simpson, Skidmore, Green and Abbey – and they followed me through the flattened fields.

We came upon a farmhouse still smoking from the shells. A single white curtain waved out of an upstairs window as though the house were trying fruitlessly to surrender. The acrid stench of the house's demise hung in the air. I think that I shall never again enjoy the smell of a bonfire warming an autumnal chill. Some things will never please me in the way they once did.

As we approached the house we fanned out, staying alert for booby traps. We moved towards the front door, our boots crunching on glass, kicking kitchen utensils, ripping plants out by their roots. You never hear birds any more in this spectral landscape. It's as though what they've seen has struck them dumb.

To the right of the door was a piece of fabric, blown, I supposed, from the inside of the house. As I got closer I saw blue coils on the fabric, steaming slightly in the freezing air. They were the guts of a young woman lying flat on her back, her long black hair mercifully obscuring her face. Her right leg stuck out at an impossible angle and her arms, too, were flung to the right, her left arm across her exposed breasts as though preserving her modesty. As my eyes travelled to the fingers of her hand, stretched, splayed, reaching for something, I saw a pink thing under a bush. A baby. He was lying on his back, unmarked, his head rolled towards his mother. I prayed that his last view of her hadn't been her intestines exploding out of her as he once had. It was dangerous to linger until we had cleared the area, so I moved on. I glanced sideways at Skidmore, who was the colour of putty, and said, 'Forwards, Skidmore. Look forwards.'

When we were certain there were no Germans still lurking, I sent the men back to our line and returned to the farmhouse. I squatted down by the woman's side and moved the hair from her face. She wasn't especially beautiful but she looked calm. Accepting, as though meeting her maker was a joyful thing. I have lost my own faith, which was anyway a feeble affair, but I know these people find succour in theirs.

Astonishingly, a single flower had survived the mayhem, a pale quince bloom still tethered to its stalk. I picked it and laid it in the woman's hair like some mad echo of Gauguin. I wanted her to look loved, as though that might mitigate her tragedy.

I sent Pollock and Weaver out later with shovels to bury her with her child. I asked them to say whatever they could remember from the funeral service over their grave. Dust to dust, I said, ashes to ashes – something like that. But say the Lord's Prayer anyway.

Four days later, Skidmore was dead, having stormed a machine-gun post on his own and killed nearly all the enemy soldiers. William recommended him for the VC.

The 11th Armoured Division, nicknamed the Black Bull, press forwards through Father's account. There are weeks when he recorded nothing and I wonder where he was. What he was doing. Maybe the Special Operations Mother told me about.

Edith appears in the penultimate volume smelling of lavender and love. As I read my father's account of their brave intimacy, I begin to chew at my cuticles. When I've finished reading it, my fingers are raw.

The last volume stares at me from the desktop, daring me to open it.

I don't want to stop but my fingers are throbbing, so I go to the bathroom. I stand with my hand under freezing cold water and catch sight of my face in the mirror. My lower lip is swollen from the fall but it isn't this that makes me look strange to myself. It is that I'm the daughter of *this* father. That the Virginia-with-a-lapsed-father has been replaced by this Virginia with a father who could love. It's as though I can no longer spell my name. As though the sheets of ice on which my history's written have melted.

I go downstairs and pour myself a large glass of Calvados. I'll take the punishment later.

The last journal wasn't completed, its last words tapering off a quarter of the way through.

On 14 April 1945 Father wrote that they were near the small town of Celle when word came through of a local truce negotiated with Germans bedded in some ten miles away. They'd been running a prison camp where typhus was raging and agreed the truce to avoid the plague decimating the armies on both sides. The Allies were to take over the camp, the German and Hungarian troops allowed to stay until they were able to move back to their lines. They were to remain under arms.

April 15th

We marched through forests of pine, the sharp tang of resin in the air, the thin spring light trickling through the needles, birdsong everywhere. The men were singing – war songs of course, but anything else that came to mind, snatches of folk songs, songs from films, the odd hymn, and sometimes they sang in the same key and sometimes not, but it didn't matter. This was the final furlong. We were all alive, and for the moment not thinking about the dead. But as we came closer to our destination, the voices subsided. The stench hacked at us more savagely than any bayonet. The trees stopped suddenly as though to persevere was presumptuous, and we saw the camp. Bergen-Belsen.

I stop reading. The book feels too hot to handle and I lay it on the desk. I've seen the pictures. Have seen the piles of bodies stripped not just of their clothes, not just of their flesh, but of their difference. Have seen the naked men and women thrown carelessly together in a ghastly bacchanal of death. Have seen the bulldozers tumbling them into pits like so much hard core. But I've never seen Father there. Never imagined his eyes seared by the horrors. For a moment

I can't bear knowing this about him and I sit sipping my drink, willing the diary to spontaneously combust. Willing myself to walk away. To leave a note for Magda, asking her to chuck away whatever she finds on my desk.

I don't of course. I can't now make him love me, but maybe the chill between us when he came back wasn't my fault. Or not entirely my fault anyway. I pick the book up.

He is meticulous in recording what he saw in the camp. Equally precise in recording what he felt when he came across the perpetrators.

I moved towards the heavy building at the end of the camp, long red banners hanging from its guttering, the black swastika brazen in its white circle halfway down. A group of men lounged smoking on the front steps, their crisp SS uniforms an insult to the depravity that lay behind me. Their revolvers sat in shiny holsters at their hips and my hand moved to my own before I checked myself. I wasn't to kill them. Orders were to co-exist with them, this enemy whom I'd been bombarding only days before.

I saw a blonde woman standing with a group of camp guards, her cap tipped perkily on her head, her jackboots giving off a lambent glow. 'That's Irma Grese,' said a Canadian soldier, following my gaze. 'She was the worst of the lot. Took pleasure in killing, in torturing the women. Sexual pleasure I mean. It's enough to drive you mad, isn't it? Girl like that. She's only twenty-one.'

Suddenly guns seemed too civilised to use on these beasts. I needed a cutlass in my hand, its edge sharp enough to fillet a leaf. I needed to charge at them, slashing and stabbing till I'd avenged the accursed victims I'd seen in the dust behind me. I turned to walk away before I, too, turned to mass murder. On the ground at my feet was a bundle of rags and I kicked at it, kicked it out of my way, kicked it against the fence where it bounced and fell on the ground.

It was a child, its baby contours as flat as its future. I fell to my knees. I howled.

My head starts to knock. I was in a waterfall, the water raining down like soft blue diamonds. I was sleeping. I was spying. I was kicked.

244

I'm spying now. I'm learning about Father, about a moment when his history crashed against my head. I put my hand to my temple. I creep its fingers across my scalp. I feel the lump, feel Mother's brush: *Oh Lord, you have been in the wars,* she says.

I'm not a doctor now, just a daughter. I can't lay my hand on his forehead. There's no remedy for death, so I can't heal him. This dark man with his dark secrets is beyond my reach, where he's always been.

It's pointless to cry. Spilled milk, spilled blood, spilled tears, it's all the same: mop it up, bleach the stains, pass the ammunition, move on.

There's a rustle behind me and a sweet smell fills the room. Ruby's mouth is in my hair. 'Come with me, *mon capitaine,*' she says and helps me to stand. Her clothes are scandalous against her emaciated body and her make-up is brash. She has a bottle of whisky in her hand, which she holds like a bludgeon. I follow her out of the study, across the landing and into my bedroom. She slides the robe over my head and touches my battered lip with her finger. She takes faded striped pyjamas from under the pillow and dresses me, the buttons fluttering like moths against my skin. She lays me on the bed gently, gently, in case I break. Sitting by my head, she cradles my head and puts the opened bottle to my lips. I suck greedily at it, but Ruby says, 'Slowly, *mon petit,* there's plenty.' She dabs at my mouth between swigs with a lavender-scented handkerchief. When the bottle is finished, she settles my head back on the pillow and arranges the bedclothes around me. She puts a hammer in my hand, switches off the light and leaves.

When I wake with the dawn and swing my feet out of bed, I see the shards of the bottle peppering the carpet. I put on my leather Moroccan slippers and crunch to the bathroom. I avoid my reflection because the mirror's been smashed. The frosted window's been smashed too, and a hammer rests, wearied, at the bottom of the battered bath. I go downstairs. The kitchen curtains have been slashed with my favourite carving knife, as though to blind the room. There are deep scratches in the worktop and a board has been stabbed through the heart near the sink.

Before I make my splendid breakfast, I burn the journals in the garden brazier. The smoke hangs over the pyre as if reluctant to leave. I get a sack from the shed and flap at it. The smoke flees over the gardens.

I'm starving.

# 1952

William takes the *Times* to his study. He closes the door quietly, as though afraid to wake the dead. He clears a space on his desk, consigns *L'Aube de la Renaissance* to the floor and his pens to the box he bought in France.

There is no other news. Yesterday George VI died in his sleep and the nation now grieves for their unexpected king. He was hurtled on to the throne the year William was hustled into marriage, both of them reluctant but compliant.

*You owe it us, lad.*

On the front page, the alderman stands in front of Queen Victoria's statue and reads the proclamation. The words freeze in history's arctic breath. The young mother in Africa is suddenly a queen, willy-nilly.

God save her anyway.

The King was sixteen years older than William is now, and he considers whether he'll make it to fifty-six. His father is seventy-two, with the vigour and spleen of a man half his age, but his sons may be blighted. Along with the factory's mantle, William wonders if he's inherited his brother's attenuated life. Sometimes he hopes he has.

There's a timid tap at the door.

'Father?' says Virginia from the other side. 'Mother says your breakfast is ready. I'm going off to school now. Mother's going shopping in two ticks.'

He hears her pad down the hall and he waits until the front door closes before he goes to the kitchen.

It feels wrong to be tucking into a fry-up with the King on his catafalque in Westminster Hall. He toys with his black pudding but leaves the rest to congeal. Eleanor will deal with it when she gets back.

When he reaches his office, Stephen telephones him.

'Just heard from Beaver,' he says. 'Major Beaver. Says there's to be a contingent of the regiment at the King's funeral. I said we'd both go. That's right, isn't it?'

'Of course,' says William. 'Let's take a few days. Might as well. Stay at that little Mayfair hotel from before.'

'Unfortunately, I'm right in the middle of that case I told you about – bally nuisance, but Rogers is off sick and there's no one else I trust. I'll raise a glass to the King, though. And to us.'

Martin will have been at work for hours, so it's safe to call Agnès. They've never managed to be together for longer than a night, so a few days together in London would be thrilling. Martin's so consumed with work he hasn't noticed his wife's absences, and Eleanor wouldn't care if she did.

Agnès is delighted. She is already inventing a reunion of her old school friends, who are coming to London for a break.

Six days later when Virginia comes back from school, she finds a note written in her father's fine italic hand propped against the hall phone.

*Eleanor – gone to London for King's funeral*, it says. *Probably back in a few days.*

She doesn't pick it up in case Mother spots that she's read a letter not addressed to her.

William and Stephen sit in the First Class compartment of the train snickering down to London. William offers his friend a cigar but Stephen pulls out his Woodbines and says ruefully, 'Can't seem to give these things up, old man. Don't quite know why – after all, I can easily afford American fags now, but Woodies bring it all back. Sometimes I wish I could fucking forget actually, especially when I wake in the night with my head chock-a-block. But at the same time, forgetting feels dishonourable somehow. As though I'd be disrespecting the dead. D'you know what I mean?'

William always knows what Stephen means. He knows what Stephen means even when he's only having a passing thought. He, too, has learned to say 'fuck' in the war, but for him it belongs on the battlefield, under fire, and sounds subversive in this well-heeled carriage.

Half an hour into their journey and after several slugs from his hip flask, Stephen falls asleep. When the train hurdles the points, his head jerks to the left and William reaches over and props him back up. He wipes a thin trail of drool from the corner of his mouth with his linen handkerchief.

At the hotel they arrange for their uniforms to be pressed and go to see their dead king. They join a queue that snakes down the road and round the block, men as well as women dabbing their eyes and sharing memories. They are grateful to this fragile man for learning to speak through his stammer, for quelling his anxiety enough to address them, for staying with his people when the bombs fell. His daughter has a hard act to follow.

They do the slow, shy shuffle of the bereaved past George's coffin and William wonders how he lived his life behind palace doors. Wonders if his comely wife and adoring daughters were enough to anaesthetise the agonies of kingship. Wonders if he ever planned his escape.

The next day, they escort the King to Paddington with their old comrades, their chins at exactly forty-five degrees, their shoulders ranked like shelves. Chopin's funeral march hangs dolefully in the air as George is loaded on to the train to Windsor like a rather large parcel for the Royal Mail. The old soldiers drift with the civilian crowds back to the centre of London.

Stephen has one beer and leaves for the hotel. 'Drink yourselves silly for me, chaps,' he says. 'Work's a fucking nuisance sometimes.'

William settles in for the duration.

Each man gives a precised account of his post-war life, but it's no more than a formality. They can't wait to get down to what binds them. Their memories. No one else in their lives has seen a comrade splintered. No one else's eyes have been cataracted by horrors.

He is drunker as he reaches his hotel than he's ever been in his life. Drunker even than in 1945, when he was sure Japan's surrender was a ruse. Sure the Nips would jump out from behind their loss of face shouting, '*Surprise!*'

The hotel porter is a kindly man who remembers the armistice thirty-four years ago and he steers William to his room, which seems not to be quite where he left it.

When he wakes up the following morning, he's wet the bed.

He sits in the hotel dining room, queasy over his kedgeree and tea. His head is chattering like a pack of antic monkeys splashing about in puddles of alcohol. Fragments of a dream keep jabbing at him. A child – there was something about a child, but he can't pin it down. He thinks of all the children he knows, but none of them ring any bells.

He debates whether he should own up to the sodden bed, but decides to brazen it out. The hotel is far too well bred to mention it. He won't be sleeping in it tonight anyway since he's booked another room for Agnès under a false name.

I've had to creep around for the past nine days. I thought Mother was going to cry when she saw the news of the King's death on our new television set, and I've never seen Mother cry. She's been wearing her black necklace and brooch a lot ever since. I think it's made of ebony, which is a tree that grows in India and Ceylon. I learned about that in geography. Father didn't cry but he looked sort of gloomy, as though he'd been told there'd been an explosion at the factory or something. He started playing sad records on the gramophone – there was sad music on the wireless too – which made me feel like life was happening in slow motion. You see it in films sometimes when a lady's about to get kissed. He doesn't chat much at the best of times but I was rather afraid to say anything to him when we met each other in case it made him angry for disturbing his gloom. I'd say, 'Excuse me, Father,' if we passed on the stairs, but anything else might have startled him.

Mother said nothing when she came home and read Father's note, but after he left we ate our supper on trays in front of the television, which isn't usually allowed.

If I say something while it's on, Mother says, 'Shh!' without look-ing at me. Even if all I want to say is, 'Please, Mother, may I be excused

– I need to go to the lavatory.' One time I jolly nearly wet my knickers because I was too afraid to ask to leave the room. I couldn't decide whether it'd be worse to wet myself or to interrupt, but in the end I avoided an accident by thinking of my biology homework.

Now Mother and I are sitting on the sofa in front of the screen flickering at the heart of its huge walnut cabinet. Mother has a black suit on and her face is made up and her hair is styled and she's sitting up awfully straight. If I sit up straight I tower above her, which doesn't seem right, so I slide down on the cushions till my head's at the level of her shoulders. I could almost rest it on them if I bent sideways. I cross my ankles like ladies do but it's jolly uncomfortable. *You're nearly fourteen now, Virginia. Try to behave like a lady.* I really do try. I'm wearing my best shoes – Mother insisted – and the patent leather reflects the pattern of the wallpaper if I move my feet a little to the left. It takes my mind off my ankles but I mustn't do it too much or Mother will think I'm fidgeting, which would be dreadfully rude in the middle of a funeral.

The King's flag-draped coffin crawls through the streets of London on its gun carriage, led by soldiers on horses with shiny breastplates and ponytails on their helmets. I've never been to London, though I went to Manchester once on a school trip, and I think it's probably quite frightening. But it doesn't look frightening with a funeral going on – it could almost be a sleepy little village. A man is describing the scene as though he thinks you've gone blind, so I look sideways to see if Mother thinks that's a bit queer. To my surprise, I see tears plopping off her face on to her blouse, though she's not making a sound. She's not snuffling and she doesn't look like a pink cauliflower like I do when I've been crying in my room. I put my hand in my pocket to find a handkerchief for her, but then I think better of it because she might want to keep her crying secret, like I do.

I'm getting bored because all that's happening is a lot of walking along streets, so I try to pick Father out in the crowds lining the route. I don't know what he's wearing but it's almost bound to include his black hat, so I scan the rows and rows of people to see if I can spot him. I can't see him or the hat. I see some men wearing funny wigs and gowns, bowing their heads as the coffin passes. I have to put my hand over my mouth to cover my smile. Fancy turning up to a funeral in fancy dress!

Then it's the end. The coffin is loaded on to a train, which takes off full of important-looking people. Maybe Father goes off with them because he's very important here in Harrogate.

Mother pulls her handkerchief from her sleeve and dabs at her eyes. She walks over to the television, clicks it off and leaves the room, holding her head very high as though there's a horrid smell under her nose. I watch the little star vanish in the middle of the screen. If I was a superhero, I'd pull it out and fill the room with starlight. I wish I was Superman. Mother won't let me read comic books because they're vulgar, but Aurora brings them into school and we look at them and imagine what superpowers we'd like to have. I'd like to have X-ray vision because then I could see my parents behind closed doors. I wonder what they'd say – I'd need super-hearing for that of course – and if they talked about me. As I leave the room, I go over to the television and stroke it like a family pet. I've always wished we could have a pet, but Mother says they make too much noise and mess.

I've just finished reading *The Mountain of Adventure* by Enid Blyton. She's my favourite writer in the whole world because her books are full of stupid grown-ups who muck things up and clever children who save the day. Aurora and I are reading our way through all her books, so the next day I go over to her house to compare notes. It's always this way round because although Mother's never said anything, I don't think she approves of her much. Her house is crammed with wild paintings and bright colours and smells of spices I've never heard of. And her family talk about the weirdest things all the time – even things that aren't very polite – and they do a lot of laughing. Cassandra, her mother, is extremely rich and extremely tall and she's got this crazy hair the same colour as Mother's, which she makes into knots and clumps with clips and clasps. She doesn't seem to care about being fashionable or anything, so she just wraps scarves round her head and shawls round her hips and isn't bothered if nothing matches. And she wears tons of jewellery so you always know when she's coming because she clatters and clanks.

Aurora and I saw her parents in the kitchen once when we came in to ask how to use the heated rollers. They were kissing by the sink, Cassandra's back arched over the worktop. They didn't hear us and we watched as Hugo's hands slid down her thighs to lift her skirt. I knew I should look somewhere else because it's rude to look at private things, but I couldn't tear my eyes away. Aurora gave a little giggle and Hugo looked over. At the time I thought he must have stuffed a banana down the front of his trousers in case he got peckish.

'Oh, there you are!' he said, a little breathlessly. 'Sorry – I was just overtaken for a moment by your gorgeous mother. Come and have a hug, darling.'

Aurora skipped over to them and they folded her into them as though she'd always been there. I envied her, although I wouldn't have called it that then because I knew I had to be grateful for what I had. Starving children and all that. But I had four helpings of Cassandra's boeuf stroganoff at suppertime and two of the crème brûlée.

'Where do you put it all, Ginny?' said Hugo. 'You must have hollow legs.'

I laughed with the rest of them but I was busy stashing away what I'd seen, like a soon-to-hibernate squirrel.

When I arrive, Aurora and I go up to her bedroom via Cassandra's dressing room. There's a huge great pile of perfumes and make-up on her dressing table next to the hair things and we scoop a selection into our skirts and totter along the corridor. Once we're in her bedroom, Aurora takes the Anglepoise lamp from her desk and the bedside light from the chest and points them to make a spotlight in front of the mirror. We spend ages experimenting with make-up and hairstyles, pulling pouty faces at our reflections, trying to look like ladies even though we're only girls. When we've finished, Aurora looks even more beautiful but I just look like I've had an accident.

Aurora goes back to the dressing room and chooses a pile of clothes in mad colours and patterns and we giggle as we try them on in front of the mirror. When Cassandra shouts up to say tea's ready (which they call dinner here), Aurora's wearing a beaded frock in turquoise chiffon and I'm wearing a sari, which is the only thing that fits me properly.

Aurora's father's already sitting at the dining table as we come in and when he sees her he stands up and comes over.

'Oh, my darling girl,' he says, 'don't you look gorgeous! You could be a film star!' He gathers her in his arms. 'Mm,' he says, 'and you smell delicious – is that Cassandra's sandalwood?' He looks over her head to where I'm standing in the doorway. 'Oh, Ginny,' he says, 'and you look lovely too.'

I know that I don't, but just for a moment I can borrow a little of his kindness. It's not like stealing or anything because I'll leave it behind when I go home.

Six weeks later, Aurora's gone. She invites me over three days before her family leave the country. We sit on her bed with our legs tangled up, and I'm getting ready to gossip about what Jennifer did today in Cookery.

'We're moving to Venezuela,' Aurora says suddenly, and I feel like I've been stabbed. 'Cassandra says she's sick of all those dreary English winters and wants to be somewhere jolly. And she likes South American music too. Says we can go to dance classes together – I can't wait! I wish you could come with us. Don't be sad,' she says.

Sad doesn't begin to describe what I'm feeling as I watch my life start to bleed. 'But you can't!' I say. 'What'll become of me? Who'll I talk to if you're not here?'

'Well, I'll write to you of course, soppy date!' Aurora says. 'We'll be pen pals – what fun that'll be! And maybe your parents will let you come and visit us over there. We're going to have a ranch thing. With horses. Hugo's going to breed them – he says it's high time Hera and Sandro and me learned to ride bare back.'

'What will I do without you?' I say. I think I'm going to be sick. 'You're my only friend.'

'I know. And you're my only friend too, but look, I wanted to give you this so that when you put it on, you'll think of me.' She pulls a pink angora jumper out of her satchel. 'It's my favourite thing in the whole wide world, so every time you wear it, it'll be like I'm giving you a hug, and every time I miss it I'll know I'm missing you.'

When I get home I try on the sweater, but I know what I'll see when I turn to the mirror. It looks as stupid on me as a bishop's mitre on a penguin, and my shoulders are stretching the knitting way beyond its limits. I take it off, find some tissue paper and wrap it up. I fold my hopes into its creases and put it in a drawer.

Aurora sends me hypercoloured postcards from time to time, to which I reply with long confessionals. But when the cards dry up, I realise I've been dumped.

*There's the girl. She's at the front door in her coat. The maroon wool one with the big buttons. The practical one. She calls out.* Just popping into town, *she calls.* Make sure you're back in time for tea – *the woman's voice comes from upstairs.* OK, *says the girl.* Don't say OK, please. It's common – *the woman's voice again.* Sorry, *says the girl and leaves the house. She goes down the drive, her heavy shoes crunching on the gravel. A damp leaf sticks to the side of the left shoe, but she doesn't bend over to flick it off. She's feeling daring today. So daring that she wouldn't even scrape her sole on the kerb if she stepped in dog muck. As she turns the corner by the hotel, she unbuttons her coat. Just a bit. Just enough to pull out the brown paper bag she's got hidden under her arm. She holds it in her left hand and buttons up the coat again. She has to stop walking because she's all fingers and thumbs. When she's wrapped up again, she walks down the hill. She's almost skipping. She's swinging the paper bag backwards and forwards by her side. She looks merry. When she gets to the park, she strides across the lawn. Big giant steps at first, then she starts to run. She can't wait. The public lavatories are open and she goes into the Ladies. She opens the door of a cubicle and goes in. She carefully turns the lock so everyone will know she's ENGAGED. The lavatory smells of disinfectant, which doesn't quite cover the smell of fart. Except ladies don't fart. They break wind and apologise, blushing. She takes off her coat and hangs it on the hook on the wall next to the graffiti that tells her that Geraldine fucks dogs. There's a picture. She's wearing a tweed skirt with side pockets, a brown jacket and a cream blouse with a tie thing at the neck. And snagged wool stockings which her suspenders struggle to accommodate – sometimes it takes several goes before she can fiddle their buttons through the loops with her large hands. She takes off her jacket and blouse and stands there in her liberty bodice. She's slightly sweaty now, but she can't wipe it off because the lavatory paper is the shiny kind, Izal, which just slips off when you try to dry yourself. You have to sort of saw back and forth after you've done something. She bends over and opens* the bag. She pulls it out with both hands, so it looks like washing on the line. She smells it. She thinks she can smell her still, even though it's been a while. She probably smells different now. Venezuelan. Whatever Venezuelan smells like. She lifts it over her head and holds it there for a second. Willing it to fit her properly this time. She's managed not to eat lots recently, so she might have shrunk enough. She lowers it and pulls it over her head. It resists at first, then grudgingly lets her head through. Her hair's messy and there are little bits of angora in it and on her nose, but she doesn't care. She pushes her arms through the armholes. The sleeves stop short of her wrists. She pulls it down to her waist. She packs her jacket and her blouse into the paper bag, which she chose because it was the biggest one under the sink. She puts her coat over her arm, picks up the bag and leaves the cubicle. She tries not to look in the mirror as she passes, but the sudden flash of colour startles her. The mirror has lost some of its silvering and is streaky. You don't want to imagine what the streaks are. She sees herself in patches, like a reflection in choppy water. She tries to admire herself. Admire herself for wearing the pink angora jumper. For wearing it in public, but for a moment she loses her nerve. Loses the daring that she felt earlier. Buck up, she says to her reflection, it might never happen.

As she walks up the High Street, she sees people looking at her. She hopes they like what they see. Tries to keep her head up, but her shoulders are beginning to shrug up to her ears. She hears giggling behind her and she knows it's because of the jumper. Not the jumper exactly, but the her-in-the-jumper. She darts into the department store. Goes in the lift up to Ladies Wear. Finds a big rack with winter coats on it and hides behind it. Her heart is pounding. She's blushing. There's a shop assistant over there who's noticed her. She tries to look unsuspicious, but she fails. The lady comes over to her. She is wearing a black suit and very high heels. Her dark hair is stuck on top of her head in shiny, shiny curls that don't look real. Can I help you? she says and the girl comes out from behind the coats. It's only polite. When she sees the jumper, when she sees the girl in the jumper, the lady's eyebrows shoot up. They're black eyebrows with a sudden angle at the top. Like black elbows, but they seem to have a life of their own, jumping like frogs up to her hair. N . . . no, it's OK – I mean, it's all right. I'm fine actually, the girl says. Just looking around. You know. The lady fixes her with a hard look from under swoops of black eyeliner. You look like you could do with a new jumper, *she says*. That one doesn't fit properly. Not quite your colour, is it? Not your style. I've borrowed it from a friend, *the girl says, a bit desperately.* She said it would keep me warm. Let's find you something else, *says the lady. Almost kindly, though her eyebrows haven't come down yet.* Look, over here, *she says, and the girl follows her over to a row of brown and cream jumpers. Sturdy things. No frivolity or jolliness there. Or style. She picks up three and leads the girl to the changing rooms. She stands outside, on guard in case the girl steals something. She looked suspicious, after all, back there behind the coats. The girl tries on all the jumpers. When she looks in the mirror, she sees herself. Her shapeless self. Dull. She's fighting back tears now. She sits on the spindly-legged chair in the cubicle and fights the tears. Swallows the sound of losing the fight. She has to fight the pink jumper, too, which is reluctant to go back on. She forces it, and feels the stitches in the left-hand shoulder give up the ghost. The seam splits. She stands up.* Shoulders back, *she tells herself.* Stand up tall, *she says, but not out loud. She gives the jumpers back to the assistant and thanks her.* I don't think so, *she says.* Not today, *and doesn't look at the lady's face in case her eyebrows leap up again. She races back to the public lavatory, her ears filled with the laughter pursuing her down the street. She tears off the jumper, puts on the blouse, which she buttons wrong, shrugs on the jacket again and sits on the lavatory seat. She doesn't care about the germs Mother goes on about.*

*I put out my hand. I rest it on her shoulder.*

You can't do it, *I say.* You can't borrow her.

She wanted me to. She wanted me to be like her.

She just wanted to leave you something to remember her by.

As if I'd forget? As if she'd ever be out of sight, out of mind?

When was the last time you heard from her?

Yesterday. I got a postcard yesterday.

Are you sure about that?

Yes. She told me she misses me horribly. And that she hates Venezuela. And that she wishes she was back here with me.

Really?

Yes. *Yes!*

?

OK, OK – no! She didn't, OK? She hasn't written for ages and ages, OK? I've sent her three letters and she hasn't written back. Not once.

She's forgotten you then.

Yes, she has. Yes, she *bloody* has. It was all rubbish. Everything she said to me about being my friend was rubbish. She didn't mean any of it. She told me lies. She told me lies all the time. Not fibs, not little fibs – big fat lies. I hate her!

Hate's a big word.

So's love. But I'd rather have hate because it makes you strong. No one's going to push you around if you're strong.

But you loved her.

*The girl snaps forwards. I put my arms round her. Her voice is muffled by the tweed.*

Yes, *she says.* Yes.


*When she gets home, she doesn't bother taking off her coat and hanging it by the front door. She takes the paper bag to her room. She sits on her bed. She pulls the jumper out and snips the bottom edge with a pair of nail scissors. She tugs at a strand of wool and the stitches pull out of each other's clutches. The knitting unravels. She kicks at the angora heap on the floor and pink fluff sticks to her shoe buckle.*

*Ruby's there. She comes and sits next to her. She stormed off when Aurora came along, but now she's back.*

I told you so, *she says.* Told you she wouldn't stick around. You're such a dope – d'you really think she wanted to be your friend? Better not try that again. Come on, let's get rid of this shitty thing.

*They bury the wool in the garden with no incantations or rites. It'll get maggoty and slimy. She hopes it rots.*


*No more distractions. She can be single-minded. She can pass her exams and leave home. She can depend on herself.*

*And Ruby. She can always depend on Ruby.*

# 1977

Gilda's mojo is back and boogying. Her friends notice. Her clients notice. Maxim-aka-Samuel notices.

'Sweetie,' he says, 'you look like you're on top of the world.'

She is. She holds it between her knees like a beach ball. She bounces it on her head. She keeps it in the air with her toes. She controls it. Her tips go up because her ladies feel cherished and Maxim's upped her wages too, so the nursery's affordable, she and her boy eat well and she could arrange a holiday if she wanted one. A hunting trip to Wales if she wanted one. Stephanie's daughter is longing to babysit Tobias, who has beguiled her as he beguiles the world, but Gilda rarely goes out and her friends learn that if they want to see her, they must come to her house and adore her baby. It's not hard. Virginia's often there, though never when anyone else is expected, and if someone pitches up by chance, she remembers an urgent task elsewhere. Gilda invites her to dinner with friends a few times, but after a bit she stops asking because there's always an excuse. It suits her to have her friend to herself anyway. One evening, as she strolls home with Tobias after buying bananas, she passes her favourite Indian restaurant. She sees Virginia sitting in the Kastoori window with her back to the street and is about to go in and show her the baby's new tooth when she sees what's going on. Sees Virginia's hunger. Sees the ten dishes she's working through. Sees her need for solitude.

She walks on.

She tries to hook her friend into novels, but Virginia's having none of it.

'No time,' she says. 'And anyway, I'm not interested in someone else's fantasies. Reality's quite enough for me, thanks very much.'

When they pass a clothes shop together, Gilda suggests going in and trying things on – just for a giggle. 'How about a make-over?' she says. 'Smarten up your wardrobe.'

'Don't think so,' says Virginia. 'Happy the way I am,' and Gilda doesn't push it.

But one lunchtime, after an overdose of cheese, she passes behind Virginia's chair and strokes her head. 'You could do such a lot with your hair,' she says, 'it's got loads of body, but it's just sitting there at the moment. Let me have a go, see what I could do – please. You could look years younger.'

'But I've always worn it this way. Means I don't have to bother with it. And why would I want to look younger?'

'Most women would.'

'But I'm not most women.'

'I know. That's what I like about you. But suppose I could make it easier to manage *and* liven it up a bit? What then?'

'I really don't want anything I have to fuss with.'

'Promise you. No fussing, no blow-drying, no product, nothing. Just a style you can wash and leave.' She runs her hands through Virginia's hair, assessing its texture.

Her touch is tender and Virginia closes her eyes. No knots or tugging either. 'Well, if you want to,' she says gruffly. 'Go on then – but I'll shave it off if I don't like it, I warn you. I'm not looking stupid.'

'As if I'd make you look stupid,' says Gilda. 'As if I'd do that to you.'

She washes Virginia's hair and massages her head with conditioner in slow, sensual strokes.

Virginia's body goes limp. 'Oh my goodness, that does feel good,' she says. 'I could almost go to sleep now. Don't stop.'

Gilda sometimes thinks Virginia must have had a vanity bypass at birth because she's never known a woman so indifferent to looking good – aside from the Sistern, that is – but this is looking promising. She finds her styling scissors and clips and they go down to the kitchen.

She sits Virginia in the middle of the room with a towel round her shoulders. 'You ready?' she asks.

'Do your worst.'

'Or maybe I'll do my best – there's a surprise!'

She combs and parts and clips the hair. Starting with the front, she feathers and thins it so that it rests in tendrils round Virginia's face, which begins to change shape. Begins to soften. As her hair gets shorter, its kinks rediscover some earlier grace and when Gilda reaches the nape, she finds a cluster of tight curls huddling at the base of her skull.

'Oh my god,' she says, 'your hair's really curly back here – who'd have known? What was it like when you were a little girl?'

Virginia is silent for a moment. She remembers his jacket with the patches at the elbow. His freckly hands. His kiss. 'It was curly,' she says. She tries to keep her voice steady. 'My mother hated it because it'd get really tangled. Specially in the morning, when I'd been tossing my head in my sleep. She'd pull the brush through it and I could feel her getting more and more irritated and hear her tutting, so I tried not to say ouch. But he liked it. He used to pat me on the head and call me Bubbles. It was the only nickname I've ever had, and it made me feel sort of ethereal, as though I could float away up to heaven. One evening, after he'd patted my head and called me Bubbles, he bent over and kissed me on the head. No one'd ever done that before, and it felt like the spot where he'd kissed me was hot. Like a tiny oven.'

Gilda is stroking the back of Virginia's neck. She strokes the baby's neck when he's fussing.

'I remember wishing I could find a saucepan lid just the right size so I could keep the spot warm forever. Or . . . or . . . keep my hand over it so the kiss would never go away.' Her voice wavers. 'But it did of course. I held my finger on the spot all the way upstairs to my bedroom, but I had a friend staying and she jogged my elbow – deliberately, I think, because she said I looked stupid – and I never found it again. I used to wish it'd been hot enough to burn me because then it would've left a scar and I could run my fingers across my scalp till I felt it again. Like running through a forest and finding a secret place where you could hide. I used to love hiding. Whenever I found another hidey-hole in the house or in the garden, I knew I'd be safe for a little while. When I was in there, all by myself, when no one could see me, I was in control. I could look out and see things. I could hear things and they wouldn't know. They wouldn't know what I knew. I'd have to come out eventually of course. Couldn't stay hidden forever. Although sometimes I wondered if they'd come looking for me if I did. If they'd notice I hadn't been around for a while. If they'd realise nothing had got broken for a while. I didn't feel lonely in the hidey-holes because I was with me. *I* was noticing *me*. I could be who I wanted to be. I could be as naughty as I liked – as wicked even. It wasn't so much out of sight, out of mind, because truthfully I don't think I was in anybody's mind, but when I was hiding I was in my own sight. In my own mind. Whatever state of mind I was in. But they had to be stolen, these moments. And they were like a string of islands. Couldn't link them up. Couldn't stitch them together to make a mainland. Anything solid.'

She's still for a few moments, then Gilda feels the muscles in her neck tightening. 'But I've got my work. I'm a doctor. I'm a good doctor. *Good.* I make things happen. I make people better. Healing, that's what I do. I don't break things at work. Don't destroy . . . don't . . . don't destroy things. Bring new life into the world. That's what I do. Not a savage. I'm *not a savage!*' She's breathing heavily and a droplet of sweat creeps down her neck.

Gilda's hand rests on Virginia's shoulder and the two women stay where they are, as though they've fused.

Tobias starts to whimper in the next room, where he's been asleep in his chair, and Virginia shrugs Gilda's hand off. 'You'd better go and see to him,' she says fiercely. 'He needs you – go on!'

'He's fine. Don't worry. He's OK for the moment and I've just got to finish off here at the back. Sit down now.'

Virginia has half risen. 'I'll come back,' she says, 'you can finish off another time.'

'No,' says Gilda firmly, 'I'll do it now, Virginia. Sit still.' She shapes the back of her friend's hair, layering it and cutting a wispy coda into the nape. She puts the scissors down and says, 'There you go.'

Virginia stands up and frantically brushes at her shoulders, getting rid of the evidence. 'Got to go,' she mutters. 'Must dash.'

'But don't you want to see what you –'

'Got a mirror at home. 'S fine. Sure it's fine. Got to go.' She hears the baby. 'See to the baby!' she says, her voice cracking. 'For Christ's sake!' and she's out of the door. She's down the path, she's along the road, running, running from what she's just done.

I have got a mirror but I don't look in it. Don't want to see what I look like skinned. What this woman looks like who gives away secrets.

Ruby's tongue snakes into my ear. 'Just write a fucking newsletter, why don't you? Shove it through everyone's fucking letter box. I told you not to leave clues and now you've blabbed like some big baby. Well, actions have consequences, Virginia, actions have consequences. I'm not going to help you with this one – you're on your own.'

I sleep fitfully, dreaming of escaping/not escaping/trying to escape. Failing. I'm naked in the dreams. I can't move my arms to cover myself up. I can't poke the eyes of the spies looking straight in my guts.

I walk into the hospital the next morning and turn heads.

'My goodness, don't you look pretty!'

'What a change, Miss Denham!'

'Hardly recognised you, Virginia – you look ten years younger.'

'Wow!'

If I could bandage my head, I would. If I could wear a hat, I would. I don't *want* to be someone they don't recognise – I don't recognise. I don't *want* to look ten years younger or pretty. But there's nowhere to hide, so I freeze. As the hours crawl by, the comments start to ping off and clatter to the ground, disarmed. I hope I'll make it through the day without making a mistake.

Without hurting anyone.

Faisal's running late. Actually, he isn't running at all because he pulled a calf muscle on the squash court last night, so every step is a painful reminder of losing. He doesn't think of himself as a competitive man, but when he plays squash, winning means more to him than is seemly. When he wins, he thanks his opponent – congratulates him on his game even – but in the locker room he talks like a killer. 'Thrashed him,' he says. 'Slaughtered the poor bastard. Wiped him out.'

Last night, he was thrashed by a banker whose sneery mien reminded him of his housemaster, so the humiliation stung. 'Get you back next time,' he said as they walked off the court. 'Won't take that one lying down,' but he looked away as he said it to avoid the other man's triumph.

He limps along the corridor towards the committee room, hoping that Anna remembered to bring along his briefcase as he'd asked her to. Hoping that he'd remembered to put the right damn papers in when he fished them out of his study last night. He glances through the small window in the door before he goes in. Everybody's there, their heads turned towards the chairman at the head of the table. He impresses himself no end with his procedures this and his policies that: it is his only talent and he milks it. There's a woman sitting on the left-hand side Faisal doesn't recognise, which is odd since the committee's composition hasn't changed since its inception. He pushes the door open and mutters apologetically over to the seat next to Anna and opposite the stranger.

Anna lays his briefcase in his lap and he smiles gratefully at her. She scribbles something on her copy of the minutes and slides it over to him. *HELLLLP!!!* it says, *I'm fighting a coma! – do something! Sing, dance – anything!*

Faisal's rummaging in his case for the agenda when the stranger opposite interrupts the chairman's peroration. Except that it isn't a stranger. When he looks up, for a moment it feels like someone's switched channels as he hears Virginia's voice, sees Virginia's form, but doesn't recognise Virginia's head. He is so used to her careless-ness about her appearance, her well-cut hair is as shocking as a poodle's head on a mutt. It's not that she's any less plain, more that it looks as if her appearance matters to her. As if she minds what other people think. Anna sees the expression on his face and pushes another note across to him. *I know*, it says, *what's going on? Is she having a funny turn? Surely she's not dating!?!?!?*

Virginia neither looks at him nor anyone else as the meeting drones on, addressing her papers when she speaks as though they were intimates, but Faisal notices how busy her hands are. How they rub at her hair and cover her head and pull at her fringe. When the meeting finishes, she shoots out of the door and is halfway down the corridor before he catches up with her.

'Virginia!' he says. 'Just wanted to say how lovely –'

'Don't say anything unless it's work, OK? Or that meeting, OK? Don't want to hear.' And she leaves him standing outside Radiography.

Gilda leaves a message on her answering machine. *Click*. 'Virginia Denham. Leave me a message. Thank you.' *Click*.

'Virginia? It's me. Gilda. Thought you said you were going to be there this evening. I was just calling to see how you are. Hope the haircut hasn't been too much of a shock. I'm sure everybody loved it – you look gorgeous. Give me a call.'

Virginia doesn't call back then. Nor does she reply to the other three messages Gilda leaves over the next fortnight. With anyone else, she'd just turn up on the doorstep with a bottle of wine and an open mind, but she doesn't think she can do that with Virginia, who clearly said more about her father than she wanted to. The father who loved her enough to give her a nickname. Gilda watched this wildlife programme once and when she saw a sea anemone snap its fronds back as it was touched, she decided she'd probably been one in a previous incarnation. Now she knows another one.

She sees the other anemone a few weeks later in Balham market. She's wearing a hat but her stooped figure is unmistakable.

Gilda walks up to her. 'Virginia,' she says, 'I've missed you.'

The friendship resumes, but Gilda is kept at arm's length. She brings the conversation round from time to time to fathers and daughters, tells her Aaron used to call her Becksy, but Virginia's unforthcoming. Gilda understands that she needs the cordon sanitaire, though not why, and feels the loss of intimacy keenly. Since the incident with the pink latex glove she's felt a connection between them that appeared solid. As though they both inhabited the same small island. Now there's a gulf and she can't bridge it.

# 1977


Saturday, 4.33 p.m.

Maxim and her friends keep asking Gilda when she's going to chris-
ten Tobias and while she's hardly going to invite god to the party, she
thinks a celebration might be in order. *This might be the bridge*, she
thinks. She calls Virginia.

'I'm going to have a naming ceremony,' she says, 'here at home.
Next month, on the twenty-fifth. I'm just planning it now – got
a poem or two and this lovely description of a baby I found in a
book recently. Couple of friends are going to read them, and
there'll be music and stuff – and obviously food and drink – and
I know you're not a fan of social events, but I need you to come
to this one. I want you to be his godmother, Virginia, sort of mark
how important you are to him and me and make sure you're part
of his life forever. Would you do it? I don't want anyone else.
Maxim's going to be the godfather, so you'll have something in
common.'

'Well, I don't do god, I think you know that.'

'Strangely, neither do I. Bit of a mystery, that, but I don't know
what else to call you. If I could think of something else, I would, but
at the moment I can't, so we'll have to steel ourselves till I do. Please
say you will.'

There's a pause. Gilda hears Virginia gathering herself.

'I've never been asked that before. Never. I've had babies named
after me – as a matter of fact there's a part of West Africa positively
swimming in Virginias – but that's quite an invitation. Let me think
about it – no, no, that's nonsense. I'd love to do it. Love to. He's a very
special little chap to me.'

'And you're special to both of us. I'm so, so happy, Virginia. You don't know how happy.'

I put the phone down. I can't go. I hate parties. Hate being stuck in a room with a group of people roaming around like chess pieces without a board. Hate the brittle chat over the drone of sex that passes for conversation. If I accept Gilda's invitation, I risk rupturing the membrane I keep between me and the world. The membrane that ballooned the other week when I was so incontinent about Dr Greenaway's kiss. Without it, I'd be exposed to the perils of an intimacy for which I yearn, but by which I am appalled. And suppose Ruby leaves me? She's done that before. Without Ruby I'm an outsider in my own life. Without Ruby I won't be me any more. Not the me I recognise. Not the me-with-Ruby I've been for as long as I can remember being me. I say out loud, 'Ruby?' It sounds like a lamb's bleat, but she's not listening.

I would never have had my own children because I might have been dangerous to them, though I can't imagine harming Tobias. But if I go to the naming, I'm not sure I've got the reserves to stay invisible.

I'll leave it till the week before.

The week before the party, Gilda's running through the order of ceremony with her friends. They're on a second bottle of wine and finding themselves hilarious when the phone rings. Gilda answers through the tail end of a giggle.

'Hello? Shhh, everybody – can't hear myself think.'

'Sounds like you're having a good time,' says Virginia. 'I'll be quick.'

'Oh, it's just the friends who're doing the readings next week. They're getting a bit frisky, the little scamps. They're really looking forward to meeting you.'

'I'm afraid it's not going to happen. I'm terribly disappointed. My secretary forgot to put an engagement in my diary, which is very unlike her, and I find I'm committed to going to a wretched dinner that evening. I'd duck out if I could, but it turns out they're going to give me some award or other, so I'm expected to make a speech. Eileen promised I'd be there apparently, but there was a crisis with one of her children and she forgot to tell me.'

Jenny nudges Karen and they stop talking when they see Gilda slump against the cooker.

'Oh, but that's awful!' she says. 'You're at the heart of the whole thing – I've told everyone so much about you and I was really hoping you'd get on with them because I know they'll love you. And Maxim goes on about meeting you all the time.'

'I know, I know. I was really looking forward to it too – and meeting your friends – but look, why don't I pop in on my way to the dinner? Before the naming ceremony starts. My thing kicks off ridiculously early and I've got a little something for Tobias. I'll raise a glass to him while I'm there. I'll come at half past five – would that be OK?'

'Of course,' says Gilda dully. 'Of course. At least there'll be a whiff of you there.'

Virginia's there at 5.29, dressed in the only grand frock she possesses, a long satin affair in three shades of bland. She's put on a pair of pointed idiot-shoes to take her from the car to Gilda's front door and as she goes up the path, her feet start low-level whingeing. She's carrying a Tesco's carrier bag, which swings against the door as she rings the bell.

Gilda tries not to look too let down. 'Hi. Glad you could pop in for a moment at least. Come in.'

Virginia drops the bag by the front door and follows Gilda, who's carrying Tobias on her hip. As they go into the kitchen he's clapping his hands, as though he knows he's the star of tonight's show. She sits him in his high chair and gives him a rusk.

'Phew! Now I can get shot of this for a moment,' she says, and takes off her plastic apron. She's wearing a floor-length white silk frock, bias cut round her hips, which floats out to a scalloped hem embroidered with daisies. Her hair is loosely pinned round her crown and she's scattered tiny white flowers over her head, as though she's grazed a blossom-heavy branch. She wears a fragile gold chain round her neck.

'You look quite, quite lovely,' says Virginia. 'But I can see why you needed the apron.'

'It's my born-again virgin look,' says Gilda. 'It's what I'm planning to be now I've given up men – well, now that I've got my own little man anyway. Looks a bit like a wedding dress too, doesn't it? Like me and Tobias are getting married – which we sort of are, aren't we, chuckle?'

The baby grins at her through rusky lips and says something that might be, 'Mama, kiss.'

She kisses his head, pops open a bottle of champagne and fills two glasses. 'You've got time for this, have you?'

'You bet!' Virginia takes the glass. 'To Tobias, then, and may his life with you continue as blessed as it's begun. And to you, Gilda, and to all the joys motherhood's bringing you.'

'And to you and your place in his life.'

They take a sip and sit down at the breakfast bar. Gilda's forefinger is running backwards and forwards under the chain.

'It's really shitty that you can't stay,' she says. 'I'm not going to lie. It's left this big gap in the middle of things. It feels like being on my own again. And I've been thinking about my mother a lot for the first time in ages. She gave me this chain when I was eleven. It had a bloody crucifix on it of course, so I sold that, but I know she loved me. She did. Just not enough to stick around with Daddy. When I look at Tobias, sometimes I find myself thinking, *how the fuck could you do that? How the fuck could you leave me?* but perhaps she felt it was just being true to herself. So when you said you couldn't come tonight, she just popped into my head and I remembered being with her when I was little and I wrote her this letter. It was really long – must've been ten pages or so – and I just poured my heart out. Told her all about Tobias and Raymond and how when he walked out, I thought I'd never be happy again. Told her why he walked out, too, so she wouldn't think it was his fault. Told her how happy I am now. Even told her about life with Graham and the others on the scene. The thing is, I don't know if she'd be shocked because I don't know what she's like now. I bet she's changed, away from the Brethren and everything, but it hurts not to know. Oh fuck! Now my make-up's going to smudge.' She grabs a piece of kitchen paper and dabs at her eyes. 'I read the letter to Tobias when I'd finished it – he looked a bit baffled, not surprisingly – then I burned it. I don't know where I'd have sent it to anyway. I think I was just writing to the mother in my head. I don't want to make you feel guilty, Virginia, because obviously you couldn't have helped it, but I really wish you were going to be here tonight.'

'I do too – and I feel very badly about it. I know I'm letting you down.'

'Well, you're not doing it deliberately.'

'No I'm not, but you'll probably wish I *would* stay away in the coming years, you know, when I take up my godmotherly duties – you won't be able to get rid of me!'

'That's just fine by me. And by him too. Oh, do you have to go?'

'I do, but first I wanted to give you something.' She goes to the front door and retrieves the carrier bag. In the kitchen she pulls out two parcels wrapped in paper covered with gurning babies, little rips here and there where she misplaced the Sellotape.

'Ooh, I love opening presents!' says Gilda. 'Look, Tobey-tobes – look what godmother Virginia's brought you!'

In the first parcel is a silver Victorian rattle, its ivory handle yellowed with age and several generations' drool.

'Have a look here,' says Virginia, pointing to the base of the sphere, and Gilda reads the engraving out aloud.

'*From Virginia to Tobias, who will rattle the world.* Oh, that's amazing! I'll read it to him when he's older. Or you can, better still.'

'There's something else to read. Open the other one.'

Gilda draws a book out of the paper, a strange creature gambolling on its cover. 'Oh my goodness,' she says, 'what's this?'

'I had one of these when I was small. It was my favourite book. I pretty much lived in the world of these patchwork people actually. I used to imagine us getting together up a mountain where no one would ever find us. Or tell us off. I hope Tobias enjoys it as much as I did – though I'm sure he won't need to go up a mountain with a bunch of weirdoes.'

When I get home, I banish the wretched satin to its plastic cover in the wardrobe and select my clothes for the evening. If I can't roister at Gilda's party, I'll have my own party here at home. Just as good. If I drink enough, I won't notice I'm alone.

Tight. It needs to be tight tonight to hold me together. I pull on the Speedo swimsuit that's two sizes too small and tug my shiny leggings up my legs. They're not quite long enough and stop mid-calf, as though too shocked by my gormless feet to continue, but they're tight enough to stop the circulation so they'll do. It's chilly, so I shrug on my black PVC bomber jacket covered in studs, and as I close its giant zip I begin to feel settled.

I stuck three bottles of champagne in the fridge before I left. I may drink them all, especially if Ruby turns up. I don't feel hungry because I ate a pot of bouillabaisse before I set off for Gilda's, but I put out chunks of salami in case I need to bite something later. I leave the mimsy little champagne glasses in the cupboard and pour the fizz into a half-pint tankard.

I sit on the kitchen floor with my back against the fridge. I raise a toast to the new godmother.

Aurora didn't have a godmother because her parents couldn't be doing with god, but I did. When I was little I was allowed to call her Auntie Edna, but on my eleventh birthday Mother said it was time to call her Mrs Russell. She used to sit with her family in the pew behind us in St Wilfred's and I'd hear her tone-deaf singing over the choir's harmonies. It was the only loud thing she did. Like all Mother's friends she was a dumpy woman, as though Mother felt her own shapeliness would stand out if she were surrounded by the shapeless. Auntie Edna had four children of her own, all older than me, so asking her to pile godmotherly duties on top of family commitments was a bit of a cheek. She showed no reluctance – not that she showed anything very much – and always gave me something worthy at birthdays. Improving, as though I were already spoiled. Cinderella's godmother improved her prospects by turning her into a beauty fit for a prince, but Mrs Russell's ambitions for me were more earthbound. *Be good. Mind your manners. Work hard. Have children.* I only missed one of her targets.

Ruby's here, sitting beside me on the floor in her combat fatigues. 'Champagne!' she says, holding out her water flask. 'Need some now!'
    'It'll taste tinny in there, Ruby.'
    'Don't care. Fill it up.'

I do as I'm told, and we sit on the floor with our feet out in front of us. I raise my glass to clink her bottle.

'To babies,' I say. 'And their godmothers.'

'Fuck off!' she says. 'Pile of steaming dogshit! Why d'you want to drink to all that bollocks?'

'Because Gilda wants me to be part of Tobias's life. Be a permanent fixture –'

'What, like the plumbing? Dream on, sunshine – you're nothing but a cash cow to her. Why won't you ever learn?'

'Don't say that! Mother used to say that!'

'Well, Mother didn't bullshit you, did she? Mother didn't play games like your fuck-face friend. Grow up, Virginia! How many times do I have to tell you – don't expect anything from anyone.'

'But she's different!' I can hear myself beginning to whine and I'm appalled. 'Gilda likes me. She asked me because she thinks I'll make a good godmother. I'll help her bring Tobias up. I'll make him feel special.' I stand up, refill my glass and open some more champagne, a Veuve Clicquot bottled in the same year Gilda was born. 'She's my friend. You've never had one, so you don't know what that means, Ruby.'

She's in my face. 'Lieutenant-General Royal Marines Ruby!' she barks. 'Show some respect, Marine!'

I stand up straight. 'Sah! Permission to join Gilda and Tobias, sah!'

'Permission denied, Marine. Weapon up! Enemy sighted!'

'Not the enemy, sah! Friendly forces, sah!' There's a gun in my hand and a knife in my face.

'Destroy them, before they destroy you. Before they make you weak. Smash them! Smash the fuckers! You're armed and dangerous, Marine – you know your duty. Do what you must.'

When I wake in the morning, my head rocking and rolling, all I can remember of the rest of the evening is dancing with Ruby in the hall under the spermy light, her buckles and straps pressing into my chest, her grenades pressing into my groin.

I drink a litre bottle of Badoit for breakfast.

# 1977

Amina's had a restless night, so at five o'clock she finally gives up trying to get back to sleep and goes down to the kitchen to make herself some coffee. She's always loved the potential of this time of day. She never minded the early morning feeds, never minded sitting on the sofa with a sleepy baby flopped over her shoulder, never minded the solitude. It was something of a relief from the populous habits of her days. She stands holding her steaming mug, looking out at the garden, and notices that the swing's rope is looking slightly frayed at the top. She must take it down before breakfast, she thinks, in case it breaks another one of her children.

Farah's walking now, and talks of her injuries as though they were some other little girl's, but Amina is sometimes stopped in her tracks by the sound of protesting brakes. She and Faisal have talked through the accident. Explored the blame, and it troubles her rarely now. But she remembers him at the hospital. Remembers seeing him on the wrong side of a closed door.

At the beginning of their marriage she used to suggest going to Pakistan, but he always pulled a plausible excuse out of the hat. Money's less tight now and his training's over, but the tickets were never bought. She sends photos of the children to Kashmir and tapes of them singing, but the only picture she has of Faisal's family is from his account, and that's out of focus. Since her father vowed that the dust of Pakistani history would never fill his shoes, she's worried from time to time that her own cultural identity has become vague. Until she sees *PAKI GO HOME* daubed on a shopkeeper's window and thinks they probably don't mean Glasgow. When she and Faisal first met, she had to explain to him what it meant when louts shouted 'goodness, gracious me' at them in the streets and waggled their idiot heads from side to side. His time at Dickens Academy had inured him to insult and he'd never seen *The Millionairess*.

When Farah was in hospital, Amina's mother came down from Glasgow to look after them all. Even in her shell-shocked state Amina was astonished when Aarya confessed one day that she'd gone into the mosque to pray while out shopping. Her no-nonsense, secular, down-to-earth mother. For Aarya, mosques were for high days and holy days, but in the face of disaster tradition jerked in like a reflex.

But in the end, Farah's restored health depended less on divine intervention, more on Virginia's. The insatiable appetite Amina observed when Virginia came to dinner seldom crosses her mind, and when it occasionally does, she simply tells herself Faisal was right. Mrs Psycho should shut up sometimes – Virginia's a friend, not a patient.

She putters around the kitchen, planning this evening's meal. When she was with them, Aarya made sure the family never starved and before she left she froze enough food to feed them for weeks, plus any greedy passer-by. Amina goes over to the freezer and takes out a biryani and a box of pakoras. *They'll thaw in time for this evening*, she thinks, and goes to the cupboard to check out the chutney situation.

It's a Sunday and they let the boys stay up later than usual last night, so they and their father are unlikely to surface for a few hours yet. Among his other talents Faisal can sleep for Britain. He's taking Shafiq and Ismail to the Granada today to see *Amar Akbar Anthony*, so they'll be occupied for most of the afternoon, keeping up their Urdu and learning the songs. If it's warm enough, she thinks, she can take Farah to the Common while they're out – avoiding the road where the accident happened – and play the games the physio says will improve her balance.

She hears a door open upstairs and a voice call out, 'Mummy?' When she goes into the hall she sees Farah standing at the top of the stairs, clutching the banister tightly.

She flaps her hand at Amina. 'Carry, Mummy? I'm still sleeping, look,' and she closes her eyes and makes comic snoring noises. She can manage the stairs perfectly well now but from time to time it suits them both to find reasons why she needs to be carried. As she bounces down the stairs on her mother's back, she chirrups happily about what she wants for breakfast and what they're going to do today.

Half an hour after Faisal and the boys leave, a monsoon bursts over Colliers Wood, so the Common is out and Amina and Farah settle down to mix some bilious coloured play dough in the kitchen. They're in the middle of making a farmyard scene featuring many lolly sticks and an egg box when the doorbell rings.

Amina leaves her daughter sitting on the floor talking to the cows and the chickens, first checking the work surfaces for anything that might tip or fall. She sees a man's silhouette in the front door's stained-glass panels and hopes it isn't the god-botherers who cloud their weekends like gnats. One look at her brown face tends to provoke especially zealous evangelism and she's too polite to shoo them away.

It's Virginia, her hair plastered to her head. 'Just thought I'd pop by,' she says. 'Wondered how Farah's getting on.'

'Oh, you poor thing – you're drenched!' says Amina. 'Come in – do you want a towel?'

Virginia's been a regular visitor since Farah came home from the hospital – usually 'just popping by' – and the little girl squeals when she comes into the kitchen, 'Look, Virginia, look! My chicky's having a ride on moo-cow!' She lifts two lumps of play dough in the air and four spindly sausage shapes drop off. 'Oh-oh!' she says. 'Moo-cow's legs fell off. Now she can't do dancing any more.'

'Shall I help you put them back on?' says Virginia. 'I am a doctor after all.'

She looks tired, almost like she's had a night out on the tiles. Amina's never thought she looked much like someone who knew where the tiles were, let alone how to have a night out on them, so she wonders.

'Are you all right, Virginia?' she asks. 'You look whacked.'

'Oh, quite all right!' Virginia says gaily. 'Went over to a friend's house last night for a quiet dinner and it all got rather late and rather rowdy. We were celebrating the arrival of a new baby – you know how it is when you're with close friends.' She drapes her dripping mac over a stool and drops on to the floor next to Farah, her legs sticking out in front of her like a small child.

'Will you have some tea or coffee?' Amina asks.

'No, thanks,' Virginia replies. 'Glass of water would be fine.'

She's always uninhibited with children, but today she's particularly inventive. She plays with Farah for an hour, telling her about life on the farm, about Misty, her favourite horse, about jumping hedges and splashing through brooks and Amina flits in and out, tweaking her house back into some sort of order. Every time she sees Virginia she feels compelled to thank her again, as though gratitude keeps them plugged into some source. Virginia always brushes it aside, but as Amina watches this lollopy woman making lolly-stick stables, the connection between her phone call to Dundee and Farah bouncing on her heels is palpable.

Virginia's still there when Faisal and the boys come in, fizzing with the gory pleasures of the film. Ismail's trying to remember the words of the title song, which every Asian shop in the neighbourhood's playing, but he can't get beyond the first verse. Shafiq starts ridiculing him, but when Faisal says sharply, 'Stop that right now!' he lays off. They all remember how the accident happened.

Sitting around the breakfast bar, Faisal and Amina are drinking good Italian coffee while Virginia gulps down a mug of hot chocolate. There's a plate that had been piled with barfi and jalebi between them. Amina catches Virginia's gaze and asks her again. 'Won't you have the last few, Virginia? Shame to let them go to waste and we've had more than enough.'

Virginia clears her throat. 'No – thank you. They were quite delicious, but I've got to dash off in a second and I'm really not hungry.' Her eyes betray her. 'Just wanted to check you've got that health authority meeting covered tomorrow afternoon, Faisal. I'm off first thing, as you know.'

'Absolutely. Hope it goes well. You're back on Wednesday, aren't you?'

'Yup – I'll be in early Wednesday morning, so we can meet up at the end of the day – is that the plan?'

'Great. Oh, you're off right now?'

Virginia is shrugging on her mac. 'Better had,' she says, 'before the skies open again.'

'Thirsty, Mummy,' says Farah, looking up from the floor. 'Can I have some milk?'

'Where did you put the milk you bought, Faisal?' asks Amina.

'Bugger! I completely forgot. I'll walk out with you, Virginia, pick some up at the Paki – *joke*, Amina!'

As they walk down the street, the soggy autumn leaves treacherous underfoot, Virginia asks him about the film.

'Oh, just the usual stuff,' he says, 'though better executed than many the machine churns out. Great songs, great actors, and none of the loose ends western films leave hanging of course. Dishonour's always avenged, the baddies suitably punished – or wiped out, mostly – and then along come the songs and dances. Rape and pillage followed by big production numbers in Alpine settings – you know the sort of thing.'

'No, I don't actually. I've never seen one. Does it remind you of home?'

'Well, only insofar as we used to watch them religiously. The zamindar – that's like a sort of country squire, or feudal landowner, perhaps – used to set up a screen in one of his fields and the whole village would gather to watch. My sisters and I used to lean up against my mum, who loved them, and even my dad stuck around till the end. The projector was run by a huge generator on the back of a truck which sounded like seventy tigers all roaring at once. It often drowned out the soundtrack when the actors weren't shouting or screaming or getting shot, but they were great family times. The only great times I remember, actually, in a fairly thin existence.'

'I don't think I've ever heard you say you've been back, have I?'

'I'm ashamed to say I never have, but I had a letter from my mother the other day that raised the issue again.'

'Oh?'

'The zamindar – or his nephew anyway – has just opened a hospital in the area after years of stalling, and now he's staffing it. For Pakistan it's incredibly well equipped, and he's taken pains to make sure the obs/gynae department's particularly high tech because of the appalling levels of infant mortality – and maternal mortality, come to that. My mother writes that I should apply for the Medical Director post, come back home, but . . .' He looks troubled.

'Is there some reason you can't?' asks Virginia.

'Well, I think I need more experience – five years at consultant level, ideally – but really I'm making excuses. My life is here, it has been for years, my children are British after all, my wife is too – well, she'd kill me if she heard me saying that, but you know what I mean – and going back to that part of my history fills me with horror. I haven't told Amina any of this, by the way. It frightens me that she might suggest I apply.'

'Where is it exactly?'

'It's in Kashmir – village called Jugnuwalla. The hospital's called the Choudry Akbar Khan Infirmary, after the old zamindar. He was my benefactor really. Made it possible for me to be walking down this street with you now. I owe him everything.'

They separate at the corner shop, Virginia walking briskly to stay ahead of the storm chasing her tail.

# 1977

I'm swaying in the egg chair in the living room when I remember Gilda rocking her baby, folding him into a love sweeter than any pastry. And Farah draped round Amina's neck, crooning into her ear. I pick up the phone and dial.

Mother sounds surprised. 'Oh, it's you! I didn't expect to hear from you until Friday. Is anything wrong?'

'No, not at all. I was just calling to see how you are. The weather's been so dire and when I saw that Yorkshire caught the worst of it, I thought I'd just check in. Make sure you're OK.'

'But why wouldn't I be? I mean, thank you and everything, but I'm fine – really. You know, life goes on as usual. Nothing new. How about you?'

'Well, I thought it was probably time I came up. Paid a visit. Maybe the weekend after next. Are you around?'

'Let me just check my diary. It's just here. Yes . . . yes, that would be fine. Will you come up on the Friday?'

'I'll drive up, but it'll be late, so don't wait up. I'll just let myself in and go to bed. I'll see you on Saturday morning.'

Mother's as mystified as I am about why I'm turning up now, but we manage to avoid mentioning it all weekend. After breakfast on Saturday, we go into the garden so I can advise her about a rose that's looking morose and she tells me about a new mulch she's discovered. This is number seven in our handbook of chats that keeps the no-man's-land between us weeded. We walk into town after lunch and Mother does a spot of shopping, looking for winter cashmeres, while I scour the charity shops. We meet in Bettys later for apple crumble and fruitcake (me) and a cream cone and lapsang (her). I've already had a dispirited ham sandwich and a bag of toffees as I walked around town and I'm looking forward to dinner, which I tell Mother I'll cook. I'm not going to eat crap.

We watch television when we've finished, first poring over the *Radio Times* because neither of us wants to waste time on trivia. We see the news, followed by a documentary about Victorian orphanages, both of them satisfyingly bleak. I look across to Mother, sitting in a chair on the other side of the room, and notice she's slightly jowly. And she's put on weight too. I wonder when that happened. When she loosened her grip on her body. After she's gone to bed, I pour myself a mighty cognac and when I've finished that one, take another glass upstairs.

In the morning, Mother is going to church. She knows I won't come, so doesn't ask.

'I'm planning to stay for Bible study afterwards,' she says, pulling on a frantically yellow overcoat and an emerald scarf, 'so I'll be a little longer than usual. I expect you can amuse yourself. I'll make us a light luncheon when I get back, before you go back down south.'

I'm sitting at the kitchen table, contemplating another mega fry-up, when I feel my trouser button lose heart and ping to the floor. It's given up trying to keep me decent and the zip's beginning to crawl downwards. I put my third breakfast on hold and go upstairs to find a needle and thread. Mother's top-floor eyrie has never been so forbidding a place as Father's study, but I still feel ill at ease as I go into the sewing room, as though I'm climbing into her wardrobe again. I go to the window to look at Harrogate rocking back on its haunches. It always laces me into its own idea of who I am like an ill-fitting corset, so I itch for London's anonymity from the moment I arrive.

I turn to the sewing basket, an old-fashioned two-storey affair in brisk wicker with a chintzy lining. As I rummage in the bottom storey for the thread, I see a package tied with red ribbon down the side of the bias binding. *Time to snoop, Detective Virginia*, Ruby whispers from behind my head. *Time to crack the case.*

I check the room, listen to the house and lift it out.

There are twelve letters, all addressed to Mother in the same handwriting, all bearing the same postmark. I know what I'm doing is wrong, but the lure of discovering something about Mother is too sweet and I sit on the floor and undo the ribbon.

I open the first letter. *Dear Mrs Denham*, it says, *I believe you are my mother*.

I can't read on because the air's been punched from my lungs. I struggle to recall my breathing. When I recover, I check the outside of the envelope to make sure it's intended for Mother. *My* mother. Mrs William Denham of Hanover House. It is, as are the others. As I read it, my shoulders slump.

The second letter is dated three weeks later.

> Dear Mummy,
> I read your letter, which came today, with such joy. I feel the same. Meeting up on Friday felt in some curious way like the first day of my life. My new life anyway. Seeing you with Saskia felt both strange and familiar, but I'm really sorry I flew off the handle like that. I'm so used to helping other people through the adoption process, I suppose I assumed I could handle this better than most. Professional arrogance probably. But when you had Saskia on your knee and you both looked so happy, I just found myself full of how it could have been if you'd kept me. I understand rationally why you gave me away of course, but it's not so easy to deal with the emotional flak. You'll have to give me time to work it through, that's all. I haven't told Sarah and Francis yet because I want this time alone with you first. And I'll have to prepare them anyway. I'm almost sure they'll be fine about it and will want to meet you, but only when they're ready. It's not going to be easy for any of us. But what a lucky girl Saskia is to have three grannies! You'll have to decide what you want her to call you, though probably she'll invent her own name when she starts to speak. Nana Nellie or something. I used to call my maternal granny Boot!
> And it was lovely to see that photo of Daddy.

I have to read them all, but it's like sticking lighted matches in my eyes. I was six when Hermia was born. Mother's Important War Work.

Her Top Secret.

I pick up the next one.

> Dearest Mummy,
> It was strange having lunch with Sarah and Francis yesterday, wasn't it? I was surprised how nervous we all were because we've talked it through often enough, and they're so broad-minded I thought they'd just warm to you immediately. Sarah called last night to say how weird she felt about all of it. She'd expected you and her to be sort of alike in some way (because you're both my mums, I suppose), so the differences took her aback. But she'll get there. We all will, and when you told me I looked like Gerald – Daddy – I was overwhelmed. Now I know that I was conceived in love and that had circumstances been different you'd have brought me up together, I feel more substantial somehow. When I look at Saskia, I can feel how tragic it must have been to give me away. Daddy sounds like a wonderful man, and the idea that my doctor father delivered me in his own surgery is almost unbearably special.

Dr Greenaway's hands that ruffled my curls and soothed my skin had held his own daughter first – even before her mother. Dr Greenaway who loved me enough to call me Bubbles. *My* Dr Greenaway.

In the following letters, Hermia's eagerness to absorb every ticking second of Mother's past thirty years spins an intimacy between them that I find unendurable. I'm mentioned only once.

> It must have been awful to have been so tethered to William by Virginia, but I'm sure you did your best with her. She sounds like a fabulously successful woman, but it's strange that she should be the doctor and not me, given my parentage, isn't it? But then

maybe not everything's down to genetics. I'm a lot like Sarah, for example – everybody says so.

When I've finished reading, I fold the letters back in their envelopes and replace them in the basket, but not before I've made a note of the address.

95, High Trees, Harrogate.

I know where that is.

I don't stay for lunch. Can't bear to be in Mother's company for even a fleeting second more. I drive down the motorway, harvesting a fury as lightless as a hurricane. I stop off at a motorway café and I block a toilet with three rolls of tissue, then scrape the car in the next bay to mine with the keys that Ruby hands me. When I get home, I pull the namby-pamby watercolours off the wall and rip them out of their frames. Ruby brings me the matches and I set fire to them in the sink. It brings me only momentary satisfaction, so I bring what few family photographs I have and add them to the conflagration.

That's more like it.

I have to eat. Now. Can't wait for anything to cook, so I find the T-bone steak that's been lording it in the fridge. I unwrap it and spread it out on the worktop. It lies there, daring me. I don't bother with a knife, but lift it with both hands to my mouth. I'm growling as my teeth tear at the flesh, eating with my mouth open as gobs of meat and spit drizzle my chin. There's blood on my face and poison in my veins. Ruby goes next door to get the rosewood box. 'We'll let the poison out,' she says as she comes back, but I want to hold on to it. I want to use it. We go upstairs and she makes for the bathroom, but I grab her sleeve and snatch the box out of her hands. She has the sense not to remonstrate. I go into the Dali room, put the box on the chest and open it. The scalpels lie there side by side, promising me vengeance. *Vengeance is mine; I will repay, saith the Lord.*

Fuck the lord. I'm after the lady.

I'm running on adrenalin as I sweep into the hospital the next morning at seven. I slept for an hour between three and four and begrudge the time spent dreaming when I could have been planning.

I look down at my surgical list. I have a photographic memory for my patients, remembering every tic and lump and sac and cyst, and can bring them back to mind as easily as sliding a scalpel through skin. Three-quarters of the way down I see her: Angela Barton, mid-thirties, plump, difficulties conceiving, severe endometriosis, lost her parents and whole family in an accident.

*Oops-a-daisy!* I think. *Clumsy clot!* I smile.

I say nothing to my team as I scrub up. Look at none of them as I snap on my gloves, march into the operating theatre and wait by the table. As they come in, I see the theatre sister raise her eyebrows to the anaesthetist, warning him not to mess with me today.

I work tirelessly down my list, speaking only to demand an instrument or issue instructions. Finally Angela Barton is wheeled in. Behind the trolley Ruby slips into the theatre and leans against the back wall, her eyes glittering over her mask. The patient's endometriosis is extensive and I work my way round her abdominal cavity with the diathermy, destroying the adhesions that have developed in all the usual places, plus a few more for luck. Not that Angela's luck is in today. The size of my hands is enough to cover what I'm doing as I cauterise the ends of her fallopian tubes with the diathermy, but I manoeuvre my body in such a way that my team's vision is further obscured, just to make sure. I close the wound and stitch it as finely as a Parisian seamstress.

'Good work, everybody, well done,' I say when I've finished. 'I think we deserve a break, don't you? Cakes are on me!'

I look over at Ruby, who's doing a victory jig by the sterilising unit. She pulls down her mask. *Congratulations*, she mouths.

I call Mother twice in the next six weeks and we talk stiffly about nothing. I tell her about work and she tells me about the WI and the charity. My precipitous visit has skewed our ordinary routine, so it passes unnoticed that we're speaking less often.

I'm vexed when the phone goes. I'm busy in the garden. I've just discovered honey fungus in one of my favourite roses and it's threatening to lay waste to all my years of hard work. I rarely speak to my godmother, so her call is perplexing.

'It's Edna Russell here, Virginia. How are you?'

'Very well, thank you. How lovely to hear from you, Mrs Russell. How's the family?'

'Everyone's fine. Alistair and Rachel have had another baby, so that makes eight grandchildren so far. They keep me pretty busy. But that's not why I'm calling. Your mother's in hospital. She's been there for three days now and she's really quite poorly. I heard she'd been admitted and went to see her this morning. She's in an oxygen tent and I was awfully shocked by how ill she looks. It's pleurisy, I think. I asked her if you knew and she said she hadn't wanted to bother you because you're always so busy, so I told her I'd call you. She tried to stop me – you know what she's like – but I said I'd do it anyway. I said I was sure you'd want to come and see her.'

'Of course.'

'When can you come?'

'I'll drive up today. Stay over tonight and come back tomorrow evening.' *Fuck.* 'Have a word with her consultant.'

'Pop over and have a cup of tea with us tomorrow, why don't you? We'll be back from church at the usual time.'

'If I can, I will. Thanks. I'll call you.'

I speak to the consultant, who tells me Mother has double pneumonia and is responding only sluggishly to treatment.

'She seems to have a rather stoical nature, doesn't she?' he says. 'Like so many of her generation. Left it far too long before seeing her GP, so she's developed quite severe empyema. We're draining the fluid to make her more comfortable, but she's causing us some concern, actually. You're coming up, are you?'

'Yes, tonight.'

'Well, do give me a call when you've seen her and we can discuss her treatment.'

I chuck the gardening tools into the shed and stomp into the house. How *dare* she! How *dare* she force me north to play the dutiful daughter! How *dare* she maintain the charade! I put three bottles of water, a change of underwear and a toothbrush into a carrier bag and go out to the car.

\*

It's after eight when I pull into the drive, so I'm spared the hospital because visiting hours finish at half past. I'm disinclined to pull the I'm-a-doctor card to see her out of hours, so I'll turn up tomorrow with the ordinary visitors.

The house is chilly, which is nothing new. I'm alone in it, which figures. I don't bother switching on the lights as I go upstairs to dump my stuff because even Mother can't move rooms around. It's too painful to sleep in my old room, so I'll sleep in the spare room among the decorous lilacs. Father's been dead two years now but hasn't left so much as a dent on this house of stillborn affection.

Ruby's sitting on the bed as I go in. She's wearing a deerstalker hat and looks idiotic.

'You look idiotic, Ruby. Take the hat off, for Christ's sake.'

'Nope. We've got more snooping to do and this is my snooper's hat. Crack the case of the missing persons.'

'Who's gone missing?'

'Oh, you know – Mother, Father – you.'

'I'm right here.'

'You're a missing person too and you know it, Detective. C'mon, let's go and sniff around.'

I take a swig of water and chuck my coat on the floor. She'll only nag, and I'm not ready for bed yet.

We start in the tasteless kitchen and the polite drawing room. Ruby opens drawers and pokes in paper piles and files and sticks her head in cupboards, but the rooms stay tight-lipped. We go down the hall to Father's study. As we go in, Ruby's singing a song about picking a pocket or two which I recognise, but can't place. The window's been replaced by a door and there are plant pots on the bookshelves and a listlessly leaking lawnmower where his desk used to sit. Mother's tiled the floor and the oil's oozing into the compost and fertiliser and bone-meal littering what was once Father's hermitage. A clatter of bamboo canes lean against the wall where I hid under the table and the smells of cigars and whisky have been replaced by the stench of chemicals.

Nothing new here.

'Nothing new here,' I say to Ruby. 'I'm getting bored – and tired. I'm going to bed.'

'Ooh, you are a droopy-drawers-party-pooper, Virginia – why can't we just have a bit of fun sometimes? I know, I know – why don't you sleep in Mother's bedroom for a change? The spare room's too dreary for words. C'mon – what a wizard wheeze!'

I half expect to be challenged as I walk across the room in my grown-up self, wishing I were back in the wardrobe.

Ruby opens its door and riffles the clothes. 'Why don't you try something on?' she says. 'She'll never know.'

'Don't be stupid – I'm about three sizes bigger than her. I'll bust anything of hers.'

'Not this,' she says, pulling a plastic coat carrier out of the cupboard. 'This'll fit anyone.'

It's Mother's fox-fur cape, and as Ruby drapes it round my shoulders I can smell something beastly beneath the familiar Arpège. I'm close to tears in its embrace, but Ruby sees my face and smacks the back of my head.

'Buck up, nit-wit!' she says. 'It's only a cape! C'mon, let's see what she's got in here.' She races over to the bedside cupboard. 'Remember the strainer for making custard?' she says, giggling. 'Remember what we did? Bet it's not there now.'

She pulls the drawer out and lays it on the bed. There's a small Bible and a tube of hand cream and a red velour eye mask inside, which Ruby flings on the floor.

'Crap!' she says. 'Ooh, but what about this?' She lifts out an envelope. 'Could be love letters.'

They're not love letters, though the photographs reek of love. Mother stands in front of the London Planetarium next to a tall, sandy woman in jeans. They're holding a little girl between them like a prize. They're all beaming, happy to be together. Happy to be on a family day out. I hardly need to turn the photo over to identify Mother's companions, but I do, just to be sure. *Hermia, Saskia and me*, Mother's written, *looking up at the stars!* There are others: a picnic in the Dales, Mother lifting Saskia up to look at monkeys in the zoo, Saskia dozing on her sleepy mother's lap on a train. Pictures of a newly minted kinship.

'And how about her bed?' Ruby's whispering in my ear, her hot breath turning to tears as it cools. 'They must have fucked here. They

288

must have made the baby here with our strainer. Fucking like bunnies, they were. At it like dogs, Virginia, after she'd packed you off to Nana's. Couldn't wait to get rid of you.'

I lunge at her, but she's too fast and dodges away.

'Fuck 'em back!' she shouts from the other side of the room. 'Get the fuckers!'

I strip the bed. I kick the bedding round the room, spitting on it as it cowers at my feet. Ruby's put a knife in my hand and I stab the sheets over and over till they're hanging on by a thread. I rip them from end to end. I tear them into tiny shreds, as though I could reduce what Mother's done to a trifle and flush it away.

But I can't. The betrayal's there in the photographs. In the fat satisfied smiles. In the ease between them. I fall asleep on the debris.

I take the rubbish to the dump in the morning. I wish I could dump the bed, but I think Mother would probably notice. I remake the bed with identical sheets and have two breakfasts and a greasy pub lunch before going to see her in hospital.

As I approach her single room, I see a tall woman leaving it, dabbing her eyes. I don't need a formal introduction. She's been to see her mother. *Mine.* Shed tears over her mother. *Mine.* 'See you tomorrow,' she's said to her mother. *Mine.*

I stand by Mother's bed. She looks a hundred years old in her sleep. Her breathing is noisy. Vulgar. She'd be mortified if she knew.

It wouldn't take much. Turn off the oxygen supply, lift the tent. Help her into the arms of her Jesus with a pillow. This pillow in my hand. The oxygen tank's right there, the dial showing it's full. I reach over to turn it off, hesitate for a moment too long and there's a nurse in the room with me. I plump up the pillow and settle it in a chair. I make myself known. 'I'm her daughter,' I say, daring her to contradict me. 'Dr Denham.'

Two days later, I'm in theatre. Ruby watches from behind the anaesthetist's head, her gloved hands soundlessly applauding as I make sure Mrs Khan won't be having any more babies. She's had three already.

Greedy pig.

# 1979

Monday, 6.55 a.m.

The alarm's gone off and Faisal struggles to wake up. He seems to have fused with the mattress overnight and his neck's aching. Yesterday's drive down from Glasgow was always going to be punishing, and the children conspired to make it worse: Farah took up projectile vomiting as though it were a competition sport and the boys started squabbling half an hour into the journey. Amina did her best to deal with them, but when they'd had to stop for the sixth time in three hours, she snapped.

'You'd better let me do the driving,' she said to Faisal, 'or I'm going to do something I'll regret.'

They swapped places and she'd calmed down by Birmingham, but Faisal cricked his neck badly when Shafiq yelped.

'Ismail punched me, Daddy!' he said, his eyes filling. 'I didn't do nuffing.'

'Ismail –' said Faisal.

'Didn't, didn't, didn't!' said Ismail. 'But-Shafiq-took-my-book-and-spat-on-it-and-that's-really-horrible-and-now-I-can't-read-it-and-it's-my-best-book-ever-so-tell-him-Daddy-tell-him!'

Already tired from the drive and the three days of wedding celebrations, Faisal's mediation skills were waning, but he admonished Ismail for punching, told Shafiq to treat books with respect, and by Luton both boys lolled sideways, dribble crusting their chins.

As soon as the car drew up outside their house, however, the children woke up and, fuelled by second and third wind, made it their mission to sabotage the unpacking.

Amina wondered how they had the energy as she stopped the boys jousting with floor mops and rescued Farah from the airing cupboard.

By the time she got to bed at two in the morning, she'd resigned herself to a short night and an overwrought morning.

There's an eruption at the bedroom door and Farah stumbles into the room, pursued by her brothers.

'Mama, Mama,' she shouts as she clambers on to the bed. 'Shaffy's gonna eat me!'

Shafiq roars at her and she gratifies him by squealing back. She settles herself on Amina's pillow, queen of her castle, while the boys straddle Faisal's legs and start to bounce,

'Ooh – go easy, boys,' he groans, 'have pity on your poor old dad. Come and give me a cuddle.' Lying on his back, his arms full of boy, Faisal closes his eyes and thanks someone, something, for the plenitude of his life. In public, he might call the someone or something Allah but in private it has no name, no history, no godly identity. He's thanking circumstantial accidents for bringing him to this place where he loves and is loved in equal measure. He turns his head to Amina. 'I'm sorry about yesterday,' he says.

Her face sets. 'Well, I don't suppose that'll be the last of it. I'm just about sick of it actually. I'm not sure you're listening to me.'

Yesterday they had one of their periodic rows about education in the middle of the wedding, upsetting them both. They are equally intransigent about their ambitions for the children and however often they revisit the subject, neither is prepared to compromise. Amina despairs.

'We don't need to buy them privilege,' she said, 'they're privileged enough already. They've got all the expectations and the prospects that come from backgrounds like ours. They're never going to fall by the wayside because we're vigilant, and we know what we're watching for, unlike the families I work with.'

'But a private school will give them structure, Amina, and more focused attention. They'll be around kids like them, which obviously makes for a better learning environment. Look at what it did for me.'

'Yeah – and look at how you hated it. Why would you wish that on them?'

'It wouldn't be like it was for me. There'd be plenty of other Asian kids there. What happened to me was decades ago and on another continent – obviously I wouldn't be pushing it if I thought they'd be as miserable as I was. Think of the friendships they'll make – friendships for life probably.'

'You mean friendships that'll help them up the greasy pole?'

'What's wrong with wanting them to succeed?'

'Standing on the heads of the great unwashed? I don't think so.'

They get the children ready for their day, but the chill between them is palpable as their histories clash.

His surgical list that day looks arduous, but he has a way of thinking himself into the state of mind that makes it doable. He locks himself into a cubicle in the men's room and closes his eyes, shutting out everything but his breathing. Each exhalation looses Faisal-the-father, Faisal-the-husband, Faisal-the-son-and-brother from their moorings and each inhalation sets Faisal-the-doctor down his centre like a steel spine. When he's finished, he walks on his doctor's feet to the theatre and scrubs his surgeon's hands free of pathogens.

Midway through the morning list, he sees a name he recognises. Three months ago, Angela Barton showed up in his clinic, having failed to get pregnant after Virginia had treated her endometriosis. He remembers her because she wept continuously through the consultation, holding a scarf to her mouth like a comfort blanket.

'I grew up in such a happy home, Doctor,' she said. 'There were four of us, me the youngest, and I don't remember a single bad thing – not one. Apart from what happened of course. I'm sure a shrink would tell me that I've rewritten history, but you've got to keep your head straight somehow, haven't you? I'd be in a nuthouse otherwise. We were on holiday in Norfolk and Mum'd switched the heating on because it'd suddenly turned freezing. I used to sleepwalk around that age – I was eight – and I must've taken myself off during the night, because in the morning I woke up in the car under a picnic blanket. I was a bit bewildered, but it'd happened before so I trotted back into the house, which was completely quiet. I went into all of their bedrooms, one after the other, because I thought they'd just overslept, but they were dead. My whole family. The boiler'd been pumping out carbon monoxide all night. I know I can never replace them, but if I managed to have a family of my own it might make me feel less dead myself. Miss Denham told me everything was fine after the operation, but nothing's happened and Derek and I are getting more and more desperate. We're ratting at each other all the time and I just know it's to do with all of this. It's like I'm crippled or something.'

While conception could be difficult after such severe endometriosis, Faisal thought it was worth having another look, so he booked the patient in for a laparoscopy.

When the theatre sister lifts Angela Barton's gown, she looks at Faisal and raises her eyebrows.

'Now, I wonder if we can guess what she's here for?'

Faisal looks down.

Just below her navel in red ink Angela has drawn a picture of a placidly smiling foetus with the word PLEASE underneath.

'Well, let's hope we can help her get what she wants,' he says, and his eyes grin above his mask.

Purkiss is assisting and sees the look in the sister's eyes. Even on a good day, his fiancée doesn't look at him like that.

Faisal makes the incision and slips the slender tube into the peritoneal cavity. He must have looked into a living body hundreds of times but he is still awed by the way the viscera collaborate to make a space where consciousness grows and sentience thrives. Whatever differences distinguish one person from the next on the outside, each is human in the same gutsy way on the inside.

According to Virginia's notes, Angela had extensive adhesions, not only in the more common locations – the uterosacral ligaments, the pelvic side walls, the ovaries – but also on the bladder and the bowel. She explained to Angela that its spread was too wide to treat laparoscopically, so she'd have to perform open surgery. After he joined the firm, Faisal often assisted her and observed her wielding the diathermy with the skill of a miniaturist. As he looks down the scope now, he once again marvels at the precision of her work. He examines the peritoneum: clear. The bowel: clear. The bladder: clear. The ovaries: clear. And then the fallopian tubes.

Instead of willowy terminal fronds he sees stumps, like hands with lopped fingers. There was no mention in Virginia's notes of any blockage or malformation, but Angela's chances of conceiving are less than nil. He moves her organs around, as though there's a way of restoring her fertility, but he knows he's looking at a blasted waste.

He closes her up, already dreading telling her what he's found. He's never forgotten finding a carcinoma the size of a grapefruit in a patient's liver when he was a junior doctor, and having to tell a 29-year-old man he'd never see thirty.

The rest of the day, Faisal stitches back prolapses and removes fibroids and wombs and cervical cells that are threatening to mutate, but Angela's stunted tubes baffle him. Growing up in a world where the only certain thing was uncertainty he's used to doubt, but this discovery unsettles him.

Early on in his career, he introduced Amina to the term 'idio-pathic', which he explained meant 'shit happens' and she chortled.

'I could use that in a million different ways,' she said, 'like "I have this idiopathic lack of time, Doctor" or "this soufflé idiopathically refuses to rise".'

But he never told her about 'iatrogenic', which means 'a doctor caused it'.

He'll ask Virginia about it when they meet. She'll know.

They pass in the corridor at the end of the day, he still in his scrubs, she already in her bulky coat.

'Got a moment?' he asks.

''Fraid I'm dashing,' she says. 'Got to put the final frills on that paper and then I'm off to Oslo before dawn tomorrow. I'm back on Thursday – not staying for the whole conference – so why don't we get together then? Anything particular you want to discuss?'

'Just a bit of a mystery, that's all. Opened up a patient today – Angela Barton, you might remember her. You treated her a couple of years ago. Extensive endometriosis. Her tubes were unaccount-ably damaged – couldn't work it out. Perhaps I could run it by you on Friday?'

'Of course. Don't remember her particularly, but you can remind me.' She looks at her watch. 'Oh Lord, sorry, got to rush,' and she speeds off, though not towards the car park.

Once the kids are in bed, Faisal and Amina sit in the living room with steaming mugs of chai. Since the children arrived they've tried to stop arrangements tyrannising their conversations, but Mary operates on Caribbean time and was half an hour late today. Then she pulled out a baked breadfruit for the family and spiked Amina's guns.

'So I couldn't have a go at her, could I?' Amina says. 'I just can't seem to get through to her that I need to get to work on time.'

'I know,' he replies, 'but you can forgive her anything when you see her with the kids, can't you?' When he comes across Mary telling Anansi stories on the sofa, one child draped over her shoulder, another nestled under her arm sucking his thumb, the third nearly swallowed up by her breasts, he sometimes feels a clenched-fist yearning in the pit of his stomach. 'She can only do what she can do, and timekeeping just isn't one of her strengths.'

They chat idly about how Shafiq's reading's progressing, then turn to their days.

'Something strange happened today,' Faisal says, 'and I'm struggling to explain it really.' He tells her about Angela Barton and how Virginia was in too much of a rush to talk it through with him.

Amina's surprised by how disconcerted he is, because she knows medical puzzles fascinate him. 'Do you think Virginia might have missed something?' she asks. 'Everyone mucks up sometimes – even someone as brilliant as her.'

'She didn't say anything,' says Faisal, 'and I'm sure she would, even passing in the corridor. You know how straight she is. She always says slips can lead to knowledge if you force yourself to examine them. But I'll have to wait till Thursday, I suppose.'

When he sees Virginia back at work, he's struck by how tired she looks. She's usually indefatigable, but dark circles hang under her eyes like bodybags.

'How was the conference?' he asks.

'Oh, you know. Same old faces, same old drug companies, nothing new.'

'How did your paper go down?'

'Pretty well. But I'm going to have to be choosy about which invitations to accept or I'll be spending the next couple of years on planes. There were two from America – one from Johns Hopkins – one from the Soviet Union, one each from Australia and New Zealand and . . . oh, two or three others. I can't remember. Thought maybe you could offer them that paper you've been writing, if it's appropriate.'

'The one on salpingectomy?'

'Yes. You've got some really original ideas in there. Think about it and let me know. I'll tell them about you. Are we planning to meet up today?'

'Absolutely.'

At Virginia's suggestion, they agree to meet at a small café round the corner from the hospital.

'Need to stretch my limbs,' she says. 'Been sitting around in lecture halls for two solid days and I'm beginning to rust.'

The café is overheated and crowded and they sit close together in a shepherd's-pie fug, Faisal with a cup of tea, Virginia with a glass of water.

'What was it that was troubling you when we chatted the other day?' she asks. 'Remind me.'

'Angela Barton. Fertility problems. You operated on her two years ago for severe endometriosis – everything seems to have gone smoothly but she hasn't managed to get pregnant.'

'Well, only thirty-five per cent of women as badly affected as her do of course. And at two years after the operation she's got very little chance. I remember her. Slightly tubby, very anxious, mid-thirties or so? Wasn't there some terrible tragedy in her life?'

Faisal sometimes thinks Virginia was born with an auxiliary memory bank because she recalls the salient features of all her patients' histories.

'That's the one. I took her in for a laparoscopy and everything seemed perfectly tidied up in the cavity, all the organs were mobile, but . . .'

'Ah yes, her tubes. I remember. Poor woman. Congenitally mal-formed, weren't they? I'd never seen anything quite that bad before. Tragic. I remember having to break the news to her. Went in to see her by myself actually, because I didn't want her to have to hear it in front of other people. She was so traumatised by losing her family, I thought she'd probably find this almost as bad. And she did, you know. She fainted straight away – out for a long time, I was quite worried – and was inconsolable when she came round. I remember sitting with her for about an hour afterwards. She talked and sobbed and sobbed and talked, and when she'd calmed down a bit, I got the psychology department to go and see her. What's she come back for this time?'

Faisal finds himself tuning into the two men behind him fulminat-ing about their boss.

'Faisal?'

'Sorry. Sorry – it's so noisy in here, I'm not sure I heard you right. You did say you told her about the state of her tubes?'

Virginia's cheeks look feverish. 'Yes, that's what I said. What's she presenting with now?' She dips a forefinger in her water and draws it along scalpel-thin lips.

'It wasn't in her notes,' says Faisal. 'About the tubal malformation, I mean. There was nothing there. I would never have opened her up if I'd seen that. It wasn't there, Virginia.'

Virginia's gaze condenses. 'I think you'll find it, if you read the notes properly, Faisal. It's not like you to miss something that obvious. Perhaps you were tired. I know how demanding small children are.'

*No, you don't*, thinks Faisal.

'Is it time to take some leave, do you think?'

'No . . . yes . . . perhaps you're right. Actually I've got to get back now – I said I'd get to Ismail's school play this evening.'

'Righto. Have a good night's sleep and I'll see you at the meeting tomorrow.'

He stumbles out of the café, leaving Virginia to pay the bill.

It's freezing outside, the sky busy with stars that feel like pins in his skin. He passes stolid Victorian houses in which people live unsur-prising lives, but tonight he finds himself wondering what's going on in there. What blood there is on the carpet. What's buried in the garden. After twenty minutes, he realises he's been walking away from the hospital and as he turns back, he tries to soothe himself. *It's OK, it's OK, it's OK. You just got it wrong, that's all. No harm done. Don't worry – everyone makes mistakes.* He almost misses the hospital entrance.

In the office, he stands in front of the cabinet, telling himself he can choose not to look at Angela's file. He can accept Virginia's explanation and move on. But he can't. He opens the drawer. He slips the buff folder out of the Bs. He takes it over to a desk and sits down heavily. If he's right, his world's about to warp.

He reads the file backwards from his own notes, written in the legible hand of someone to whom English isn't native. He reads slowly. He can wait to get to Virginia's. When finally he sees her wonky handwriting, he realises he'd been holding his breath. He exhales and starts to read.

*Endometriosis diathermed from uterosacral ligaments, pelvic sidewalls, ovaries, bladder & bowel. Uterus healthy. Ovaries healthy. Congenital malformation of f. tubes, rendering both non-functional. Patient very upset. Psych. Department contacted.* The last three sentences are in darker ink than the rest, the writing more legible, the words more determined. He reads it again. And again. And again, as though he could exhaust it. But Virginia's lie stays stubbornly on the page.

He closes the file and puts it back in the drawer.

When he gets home, he pleads fatigue and a touch of migraine and takes himself to bed while the others go off to Ismail's play. The jabber of voices fades as they shut the front door and he gets up and roams the house as though he's been blinded. Blindness would be a blessed relief. As would deafness – or becoming a mute. This house has been his sanctuary, but he could now be swimming with sharks. He can't wheedle doubt into what he knows. Can't blink away the truth.

Virginia has deliberately maimed a patient.

*Above all, do no harm.* Hippocrates never said it, but the injunction lies at the heart of the oath he composed twenty-four centuries ago. As though a doctor would. As though modern medicine's patriarch could imagine a doctor harming the sick.

Faisal imagines it now.

He tells Amina everything, but he can't tell her this. If he tells her, it will be real.

His dreams are full of knives, and he wakes at three in the morning convinced he's killed someone. He takes himself away from his wife in case he's dangerous.

In the living room he sits on the sofa, holding the cushion Amina made out of fabric his mother embroidered. As his fingers trip across the threads, the zamindar comes to mind. Since coming to England the shame of his broken promise has played in his mind like a contrapuntal theme. However successful he's become in the British system, however deep are his British children's roots, the hectoring voice of his conscience can always unsteady him. He watches his children grow in Iftikhar soil and nods like a car mascot when Amina's father inveighs against Pakistan. The country he's betrayed.

Virginia's mendacity is another tug at the rug he's trying to stand on. He can pray in aid neither the Islam he absorbed as a child, nor the medical ethics he absorbed as a student, each as obdurate as the other.

And then there's Farah.

That she is able to walk is a tribute to Farooqi's genius, but Farooqi would never have been there without Virginia. Farah's accident made her Virginia's patient by proxy and he owes her a parent's gratitude. Whatever she's done to Angela Barton – whyever she's done it – she averted a tragedy at his family's heart and the moral compromise he's facing feels like a creeper round his head, its suckers sapping his resolve. His shame about abandoning Kashmir continues to harry him, but no one will die if he stays. Virginia's a different matter. He can't be certain she won't do it again, but maybe he can monitor her. Maybe he can ask after her patients, read through her files, watch for a flicker when she talks about fertility. He picks at the fringe of the cushion and it unravels in his hand. He loops the silk round his finger and pulls it tight.

He's beginning to convince himself that this was a one-off. A moment of temporary madness. It happens. Amina marked her behaviour at dinner that time so he'll tell her about Virginia's behaviour at work, saying only that she's been stressed lately and that he's worried. Mrs Psycho will know.

Virginia's actions have restored Farah's future and that simple equation is tending to override his qualms. He knows that deciding not to report her deracinates him from his obligations, but he shuts down his conscience. Farah's alive. That's all there is. Faisal's in awe of Virginia's technical brilliance, but he knows something of her warmth too. The young woman he looked out for every day on his way to and from work had evoked the tenderness he'd noticed when he saw them together on the hospital bed. When he'd mentioned her to Virginia a few days later, she'd blushed slightly.

'Oh yes,' she'd said, 'Gilda. She's the daughter of my cleaning lady, and I promised her mother I'd keep an eye out for her when she came in. Her mum tells me she's doing well now, though she had a jolly rough time to begin with. I haven't seen her since we discharged her, but I hear how she's doing from time to time.'

When Amina gets up, she's concerned by how haggard he looks, but he assures her the migraine's run its course and that he's fine to go to work.

'Bit of a nuisance, that,' he says. 'Never had one before, but there's always a first time, I suppose.'

The ethical compromise is a first too.

# 1979

A week later, Faisal's in the staff room, resting his head against the back of the banquette with his eyes closed. He's had to shift along from where the stuffing's oozing out of a split, but even this section has all the charm of sitting on a peeled hard-boiled egg. His brackish cup of coffee has run out of steam on the side table, but he is anyway disinclined to drink it. He's exhausted. He's been on the labour ward for twelve hours straight. A young girl went into labour at thirty-two weeks and he battled to save both her and her baby when it became clear that she was suffering from placenta accreta and was haemorrhaging. He performed a Caesarean and a hysterectomy with economy and speed, focusing on saving the mother's life while his paediatric colleagues revived the pale streak of infant he'd just delivered. When he checked up on them in their respective ICUs half an hour ago, he thought the odds were just about in their favour. Some time ago he'd assisted Virginia in the same procedure and learned tricks from her that he put into action today. His patient had reasons to be grateful to her.

He should go home – he's late already – but his limbs have fossilised. Perhaps he could sleep here. Just for ten minutes. A dream pokes its head round the corner.

Someone crashes into the staff room.

'Well, there you are, Dr Usman!' cries Purkiss. 'Sleeping on the job? Want some coffee?'

Faisal wearily opens his eyes. 'Thanks, but no thanks. I've got some here.'

Purkiss peers at his cup. 'Christ, it's gone into rigor mortis!' he says. 'Stay right there – I'll get you fresh. Bloody hell, I'm knackered!'

Faisal pulls himself upright and tries to look attentive. 'How's your day been?' he enquires politely when Purkiss has brought their coffee over.

'Oh, you know, same old, same old. Clinic went on forever. That locum consultant can bore for Britain. Well, India actually – sometimes he was practically bloody unintelligible. He's only marginally more intelligent than a sock and I had to interpret quite a lot of what he was saying, which doubled the length of every appointment, so we didn't finish till three. All fairly routine stuff except for this one patient – um, Salima Khan, I think.' He picks up his coffee and plunks his feet on the table. 'Lady Miss Denham treated a couple of years ago. Went in to deal with ovarian cysts. Everything hunky-dory afterwards, but she's been trying for a baby ever since and it hasn't happened.'

Faisal's body tenses.

'Consultant had a look last week and found her fallopian tubes were completely wrecked – looked like they'd been cauterised, he said. No history of ectopic pregnancy, no mention of abnormality after the first operation – nada. Nix. Complete mystery. Had to tell the poor soul today that she'd have to whistle for more children. Mind you, she's got three already, but she's Asian, so it's a big deal for them, isn't it?'

'You mean for us?'

'Oh sorry, sorry. I always forget you're of that persuasion. And I mean that as a compliment.'

Faisal doesn't know where to begin with that, so he says nothing. He extricates himself from Purkiss and goes up to the office. He needs to make sure.

What he reads in Salima Khan's file makes him sure.

He cycles home, wobbling dangerously down Blackshaw Road.

Amina and Farah are making words with letter cards on the living-room floor when Faisal gets home.

'Oh, you do look tired,' Amina says. 'You're not coming down with another migraine, are you? How's your head?'

His head is full of snakes. 'A bit achy,' he says, 'but I'll be better after some food. Just need to sort a couple of things out before we eat. Can I do anything?'

'No, no, it's all under control. I'll call you when dinner's ready. Show Daddy what you've done, hen. You've been such a clever girl.'

'Look, Daddy,' says Farah, 'I did it all by my own,' and she points to the sentence she's made on the floor. BABY SMILES 'AT MUMMY, it says, AND MUMMY MAKES BABY HER LUNCH.

'It's like the picture in my book,' she says, bringing the book over to Faisal. 'Here. The mummy's feeding the baby with that green stuff and I don't think he likes it. I want a baby as well – can we have a baby soon, Daddy?'

Amina sits back against the sofa and grins at Faisal. She's been working on him to try for a fourth.

'I don't know about that,' he says. 'Perhaps we could get a puppy instead.'

'Yeah, yeah, yeah!' says Farah, grabbing his hands and bouncing like a pogo stick. 'Puppy, puppy, puppy, pup, pup, pup!'

'Traitor!' says Amina, getting up. 'Never promise what you can't deliver,' and she kisses him as she passes. 'C'mon, Farah. Clear up the cards and come and help me make dinner. You can wash the vegetables and stir the sauce – how about that?'

He sits in his study, surrounded by the evidence of his life. Pictures of the children are propped up against his books and he and his bride smile from a silver frame on his desk. On a good day he can take credit for this, <u>for</u> his hard work, for his children's security, but on a bad day he feels like he's crossing a canyon on a cobweb. He understands what it is to be an outsider. Without being able to articulate it, there's something about Virginia that he recognises in himself, so it's as though ripping off her camouflage will jeopardise his own. He has willingly swapped his Kashmiri obligations for his British profession, but he remembers the accusation in Omar's eyes as he left for the last time.

Purkiss is radiantly unaware of what Virginia's done, so it falls to him to unmask her. His mentor. He's not sure he can do it.

When the children are in bed, he and Amina sit in the kitchen, chatting about today's news. Over the last four years, the Yorkshire Ripper's been murdering women in the north, leaving them tangled and mangled on wasteland as bleak as their profession. Then two years ago, he killed a sixteen-year-old girl and Britain sat up and blinked. This victim was no easy-to-dismiss drug-addled whore: she was barely out of childhood when two other kids found her body. In a playground, where they'd gone to muck around. Suddenly this wasn't pond life preying on pond life but Evil destroying Innocence, and the press bayed for blood. The Ripper has recently been attacking blameless women again, including a university student, and the reports seethe with righteous anger.

Amina tells her husband how the killer is stalking her clients' minds.

'Two of my girls were talking about it today,' she says. 'One of them – she's just coming up to sixteen – says she absolutely knows he's down here. She says she feels like her legs have been paralysed, so that when he comes for her in his van – she's positive he drives a green van for some reason – she won't be able to run away. She's always felt like damaged goods anyway, so part of her feels she'd deserve it if he killed her. I mean, I can tell her he only operates in the north, I can tell her there *are* bad men out there but she just needs to take ordinary precautions, that kind of stuff, but she's fixated on the idea that he's targeting her. I suppose in a perverse sort of way it makes her feel special.'

'Do you think she's being picked on by the other girls?'

'Well, she's pretty much an outcast anyway, so it wouldn't take much for her to be an even bigger target. And then in my other school there's this poor wee lassie whose mum actually is a prostitute, so she's terrified she'll come home one day and find her in pieces. She keeps saying, "She'll be all minced up, miss, like school dinners and everything."'

Faisal falls silent. He looks up at the light, then down at the table. His fingers rub at the wood, as though trying to erase the blemishes.

'Faisal?' says Amina. 'Are you OK, hen?'

He doesn't look up. 'Yeah, yeah, I'm fine, I'm fine. Just thinking about the Ripper really. You know, what awful things one human being can do to another. Well, you know better than I do about that, I suppose, but the trouble is, you can't always spot evil just by looking at people, can you? I mean, you couldn't pick out a serial killer in a crowd. And I suppose it's conceivable that terrible things could even be done by educated people. Look at whatever his name was – that doctor – in the concentration camps.'

'Mengele?'

'Yes. Not exactly what you'd expect from someone dedicated to healing, was it, all those experiments?' He puts his hand over his eyes.

'What's going on here – what is it, Faisal?'

Faisal's dam bursts. 'Something's happening at work that I'm finding rather difficult,' he says. 'Well, that's a bit of an understatement. It looks like . . . it seems like . . . I'm not sure I can talk about it actually.'

Amina reaches across the table and takes his hand. 'It's OK,' she says, 'just tell me. It's OK.'

'Well, I will tell you, but you probably won't believe it. *I'm* finding it hard to believe, frankly.' He pauses. He looks up at her. 'It's Virginia,' he says, 'I . . . I think – no, there's no "think" about it really – I *know* she's been deliberately damaging her patients. I've seen the files. She sterilised two patients with a diathermy during their operations, Amina – two patients who were desperate to have babies. I've got no idea why she did it. How she *could* do it. And then she doctored one of the files to cover it up. I . . . I feel like the earth's splintering under my shoes. What am I going to do?'

Amina looks aghast.

'I know, I know,' he says, 'it doesn't seem possible, does it? I mean, she's the most dedicated doctor I've ever known – think of what she did for Farah, for heaven's sake – but something must have happened to her, you know? When I found out about the first one, I managed to persuade myself that it must have been a moment of madness or something. That if I just watched her really closely, I'd know if she'd gone crazy. I . . . I thought I could just run it by you without saying exactly what was going on, as though she was another patient or something and you'd explain her psychology to me and I'd be able to – I don't know – stop her or something. I thought I could tell if she was going to do it again.'

'When was this?'

'A week ago.'

'For god's sake, why didn't you tell me?'

'I suppose I sort of thought that if I told you, I'd have to do something about it. Take action, you know? Expose her. And if I reported her, I knew I'd be destroying one of the finest doctors I know. Help me here, Amina. I think I'm going mad.'

'You're not going mad, hen, but she may be. You *must* report what she's done. You don't have a choice. One sterilisation could be an accident, I suppose – though the cover-up is serious – but two has to be deliberate. You're the medic, but even I know this doesn't happen by chance. You've got to tell the authorities – supposing she does it to somebody else?'

Faisal does his best to argue himself out of taking that next step. Every day is haunted by the decision not to expose Virginia. Not that day anyway. Every day he vascillates between the consequences of speaking out and the consequences of silence. Every day he wonders if she's done it again. When he meets Anna in a corridor and she tells him – at some length – about a conversation she had with her heroine the day before, he nods and smiles and agrees. Yes, she *is* extraordinary. Yes, she *is* unique.

No, absolutely, no one's doing what she's doing.

He goes to the filing cabinet over and over, as though visiting a sister in jail, and Mrs Khan's file begins to fall open at the right place every time. The successful surgery is recorded in Virginia's inimitable hand, as is the follow-up appointment bringing the treatment to an end. There's no mention of the fallopian tubes.

He mentions the patient – casually, chattily – one evening in the staff room, aware of a tremor in his voice. They're alone, other doctors having sensibly gone home.

'Purkiss told me a strange thing recently,' he says. 'Patient you operated on some time ago – might have been a couple of years or so? – ovarian cysts. Name of Salima Khan. Sure you remember.'

Virginia swirls her water around in its paper cup. 'Um, yes, I think so. Small woman, three children closely spaced, rather fierce husband?'

'Well, I haven't seen her myself, but I'm sure you're right. She came back recently. Seen by Patel. Complaining about not being able to get pregnant.'

'Oh god, that man's a complete bloody incompetent! He really should be drummed out of the profession PDQ – become a car mechanic or something.'

'You're probably right. But he opened her up to see what was going on and he found that her tubes were terminally damaged. Like they'd been cauterised, Purkiss said. Rather like that other patient I discussed with you – do you remember? Angela Barton.'

'Oh yes, she was the one with the congenital malformation, wasn't she? Whose family died?'

'That's the one.'

'D'you know, I remember thinking then that it was an extraordinary thing to come across the same pathology in two women in such quick succession. Some doctors probably never see that in their whole career. Just my luck to defy the odds.'

'But she'd conceived three times before, so how could that be?'

'Oh, she'd had severe chronic chlamydia. For years probably. Untreated of course. Tragic for her, poor woman, because she badly needed a son, having had three daughters. Her wretch of a husband was demanding an heir – I despair sometimes. But weren't you going to tell me about that patient you saw the other day with Sheehan syndrome?'

As Faisal approaches the filing cabinet the next day, it seems to be shrouded in doomy clouds. He opens the drawer. Mrs Khan isn't there. His heart hiccoughs. She's taken the file. *Wrong drawer, idiot. Next drawer down.* His fingers crawl towards the file. He knows what he'll see. He ambles through the pages backwards from Patel's notes. Turning the last page, he involuntarily closes his eyes. He forces them open. There's her writing, pressed hurriedly into the page. *Severe tubal damage*, it says, *Chronic untreated chlamydia. Patient informed further conception impossible.*

He only reads it once.

Amina is trying to be reasonable. Trying to keep her cool and let Faisal do things at his own pace, but she wants to shove him. Wants to say, Do *something, for Christ's sake – don't be such a bloody wimp!*

But he says he needs more time to think. He continues to go to work, continues to meet daily with Virginia, but the decision to annihilate her seems to be beyond him.

Sometimes Amina thinks she should just tell the authorities herself. Anonymously of course, but they'd have to investigate. Faisal would be off the hook then. She's worried by his weight loss and his lassitude and by the nights he spends in the study, pulling books off the shelf as though he'll find an answer in their pages. She sometimes finds him asleep on his desk in the morning, the outline of a cover bold against his cheek. Finally she surprises him with the holiday she's booked and paid for without consulting him. She's found a package to a child-friendly hotel in Lanzarote for a week in November and presents it to him as a fait accompli.

'But what about school?' he says. 'We can't pull the boys out in term time.'

'Where, and on what tablets of stone, does it say that their heads will explode if they miss a week?' she asks. 'Think of it as part of their education – think how much they'll learn about Spanish island culture.'

'In a hotel with a pool in a walled compound? I'm thinking not much.'

'Well, what I'm thinking is, the week'll give you time to think about what to do about Virginia – because you must do something, mustn't you? And *soon*. I bet you'll find it easier to decide when you're away from it all, and we can talk about it as much as you like. And Ismail can take his books with him and read by the pool – imagine how many he'll get through without distractions.'

'Like the pool isn't a distraction?' He smiles. 'Actually, I think I could be distracted quite easily. Let's do it then.'

November 3rd is circled in red on the kitchen calendar, and one day he finds that Shafiq has drawn a picture underneath it of a family in various shades of brown on a beach next to a turquoise sea. He tracks down his swimming trunks.

# 1979

One Saturday a fortnight before Hermia's thirty-fifth birthday, Eleanor treats her to lunch after they've spent the morning melting in the Royal Baths. Over the past two years, Eleanor's face has softened with the extra pounds that have inched round her body. She has curvy hips now, and a bosom, and a sorority of loose dresses and embroidered cardigans hang in her wardrobe above shoes that trade elegance for comfort. Jonathan is joining them after Saskia's gym class, but for the moment mother and daughter are alone.

'I've been thinking about what to get you for your birthday,' Eleanor says. 'We've known each other two and a half years now and I wanted to get you something special.'

'Oh really, Mummy, I don't need anything. We've got far too much clutter at home anyway, so let's just go out for lunch or something – or, better still, come to dinner with us. It's not as if it's a specially significant birthday or anything.'

'Well, if that's what you'd prefer. But I've got a great idea. How about a day trip to York?'

As they drive down to York, the thunderstorm that made Saskia squeal moves on to scare some other small child and the skies clear. October's copper light burnishes the puddles on the road and Eleanor feels sure it's an augury. A few miles on, her tender history is waiting for them, hanging on a wall.

I arrive at my hotel earlier than expected, and the receptionist is all smiles and apologies.

'Very sorry, Dr Denham, but the chambermaid's still up there getting your room ready. May we offer you some coffee in the lounge while you wait? I'll come and tell you when she's finished.'

'Yes, that's fine. Perhaps I can leave my case somewhere, can I?'

'Absolutely. I'll put it in the room back here.'

'And actually, thinking about it, I'm going to have a bit of a wander. Get some fresh air. I've been cooped up on a train for hours. I'm sure York runs to coffee shops.'

I've always liked York with its venerable antiquity and serial settlers: its Anglo-Saxons, its Romans and its Christians. The conference is to be held at the university two days before the students rollick back after the summer and I'm looking forward to meeting up again with Chi Su Yi, who's giving a paper on the genetic predispositions of her Solomon Islands patients. She's a feisty woman who takes no prisoners and when we meet up at conferences we spend as much time together as we can. We share a single-mindedness about our work and a rage with the phallocrats governing health in our respective countries, so our conversations are always spirited affairs.

I amble towards the town centre. I'll probably wander through the cathedral, buy a paper and sit in a coffee shop, drifting pleasantly. I see from a hoarding that the Yorkshire Ripper's back in the headlines. Like everyone else I've wondered why he hates women so, but it's only an extreme end of the misogyny I've battled all my life, so I haven't wasted time speculating.

It's too balmy a day to be indoors, so I buy a paper and make for Dean's Park. I'll look for a present for Tobias after I've had a little sit-down. It's not his birthday or anything, but as his godmother I'm free to spoil him rotten. He's a chatty, cuddly, delightful little boy whose curiosity is unbounded, so I'll look for some books about wild animals, which is his latest passion – Gilda and I can point them out at the zoo next week. I realise I've forgotten my toothbrush and toothpaste, so I pop into Boots to replace them. As I'm leaving the shop, I have my eyes down while putting my purchases in my handbag and nearly tread on the heels of a woman passing by. I'm about to apologise, but she's so deep in conversation with her companion that she hasn't noticed the near-collision. They continue walking down the shopping precinct, a small girl hopping along beside them.

I lean against the shop window as I watch Mother walk through York with her daughter and granddaughter. I haven't seen her for a while but we talk on the phone at our usual times. The conversation Mother's having with Hermia is of a different order, their body language speaking volumes. Saskia pinballs back and forth from her hopping to her mother, and at one point Mother says something that makes her laugh so wildly she doubles over.

They're about to disappear round a corner and I stand outside the shop, paralysed with indecision. Following them, spying on them, might expose me, but not following, not spying, is inconceivable. I raise my handbag up to my face and follow them, darting in and out of doorways like an escaped lunatic.

Eleanor's excitement is ratcheting up as they approach St Helen's Square and when they round the corner, Saskia races ahead of them and pushes her face against the window.

'Over here, Nana Lelly!' she calls to Eleanor. 'Ooh, look at these strawberry cakes! Can we go in here? Pleasepleasepleaseplease?'

'That's exactly where we're going, Sassy – how clever of you to find it! Why don't you pop inside and ask the nice lady if she's got a table for us?'

Bettys huffs its sweet breath in their faces as they go in. The tables have been rearranged since the last time she was there, and Hermia sees her face cloud.

'Are you looking for something particular, Mummy?'

'No, it's OK. The thing that's really important is still here, thank goodness. Look, there's a table free over there.'

I position myself outside by the window, from where I can see them sitting. There's a pyramidal display of cakes in the window that will just about conceal me if I duck in time.

When they've placed their order, Mother seems to launch into a story, Hermia's head inclining towards her, her body motionless. Saskia's playing with the spoons and when she taps one of them on Hermia's plate, her mother puts her hand on her arm without look-ing at her and she subsides back in her chair. The sandwiches and drinks come but are ignored as Mother continues talking, Hermia continues listening. Finally Mother sits forwards and points towards the bar. There's a large, ornately framed mirror on the wall behind it, and a young man's polishing glasses and stacking them on the shelves beneath. Mother looks at Hermia, who nods. She says something to Saskia and the little girl smiles broadly and helps herself to a stack of sandwiches.

The two women go over to the bar and talk to the man, who puts down his cloth. He fetches another man from the front of the shop and they carry two chairs behind the bar. Together, and with difficulty, they lift the mirror off its hook and place it on the floor in front of the women. Mother says something and stands back as the men turn the mirror to face the bar. The two women hold hands as they squat down. From this distance I can't see what they're looking at, but Mother's finger is pointing here and there on the mirror's black back with a strange liveliness. As it moves to the bottom right-hand corner her other hand moves to her chest, just above the heart, and her finger stops. Hermia looks for a long time, shaking her head slowly. She turns to her mother and her lips move. Mother dabs her eyes and they embrace. They stand up and walk back to their table, their arms round each other as though walking might otherwise be impossible. When they sit back down, Saskia points to her empty plate and says something that makes her mother and grandmother laugh.

I go slowly back to my hotel. The sun has clouded over and a storm grumbles overhead. It seems fitting.

95, High Trees. I know where that is.

# 1979

Ruby's sitting in the passenger seat as we head north, tapping her foot on the floor. It's irritating me but I don't say anything. I'd be tapping my foot too if I wasn't driving. We spent last night getting everything together and even though I'd made a list, I worried that I might have forgotten something. This isn't a rehearsal.

When Ruby arrived, she was wearing a blue boiler suit with *Northern Energy* embroidered on the breast pocket. Her baseball cap was pulled down over her forehead and she was wearing heavy work boots scuffed at the toe and carrying a canvas holdall. My cap and suit and boots, bought from a surplus store, were piled by the fridge and everything on the list was laid out on the kitchen floor.

Ruby took over the list in a head girlish way and leaned against the cooker, directing operations. 'Now, Mr Virginia, let's do it from the top. Plastic sheet? – check. Scalpels? – check. Gauze? – check. Sutures? – check. Potassium chloride? – check. Syringes? – check. Barbiturates? – barbiturates?'

'Oh Christ, they're still in my briefcase.'

I rattled the pot as I came back into the kitchen.

'You can't be forgetting those, Mr V. Whatever were you thinking? We've only got one stab at this, remember.' She chuckled. 'Now, where was I? Oh yes, barbiturates? – check. Scrubs? – check. Gloves? – check. Spare knickers?'

I looked at her. 'Why do I need spare underwear?'

'In case you pee yourself!' She saw my face. 'Just a joke, OK? You're not going to pee yourself, OK? Get a grip, for heaven's sake!'

*

313

As we travel, the holdall's sliding around the boot as though it's alive. As though it has a mind of its own, and at a service station near Leicester I secure it with the safety belt on the back seat. As I drive on, I check it from time to time in the rear-view mirror as if it were a fretful toddler.

I park the car a block away from the commercial vehicle hire company in Leeds. They have the white Austin van ready for me and as I stride out of the office, the receptionist calls out, 'Thanks for your business. Hope it does the job.'

When we start seeing signs for Harrogate, Ruby says, 'Now, keep your eyes peeled from now on, Mr V. For Mother, obviously, but for anyone else who might recognise you as well. Mind you, I bet you didn't have a beard last time they saw you.' She leans over to tug at my chin.

'Lay off, Mr Ruby,' I say. 'I glued it on really firmly. It'll hurt if you tear it off.'

'Sorry. Just kidding around. Just lightening the atmosphere a bit.'

'Well, don't. I like this atmosphere, OK?'

As we approach High Trees, I pull over and check my face in the mirror. I've probably been a bit heavy-handed with the dark foundation, but the receptionist at the hire company didn't look startled when I walked in, so I suppose the false black eyebrows and the wig sticking out from under the cap must have convinced him. That, or van drivers round here tend to pile on the slap. I pull my cap down a further centimetre. It means I have to raise my chin uncomfortably high to drive, but it's better than anyone getting a good look at my face.

I turn into High Trees and a cloud scuds across the face of the sun. The street is named after the green sward that separates one side of the road from the other, a sentinel of ancient cedars standing guard down its spine. A sudden sharp breeze buffets their canopies and they rustle busily. The road is bracing itself.

Number 95 is in a little group of late-nineteenth-century houses rather smaller than the Edwardian piles at the other end. They're detached, with long, well-tended front gardens. I park, get out of the van and reach into the holdall for my latex gloves. I slip them on and snap the wrists. I check the rest of the bag's contents in the same way I'd check my documents before travelling.

*Ticket? Money? Passport?*
*Scalpel? Syringe? Sutures?*

'All present and correct, Mr Virginia,' says Ruby at my elbow. 'Let's go.'

I carefully shut the gate behind me and walk up the garden path. I knock on the front door. I ring the bell, just to be sure. If she's not there today, we've got sleeping bags in the back.

Hermia's been looking forward to her day off. She hasn't taken all her annual leave this year, so she's had to cram it in before her leave year ends at Christmas. Saskia is at school until 3.30, so she has the whole day to herself. When she's picked her up, they're going swimming and then joining Nana Lelly for tea. Mummy says she's got a surprise for them, which Hermia thinks is probably tickets for the pantomime they talked about last time they met – Saskia will be delirious.

She deliberately didn't plan anything else, luxuriating in the amorphous day ahead. She'll do whatever she fancies: reading or playing solitaire or dozing in front of crappy daytime television, maybe painting her nails. Doing handstands maybe. She's making a pot of tea in the kitchen when she hears the van door slam in the road outside and her gate squeak. She reminds herself to oil it, but not today. The knock on the door is imperious and she's mildly irritated when the bell rings too. *I'm coming, I'm coming*, she thinks, *keep your flipping hair on!*

A tall man is standing at the door, dressed in a blue boiler suit and a baseball cap. She can't see much of his face because of the beard, but when he speaks his voice is curiously light.

'Hermia?' he says.

'Yes?'

'I'm your sister. Virginia.'

'Oh my lord, I thought you were a man! But what are you doing here? And why are you . . . oh, I'm sorry, that's so rude. I'm just a bit shocked, that's all – this is terribly unexpected. But Mummy's told me about you of course – do come in.'

When Hermia fails to show up at the end of the school day, Saskia's teacher doesn't immediately worry. She knows what Hermia does

315

for a living and that there are sometimes emergencies or things beyond her control – like a court sitting late, for example, or a last-minute report. She and Saskia wait in the classroom reading books, but when 4.30 comes and goes she leaves her there and goes to the office. She tries the home number three times and Hermia's emollient voice kicks in, inviting her to leave a message. She flips Saskia's record card over and finds Jonathan's number.

He arrives fifteen minutes later, looking harried.

'I'm so sorry, Mrs Benson. I've got no idea why Hermia didn't turn up. She's taken a day's leave today, so maybe she's dozed off or something.'

But when he goes into his house, when he sees her on the floor, when he sees what's been done to her, he know's she's not asleep. There's a scream and for a moment he's not sure if it's him or Saskia. He gathers his daughter up, pushing her face into his chest as he staggers to the kitchen. He dials 888. When it doesn't connect, he tries again. 999 this time.

Chief Inspector Hughes has been in the force for twenty-seven years and thought he'd seen the gamut of bad things done by bad people, but here in Hermia's living room her killer's reinvented the wheel. The sergeant is shaking his head.

'He's come up here, hasn't he, sir? Perhaps it got too hot for him down there. We'd best get in contact with the Prostitute Murder Squad, hadn't we?'

Hughes rubs his forehead. 'I'm not sure, Sergeant. Doesn't look to me like his usual style – as far as I know, anyway. There's no stab wounds, her pubic area's not been mutilated and she doesn't seem to have been beaten. The Ripper's rather partial to a ball peen hammer, but her head's OK. Most likely this is a copycat at work, but there's no forced entry, so she must have known him.'

Smoothed by the infinite calm of death, Hermia's face is beautiful, her hair floating round her head like a summer cumulus. She's lying on her back on the beige wool carpet they've just had laid, looking as though she were just resting after a busy day's work. Her hands are crossed over her chest and her legs lie close together: were she carved

316

in marble or in alabaster, she could have been a saintly sculpture on a tomb. She has no clothes on but looks unembarrassed to be leaving life as naked as she arrived. Her body is smooth and clean, as if she's lately stepped out of a bath leaving no puddles of blood or sweat or tears in her wake.

Only the wound spoils what would have been a peaceful scene. On her lower abdomen, on top of a neatly closed bikini-line incision, rests her womb, glistening in the voyeuristic police lights. It could have been a little fist, surprised at finding itself outside the body, tethered to Hermia's skin in a row of stitches so fine they're practically invisible. It could have grown there suddenly, like a puffball in a hedgerow.

'This isn't any ordinary killer,' Hughes says. 'This guy knew what he was doing. The Ripper couldn't have done this – but then, who knows? Maybe he's been teaching himself surgery in his spare time. When was the last one – September, wasn't it? That student. She wasn't a tart either.' He's three years off retirement and the prospect of playing a part in the biggest manhunt in British criminal history is thrilling. He's been worried that retirement might turn out to be boring, but this'll be leaving in hyperbolic style – he might even become a household name. For a while at least.

The post-mortem reveals the presence of barbiturates in Hermia's blood and forensics find more at the bottom of her *Greatest Mummy In The World* mug. There's a puncture wound in the crook of her right arm where the potassium was administered. She was dead when she was turned inside out, which seems an oddly compassionate act, given the killer's intentions. As the pathologist slices her down the middle, he marvels at the killer's handiwork. It makes his own look crude, like a provincial butcher next to a big-city surgeon. 'This can't be the Ripper,' he says to his assistant, 'this guy's brilliant. He must be a medic of some sort – not that a doctor'd ever do something like this.'

The car-hire receptionist's description spills out across the airwaves: a tall, swarthy, bearded man with long limbs, big hands and a high tenor voice, he says when he gets his fifteen minutes of fame. 'I thought there was something funny about him at the time, but not a murderer – no, never a murderer. Not standing in my office bold as brass.' The description chimes with the patchy accounts given by

Ripper survivors, so there's room still for speculation that the same man is responsible for this sedate little town's tragedy.

It doesn't seem possible. Not here, but women stay indoors for weeks afterwards and bewildered husbands cruise Tesco with lists in their hands, looking for bleach. A pall of fear hangs over Harrogate like a sinister aurora borealis, and people suspect their own shadows as they pass down the streets.

Four days after I've dealt with Mother's Important War Work, I'm sitting in my living room surrounded by newspapers. Being a *Guardian* reader, the pile of tabloids on the coffee table is offending me, but I need to know what everybody's thinking. Largely they're thinking the same thing as the Ripper hits the headlines again. The police are trying to calm the hysteria with daily press conferences, but to little avail: everyone wants to know what he's done this time. And why. The police aren't telling. Chief Inspector Hughes, blinking nervously in the television lights, says only that Hermia's body has been mutilated. 'I've been in the force twenty-seven years,' he says, 'and this is the worst I've ever seen. But someone knows this man. Someone may have washed his clothes. For heaven's sake, I appeal to you to come forward and prevent this happening to some other poor woman.'

I read all the accounts, all the op-eds, until I'm satiated. Satisfied by what they don't know. I gather up the newspapers and take them into the garden. In the brazier the charred remains of my scrubs need finishing off and the paper will rekindle the blaze. I set it all alight, adding a small pile of dead twigs, and stand back. The sparks frisk in the air like fiery midges and the evidence hisses as it obediently turns to ash. When it begins to subside, I go back into the house. I haven't spoken to Mother yet. I'll telephone her on Friday as usual and listen for anything untoward in her voice. Tremors of shock or anguish or disbelief maybe – of denial even – but not accusation. I don't expect to hear accusation.

The next day, I'm catching up on paperwork in my office at the hospital when Eileen rings through.

'It's Harrogate hospital, Miss Denham. They say it's urgent.'

'OK, Eileen, stick them through. Hello?'

'Miss Denham? This is staff nurse Bird in the A&E department. I'm afraid I'm calling with bad news. We admitted your mother this morning. She'd taken an overdose – we don't know yet what of – and her cleaner found her this morning when she turned up for work.'

'Is she . . .?'

'She's alive, I'm glad to say, but she's really pretty poorly. We pumped her as soon as she got here and she's now in ICU. The best I can say is that she's stable. As you know, the next few hours are critical, but Dr Larson – that's the consultant – thinks there's a fair chance she'll pull through. I expect you'd like to speak to him.'

'Yes. Yes, I would, after we've finished. What else can you tell me?'

'Well, there was a note – a suicide note, I suppose – in her pocket. We found it when we were prepping her. I've got it here.'

'Would you be kind enough to read it to me?'

'I will, but it's a bit of a strange one. Mrs Bailey, her cleaner, gave us your number and said you were Mrs Denham's only child, but she says in the note – well, I'll read it to you. See what you think.' There was a faint rustle at the other end of the phone. The nurse clears her throat. 'I hope you won't find this too upsetting,' she says.

'No, no, I'm fine. Please go ahead.'


To whoever finds me

I'm really sorry to give you such a shock and I hope it hasn't been messy, but I can't go on any more. Life often felt pretty pointless before I got my real daughter back, but I never thought dying would solve anything. It does now. When Hermia found me, I remembered that I'd been a mother once – briefly, before they took her away – and that I'd known how to love. And I did so love her father. My beautiful Gerald.

But now the Ripper's snatched her away and with it my happiness. Since Wednesday, all I've thought about is death. Her death and now my death, and I truly hope I've taken enough pills to make sure I don't wake up. I'm feeling sleepy now, so I apologise if my writing's getting a bit scatty, but I'm sure you'll get the gist. This wasn't an accident.

I don't think I shall be much missed – the only people who would miss me are ahead of me now, and I feel sure we'll meet up in a place where there is only peace and the freedom to be together. Where God holds us all in his arms.

I'm really sorry to cause so much trouble. I'm not in the habit of doing this.

Yours sincerely,

Eleanor Denham

PS. You'll find my will with my solicitor, Mr Stephen Keen, of Stephen Keen and Co., Bradford.

I check my smile in case it can be heard in my voice. 'Please keep it for me,' I say, 'for when I come up. Now, can I speak to Dr Larson?'

There's a lot to organise, and I plough through my paperwork as I make lists and phone calls and write letters. I take particular care with the last letter, rewriting it several times to make sure I get it right. I hear the nation celebrating the defeat of a papist plot outside the window, the city skies bursting with frantic sparks. Everyone's gone home when I emerge from my room, so I leave the envelope on Eileen's desk, propped up against the photograph of her and her children in Paris.

I stay up all night, sorting and disposing and ordering and counting, humming as I move round the house making choices.

Just as I'm leaving at lunchtime the next day, the phone rings. I close the door behind me and lock it. The answerphone kicks in.

'Dr Denham? This is Nick Larson. I'm glad to say your mother's regained consciousness. I've called in the psychiatric department. You can speak to them when they've seen her. I imagine you're on your way up here, so I'll see you soon.'

*Click.*

# 1979

At the hotel, Faisal has steered clear of the English newspapers in the lobby, but the banner headlines are unavoidable. RIPPER STRIKES AGAIN! RIPPER'S VICTIM NOT PROSTITUTE! they shout, claiming Hermia as one of their own. He mentions it idly to Amina as they lounge by the pool.

'Oh god,' she groans, 'who is it this time?'

'Don't know. Just saw the headlines. Seems a long way away, doesn't it? But it's a kind of reminder that we've got to get back to reality sometime. I'm nearly ready to go home actually – how about you?'

'Oh, I don't think so. These last few days have convinced me I was born to be a sybarite.'

'How about I give you another back rub then? The cream's just down here. Oh, well done, Farah!'

Farah's sitting on the edge of the children's pool dipping her toes in the water, her brothers on either side of her. The scar is dark pink against her brown skin and reminds Faisal every time he sees it. She conquers her fear of water that day and they slowly deflate her water wings as she flaps about in the pool, staying afloat. When she manages two doggy-paddled yards unaided, the family celebrate with gooey pastries bought in a nearby village.

Farah jumps up and down when she sees them. 'How many do I get if I swim right across the pool?' she asks. 'Can I have fifteen?'

Faisal's joints feel limber, as though they've been oiled, and he and Amina make love most nights as if time no longer ticks. When he's ready, they talk about what he will do about Virginia when they return and he tells her that it feels like a killing. She understands, and holds him when he weeps.

As they tumble through their front door at the end of the holiday they see the answerphone winking on the hall stand.

'Oh, let's just concentrate on getting the kids to bed, shall we?' says Amina. 'It's not the end of the world if we leave the messages till later. Tomorrow morning even.'

But Faisal can't resist the machine's siren call, his doctor's mind always alert for an emergency. When they've settled the children, he plays the messages back. They're mostly routine – invitations to birthday parties for Shafiq and Ismail, an optician's appointment for Amina, Mary saying she was unwell – but there's a call from the hospital, dated three days after they'd left, that sounds urgent. 'Dr Usman? This is Eileen. I need to talk to you as soon as you get back. Something rather important has cropped up. I hope you've had a really good holiday. See you soon.' He hopes Purkiss hasn't screwed up, but he feels rested enough to deal with anything and falls asleep easily.

The turbulence is palpable as he walks into the department the following day. His colleagues manage a polite enquiry after his holiday before bowling him the googly. Virginia's resigned. Eileen opened the letter when she got in, surprised by the envelope. Usually when Virginia left her notes, they were on Post-its on her phone or bits of scrap paper tucked under her photograph. There were two letters inside, one addressed to her, thanking her for all her support and efficiency and good humour over the years, signed Virginia, the other a formal letter of resignation. Neither revealed where she'd gone or what precipitated her going, and rumours swarmed around like locusts. She was terminally ill; she'd been poached by America; she'd had a breakdown; she was in financial trouble – but never running off with a man or making a mistake. Neither was conceivable.

The authorities brought in a locum consultant while Faisal was away but they ask him to act up when he returns. Providing he works as effectively in the role as he has as second-in-command, everyone knows he's a shoe-in when the post's formally advertised.

The day is congested with meetings and briefings and patients, so he can't call Amina. He feels the loss of his mentor as a faint ache at the base of his skull, but has no time to think about it or talk about anything other than the detritus she's left behind.

When she hears his key in the lock after work, Farah bounces to the front door. 'Daddy, Daddy, Daddy – guess what I did today?'

He bends over and kisses her head. 'Tell me later, Farah,' he says, 'I just need to talk to Mummy for a moment.' He doesn't say hello to his wife as he walks into the kitchen. 'Virginia's resigned,' he says. 'Didn't tell anyone in advance, just left a letter for her secretary and took off.'

'Dear god – where's she gone?'

'No one knows. All her stuff's still in her office, her files are in order, she finished off all her correspondence – she just disappeared, no working her notice, no sorting out her pension, nothing.'

'Has she had a breakdown or something?'

'There's nothing to indicate that, but it's so uncharacteristic, perhaps it is what happened. Eileen says her mother'd made a suicide attempt and the hospital kept phoning to check she was on her way, but she never showed.'

'Oh my god,' says Amina, as the thought occurs to Faisal too, 'maybe it was those patients. Maybe she realised you didn't believe her. She'd know she'd lose everything – and her work was all she had.'

'And the awful part of it is, it's a fantastic relief. Because now she's taken herself off I don't have to shop her. For the moment at least. I'm rather ashamed of that.'

Farah races in from the living room and throws herself at Faisal's leg. '*Daddy!*' she says. 'Come and see what I've done!'

Six months later, Faisal picks up a letter from his mother from the kitchen worktop. He's been a consultant for three months now and his days are crammed with medical and administrative conundrums which he finds taxing, but largely soluble. The children are busy with homework and television and Amina's trying to finish off a report before the final straits of the day, so he takes the aerogramme up to his study with a cup of coffee and slits it open with the letter knife he bought in the Canaries.

His mother lists the news of his sisters assiduously – their children, their husbands, their complaints – before telling him the big news.

> So, finally we have a new hospital director, coming all the way from England. The infirmary has been waiting patiently until now, but your father says it is like a family: now it has a head, it will walk a straight path. It could have been you, my son, but we know that you have more work to do there before you can come home. Insha'allah all will be well now with Rana, who still suffers with her woman's pains.

He thought he'd long ago silenced shame's nagging voice in his head, but it pipes up again now. It's time he tells his mother he's never coming back, tells her to give up hope, and he reaches for his pen.

Rana feels her stomach lurch as she walks up the steps of the hospital, its grandiose portico soaring over her as she goes through the door. She's suffered the sharp stabs of pain and the heavy loss of blood for so long, she's almost too frightened to believe this new doctor might cure her, but her neighbour's been relieved of similar symptoms and thinks the doctor walks on water.

The air-conditioned cool of the hospital's interior slaps her in the face as she walks into the foyer and over to the desk rising from the marble floor like a stately ocean liner. The medical clerk is a kindly woman who recognises fear when she sees it.

'We are expecting you, Mrs Husain. Welcome. Go through the double doors on your left and take a seat in the waiting room. You'll find a water cooler in there – please help yourself.'

Rana sits in the moulded plastic chair, beads of water trickling down her fingers from the beaker. She jumps when a nurse bustles up to her.

'Rana?' the nurse says. 'Doctor will see you now.'

As she walks through the door, the doctor is looking out of the window at the barren hills in the distance, brutalised by the sun.

'Dr Redford?' Rana says timidly, hovering by the patient's chair.

Virginia turns round.

'Rana,' she says, 'please take a seat.'

# Acknowledgements

My embarrassingly long CV mysteriously doesn't include obstetrician/gynaecologist, so I've depended on the comfort of experts to write this book. Professor Janice Rymer and Dr Anthony Kenney, both eminent in the field, have been unstinting both with their erudition and their tolerance of my simple-minded mistakes. I have reluctantly concluded that I have no future in the profession. Sad but true. The redoubtable Betty Parsons, who has seen generations of women through their pregnancies, regaled me with her ideas and experiences, which made me wish I'd known her when I was having babies. Mistress Absolute has been my guide through what in the 1970s was known as the SM scene (now BDSM) with wit, warmth and intelligence, and in particular has helped me understand the nature of the desire. What it feels like. I am grateful to the Wellcome Foundation – especially Ruth Blue – for access to their astounding archive, which I greedily consumed in one of their airy viewing rooms. Who knew such wealth was available? I find that I write best when untethered from my ordinary life and am indebted to Emma and Josep Alsina-Olaizola for lending me their Barcelona flat, where I have holed up, gone slightly barmy, and written some of this book. Perhaps the barmiest parts.

And then to friends – expert friends – who generously contributed to my knowledge and eased the sometimes rocky process of writing this book. Jo Cameron gave me her knowledge of Sierra Leone and her friendship, Melanie Hart her fine psychoanalytic take on my characters and her friendship, Michael Parsons his experiences as a medical student and his friendship, Wayne Milstead and Andrew MacKenzie their structural skills and their friendship, Jan Woolf and Alice Owens their sensitive reading of extracts and their friendship, Shah Husain her understanding of South Asian culture and her friendship and Jenny Uglow her understanding of the ways of publishing and her friendship.

I have especially needed their friendship.

Jonny Geller, my agent, is an unfailing support and has buoyed me up when I was in danger of going under, but never in any vapid 'darling-you-were-wonderful' way. He survived earlier drafts of the book and offered me comments that slid me further along the learning curve on which I'm trying to stay upright. Juliet Annan, my editor, has applied herself heroically and has helped whip it into the shape it's in now. As it were. And Jenny Lord, her assistant editor, is a generous and merry presence.

Michael, Cassie, Clea, Alessia and Luca are at the front of the book, and here they are again at the end. They bookend my life and enrich it every time I take a new breath.